*The Ancient
Mysteries Reader*

The Ancient
Mysteries Reader

edited by
PETER HAINING

Illustrated by Christopher Scott

DOUBLEDAY & COMPANY, INC.

GARDEN CITY, N.Y.

Library of Congress Cataloging in Publication Data

Main entry under title:

The Ancient mysteries reader

Includes index
CONTENTS: Subterranean worlds: Poe, E. A. MS. found in a
bottle. Bulwer-Lytton, E. The coming race.—Prehistoric man: Wells,
H. G. The grisly folk. Hearn, L. The mound builders.—Mythology:
Machen, A. The shining pyramid. Lovecraft, H. P. The call of
Cthulhu. [etc.]
    1. Fantastic fiction, American. 2. Fantastic fiction, English. I. Hain-
ing, Peter.
PZ1.A5713   [PS648.F3]   823'.0872
ISBN 0-385-09867-7
Library of Congress Catalog Card Number 74-18802

SC
ANC

The editor wishes to extend his thanks to the following authors, publishers
and agents for permission to include copyright material in this collection:

"The Grisly Folk" by H. G. Wells. Reprinted from *The Short Stories of H. G.
Wells* by permission of the executors of H. G. Wells.

"The Call of Cthulhu" by H. P. Lovecraft. Copyright 1928 by The Popular
Fiction Publishing Company for *Weird Tales;* copyright renewed 1945 by
August Derleth and Donald Wandrei and reprinted by permission of the Scott
Meredith Literary Agency.

"The Terror of Blue John Gap" by Sir Arthur Conan Doyle. Reprinted from
The Collected Short Stories of Sir Arthur Conan Doyle by permission of the
author's estate.

"A New God Was Born" by B. Traven. Copyright © 1966 by Harper & Row
for *The Collected Stories of B. Traven* and reprinted with their permission.

H-12623

There has been noticeable within the last few years a strong inclination on the part of scientific men to investigate old mysteries and legends in a serious new light, and to evince a real interest in stories which, a quarter of a century ago, were considered only suited for the young, except in their historical bearings as illustrating the ignorance and credulity of our forefathers.

LAFCADIO HEARN
December 1878.

Contents

Introduction

Mankind loves mystery. From our stumbling toward basic knowledge in primitive times to the present day of so-called rationality, the sense of wonder about things just beyond the range of comprehension is one of the most powerful of all human emotions. It was Arthur Machen, the revered Welsh mystic and storyteller (and who should know better of such things than the legend-haunted Welsh?), who wrote, close on fifty years ago: "Man is so made that all his true delight arises from the contemplation of mystery, and save by his own frantic and invincible folly, mystery is never taken from him; it rises within his soul, a well of joy unending."

Mystery is, of course, many things to many people: a puzzle over the meaning of existence, a debate on the ways of nature, an attempt to assess the course of history—it can be applied to almost any facet of life and certainly much of human psychology. It is a topic endlessly evolving, endlessly intriguing.

In the last century, give or take a few years, we have begun to take a particular and much wider interest in the very oldest of our mysteries: how the earth was formed, how life began, what primitive man did, and how the world as we know it came about. But what distinguishes this latest interest from the many previous studies of the past, are the totally new theories and points of view we have brought to bear on the issues concerned. Gone are the traditionally held views, swept aside are the centuries-old conclusions. In their place—or perhaps one should say, standing shoulder to shoulder—has emerged a whole new body of theories which, right or wrong, cannot fail to excite and stimulate even the most reserved traditionalist. Arrived at by a combination of man's increased reasoning power and the new scientific and technological equipment now at his command, they present ancient mysteries in a totally new light . . .

A light which proposes that the Earth *might* be hollow, that ancient civilizations *might* have possessed knowledge far in advance of our own, that the great monoliths of the past *might* have been vastly complex computers able to divine the future, and—most remarkable of all—that God himself *might* have been a spaceman.

As I write these words, discovery follows discovery to substantiate our right to question even the most strongly held view or most tenuous theory. Hardly a day passes without new light being shed on some old mystery. For example, I select at random this item from the London Sunday *Express* of August 12, 1973:

ONE IN THE EYE FOR DISBELIEVERS

Sofia: The complete skeleton of a Cyclops—the one-eyed creature of Greek mythology—has been discovered by Bulgarian archaeologists, an official report from Sophia claims.

The discovery was made during excavations near Razlog in southwestern Bulgaria.

The skull, it is claimed, had only one eye socket which was placed directly over the nose, and the skeleton measured five foot eleven inches high.

There is fiction, after centuries of disbelief, becoming—in a moment —fact. And who is to say that the work of international scientist-writers such as Dr. Willy Ley, Professor Thor Heyerdahl, Dr. Immanuel Velikovsky, Professor Fred Hoyle, Dr. Isaac Asimov, and the archaeologist Erich von Daniken, will not lead to the unraveling of still more complex and enduring ancient mysteries?

It is not only the scientists, astronomers and archaeologists who have deliberated over these mysteries: writers of fiction, too, have found them a rich vein of ideas and possibilities to work. Fantasy writers in particular have been drawn to this new contemplation of our past, and through their own imagination, talent—and, in some cases, genius—have propounded their own theories: partly as entertainment (for all stories must fulfill this qualification) and partly as a stimulus to further thought.

In THE ANCIENT MYSTERIES READER I have tried to bring together the most entertaining and thought-provoking short stories which deal with this facet of mystery. In a sentence, herein you will find famous writers of fantasy speculating on old mysteries. A collection, indeed, of fiction that might just prove to be fact!

The stories which I have assembled are specifically the work of American and English writers, and cover the period from Edgar Allan Poe to Gerald Kersh. Within this time span, as you will see, most of the important mysteries of our existence—from the nature of the planet on which we live to the startling thought that we might all be of extraterrestrial origin—have been formulated and advanced. The book therefore provides a conducted tour, albeit somewhat brief, of modern speculations through some of the most exciting fictional interpretations in the English language.

Of course, restrictions of space and availability—not to mention a desire to avoid duplication—have meant that many famous authors are omitted who perhaps ought to be here: important figures in the field of literary speculation like Rider Haggard, Fitz-James O'Brien, E. F. Benson, Ambrose Bierce, Robert Graves, Fritz Leiber, Arthur C. Clarke, and many more—not forgetting the great master, Jules Verne, who had to be excluded by virtue of his nationality, but whose presence can be sensed on almost every page.

All the stories are rooted in fact, and some, you will find, have actually inspired scientific and lay activity. It has given me particular pleasure to be able to select so many stories that are not available elsewhere, and all of which have not been brought together in a collection such as this before.

Finally, I hope that this book, and all those whose work is represented herein, will serve in some modest way to encourage man in his quest for awareness and knowledge—both of himself and the universe in which he lives.

PETER HAINING

Birch Green, Essex

August 1974

The Ancient
Mysteries Reader

I

SUBTERRANEAN
WORLDS

***

MS. Found in a Bottle
By Edgar Allan Poe

The Coming Race
By Edward Bulwer-Lytton

1

The nature of the planet on which we live has been one of the most ancient and intriguing of all mysteries—a mystery that has engrossed man virtually since he first stood upright on the Earth. Much of the surface of the globe has, of course, now been explored and charted, but it is the interior and its substance which still puzzles scientists and laymen alike. Scientists, over many generations, have plumped for the view that the Earth is solid, built up of varying layers of rocks with a molten core. Others contend it is hollow and could contain not only continents but life-forms, too. The most popular version of the hollow-earth theory maintains that there are gigantic holes at the North and South Poles which lead to a vast, unknown world peopled—according to several different schools of thought—by "wee folk," giants, animal-men or gentle, supremely wise beings who could be the survivors of the sunken continents of Atlantis or Mu. The most famous public figure associated with this theory was the American aviator Rear Admiral Richard E. Byrd, who claimed in February 1947 to have flown *beyond* the North Pole "into the polar opening leading to the hollow interior of the Earth, traversing an iceless region of mountains, lakes, rivers, green vegetation and animal life." This, said Byrd, was "the center of the Great Unknown." Despite further expeditions to both Poles, Rear Admiral Byrd and his theories received little serious attention, and even his insistence that whoever first reached this new world would become "the greatest power on Earth" fell on deaf ears throughout the rest of his life. The hollow-earth history is full of other strongly advanced claims which have been steadfastly ignored—such as the report by the Norwegian Olaf Jansen, who at the turn of the century claimed to have accidentally sailed his fishing boat into the interior of the Earth through one of the holes and there spent two years with a race of twelve-foot-high giants, far advanced technologically over the surface dwellers, who taught him their language and ways. When Olaf returned to the surface in his boat, he was picked up by a fishing smack, and, on retelling his story, was quickly dismissed as mad. The same label has also been directed at proponents of the theory that the phenomena known as Flying Saucers have their origin in the hollow Earth and are the means whereby the subterranean

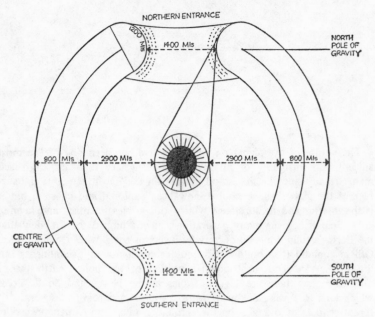

The Hollow Earth as visualized by one of its leading proponents, Marshall B. Gardner, in 1920.

dwellers observe humanity's activities. The controversy has, naturally, been the subject of a great many studies—some factual evaluations of the evidence, others wild flights of fancy and speculation. Because of the enduring interest in the theory—in America, particularly—it is hardly surprising to find that the great master of modern fantasy, the man who brought the macabre story out of its Gothic limitations into the freedom of modern expression, *Edgar Allan Poe* (1809–49), should have utilized it in his work. At the time Poe was writing, the American public was marveling over the exploits of a certain Captain John Symmes, who had distinguished himself in the War of Independence, and thereafter took to dabbling in science, making the bold proclamation that Newton's theory of gravity was incorrect! Objects on the Earth, he said, were dependent for their movement on an aerial plastic fluid invisible to the eye. He was also the first man to advance the theory that the hollow Earth could be entered by holes which were situated at the Poles. "I declare," he wrote in 1818 in a pamphlet sent to influential people throughout America, "that the earth is hollow, habitable within, and it is open at the Pole twelve or sixteen degrees. I pledge my life in support of this truth, and am ready to explore the hollow if the world will support and aid me in the undertaking." Authority, predictably, reacted with indifference, but the general public seemed to be rather intrigued, so Symmes immediately began a lengthy coast-to-coast lecture tour. For the remainder of his life he sought vainly to raise money for an expedition, but in the end the strain proved too much and he died of exhaustion in 1829. Symmes's work was not to be forgotten, however, for the whole concept of a hollow Earth had caught the imagination of the great storyteller Edgar Allan Poe, and was utilized by him for a now-classic short story, "MS. Found in a Bottle," published in 1833 in the *Baltimore Saturday Visitor*. Nor was this the end of Poe's fascination, for he returned to the argument about a subterranean world in two other tales: "The Narrative of A. Gordon Pym" (1838) and "The Unparalleled Adventures of One Hans Pfall" (1840). Symmes's claims also aroused much interest in Europe, and a little later Jules Verne took up the idea once more for his most famous novel, *Journey to the Center of the Earth* (1864). Thus it was that this theory of the Earth, and the writings of these two men, opened up a new era of literary speculation on ancient mysteries. And stories like the one reprinted here became landmarks in the history of fantasy fiction.

MS. FOUND IN A BOTTLE
Edgar Allan Poe

Of my country and of my family I have little to say. Ill usage and length of years have driven me from the one, and estranged me from the other. Hereditary wealth afforded me an education of no common order, and a contemplative turn of mind enabled me to methodise the stories which early study diligently garnered up. Beyond all things, the works of the German moralists gave me a great delight; not from my ill-advised admiration of their eloquent madness, but from the ease with which my habits of rigid thought enabled me to detect their falsities. I have often been reproached with the aridity of my genius; a deficiency of imagination has been imputed to me as a crime; and the Pyrrhonism of my opinions has at all times rendered me notorious. Indeed, a strong relish for physical philosophy has, I fear, tinctured my mind with a very common error of this age—I mean the habit of referring occurrences, even the least susceptible of such reference, to the principles of that science. Upon the whole, no person could be less liable than myself to be led away from the severe precincts of truth by the *ignes fatui* of superstition. I have thought proper to premise thus much, lest the incredible tale I have to tell should be considered rather the raving of a crude imagination, than the positive experience of a mind to which the reveries of fancy have been a dead letter and a nullity.

After many years spent in foreign travel, I sailed in the year 18—, from the port of Batavia, in the rich and populous island of Java, on a voyage to the Archipelago of the Sunda islands. I went as passenger—having no other inducement than a kind of nervous restlessness which haunted me as a fiend.

Our vessel was a beautiful ship of about four hundred tons, copper-fastened, and built at Bombay of Malabar teak. She was freighted with cotton-wool and oil, from the Lachadive islands. We had also on board coir, jaggeree, ghee, cocoa-nuts, and a few cases of opium. The stowage was clumsily done, and the vessel consequently crank.

We got under way with a mere breath of wind, and for many days stood along the eastern coast of Java, without any other incident to beguile the monotony of our course than the occasional meeting with some of the small grabs of the Archipelago to which we were bound.

One evening, leaning over the taffrail, I observed a very singular isolated cloud, to the N. W. It was remarkable, as well for its colour, as from its being the first we had seen since our departure from Batavia. I watched it attentively until sunset, when it spread all at once to the eastward and westward, girting in the horizon with a narrow strip of vapour, and looking like a long line of low beach. My notice was soon afterwards attracted by the dusky-red appearance of the moon, and the peculiar character of the sea. The latter was undergoing a rapid change, and the water seemed more than usually transparent. Although I could distinctly see the bottom, yet, heaving the lead, I found the ship in fifteen fathoms. The air now became intolerably hot, and was loaded with spiral exhalations similar to those arising from heated iron. As night came on, every breath of wind died away, and a more entire calm it is impossible to conceive. The flame of a candle burned upon the poop without the least perceptible motion, and a long hair, held between the finger and thumb, hung without the possibility of detecting a vibration. However, as the captain said he could perceive no indication of danger, and as we were drifting in bodily to shore, he ordered the sails to be furled, and the anchor let go. No watch was set, and the crew, consisting principally of Malays, stretched themselves deliberately upon deck. I went below—not without a full presentiment of evil. Indeed, every appearance warranted me in apprehending a simoom. I told the captain my fears; but he paid no attention to what I said, and left me without deigning to give a reply. My uneasiness, however, prevented me from sleeping, and about midnight I went upon deck. As I placed my foot upon the upper step of the companion-ladder, I was startled by a loud, humming noise, like that occasioned by the rapid revolution of a mill-wheel, and before I could ascertain its meaning, I found the ship quivering to its centre. In the next instant, a wilderness of foam hurled us upon our beam-ends, and, rushing over us fore and aft, swept the entire decks from stem to stern.

The extreme fury of the blast proved, in a great measure, the salvation of the ship. Although completely water-logged, yet, as her masts had gone by the board, she rose, after a minute, heavily from the sea, and, staggering awhile beneath the immense pressure of the tempest, finally righted.

By what miracle I escaped destruction, it is impossible to say. Stunned by the shock of the water, I found myself, upon recovery, jammed in between the stern-post and rudder. With great difficulty I gained my feet, and looking dizzily around, was at first struck with the idea of our being among breakers; so terrific, beyond the wildest imagination, was the whirlpool of mountainous and foaming ocean within which we were engulfed. After a while, I heard the voice of an old Swede, who had shipped with us at the moment of leaving port. I hallooed to him with all my strength, and presently he came reeling aft. We soon discovered that we were the sole survivors of the accident. All on deck, with the exception of ourselves, had been swept overboard; the captain and mates must have perished as they slept, for the cabins were deluged with water. Without assistance, we could expect to do little for the security of the ship, and our exertions were at first paralysed by the momentary expectation of going down. Our cable had, of course, parted like pack-thread, at the first breath of the hurricane, or we should have been instantaneously overwhelmed. We scudded with frightful velocity before the sea, and the water made clear breaches over us. The frame-work of our stern was shattered excessively, and, in almost every respect, we had received considerable injury; but to our extreme joy we found the pumps unchoked, and that we had made no great shifting of our ballast. The main fury of the blast had already blown over, and we apprehended little danger from the violence of the wind; but we looked forward to its total cessation with dismay, well believing, that in our shattered condition, we should inevitably perish in the tremendous swell which would ensue. But this very just apprehension seemed by no means likely to be soon verified. For five entire days and nights—during which our only subsistence was a small quantity of jaggeree, procured with great difficulty from the forecastle—the hulk flew at a rate defying computation, before rapidly succeeding flaws of wind, which without equalling the first violence of the simoom, were still more terrific than any tempest I had before encountered. Our course for the first four days was, with trifling variations, S. E. and by S.; and we must have run down the coast of New Holland. On the fifth day the cold became extreme, although the wind had hauled round a point more to the northward. The sun arose with a sickly yellow lustre, and clambered a very few degrees above the horizon—emitting no decisive light. There were no clouds apparent, yet the wind was upon the increase, and blew with a fitful and unsteady fury. About noon, as nearly as we could guess, our attention was again arrested by the appearance of the sun. It gave out no light, properly so called, but a dull and sullen glow without reflection, as if all its rays were polarised. Just before sinking within the turgid sea, its central fires suddenly went out, as if hurriedly extinguished by some unaccountable power. It was a dim, silver-like rim, alone, as it rushed down the unfathomable ocean.

We waited in vain for the arrival of the sixth day—that day to me has not arrived—to the Swede, never did arrive. Thenceforward we were enshrouded in pitchy darkness, so that we could not have seen an object at twenty paces from the ship. Eternal night continued to envelop us, all unrelieved by the phosphoric sea-brilliancy to which we had been accustomed in the tropics. We observed, too, that, although the tempest continued to rage with unabated violence, there was no longer to be discovered the usual appearance of surf, or foam, which had hitherto attended us. All around were horror, and thick gloom, and a black sweltering desert of ebony. Superstitious terror crept by degrees into the spirit of the old Swede, and my own soul was wrapped up in silent wonder. We neglected all care of the ship, as worse than useless, and securing ourselves, as well as possible, to the stump of the mizen-mast, looked out bitterly into the world of ocean. We had no means of calculating time, nor could we form any guess of our situation. We were, however, well aware of having made farther to the southward than any previous navigators, and felt great amazement at not meeting with the unusual impediments of ice. In the meantime every moment threatened to be our last—every mountainous billow hurried to overwhelm us. The swell surpassed anything I had imagined possible, and that we were not instantly buried is a miracle. My companion spoke of the lightness of our cargo, and reminded me of the excellent qualities of our ship; but I could not help feeling the utter hopelessness of hope itself, and prepared myself gloomily for that death which I thought nothing could defer beyond an hour, as with every knot of way the ship made, the swelling of the black stupendous seas became more dismally appalling. At times we gasped for breath at an elevation beyond the albatross—at times became dizzy with the velocity of our descent into some watery hell, where the air grew stagnant, and no sound disturbed the slumbers of the kraken.

We were at the bottom of one of these abysses, when a quick scream from my companion broke fearfully upon the night. "See! see!" cried he, shrieking in my ears, "Almighty God! see! see!" As he spoke, I became aware of a dull, sullen glare of red light which streamed down the sides of the vast chasm where we lay, and threw a fitful brilliancy upon our deck. Casting my eyes upwards, I beheld a spectacle which froze the current of my blood. At a terrific height directly above us, and upon the very verge of the precipitous descent, hovered a gigantic ship, of perhaps four thousand tons. Although upreared upon the summit of a wave more than a hundred times her own altitude, her apparent size still exceeded that of any ship of the line or East Indiaman in existence. Her huge hull was of a deep dingy black, unrelieved by any of the customary carvings of a ship. A single row of brass cannon protruded from her open ports, and dashed from their polished surfaces the fires of innumerable battle-lanterns which swung to and fro about her rigging. But what mainly inspired us with horror and astonishment, was that she bore up under a press of sail in the very teeth of that supernatural sea, and of that ungovernable hurricane. When we first discovered her, her bows were alone to be seen, as she rose slowly from the dim and horrible gulf beyond her. For a moment of intense terror she paused upon the giddy pinnacle, as if in contemplation of her own sublimity, then trembled and tottered, and—came down.

At this instant, I know not what sudden self-possession came over my spirit. Staggering as far aft as I could, I awaited fearlessly the ruin that was to overwhelm. Our own vessel was at length ceasing from her struggles, and sinking with her head to the sea. The shock of the descending mass struck her, consequently, in that portion of her frame which was nearly under water, and the inevitable result was to hurl me, with irresistible violence, upon the rigging of the stranger.

As I fell, the ship hove in stays, and went about; and to the confusion ensuing I attributed my escape from the notice of the crew. With little difficulty I made my way, unperceived, to the main hatchway, which was partially open, and soon found an opportunity of secreting myself in the hold. Why I did so I can hardly tell. An indefinite sense of awe, which at first sight of the navigators of the ship had taken hold of my mind, was perhaps the principle of my concealment. I was unwilling to trust myself with a race of people who had offered, to the cursory glance I had taken, so many points of vague novelty, doubt, and apprehension. I therefore thought proper to contrive a hiding-place in the hold. This I did by removing a small portion of the shifting-boards, in such a manner as to afford me a convenient retreat between the huge timbers of the ship.

I had scarcely completed my work, when a footstep in the hold forced me to make use of it. A man passed by my place of concealment with a feeble and unsteady gait. I could not see his face, but had an opportunity of observing his general appearance. There was about it an evidence of great age and infirmity. His knees tottered beneath a load of years, and his entire frame quivered under the burthen. He muttered to himself, in a low broken tone, some words of a language which I could not understand, and groped in a corner among a pile of singular-looking instruments and decayed charts of navigation. His manner was a wild mixture of the peevishness of second childhood and the solemn dignity of a God. He at length went on deck, and I saw him no more.

*   *   *

A feeling, for which I have no name, has taken possession of my soul—a sensation which will admit of no analysis, to which the lessons of bygone time are inadequate, and for which I fear futurity itself will offer me no key. To a mind constituted like my own, the latter consideration is an evil. I shall never—I know that I shall never—be satisfied with regard to the nature of my conceptions. Yet it is not wonderful that these conceptions are indefinite, since they have their origin in sources so utterly novel. A new sense—a new entity is added to my soul.

*   *   *

It is long since I first trod the deck of this terrible ship, and the rays of my destiny are, I think, gathering to a focus. Incomprehensible men! Wrapped up in meditations of a kind which I cannot divine, they pass me by unnoticed. Concealment is utter folly on my part, for the people *will not* see. It was but just now that I passed directly before the eyes of the mate; it was no long while ago that I ventured into the captain's own private cabin, and took thence the materials with which I write, and have written. I shall from time to time continue this journal. It is true that I may not find an opportunity of transmitting it to the world, but I will not fail to make the endeavour. At the last moment I will enclose the MS. in a bottle, and cast it within the sea.

*   *   *

An incident has occurred which has given me new room for meditation. Are such things the operation of ungoverned chance? I had ventured upon deck and thrown myself down, without attracting any notice, among a pile of ratlin-stuff and old sails, in the bottom of the yawl. While musing upon the singularity of my fate, I unwittingly daubed with a tar-brush the edges of a neatly-folded studding-sail which lay near me on a barrel. The studding-sail is now bent upon the ship, and the thoughtless touches of the brush are spread out into the word DISCOVERY.

I have made many observations lately upon the structure of the vessel. Although well armed, she is not, I think, a ship of war. Her rigging, build, and general equipment, all negative a supposition of this kind. What she *is not,* I can easily perceive; what she *is,* I fear it is impossible to say. I know not how it is, but in scrutinising her strange model and singular cast of spars, her huge size and overgrown suits of canvas, her severely simple bow and antiquated stern, there will occasionally flash across my mind a sensation of familiar things, and there is always mixed up with such indistinct shadows of recollection, an unaccountable memory of old foreign chronicles and ages long ago.

*   *   *

I have been looking at the timbers of the ship. She is built of a material to which I am a stranger. There is a peculiar character about the wood which strikes me as rendering it unfit for the purpose to which it has been applied. I mean its extreme *porousness,* considered independently of the worm-eaten condition which is a consequence of navigation in these seas, and apart from the rottenness attendant upon age. It will appear, perhaps, an observation somewhat over-curious, but this wood would have every characteristic of Spanish oak, if Spanish oak were distended by any unnatural means.

In reading the above sentence, a curious apothegm of an old

weather-beaten Dutch navigator comes full upon my recollection. "It is as sure," he was wont to say, when any doubt was entertained of his veracity, "as sure as there is a sea where the ship itself will grow in bulk like the living body of the seaman."

*   *   *

About an hour ago I made bold to trust myself among a group of the crew. They paid me no manner of attention, and, although I stood in the very midst of them all, seemed utterly unconscious of my presence. Like the one I had at first seen in the hold, they all bore about them the marks of a hoary old age. Their knees trembled with infirmity; their shoulders were bent double with decrepitude; their shrivelled skins rattled in the wind; their voices were low, tremulous, and broken; their eyes glistened with the rheum of years; and their grey hairs streamed terribly in the tempest. Around them, on every part of the deck, lay scattered mathematical instruments of the most quaint and obsolete construction.

*   *   *

I mentioned, some time ago, the bending of a studding-sail. From that period, the ship, being thrown dead off the wind, has continued her terrific course due south, with every rag of canvas packed upon her, from her truck to her lower studding-sail booms, and rolling every moment her top-gallant yard-arms into the most appalling hell of water which it can enter into the mind of man to imagine. I have just left the deck, where I find it impossible to maintain a footing, although the crew seem to experience little inconvenience. It appears to me a miracle of miracles that our enormous bulk is not swallowed up at once and for ever. We are surely doomed to hover continually upon the brink of eternity, without taking a final plunge into the abyss. From billows a thousand times more stupendous than any I have ever seen, we glide away with the facility of the arrowy sea-gull; and the colossal waters rear their heads above us like demons of the deep, but like demons confined to simple threats, and forbidden to destroy. I am led to attribute these frequent escapes to the only natural cause which can account for such effect. I must suppose the ship to be within the influence of some strong current, or impetuous undertow.

*   *   *

I have seen the captain face to face, and in his own cabin—but, as I expected, he paid me no attention. Although in his appearance there is, to a casual observer, nothing which might bespeak him more or less than man, still a feeling of irrepressible reverence and awe mingled with the sensation of wonder with which I regarded him. In stature, he is nearly my own height; that is, about five feet eight inches. He is of a well-knit and compact frame of body, neither robust nor remarkable otherwise. But it is the singularity of the expression which reigns upon the face—it is the intense, the wonderful, the thrilling evidence of old age so utter, so extreme, which excites within my spirit a sense—a sentiment ineffable. His forehead, although little wrinkled, seems to bear upon it the stamp of a myriad of years. His grey hairs are records of the past, and his greyer eyes are sybils of the future. The cabin floor was thickly strewn with strange, iron-clasped folios, and mouldering instruments of science, and obsolete long-forgotten charts. His head was bowed down upon his hands, and he pored, with a fiery, unquiet eye, over a paper which I took to be a commission, and which, at all events, bore the signature of a monarch. He muttered to himself—as did the first seaman whom I saw in the hold—some low peevish syllables of a foreign tongue; and although the speaker was close at my elbow, his voice seemed to reach my ears from the distance of a mile.

*   *   *

The ship and all in it are imbued with the spirit of Eld. The crew glide to and fro like the ghosts of buried centuries; their eyes have an eager and uneasy meaning; and when their fingers fall athwart my path in the wild glare of the battle-lanterns, I feel as I have never felt before, although I have been all my life a dealer in antiquities, and have imbibed the shadows of fallen columns at Balbec, and Tadmor, and Persepolis, until my very soul has become a ruin.

*   *   *

When I look around me, I feel ashamed of my former apprehensions. If I trembled at the blast which has hitherto attended us, shall I not stand aghast at a warring of wind and ocean, to convey any idea of which, the words tornado and simoom are trivial and ineffective? All in the immediate vicinity of the ship is the blackness of eternal night, and a chaos of foamless water; but, about a league on either side of us, may be seen, indistinctly, and at intervals, stupendous ramparts of ice, towering away into the desolate sky, and looking like the walls of the universe.

*   *   *

As I imagined, the ship proves to be in a current—if that appellation can properly be given to a tide which, howling and shrieking by the white ice, thunders on to the southward with a velocity like the headlong dashing of a cataract.

To conceive the horror of my sensations is, I presume, utterly impossible; yet a curiosity to penetrate the mysteries of these awful regions predominates even over my despair, and will reconcile me to the most hideous aspect of death. It is evident that we are hurrying on-wards to some exciting knowledge—some never-to-be-imparted secret, whose attainment is destruction. Perhaps this current leads us to the southern pole itself. It must be confessed that a supposition apparently so wild has every probability in its favour.

*   *   *

The crew pace the deck with unquiet and tremulous step; but there is upon their countenance an expression more of the eagerness of hope than of the apathy of despair.

In the meantime the wind is still in our poop, and, as we carry a crowd of canvas, the ship is at times lifted bodily from out the sea! Oh, horror upon horror!—the ice opens suddenly to the right, and to the left, and we are whirling dizzily, in immense concentric circles, round and round the borders of a gigantic amphitheatre, the summit of whose walls is lost in the darkness and the distance. But little time will be left me to ponder upon my destiny! The circles rapidly grow small—we are plunging madly within the grasp of the whirlpool—and amid a roaring, and bellowing, and thundering of ocean and tempest, the ship is quivering—oh God! and——going down!

Note.—The "MS. Found in a Bottle" was originally published in 1831; and it was not until many years afterwards that I became acquainted with the maps of Mercator, in which the ocean is represented as rushing, by four mouths, into the (northern) Polar Gulf, to be absorbed into the bowels of the earth; the Pole itself being represented by a black rock, towering to a prodigious height.

2

Without much doubt, the most controversial story dealing with the theory of life in the interior of the Earth is Edward Bulwer-Lytton's *The Coming Race*, published in 1871 in *Blackwood's Magazine*. Although perhaps not as well written as Poe's "MS. Found in a Bottle" or as exciting as Verne's *Journey to the Center of the Earth*, this bizarre little novel, which has been a collector's item for nearly a century, has an important place in occult history and is said to have been a primary influence on Adolf Hitler and the Nazi party. In his book, *Lord Edward George Bulwer-Lytton* (1803–73) drew on the old legends to describe a race of advanced beings, or *Vril-ya*, living in caverns beneath the surface of the Earth and planning to emerge at a suitable moment and conquer the world. The author was himself a member of several occult societies which acknowledged the existence of "Supreme Beings" who could order the way of the world. At the time of its publication, *The Coming Race* attracted little attention: Lord Lytton was, after all, far better known as a historical novelist, and such literary detours passed almost without comment. (He did, however, write several other stories about the supernatural which have preserved his name, including *Zanoni*, published in 1842, and the much-anthologized *A Strange Story*.) Consequently, but for Hitler's rise to power, it might today be a forgotten work. Lytton always acknowledged the book to be mostly fiction, but the high-ranking Nazis, steeped as they were in superstition and paganism, believed it to be fact. "So convinced were they of the actuality of Bulwer-Lytton's *Vril*-race," Dr. Willy Ley, the renowned scientist, has written, "that they formed 'The *Vril* Society' or 'Luminous Lodge.' They believed that this super-race would emerge one day, and therefore set about developing their own *Vril*-power (or energy) so that they might be the equals and not the slaves of the subterraneans." Dr. Ley's contentions have been more than substantially supported by records, found after the fall of the Third Reich, which show that Hitler organized several expeditions to find the tunnel entrances to the inner world—which he believed were somewhere in Europe—and had done considerable research into Bulwer-Lytton's life in the hope that clues could be found as to where and when the author himself had actually visited the caves. Reading *The Coming Race,* one can understand its attraction for a man like Hitler: it portrays a super-race, overlorded by a dictator or *Tur,* who consider democracy as "one of the crude and ignorant experiments which belong to the infancy of political science." These people place little value on personal riches and material gains, recognize the power of women in creating a super-race, and exploit the inherent ruthlessness of children for political ends. On this novel, a historical writer's fantasy, the Third Reich was in part built. (In his obsession with the story, Hitler actually believed he saw one of these underworld dwellers on several occasions. "The new man is living amongst us now!" he told Hermann Rauschning, the Governor of Danzig. "He is here! I will tell you a secret. I have seen the new man. He is intrepid and cruel. I was afraid of him.") Bulwer-Lytton saw his concept quite differently: "I did not mean *Vril* for mesmerism," he wrote, "but for electricity, developed into uses as yet only dimly guessed, and including whatever there may be genuine in mesmerism, which I hold to be a mere branch current of the one great fluid pervading all nature." The story of *The Coming Race* is told by a wealthy young American who wanders the Earth in search of adventure and unexpectedly stumbles across the entrance to the subterranean world while exploring a mine—the location of which is left teasingly unstated. Down, down he travels until he comes into a new world of almost Eastern beauty, where he is taken into the care of one of the most important men. It is through this man, and his daughter Zee (who eventually is to help him escape so that he can reveal his amazing discovery to the world), that he learns the ways of the super-race and their extraordinary *Vril*-power. The episode which I have selected from this rare book is both evocative of the work as a whole and contains many of the elements which so influenced Hitler and the Nazis . . .

THE COMING RACE
Edward Bulwer-Lytton

A room to myself was assigned to me in this land beneath the surface. It was prettily and fantastically arranged, but without any of the splendour of metal work or gems which were displayed in the more public apartments. The walls were hung with a variegated matting made from the stalks and fibres of plants, and the floor carpeted with the same.

The apartment and its appurtenances indeed had a character, if strange in detail, still familiar as a whole, to modern notions of luxury, and would have excited admiration if found attached to the apartments of an English duchess or fashionable French author. Before I arrived this was Zee's chamber; she had hospitably assigned it to me.

Some hours after waking up, I was lying alone on my couch trying to fix my thoughts on conjecture as to the nature and genius of the people amongst whom I was thrown, when my host and his daughter Zee entered the room. My host, still speaking my native language, inquired, with much politeness, whether it would be agreeable to me to converse, or if I preferred solitude. I replied, that I should feel much honoured and obliged by the opportunity offered me to express my gratitude for the hospitality and civilities I had received in a country to which I was a stranger, and to learn enough of its customs and manners not to offend through ignorance.

As I spoke, I had of course risen from my couch; but Zee, much to my confusion, curtly ordered me to lie down again, and there was something in her voice and eye, gentle as both were, that compelled my obedience. She then seated herself unconcernedly at the foot of my bed, while her father took his place on a divan a few feet distant.

"But what part of the world do you come from," asked my host, "that we should appear so strange to you, and you to us? I have seen individual specimens of nearly all the races differing from our own, except the primeval savages who dwell in the most desolate and remote recesses of uncultivated nature, unacquainted with other light than that they obtain from volcanic fires, and contented to grope their way in the dark, as do many creeping, crawling, and even flying things. But certainly you cannot be a member of those barbarous tribes, nor, on the other hand, do you seem to belong to any civilised people."

I was somewhat nettled at this last observation, and replied that I had the honour to belong to one of the most civilised nations of the earth; and that, so far as light was concerned, while I admired the ingenuity and disregard of expense with which my host and his fellow-citizens had contrived to illumine the regions unpenetrated by the rays of the sun, yet I could not conceive how any who had once beheld the orbs of heaven could compare to their lustre the artificial lights invented by the necessities of man. But my host said he had seen specimens of most of the races differing from his own, save the wretched barbarians he had mentioned. Now, was it possible that he had never been on the surface of the earth, or could he only be referring to communities buried within its entrails?

My host was for some moments silent; his countenance showed a degree of surprise which the people of that race very rarely manifest under any circumstances, howsoever extraordinary. But Zee was more intelligent, and exclaimed, "So you see, my father, that there is truth in the old tradition; there always is truth in every tradition commonly believed in all times and by all tribes."

"Zee," said my host, mildly, "you belong to the College of Sages, and ought to be wiser than I am; but, as chief of the Light-preserving Council, it is my duty to take nothing for granted till it is proved to the evidence of my own senses." Then, turning to me, he asked me several questions about the surface of the earth and the heavenly bodies; upon which, though I answered him to the best of my knowledge, my answers seemed not to satisfy nor convince him. He shook his head quietly, and, changing the subject rather abruptly, asked how I had come down from what he was pleased to call one world to the other. I answered, that under the surface of the earth there were mines containing minerals, or metals, essential to our wants and our progress in all arts and industries; and I then briefly explained the manner in which, while exploring one of these mines, I had obtained a glimpse of the strange regions into which I had now descended.

My host then proceeded to question me as to the habits and modes of life among the races on the upper earth, more especially among those considered to be the most advanced in that civilisation which he was pleased to define "the art of diffusing throughout a community the tranquil happiness which belongs to a virtuous and well-ordered household." Naturally desiring to represent in the most favourable colours the world from which I came, I touched but slightly, though indulgently, on the antiquated and decaying institutions of Europe, in order to expatiate on the present grandeur and prospective pre-eminence of that glorious American Republic, in which Europe enviously seeks its model and tremblingly foresees its doom. Selecting for an example of the social life of the United States that city in which progress advances at the fastest rate, I indulged in an animated description of the moral habits of New York. Mortified to see, by the faces of my listeners, that I did not make the favourable impression I had anticipated, I elevated my theme; dwelling on the excellence of democratic institutions, their promotion of tranquil happiness by the government of party, and the mode in which they diffused such happiness throughout the community by preferring, for the exercise of power and the acquisition of honours, the lowliest citizens in point of property, education, and character. Fortunately recollecting the peroration of a speech, on the purifying influences of American democracy and their destined spread over the world, made by a certain eloquent senator (for whose vote in the Senate a Railway Company, to which my two brothers belonged, had just paid 20,000 dollars), I wound up by repeating its glowing predictions of the magnificent future that smiled upon mankind—when the flag of freedom should float over an entire continent, and two hundred millions of intelligent citizens, accustomed from infancy to the daily use of revolvers, should apply to a cowering universe the doctrine of the Patriot Monroe.

When I had concluded, my host gently shook his head, and fell into a musing study, making a sign to me and his daughter to remain silent while he reflected. And after a time he said, in a very earnest and solemn tone, "If you think, as you say, that you, though a stranger, have received kindness at the hands of me and mine, I adjure you to reveal nothing to any other of our people respecting the world from which you came, unless, on consideration, I give you permission to do so. Do you consent to this request?"

"Of course I pledge my word to it," said I, somewhat amazed; and I extended my right hand to grasp his. But he placed my hand gently on his forehead and his own right hand on my breast, which is the custom among this race in all matters of promise or verbal obligations. Then turning to his daughter, he said, "And you, Zee, will not repeat to any one what the stranger has said, or may say, to me or to you, of a world other than our own." Zee rose and kissed her father on the temples, saying, with a smile, "A Gy's tongue is wanton, but love can fetter it fast. And if, my father, you fear lest a chance word from me or yourself could expose our community to danger, by a desire to explore a world beyond us, will not a wave of the *vril,* properly impelled, wash even the memory of what we have heard the stranger say out of the tablets of the brain?"

"What is vril?" I asked.

Therewith Zee began to enter into an explanation of which I understood very little, for there is no word in any language I know which is an exact synonym for vril. I should call it electricity, except that it comprehends in its manifold branches other forces of nature, to which, in our scientific nomenclature, differing names are assigned, such as magnetism, galvanism, &c. These people consider that in vril they have arrived at the unity in natural energic agencies, which has been conjectured by many philosophers above ground, and which Faraday thus intimates under the more cautious term of correlation:—

"I have long held an opinion," says that illustrious experimentalist, "almost amounting to a conviction, in common, I believe, with many other lovers of natural knowledge, that the various forms under which the forces of matter are made manifest have one common origin; or, in other words, are so directly related and mutually dependent, that they are convertible, as it were, into one another, and possess equivalents of power in their action."

These subterranean philosophers assert that, by one operation of vril, which Faraday would perhaps call 'atmospheric magnetism,' they can influence the variations of temperature—in plain words, the weather; that by other operations, akin to those ascribed to mesmerism, electro-biology, odic force, &c., but applied scientifically through vril conductors, they can exercise influence over minds, and bodies animal and vegetable, to an extent not surpassed in the romances of our mystics. To all such agencies they give the common name of vril. Zee asked me if, in my world, it was not known that all the faculties of the mind could be quickened to a degree unknown in the waking state, by trance or vision, in which the thoughts of one brain could be transmitted to another, and knowledge be thus rapidly interchanged. I replied, that there were among us stories told of such trance or vision, and that I had heard much and seen something of the mode in which they were artificially effected, as in mesmeric clairvoyance; but that these practices had fallen much into disuse or contempt, partly because of the gross impostures to which they had been made subservient, and partly because, even where the effects upon certain abnormal constitutions were genuinely produced, the effects, when fairly examined and analysed, were very unsatisfactory—not to be relied upon for any systematic truthfulness or any practical purpose, and rendered very mischievous to credulous persons by the superstitions they tended to produce. Zee received my answers with much benignant attention, and said that similar instances of abuse and credulity had been familiar to their own scientific experience in the infancy of their knowledge, and while the properties of vril were misapprehended, but that she reserved further discussion on this subject till I was more fitted to enter into it. She contented herself with adding, that it was through the agency of vril, while I had been placed in the state of trance, that I had been made acquainted with the rudiments of their language; and that she and her father, who, alone of the family, took the pains to watch the experiment, had acquired a greater proportionate knowledge of my language than I of their own; partly because my language was much simpler than theirs, comprising far less of complex ideas; and partly because their organisation was, by hereditary culture, much more ductile and more readily capable of acquiring knowledge than mine. At this I secretly demurred; and having had, in the course of a practical life, to sharpen my wits, whether at home or in travel, I could not allow that my cerebral organisation could possibly be duller than that of people who had lived all their lives by lamplight. However, while I was thus thinking, Zee quietly pointed her forefinger at my forehead and sent me to sleep.

*   *   *

It was not for some time, and until, by repeated trances, if they are so to be called, my mind became better prepared to interchange ideas with my entertainers, and more fully to comprehend differences of manners and customs, at first too strange to my experience to be seized by my reason, that I was enabled to gather the following details respecting the origin and history of this subterranean population, as portion of one great family race called the Ana.

According to the earliest traditions, the remote progenitors of the race had once tenanted a world above the surface of that in which their descendants dwelt. Myths of that world were still preserved in their archives, and in those myths were legends of a vaulted dome in which the lamps were lighted by no human hand. But such legends were considered by most commentators as allegorical fables. According to these traditions the earth itself, at the date to which the traditions ascend, was not indeed in its infancy, but in the throes and travail of transition from one form of development to another, and subject to many violent revolutions of nature. By one of such revolutions, that portion of the upper world inhabited by the ancestors of this race had been subjected to inundations, not rapid, but gradual and uncontrollable, in which all, save a scanty remnant, were submerged and perished. Whether this be a record of our historical and sacred Deluge, or of some earlier one contended for by geologists, I do not pretend to conjecture; though, according to the chronology of this people as compared with that of Newton, it must have been many thousands of years before the time of Noah. On the other hand, the account of these writers does not harmonise with the opinions most in vogue among geological authorities, inasmuch as it places the existence of a human race upon earth at dates long anterior to that assigned to the terrestrial formation adapted to the introduction of mammalia. A band of the ill-fated race, thus invaded by the Flood, had, during the march of the waters, taken refuge in caverns amidst the loftier rocks, and, wandering through these hollows, they lost sight of the upper world for ever. Indeed, the whole face of the earth had been changed by this great revulsion; land had been turned into sea—sea into land. In the bowels of the inner earth even now, I was informed as a positive fact, might be discovered the remains of human habitation—habitation not in huts and caverns, but in vast cities whose ruins attest the civilisation of races which flourished before the age of Noah, and are not to be classified with those genera to which philosophy ascribes the use of flint and the ignorance of iron.

The fugitives had carried with them the knowledge of the arts they had practised above ground—arts of culture and civilisation. Their earliest want must have been that of supplying below the earth the light they had lost above it; and at no time, even in the traditional period, do the races, of which the one I now sojourned with formed a tribe, seem to have been unacquainted with the art of extracting light from gases, or manganese, or petroleum. They had been accustomed in their former state to contend with the rude forces of nature; and indeed the lengthened battle they had fought with their conqueror Ocean, which had taken centuries in its spread, had quickened their skill in curbing waters into dikes and channels. To this skill they owed their preservation in their new abode. "For many generations," said my host, with a sort of contempt and horror, "these primitive forefathers are said to have degraded their rank and shortened their lives by eating the flesh of animals, many varieties of which had, like themselves, escaped the Deluge, and sought shelter in the hollows of the earth; other animals, supposed to be unknown to the upper world, those hollows themselves produced."

When what we should term the historical age emerged from the twilight of tradition, the Ana were already established in different communities, and had attained to a degree of civilisation very analogous to that which the more advanced nations above the earth now enjoy. They were familiar with most of our mechanical inventions, including the application of steam as well as gas. The communities were in fierce competition with each other. They had their rich and their poor; they had orators and conquerors; they made war either for a domain or an idea. Though the various states acknowledged various forms of government, free institutions were beginning to preponderate; popular assemblies increased in power; republics soon became general; the democracy to which the most enlightened European politicians look forward as the extreme goal of political advancement, and which still prevailed among other subterranean races, whom they despised as barbarians, the loftier family of Ana, to which belonged the tribe I was visiting, looked back to as one of the crude and ignorant experiments which belong to the infancy of political science. It was the age of envy and hate, of fierce passions, of constant social changes more or less violent, of strife between classes, of war between state and state. This phase of society lasted, however, for some ages, and was finally brought to a close, at least among the nobler and more intellectual populations, by the gradual discovery of the latent powers stored in the all-permeating fluid which they denominate Vril.

According to the account I received from Zee, who, as an erudite professor in the College of Sages, had studied such matters more diligently than any other member of my host's family, this fluid is capable of being raised and disciplined into the mightiest agency over all forms of matter, animate or inanimate. It can destroy like the flash of lightning; yet, differently applied, it can replenish or invigorate life, heal, and preserve, and on it they chiefly rely for the cure of disease, or rather for enabling the physical organisation to re-establish the due equilibrium of its natural powers, and thereby to cure itself. By this agency they rend way through the most solid substances, and open valleys for culture through the rocks of their subterranean wilderness. From it they extract the light which supplies their lamps, finding it steadier, softer, and healthier than the other inflammable materials they had formerly used.

But the effects of the alleged discovery of the means to direct the more terrible force of vril were chiefly remarkable in their influence upon social polity. As these effects became familiarly known and skilfully administered, war between the Vril-discoverers ceased, for they brought the art of destruction to such perfection as to annul all superiority in numbers, discipline, or military skill. The fire lodged in the hollow of a rod directed by the hand of a child could shatter the strongest fortress, or cleave its burning way from the van to the rear of an embattled host. If army met army, and both had command of this agency, it could be but to the annihilation of each. The age of war was therefore gone, but with the cessation of war other effects bearing upon the social state soon became apparent. Man was so completely at the mercy of man, each whom he encountered being able, if so willing, to slay him on the instant, that all notions of government by force gradually vanished from political systems and forms of law. It is only by force that vast communities, dispersed through great distances of space, can be kept together; but now there was no longer either the necessity of self-preservation or the pride of aggrandisement to make one state desire to preponderate in population over another.

The Vril-discoverers thus, in the course of a few generations, peacefully split into communities of moderate size. The tribe amongst which I had fallen was limited to 12,000 families. Each tribe occupied a territory sufficient for all its wants, and at stated periods the surplus population departed to seek a realm of its own. There appeared no necessity for any arbitrary selection of these emigrants; there was always a sufficient number who volunteered to depart.

These subdivided states, petty if we regard either territory or population,—all appertained to one vast general family. They spoke the same language, though the dialects might slightly differ. They intermarried; they maintained the same general laws and customs; and so important a bond between these several communities was the knowledge of vril and the practice of its agencies, that the word A-Vril was synonymous with civilisation; and Vril-ya, signifying "The Civilised Nations," was the common name by which the communities employing the uses of vril distinguished themselves from such of the Ana as were yet in a state of barbarism.

The government of the tribe of Vril-ya I am treating of was apparently very complicated, really very simple. It was based upon a principle recognised in theory, though little carried out in practice, above ground—viz., that the object of all systems of philosophical thought tends to the attainment of unity, or the ascent through all intervening labyrinths to the simplicity of a single first cause or principle. Thus in politics, even republican writers have agreed that a benevolent autocracy would insure the best administration, if there were any guarantees for its continuance, or against its gradual abuse of the powers accorded to it. This singular community elected therefore a single supreme magistrate styled Tur; he held his office nominally for life, but he could seldom be induced to retain it after the first approach of old age. There was indeed in this society nothing to induce any of its members to covet the cares of office. No honours, no insignia of higher rank were assigned to it. The supreme magistrate was not distinguished from the rest by superior habitation or revenue. On the other hand, the duties awarded to him were marvellously light and easy, requiring no preponderant degree of energy or intelligence. There being no apprehensions of war, there were no armies to maintain;

being no government of force, there was no police to appoint and direct. What we call crime was utterly unknown to the Vril-ya; and there were no courts of criminal justice. The rare instances of civil disputes were referred for arbitration to friends chosen by either party, or decided by the Council of Sages, which will be described later. There were no professional lawyers; and indeed their laws were but amicable conventions, for there was no power to enforce laws against an offender who carried in his staff the power to destroy his judges. There were customs and regulations to compliance with which, for several ages, the people had tacitly habituated themselves; or if in any instance an individual felt such compliance hard, he quitted the community and went elsewhere. There was, in fact, quietly established amid this state, much the same compact that is found in our private families, in which we virtually say to any independent grown-up member of the family whom we receive and entertain, "Stay or go, according as our habits and regulations suit or displease you." But though there were no laws such as we call laws, no race above ground is so law-observing. Obedience to the rule adopted by the community has become as much an instinct as if it were implanted by nature. Even in every household the head of it makes a regulation for its guidance, which is never resisted nor even cavilled at by those who belong to the family. They have a proverb, the pithiness of which is much lost in this paraphrase, "No happiness without order, no order without authority, no authority without unity." The mildness of all government among them, civil or domestic, may be signalised by their idiomatic expressions for such terms as illegal or forbidden—viz., "It is requested not to do so-and-so." Poverty among the Ana is as unknown as crime; not that property is held in common, or that all are equals in the extent of their possessions or the size and luxury of their habitations: but there being no difference of rank or position between the grades of wealth or the choice of occupations, each pursues his own inclinations without creating envy or vying; some like a modest, some a more splendid kind of life; each makes himself happy in his own way. Owing to this absence of competition, and the limit placed on the population, it is difficult for a family to fall into distress; there are no hazardous speculations, no emulators striving for superior wealth and rank. No doubt, in each settlement all originally had the same proportions of land dealt out to them; but some, more adventurous than others, had extended their possessions farther into the bordering wilds, or had improved into richer fertility the produce of their fields, or entered into commerce or trade. Thus, necessarily, some had grown richer than others, but none had become absolutely poor, or wanting anything which their tastes desired. If they did so, it was always in their power to migrate, or at the worst to apply, without shame and with certainty of aid, to the rich; for all the members of the community considered themselves as brothers of one affectionate and united family. More upon this head will be treated of incidentally as my narrative proceeds.

The chief care of the supreme magistrate was to communicate with certain active departments charged with the administration of special details. The most important and essential of such details was that connected with the due provision of light. Of this department my host, Aph-Lin, was the chief. Another department, which might be called the foreign, communicated with the neighbouring kindred states, principally for the purpose of ascertaining all new inventions; and to a third department, all such inventions and improvements in machinery were committed for trial. Connected with this department was the College of Sages—a college especially favoured by such of the Ana as were widowed and childless, and by the young unmarried females, amongst whom Zee was the most active, and, if what we call renown or distinction was a thing acknowledged by this people (which I shall later show it is not), among the most renowned or distinguished. It is by the female Professors of this College that those studies which are deemed of least use in practical life—as purely speculative philosophy, the history of remote periods, and such sciences as entomology, conchology, &c.—are the more diligently cultivated. Zee, whose mind, active as Aristotle's, equally embraced the largest domains and the minutest details of thought, had written two volumes on the parasite insect that dwells amid the hairs of a tiger's* paw, which work was considered the best authority on that interesting subject. But the researches of the sages are not confined to such subtle or elegant studies. They comprise various others more important, and especially the properties of vril, to the perception of which their finer nervous organisation renders the female Professors eminently keen. It is out of this college that the Tur,

* The animal here referred to has many points of difference from the tiger of the upper world. It is larger, and with a broader paw, and still more receding frontal. It haunts the sides of lakes and pools, and feeds principally on fishes, though it does not object to any terrestrial animal of inferior strength that comes in its way. It is becoming very scarce even in the wild districts, where it is devoured by gigantic reptiles. I apprehend that it clearly belongs to the tiger species, since the parasite animalcule found in its paw, like that found in the Asiatic tiger's, is a miniature image of itself.

or chief magistrate, selects Councillors, limited to three, in the rare instances in which novelty of event or circumstance perplexes his own judgment.

There are a few other departments of minor consequence, but all are carried on so noiselessly and quietly that the evidence of a government seems to vanish altogether, and social order to be as regular and unobtrusive as if it were a law of nature. Machinery is employed to an inconceivable extent in all the operations of labour within and without doors, and it is the unceasing object of the department charged with its administration to extend its efficiency. There is no class of labourers or servants, but all who are required to assist or control the machinery are found in the children, from the time they leave the care of their mothers to the marriageable age, which they place at sixteen for the Gy-ei (the females), twenty for the Ana (the males). These children are formed into bands and sections under their own chiefs, each following the pursuits in which he is most pleased, or for which he feels himself most fitted. Some take to handicrafts, some to agriculture, some to household work, and some to the only services of danger to which the population is exposed; for the sole perils that threaten this tribe are, first, from those occasional convulsions within the earth, to foresee and guard against which tasks their utmost ingenuity—irruptions of fire and water, the storms of subterranean winds and escaping gases. At the borders of the domain, and at all places where such peril might be apprehended, vigilant inspectors are stationed with telegraphic communication to the hall in which chosen sages take it by turns to hold perpetual sittings. These inspectors are always selected from the elder boys approaching the age of puberty, and on the principle that at that age observation is more acute and the physical forces more alert than at any other. The second service of danger, less grave, is in the destruction of all creatures hostile to the life, or the culture, or even the comfort, of the Ana. Of these the most formidable are the vast reptiles, of some of which antediluvian relics are preserved in our museums, and certain gigantic winged creatures, half bird, half reptile. These, together with lesser wild animals, corresponding to our tigers or venomous serpents, it is left to the younger children to hunt and destroy; because, according to the Ana, here ruthlessness is wanted, and the younger a child the more ruthlessly he will destroy. There is another class of animals in the destruction of which discrimination is to be used, and against which children of intermediate age are appointed —animals that do not threaten the life of man, but ravage the produce of his labour, varieties of the elk and deer species, and a smaller creature much akin to our rabbit, though infinitely more destructive to crops, and much more cunning in its mode of depredation. It is the first object of these appointed infants, to tame the more intelligent of such animals into respect for enclosures signalised by conspicuous landmarks, as dogs are taught to respect a larder, or even to guard the master's property. It is only where such creatures are found untamable to this extent that they are destroyed. Life is never taken away for food or for sport, and never spared where untamably inimical to the Ana. Concomitantly with these bodily services and tasks, the mental education of the children goes on till boyhood ceases. It is the general custom, then, to pass through a course of instruction at the College of Sages, in which, besides more general studies, the pupil receives special lessons in such vocation or direction of intellect as he himself selects. Some, however, prefer to pass this period of probation in travel, or to emigrate, or to settle down at once into rural or commercial pursuits. No force is put upon individual inclination.

*   *   *

The word Ana (pronounced broadly *Arna*) corresponds with our plural *men;* An (pronounced *Arn*), the singular, with *man*. The word for woman is Gy (pronounced hard, as in Guy); it forms itself into Gy-ei for the plural, but the G becomes soft in the plural, like Jy-ei. They have a proverb to the effect that this difference in pronunciation is symbolical, for that the female sex is soft collectively, but hard to deal with in the individual. The Gy-ei are in the fullest enjoyment of all the rights of equality with males, for which certain philosophers above ground contend.

In childhood they perform the offices of work and labour impartially with boys; and, indeed, in the earlier age appropriated to the destruction of animals irreclaimably hostile, the girls are frequently preferred, as being by constitution more ruthless under the influence of fear or hate. In the interval between infancy and the marriageable age familiar intercourse between the sexes is suspended. At the marriageable age it is renewed, never with worse consequences than those which attend upon marriage. All arts and vocations allotted to the one sex are open to the other, and the Gy-ei arrogate to themselves a superiority in all those abstruse and mystical branches of reasoning, for which they say the Ana are unfitted by a duller sobriety of understanding, or the routine of their matter-of-fact occupations, just as young

ladies in our own world constitute themselves authorities in the sub-
tlest points of theological doctrine, for which few men, actively engaged in worldly business, have sufficient learning or refinement of intellect. Whether owing to early training in gymnastic exercises or to
their constitutional organisation, the Gy-ei are usually superior to the
Ana in physical strength (an important element in the consideration
and maintenance of female rights). They attain to loftier stature, and
amid their rounder proportions are embedded sinews and muscles as
hardy as those of the other sex. Indeed they assert that, according to
the original laws of nature, females were intended to be larger than
males, and maintain this dogma by reference to the earliest formations
of life in insects, and in the most ancient family of the vertebrata—viz.,
fishes—in both of which the females are generally large enough to
make a meal of their consorts if they so desire. Above all, the Gy-ei
have a readier and more concentred power over that mysterious fluid
or agency which contains the element of destruction, with a larger portion of that sagacity which comprehends dissimulation. Thus they can
not only defend themselves against all aggressions from the males, but
could, at any moment when he least suspected his danger, terminate
the existence of an offending spouse. To the credit of the Gy-ei no instance of their abuse of this awful superiority in the art of destruction
is on record for several ages. The last that occurred in the community
I speak of appears (according to their chronology) to have been about
two thousand years ago. A Gy, then in a fit of jealousy, slew her
husband; and this abominable act inspired such terror among the
males that they emigrated in a body and left all the Gy-ei to themselves. The history runs that the widowed Gy-ei, thus reduced to
despair, fell upon the murderess when in her sleep (and therefore
unarmed), and killed her, and then entered into a solemn obligation
amongst themselves to abrogate for ever the exercise of their extreme
conjugal powers, and to inculcate the same obligation for ever and
ever on their female children. By this conciliatory process, a deputa-
tion despatched to the fugitive consorts succeeded in persuading many
to return, but those who did return were mostly the elder ones. The
younger, either from too craven a doubt of their consorts, or too
high an estimate of their own merits, rejected all overtures, and,
remaining in other communities, were caught up there by other mates,
with whom perhaps they were no better off. But the loss of so large a
portion of the male youth operated as a salutary warning on the Gy-ei,
and confirmed them in the pious resolution to which they had pledged

themselves. Indeed it is now popularly considered that, by long hereditary disuse, the Gy-ei have lost both the aggressive and the defensive
superiority over the Ana which they once possessed, just as in the inferior animals above the earth many peculiarities in their original formation, intended by nature for their protection, gradually fade or become
inoperative when not needed under altered circumstances. I should be
sorry, however, for any An who induced a Gy to make the experiment
whether he or she were the stronger.

From the incident I have narrated, the Ana date certain alterations
in the marriage customs, tending, perhaps, somewhat to the advantage
of the male. They now bind themselves in wedlock only for three
years; at the end of each third year either male or female can divorce
the other and is free to marry again. At the end of ten years the An has
the privilege of taking a second wife, allowing the first to retire if she
so please. These regulations are for the most part a dead letter; di-
vorces and polygamy are extremely rare, and the marriage state now
seems singularly happy and serene among this astonishing people;–the
Gy-ei, notwithstanding their boastful superiority in physical strength
and intellectual abilities, being much curbed into gentle manners by
the dread of separation or of a second wife, and the Ana being very
much the creatures of custom, and not, except under great aggrava-
tion, liking to exchange for hazardous novelties faces and manners to
which they are reconciled by habit. But there is one privilege the Gy-ei
carefully retain, and the desire for which perhaps forms the secret motive of most lady asserters of woman rights above ground. They claim
the privilege, here usurped by men, of proclaiming their love and urging their suit; in other words, of being the wooing party rather than the
wooed. Such a phenomenon as an old maid does not exist among the
Gy-ei. Indeed it is very seldom that a Gy does not secure any An upon
whom she sets her heart, if his affections be not strongly engaged elsewhere. However coy, reluctant, and prudish, the male she courts may
prove at first, yet her perseverance, her ardour, her persuasive powers,
her command over the mystic agencies of vril, are pretty sure to run
down his neck into what we call "the fatal noose." Their argument for
the reversal of that relationship of the sexes which the blind tyranny of
man has established on the surface of the earth, appears cogent, and is
advanced with a frankness which might well be commended to impar-
tial consideration. They say, that of the two the female is by nature of
a more loving disposition than the male—that love occupies a larger
space in her thoughts, and is more essential to her happiness, and that

therefore she ought to be the wooing party; that otherwise the male is a shy and dubitant creature—that he has often a selfish predilection for the single state—that he often pretends to misunderstand tender glances and delicate hints—that, in short, he must be resolutely pursued and captured. They add, moreover, that unless the Gy can secure the An of her choice, and one whom she would not select out of the whole world becomes her mate, she is not only less happy than she otherwise would be, but she is not so good a being, that her qualities of heart are not sufficiently developed; whereas the An is a creature that less lastingly concentrates his affections on one object; that if he cannot get the Gy whom he prefers he easily reconciles himself to another Gy; and, finally, that at the worst, if he is loved and taken care of, it is less necessary to the welfare of his existence that he should love as well as be loved; he grows contented with his creature comforts, and the many occupations of thought which he creates for himself.

Whatever may be said as to this reasoning, the system works well for the male; for being thus sure that he is truly and ardently loved, and that the more coy and reluctant he shows himself, the more the determination to secure him increases, he generally contrives to make his consent dependent on such conditions as he thinks the best calculated to insure, if not a blissful, at least a peaceful life. Each individual An has his own hobbies, his own ways, his own predilections, and, whatever they may be, he demands a promise of full and unrestrained concession to them. This, in the pursuit of her object, the Gy readily promises; and as the characteristic of this extraordinary people is an implicit veneration for truth, and her word once given is never broken even by the giddiest Gy, the conditions stipulated for are religiously observed. In fact, notwithstanding all their abstract rights and powers, the Gy-ei are the most amiable, conciliatory, and submissive wives I have ever seen even in the happiest households above ground. It is an aphorism among them, that "where a Gy loves it is her pleasure to obey." It will be observed that in the relationship of the sexes I have spoken only of marriage, for such is the moral perfection to which this community has attained, that any illicit connection is as little possible amongst them as it would be to a couple of linnets during the time they agreed to live in pairs.

*　　　*　　　*

Nothing had more perplexed me in seeking to reconcile my sense to the existence of regions extending below the surface of the earth, and habitable by beings, if dissimilar from, still, in all material points of organism, akin to those in the upper world, than the contradiction thus presented to the doctrine in which, I believe, most geologists and philosophers concur—viz., that though with us the sun is the great source of heat, yet the deeper we go beneath the crust of the earth, the greater is the increasing heat, being, it is said, found in the ratio of a degree for every foot, commencing from fifty feet below the surface. But though the domains of the tribe I speak of were, on the higher ground, so comparatively near to the surface, that I could account for a temperature, therein, suitable to organic life, yet even the ravines and valleys of that realm were much less hot than philosophers would deem possible at such a depth—certainly not warmer than the south of France, or at least of Italy. And according to all the accounts I received, vast tracts immeasurably deeper beneath the surface, and in which one might have thought only salamanders could exist, were inhabited by innumerable races organised like ourselves. I cannot pretend in any way to account for a fact which is so at variance with the recognised laws of science, nor could Zee much help me towards a solution of it. She did but conjecture that sufficient allowance had not been made by our philosophers for the extreme porousness of the interior earth—the vastness of its cavities and irregularities, which served to create free currents of air and frequent winds—and for the various modes in which heat is evaporated and thrown off. She allowed, however, that there was a depth at which the heat was deemed to be intolerable to such organised life as was known to the experience of the Vril-ya, though their philosophers believed that even in such places life of some kind, life sentient, life intellectual, would be found abundant and thriving, could the philosophers penetrate to it. "Wherever the All-Good builds," said she, "there, be sure, He places inhabitants. He loves not empty dwellings." She added, however, that many changes in temperature and climate had been effected by the skill of the Vril-ya, and that the agency of vril had been successfully employed in such changes. She described a subtle and life-giving medium called Lai, which I suspect to be identical with the ethereal oxygen of Dr. Lewins, wherein work all the correlative forces united under the name of vril; and contended that wherever this medium could be expanded, as it were, sufficiently for the various agencies of vril to have ample play, a temperature congenial to the highest forms of life could be secured. She said also, that it was the belief of their naturalists that flowers and vegetation had been produced originally (whether developed from seeds borne from the surface of the earth in the earlier convulsions of nature, or imported by the tribes that first sought refuge in cavernous hollows) through the operations of the light constantly brought to bear on them, and the gradual improvement in culture. She said also, that since the vril light had superseded all other light-giving bodies, the colours of flower and foliage had become more brilliant, and vegetation had acquired larger growth.

II

PREHISTORIC MAN

***

The Grisly Folk
By H. G. Wells

The Mound Builders
By Lafcadio Hearn

3

The origin of mankind is a topic perhaps every bit as fascinating as that of the planet on which we live. Scientists and archaeologists have pondered for centuries on the bones and relics of bygone eras, attempting to discover from them how prehistoric man evolved and what kind of environment and society he existed in. Many great studies have shown different kinds of evolution in different parts of the world, and the migratory tendency of man has led to complex strains and a puzzling genealogy. Nevertheless, modern science has, with some assurance, explained much about primitive man's life, but remains puzzled at some of his achievements. Strange monuments, carvings and even relics bear silent witness to accomplishments we can still only guess at. It is a facet of history that can hardly have failed to excite the imagination of writers of scientific bent—none more so than the most famous of all science writers, H. G. Wells, author of such classics as *The Time Machine* (1895) and *War of the Worlds* (1898). *Herbert George Wells* (1866–1946) began life as a restless and rather unsuccessful science student. "The young Wells' mind," his biographer Vincent Brome has written, "was temperamentally hostile to the slow minutiae of the scientific approach, but perfectly at home with word pictures and sweeping visions." It was this vision and ability to conject on scientific mysteries that in time was to draw him from study and turn to writing, and later make him one of the most widely read authors of his period. It is perhaps a little difficult today to fully appreciate just how remarkable many of Wells's predictions and theories were. Yet, if we turn to his *Experiment in Autobiography* (1934), he makes the task a little easier by describing the world as it was when he came into it. "One did not see all round it in those days," he wrote. "It had mystery at its North and South Poles and Darkest Africa or its equator. Poe's 'Narrative of A. Gordon Pym,' for instance, tells us what a very intelligent mind could imagine about the South Polar regions . . . and the poor old earth had a hard crust and a molten interior and naturally suffered from chronic indigestion. It has since solidified considerably." In his stories Wells utilized his knowledge of science brilliantly— "he knew just how to unlock the excitements, the imaginative worlds, buried beneath dull scientific data," says Vincent Brome. Then, after a time, as Wells himself notes, "I became quite dexterous at evolving incidents and anecdotes from little possibilities of a scientific or quasi-scientific sort. I had no idea in those energetic, needy days of the little tips I was giving." Throughout his life, Wells was undoubtedly as interested in the past as he was in the future (although much of his writing was devoted to the latter), and prehistory caused him much thought and delight, as the colorful paintings daubed all over the walls of his garage bore witness. These depicted the dawn of civilization from the beetle-like Trilobites to man, and were painted—to quote one viewer—"with something of the elemental vigor of our prehistoric forebears!" Wells also wrote stories about early man, including the ingenuous re-creation "The Grisly Folk," which appears here; its first appearance was in 1904 in *The Strand Magazine*. It is yet one more reason for believing that Wells had more than a little justification (even if he was lacking in suitable modesty) for claiming in a letter to Arnold Bennett: "There is something other than either story writing or artistic merit which has emerged through the series of my books—something one might regard as a new system of ideas—thought."

THE GRISLY FOLK
H. G. Wells

"Can these bones live?"

Could anything be more dead, more mute and inexpressive to the inexpert eye than the ochreous fragments of bone and the fractured lumps of flint that constitute the first traces of something human in the world? We see them in the museum cases, sorted out in accordance with principles we do not understand, labelled with strange names. Chellean, Mousterian, Solutrian and the like, taken mostly from the places Chelles, La Moustier, Solutre, and so forth where the first specimens were found. Most of us stare through the glass at them, wonder vaguely for a moment at that half-savage, half-animal past of our race, and pass on. "Primitive man," we say. "Flint implements. The mammoth used to chase him." Few of us realise yet how much the subtle indefatigable cross-examination of the scientific worker has been extracting from the evidence of these rusty and obstinate witnesses during the last few years.

One of the most startling results of this recent work is the gradual realisation that great quantities of these flint implements and some of the earlier fragments of bone that used to be ascribed to humanity are the vestiges of creatures, very manlike in many respects, but not, strictly speaking, belonging to the human species. Scientific men call these vanished races man (*Homo*), just as they call lions and tigers cats (*Felis*), but there are the soundest reasons for believing that these earlier so-called men were not of our blood, not our ancestors, but a strange and vanished animal, like us, akin to us, but different from us, as the mammoth was like, and akin to, and yet different from, the elephant. Flint and bone implements are found in deposits of very considerable antiquity; some in our museums may be a million years old or more, but the traces of really human creatures, mentally and anatomically like ourselves, do not go back much earlier than twenty or thirty thousand years ago. True men appeared in Europe then, and we do not know whence they came. These other tool-using, fire-making animals, the things that were like men and yet were not men, passed away before the faces of the true men.

Scientific authorities already distinguish four species of these pseudo-men, and it is probable that we shall learn from time to time of other species. One strange breed made the implements called Chellean. These are chiefly sole-shaped blades of stone found in deposits of perhaps 300,000 or 400,000 years ago. Chellean implements are to be seen in any great museum. They are huge implements, *four or five times as big as those made by any known race of true men,* and they are not ill made. Certainly some creature with an intelligent brain made them. Big clumsy hands must have gripped and used these rocky chunks. But so far only one small fragment of a skeleton of this age has been found, a very massive chinless lower jawbone, with teeth rather *more* specialised than those of men to-day. We can only guess what strange foreshadowing of the human form once ate with that jaw, and struck at its enemies with those big but not unhandy flint blades. It may have been a tremendous fellow, probably much bigger in the body than a man. It may have been able to take bears by the scruff and the sabre-toothed lion by the throat. We do not know. We have just these great stone blades and that bit of a massive jaw and—the liberty to wonder.

Most fascinating riddle of all these riddles of the ages of ice and hardship, before the coming of the true men, is the riddle of the Mousterian men, because they were perhaps still living in the world when the true man came wandering into Europe. They lived much later than those unknown Chellean giants. They lived thirty or forty thousand years ago—a yesterday compared with the Chellean time. These Mousterians are also called Neandertalers. Until quite recently it was supposed that they were true men like ourselves. But now we begin to realise that they were different, so different that it is impossible that they can be very close relations of ours. They walked or shambled along with a peculiar slouch, they could not turn their heads up to the sky, and their teeth were very different from those of true men. One oddity about them is that in one or two points they were less like apes than we are. The dog tooth, the third tooth from the middle, which is so big in the gorilla, and which in man is pointed and still quite distinct from the other teeth, is not distinct at all in the Neandertaler. He had a very even row of teeth, and his cheek teeth also were very unlike ours, and less like the apes' than ours. He had more face and less brow than true men, but that is not because he had a lesser brain; his brain was as big as a modern man's but it was different, bigger behind and smaller in front, so that probably he thought and behaved differently from us. Perhaps he had a better memory and less reasoning power than real men, or perhaps he had more nervous energy and less intelligence. He had no chin, and the way his jawbones come together below make it very doubtful if he could have used any such sounds in speech as we employ. Probably he did not talk at all. He could not hold a pin between his finger and thumb. The more we learn about this beast-man the stranger he becomes to us and the less like the Australoid savage he was once supposed to be.

And as we realise the want of any close relationship between this ugly, strong, ungainly, manlike animal and mankind, the less likely it becomes that he had a naked skin and hair like ours and the more probable that he was different, and perhaps bristly or hairy in some queer inhuman fashion like the hairy elephant and the woolly rhinoceros who were his contemporaries. Like them he lived in a bleak land on the edge of the snows and glaciers that were even then receding northward. Hairy or grisly, with a big face like a mask, great brow ridges and no forehead, clutching an enormous flint, and running like a baboon with his head forward and not, like a man, with his head up, he must have been a fearsome creature for our forefathers to come upon.

Almost certainly they met, these grisly men and the true men. The true man must have come into the habitat of the Neandertaler, and the two must have met and fought. Some day we may come upon the evidences of this warfare.

Western Europe, which is the only part of the world that has yet been searched with any thoroughness for the remains of early men, was slowly growing warmer age by age; the glaciers that had once covered half the continent were receding, and wide stretches of summer pasture and thin woods of pine and birch were spreading slowly over the once icy land. South Europe then was like northern Labrador to-day. A few hardy beasts held out amidst the snows; the bears hibernated. With the spring grass and foliage came great herds of reindeer, wild horses, mammoth, elephant, and rhinoceros, drifting northward from the slopes of the great warm valley that is now filled up with water—the Mediterranean Sea. It was in those days before the ocean waters broke into the Mediterranean that the swallows and a multitude of other birds acquired the habit of coming north, a habit that now-adays impels them to brave the passage of the perilous seas that flow over and hide the lost secrets of the ancient Mediterranean valleys. The grisly men rejoiced at the return of life, came out of the caves in which they had lurked during the winter, and took their toll of the beasts.

These grisly men must have been almost solitary creatures.

The winter food was too scanty for communities. A male may have gone with a female or so; perhaps they parted in the winter and came together in the summer; when his sons grew big enough to annoy him, the grisly man killed them or drove them off. If he killed them he may have eaten them. If they escaped him they may have returned to kill him. The grisly folk may have had long unreasoning memories and very set purposes.

The true men came into Europe, we know not whence, out of the South. When they appeared in Europe their hands were as clever as ours; they could draw pictures we still admire, they could paint and carve; the implements they made were smaller than the Mousterian ones, far smaller than the Chellean, but better made and more various. They wore no clothes worth speaking of, but they painted themselves and probably they talked. And they came in little bands. They were already more social than the Neandertaler; they had laws and self-restraints; their minds had travelled a long way along that path of adaptation and self-suppression which has led to the intricate mind of man to-day with its concealed wishes, its confusions, and laughter and the fantasies and reveries and dreams. They were already held together, these men, and kept in order by the strange limitations of tabu.

They were still savages, very prone to violence and convulsive in their lusts and desires; but to the best of their poor ability they obeyed laws and customs already immemorably ancient, and they feared the penalties of wrong-doing. We can understand something of what was going on in their minds, those of us who can remember the fears, desires, fancies and superstitions of our childhood. Their moral struggles were ours—in cruder forms. They were our kind. But the grisly folk we cannot begin to understand. We cannot conceive in our different minds the strange ideas that chased one another through those queerly shaped brains. As well might we try to dream and feel as a gorilla dreams and feels.

We can understand how the true men drifted northward from the lost lands of the Mediterranean valley into the high Spanish valleys and the south and centre of France, and so on to what is now England —for there was no Channel then between England and France—and eastward to the Rhineland and over the broad wilderness which is now the North Sea, and the German plain. They would leave the snowy wilderness of the Alps, far higher then and covered with great glaciers, away on their right. These people drifted northward for the very good reason that their kind was multiplying and food diminishing. They would be oppressed by feuds and wars. They had no settled homes; they were accustomed to drift with the seasons, every now and then some band would be pushed by hunger and fear a little farther northward into the unknown.

We can imagine the appearance of a little group of these wanderers, our ancestors, coming over some grassy crest into these northern lands. The time would be late spring or early summer, and they would probably be following up some grazing beasts, a reindeer herd or horses.

By a score of different means our anthropologists have been able to reconstruct the particulars of the appearance and habits of these early pilgrim fathers of mankind.

They would not be a very numerous band, because if they were there would be no reason why they should have been driven northward out of their former roving grounds. Two or three older men of thirty or so, eight or ten women and girls with a few young children, a few lads between fourteen and twenty, might make up the whole community. They would be a brownish brown-eyed people with wavy dark hair;

the fairness of the European and the straight blue-black hair of the Chinaman had still to be evolved in the world. The older men would probably lead the band, the women and children would keep apart from the youths and men, fenced off by complex and definite tabus from any close companionship. The leaders would be tracking the herd they were following. Tracking was then the supreme accomplishment of mankind. By signs and traces that would be invisible to any modern civilised eye, they would be reading the story of the previous day's trek of the herd of sturdy little horses ahead of them. They would be so expert that they would go on from one faint sign to another with as little delay as a dog who follows a scent.

The horses they were following were only a little way ahead—so the trackers read the signs—they were numerous and nothing had alarmed them. They were grazing and moving only very slowly. There were no traces of wild dog or other enemies to stampede them. Some elephants were also going north, and twice our human tribe had crossed the spoor of woolly rhinoceros roaming westward.

The tribe travelled light. They were mainly naked, but all of them were painted with white and black and red and yellow ochre. At this distance of time it is difficult to see whether they were tattooed. Probably they were not. The babies and small children were carried by the women on their backs in slings or bags made of animal skins, and perhaps some or all of them wore mantles and loin bands of skin and had pouches and belts of leather. The men had stone-pointed spears, and carried sharpened flints in their hands.

There was no Old Man who was lord and master and father of this particular crowd. Weeks ago the Old Man had been charged and trampled to a jelly by a great bull in the swamp far away. Then two of the girls had been waylaid and carried off by the young men of another larger tribe. It was because of these losses that this remnant was now seeking new hunting grounds.

The landscape that spread before the eyes of this little band as they crested the hill was a bleaker, more desolate and altogether unkempt version of the landscape of western Europe to-day. About them was a grassy down athwart which a peewit flew with its melancholy cry. Before them stretched a great valley ridged with transverse purple hills over which the April cloud-shadows chased one another. Pinewoods and black heather showed where these hills became sandy, and the valleys were full of brown brushwood, and down their undrained troughs ran a bright green band of peaty swamps and long pools of weedy water. In the valley thickets many beasts lurked unseen, and where the winding streams had cut into the soil there were cliffs and caves. Far away along the northern slopes of the ridge that were now revealed, the wild ponies were to be seen grazing.

At a sign from the two leaders the little straggle of menfolk halted, and a woman who had been chattering in subdued tones to a little girl became silent. The brothers surveyed the wide prospect earnestly.

"Ugh!" said one abruptly and pointed.

"Ugh!" cried his brother.

The eyes of the whole tribe swung round to the pointing finger.

The group became one rigid stare.

Every soul of them stood still, astonishment had turned them into a tense group of statuettes.

Far away down the slope with his body in profile and his head turned towards them, frozen by an equal amazement, stood a hunched grey figure, bigger but shorter than a man. He had been creeping up behind a fold in the ground to peer at the ponies; and suddenly he had turned his eyes and seen the tribe. His head projected like a baboon's. In his hand he carried what seemed to the menfolk a great rock.

For a little while this animal scrutiny held discoverers and discovered motionless. Then some of the women and children began to stir and line out to see the strange creature better. "Man!" said an old crone of forty. *"Man!"* At the movement of the women the grisly man turned, ran clumsily for a score of yards or so towards a thicket of birch and budding thorn. Then he halted again for a moment to look at the newcomers, waved an arm strangely, and then dashed into cover.

The shadows of the thicket swallowed him up, and by hiding him seemed to make him enormous. It identified itself with him, and watched them with his eyes. Its tree stems became long silvery limbs, and a fallen trunk crouched and stared.

It was still early in the morning, and the leaders of the tribe had hoped to come up with the wild ponies as the day advanced and perhaps cut one off and drive it into difficulties among the bushes and swampy places below, and wound it and follow it up and kill it. Then they would have made a feast, and somewhere down in the valley they would have found water and dry bracken for litter and a fire before night. It had seemed a pleasant and hopeful morning to them until this moment. Now they were disconcerted. This grey figure was as if the sunny morning had suddenly made a horrible and inexplicable grimace.

The whole expedition stood gazing for a time, and then the two leaders exchanged a few words. Waugh, the elder, pointed. Click, his brother, nodded his head. They would go on, but instead of slanting down the slopes towards the thickets they would keep round the ridge.

"Come," said Waugh, and the little band began to move again. But now it marched in silence. When presently a little boy began a question his mother silenced him by a threat. Everybody kept glancing at the thickets below.

Presently a girl cried out sharply and pointed. All started and stopped short.

There was the grisly thing again. It was running across an open space, running almost on all fours, in joltering leaps. It was hunch-backed and very big and low, a grey hairy wolf-like monster. At times its long arms nearly touched the ground. It was nearer than it had been before. It vanished amidst the bushes again. It seemed to throw itself down among some red dead bracken. . . .

Waugh and Click took counsel.

A mile away was the head of the valley where the thickets had their beginning. Beyond stretched the woldy hills, bare of cover. The horses were grazing up towards the sun, and away to the north the backs of a herd of woolly rhinoceros were now visible on a crest—just the ridges of their backs showing like a string of black beads.

If the tribe struck across those grassy spaces, then the lurking prowler would have either to stay behind or come into the open. If he came into the open the dozen youths and men of the tribe would know how to deal with him.

So they struck across the grass. The little band worked round to the head of the valley, and there the menfolk stayed at the crest while the women and children pushed on ahead across the open.

For a time the watchers remained motionless, and then Waugh was moved to gestures of defiance. Click was not to be outdone. There were shouts at the hidden watcher, and then one lad, who was something of a clown, after certain grimaces and unpleasant gestures, obliged with an excellent imitation of the grey thing's lumbering run. At that, scare gave place to hilarity.

In those days laughter was a social embrace. Men could laugh, but there was no laughter in the grisly pre-man who watched and wondered in the shadow. He marvelled. The men rolled about and guffawed and slapped their thighs and one another. Tears ran down their faces.

Never a sign came from the thickets.

"Yahah," said the menfolk. "Yahah! Bzzzz. Yahah! Yah!"

They forgot altogether how frightened they had been.

And when Waugh thought the women and children had gone on a sufficient distance, he gave the word for the men to follow them.

In some such fashion it was that men, our ancestors, had their first glimpse of the pre-men of the wilderness of western Europe. . . .

The two breeds were soon to come to closer quarters.

The newcomers were pushing their way into the country of these grisly men. Presently came other glimpses of lurking semi-human shapes and grey forms that ran in the twilight. In the morning Click found long narrow footprints round the camp. . . .

Then one day one of the children, eating those little green thorn-buds that rustic English children speak of as bread and cheese, ventured too far from the others. There was a squeal and a scuffle and a thud, and something grey and hairy made off through the thickets carrying its victim, with Waugh and three of the younger men in hot pursuit. They chased the enemy into a dark gully, very much overgrown. This time it was not a solitary Neandertaler they had to deal with. Out of the bushes a big male came at them to cover the retreat of his mate, and hurled a rock that bowled over the youth it hit like a nine-pin, so that thereafter he limped always. But Waugh with his throwing spear got the grey monster in the shoulder, and he halted snarling.

No further sound came from the stolen child.

The female showed herself for a moment up the gully, snarling, bloodstained, and horrible, and the menfolk stood about afraid to continue their pursuit, and yet not caring to desist from it. One of them was already hobbling off with his hand to his knee.

How did that first fight go?

Perhaps it went against the men of our race. Perhaps the big Neandertaler male, his mane and beard bristling horribly, came down the gully with a thunderous roar, with a great rock in either hand. We do not know whether he threw those big discs of flint or whether he smote with them. Perhaps it was then that Waugh was killed in the act of running away. Perhaps it was bleak disaster then for the little tribe. Short of two of its members it presently made off over the hills as fast as it could go, keeping together for safety, and leaving the wounded youth far behind to limp along its tracks in lonely terror.

Let us suppose that he got back to the tribe at last—after nightmare hours.

Now that Waugh had gone, Click would become Old Man, and he made the tribe camp that night and build their fire on the high ridges among the heather far away from the thickets in which the grisly folk might be lurking.

The grisly folk thought we knew not how about the menfolk, and the men thought about the grisly folk in such ways as we can understand; they imagined how their enemies might act in this fashion or that, and schemed to circumvent them. It may have been Click who had the first dim idea of getting at the gorge in which the Neandertalers had their lair, from above. For as we have said, the Neandertaler did not look up. Then the menfolk could roll a great rock upon him or pelt him with burning brands and set the dry bracken alight.

One likes to think of a victory for the human side. This Click we have conjured up had run in panic from the first onset of the grisly male, but as he brooded by the fire that night he heard again in imagination the cry of the lost girl, and he was filled with rage. In his sleep the grisly male came to him and Click fought in his dreams and started awake stiff with fury. There was a fascination for him in that gorge in which Waugh had been killed. He was compelled to go back and look again for the grisly beasts, to waylay them in their tracks, and watch them from an ambush. He perceived that the Neandertalers could not climb as easily as the menfolk could climb, nor hear so quickly, nor dodge with the same unexpectedness. These grisly men were to be dealt with as the bears were dealt with, the bears before whom you run and scatter, and then come at again from behind.

But one may doubt if the first human group to come into the grisly land was clever enough to solve the problems of the new warfare. Maybe they turned southward again to the gentler regions from which they had come, and were killed by or mingled with their own brethren again. Maybe they perished altogether in that new land of the grisly folk into which they had intruded. Yet the truth may be that they even held their own and increased. If they died there were others of their kind to follow them and achieve a better fate.

That was the beginning of a nightmare age for the little children of the human tribe. They knew they were watched.

Their steps were dogged. The legends of ogres and man-eating giants that haunt the childhood of the world may descend to us from

those ancient days of fear. And for the Neandertalers it was the beginning of an incessant war that could end only in extermination.

The Neandertalers, albeit not so erect and tall as men, were the
heavier, stronger creatures, but they were stupid, and they went alone
or in twos and threes; the menfolk were swifter, quicker-witted, and
more social—when they fought they fought in combination. They lined
out and surrounded and pestered and pelted their antagonists from
every side. They fought the men of that grisly race as dogs might fight
a bear. They shouted to one another what each should do, and the
Neandertaler had no speech; he did not understand. They moved too
quickly for him and fought too cunningly.

Many and obstinate were the duels and battles these two sorts of
men fought for this world in that bleak age of the windy steppes, thirty
or forty thousand years ago. The two races were intolerable to each
other. They both wanted the caves and the banks by the rivers where
the big flints were got. They fought over the dead mammoths that had
been bogged in the marshes, and over the reindeer stags that had been
killed in the rutting season. When a human tribe found signs of the
grisly folk near their cave and squatting place, they had perforce to
track them down and kill them; their own safety and the safety of their
little ones was only to be secured by that killing. The Neandertalers
thought the little children of men fair game and pleasant eating.

How long the grisly folk lived on in that chill world of pines and
silver birch between the steppes and the glaciers, after the true menfolk came, we do not know. For ages they may have held out, growing
more cunning and dangerous as they became rare. The true men
hunted them down by their spoor and by their tracks, and watched for
the smoke of their fires, and made food scarce for them.

Great Paladins arose in that forgotten world, men who stood forth
and smote the grey man-beast face to face and slew him. They made
long spears of wood, hardened by fire at the tips; they raised shields of
skin against his mighty blows. They struck at him with stones on cords,
and slung them at him with slings. And it was not simply men who
withstood the grisly beast but women. They stood over their children;
they stood by their men against this eerie thing that was like and yet
not like mankind. Unless the *savants* read all the signs awry, it was the
women who were the makers of the larger tribes into which human
families were already growing in those ancient times. It was the woman's subtle, love-guided wits which protected her sons from the fierce
anger of the Old Man, and taught them to avoid his jealousy and

wrath, and persuaded him to tolerate them and so have their help against the grisly enemy. It was woman, says Atkinson, in the beginning of things human, who taught the primary tabus, that a son must go aside out of the way of his stepmother, and get himself a wife from another tribe, so as to keep the peace within the family. She came between the fratricides, and was the first peacemaker. Human societies in their beginnings were her work, done against the greater solitariness, the lonely fierceness of the adult male. Through her, men learnt the primary co-operation of sonship and brotherhood. The grisly folk had not learnt even the rudest elements of co-operation, and mankind had already spelt out the alphabet of a unity that may some day comprehend the whole earth. The menfolk kept together by the dozen and by the score. By ones and twos and threes therefore the grisly folk were beset and slain, until there were no more of them left in the world.

Generation after generation, age after age, that long struggle for existence went on between these men who were not quite men and the men, our ancestors, who came out of the South into western Europe. Thousands of fights and hunts, sudden murders and headlong escapes there were amidst the caves and thickets of that chill and windy world between the last age of glaciers and our own warmer time. Until at length the last poor grisly was brought to bay and faced the spears of his pursuers in anger and despair.

What leapings of the heart were there not throughout that long warfare! What moments of terror and triumph! What acts of devotion and desperate wonders of courage! And the strain of the victors was our strain; we are lineally identical with those sun-brown painted beings who ran and fought and helped one another, the blood in our veins glowed in those fights and chilled in those fears of the forgotten past. For it was forgotten. Except perhaps for some vague terrors in our dreaming life and for some lurking element of tradition in the legends and warnings of the nursery, it has gone altogether out of the memory of our race. But nothing is ever completely lost. Seventy or eighty years ago a few curious *savants* began to suspect that there were hidden memories in certain big chipped flints and scraps of bone they found in ancient gravels. Much more recently others have begun to find hints of remote strange experiences in the dreams and odd kinks in modern minds. By degrees these dry bones begin to live again.

This restoration of the past is one of the most astonishing adventures of the human mind. As humanity follows the gropings of scientific men among these ancient vestiges, it is like a man who turns over the yellow pages of some long-forgotten diary, some engagement book of his adolescence. His dead youth lives again. Once more the old excitements stir him, the old happiness returns. But the old passions that once burnt, only warm him now, and the old fears and distresses signify nothing.

A day may come when these recovered memories may grow as vivid as if we in our own persons had been there and shared the thrill and the fear of those primordial days; a day may come when the great beasts of the past will leap to life again in our imaginations, when we shall walk again in vanished scenes, stretch painted limbs we thought were dust, and feel again the sunshine of a million years ago.

4

Although America is regarded as one of the youngest civilizations of the world, it has in fact a history of human habitation dating back to antiquity. It possesses a variety of relics of these early men too, although it is only during the last one hundred years or so that extensive inquiry into their history has been carried out. Probably the two most famous sites of prehistoric man are the megaliths in New England and the extraordinary "mounds" in Ohio. The stone constructions in New England are situated on the appropriately named "Mystery Hill" in North Salem, New Hampshire, and consist of twenty-two structures and stone fragments. The majority opinion concerning their origin is that they were the handiwork of Celtic or northwest European peoples, because of their similarity to stone communities found in the Orkneys and chambered tombs in Brittany, France. It is also believed that details of their existence were suppressed by the early Puritan colonists, as they were thought to be relics of some old pagan religion. Hence, study of them has only commenced in comparatively recent times. (Another theory advanced by Harvard professor Eben Horsford in 1892 is that the stones were the last fragments of the vast lost city of Norumbega for which the French explorer Samuel de Champlain, and many other voyagers, sought in vain.) The ancient mounds found in Ohio, however, are a rather different example of primitive construction, and from them it has been possible to assemble facts about both their construction and the remarkable people responsible for their creation. "The Mound Builders"—as these people are known—have been a source of study for archaeologists and authors, among whose ranks was the eccentric but highly talented writer of macabre stories *Lafcadio Hearn* (1850–1904). A chronicler of ghosts and ghouls, murders and grave robbers, Hearn was also a passionate student of prehistoric peoples, and his writing career is dotted with stories of ancient civilizations. Some of his best work in the genre was done while he lived and worked in Cincinnati (contributing to the local *Enquirer* and *Commercial*), and this is mainly attributable to the relics of "The Mound Builders" which proliferated in the district. In one article, "The World's Worship," he demonstrated his absorption in the subject by describing the mounds as being in the form of "serpents winding for miles over level plains, or coiled in rings of circumference vast as a city walled up to heaven, in pursuing some prey—a tortoise perhaps in the form of a hillock." Apart from personal observation, Hearn had at his command "scholarship and the facility for classical and curious research," which, according to his biographer Albert Mordell, enabled him to advance theories and opinions "far bolder and more exciting than any contemporary." In an article entitled "The Precursor of Man," for instance, he suggested that the Basque peoples had descended from the Cro-Magnons, while in "Celestial Geology" he thought it might be possible to reconstruct a dead planet from meteoric stones, and in "Eye Transplantations" he speculated on the transplanting of an animal's eye into a human socket. (Hearn himself had dreadful eyesight and was more than

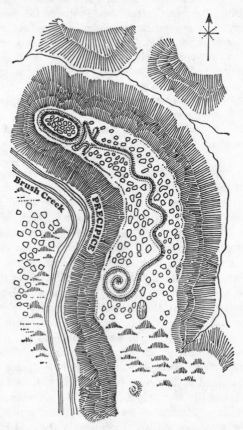

The Great Serpent Mound in Ohio, mentioned by Lafcadio Hearn.

once referred to disparagingly as "that myopic half-blind writer.") Mordell also likens Hearn to his contemporary H. G. Wells in several respects. "It was the imaginative and speculative problems opened up by science which fascinated him," Mordell has written. "He occasionally indulged in too fanciful speculations, but he often showed intuition in scientific prognostications in which future discoveries have borne him out. He was, for instance, one of the few who realized the great factor electricity would play, and wrote several editorials on the subject." Perhaps he was never more accomplished, however, than when dealing with his beloved ancient civilizations, as the contribution here will show. This story first appeared in the Cincinnati *Enquirer* in 1878.

THE MOUND BUILDERS
Lafcadio Hearn

Over the face of the country, throughout Ohio and the adjoining States, the extinct race of giant men who disputed their daily food with a race of monster animals, extinct like themselves, have written a mystic record of their existence in hieroglyphics perhaps uninterpretable, yet everlasting and indestructible save by some vast cataclysm. The mighty characters of this ancient record are not less imposing than the eternal hills themselves. A French theorist, who believed in the plurality of worlds and the possibility of holding communication with the inhabitants of other planets, once advocated the formation of enormous mounds, mathematically shaped, upon some sterile plain, to serve as a Universal Alphabet—for the language of mathematics must be the same in all spheres peopled by intelligent beings. The mountainous alphabet of the dead Nation whom we call Mound-builders offers a practical realization of the French author's idea,—excepting, perhaps, the fact of mathematical form. They wrote upon the face of the earth in such mighty bas-relief, that their hieroglyphics were once regarded as natural hills. Then it was gradually found that these hills possessed strangely unnatural forms. Some coiled in a serpentine circuit, curve within curve for miles, like ophidian monsters of the pre-Adamite age. Some presented the form of a huge tortoise fleeing from the open mouth of a pursuing serpent, whose writhing bulk shadowed the land at sundown for many thousand feet. Some were discovered to be grotesque imitations of the forms of birds or deer. Some represented nude prehistoric Man himself in monstrous effigy, and one has been found in colossal mimicry of a spider with vast legs extending over acres of ground. The serpent symbol was a favorite device, and in Adams County, Ohio, may be observed the hilly outline of a half-coiled serpent upwards of a thousand feet in length, which seems about to swallow an egg. But the greater number of mounds were found to be terraced or truncated, as though having once formed substructures for immense temples, which being built of some more perishable material than the Mexican teocallis, have disappeared without leaving a trace. Earthworks of the most extraordinary design are likewise visible throughout the State. At Miamisburg, Brownsville, Liberty, Cedarbank, Marietta, and several places in Pike and Adams Counties, Ohio, mounds have excited the curiosity of archaeologists in every civilized country. The great mound at Miamisburg is no less than sixty-eight feet high and eight hundred and fifty-two feet in circumference at the base.

And this dead race of giants who fought with hairy mammoths and enormous cave bears, and perhaps that mastodon whose colossal bones to-day dwarf into comparative delicacy the elephant's rugged skeleton—this race, who bowed before the writhing form of the serpent, and perhaps beheld the megatherium, the plesiosaurus and the monstrous brood of the earth's first-born—who were they? It is at least generally recognized that they were not Indians. Their monumental record little resembles that of the Aztec people; and indeed no other American Nation has left traces satisfactorily analogous to those left by the Mound-builders. But it is worthy of note that very similar remains have been left by the European Mound-builders. Both used similar weapons of defense; both were serpent-worshipers; both struggled with nature for a rude existence in the Stone Age—perhaps, according to the reckoning of one famous philologist, twenty thousand years ago. The arrowheads of the earliest European races are exact counterparts of those used by the earliest American people, and the serpent-mounds of Ohio and Kentucky are strangely similar in design to the ophite temples of weird Karnac or rocky Stonehenge. Again, the Mound-builders of both hemispheres appear to have been sun-worshipers, and carven disks representing the sun have been found in their graves. But it would appear that the Mound-builders who peopled the Mississippi Valley passed up north and west from the Gulf. Their rude stone implements are mostly wrought from rock which is not found in the region where they have left their mightiest traces. Obsidian, a volcanic product of adamantine density, from which many of their weapons and utensils have been manufactured, is found no nearer to the Mississippi Valley than the Mexican mountains of Cerro Gordo. The Ohio relics of stone are almost all made from material which can not be found in any part of the State. Many arrowheads from the Cincinnati district, for instance, are wrought out of a species of moss-agate almost peculiar to Colorado.

A highly interesting theory of the origin of the Mound-builders, is connected with the most awful and most wonderful of all historic traditions—the ancient Legend of Atlantis, whereof Plato and other ancient writers spake weirdly and dreamfully. Even in their day, it was probably but the echo of a most remote tradition, handed down through the ages. Classic travelers said that toward the setting sun, far beyond the pillars of Hercules, lay a great, fair island, in the midst of the Unknown Sea, and beyond, yet another island; and still beyond, the foam-kissed shore of the unknown land which girdled the ocean. The first fair island was called Atlantis, and it contained four great kingdoms, with principalities and palaces innumerable. No such island, as geographically described by these writers, has any place in the world, although the researches of modern travelers confirm many long-doubted statements written in the classic ages. But the Aztecs and other ancient races had a dim tradition of such an island, and of a frightful cataclysm which destroyed it, even as the classic authors had written. And some modern theorists believe that there was an Atlantis, inhabited by mighty and wealthy nations.

In fine, there is not wanting testimony to support the opinion that the present continent of America once extended into the Atlantic Ocean as far as the Madeira Islands; that these islands themselves are actually but the summits of a prehistoric mountain chain, which once shadowed Atlantis and its cities; that the ocean gradually divided this lost land into two or more islands, and that the condition of things spoken of by Plato really existed. Then came some calamity so overwhelming and frightful that we can form no adequate conception of it, when the islands and their cities were in one short night lost from the face of the earth. Tradition speaks of terrific earthquakes, of a raging sea eating up the land, of rivers of fire breaking forth from the entrails of the rocks and devouring cities, with their peoples. Some few perhaps escaped to record the calamity in this fearful tradition, which has lived perhaps through ten thousand years.

It is likewise supposed that it was from Northern Europe to Atlantis, and thence overland, or by short sea-journeys, to the continent beyond—that the Mound-builders came with their cattle.

[It is known that an animal very similar to the American bison once existed in Northern Europe.]

When the Aztecs were questioned by Spanish discoverers as to their ancestry, they replied that they were the children of bearded strangers, with pale skins, who came from the remote East—from the rising sun. Perhaps those pale-skinned strangers were the emigrant Mound-builders, and perhaps thousands upon thousands of years in this western climate permanently bronzed the skins and sharpened the features, and dwarfed the physique of their progeny. We do not hint at these theories because they have any great weight of probability, but simply because they are interesting. The birthplace of the human race might have been, not in the Far East, but in the Far West, or in some lost continent. And here it is worthy of note that in some of the Pacific islands are visible remains not altogether unlike the mounds of the Mound-builders. Perhaps there was also an Atlantis in the Pacific; for the language of Tahiti is recognizably similar to the tongue of Malay.

We can hardly form any satisfactory opinion in regard to the physical characteristics of this primitive race, except that extraordinary strength, activity and endurance must have been necessary to human existence amid such rude conditions. Deep in the heart of their mystic mounds, skeletons have been found, but so completely decayed that the mere contact of the outer air destroyed even their form. It has yet been found impossible to obtain a correct outline of such a skeleton, much less of the entire body, which has been frequently done at Pompeii. Yet skeletons nearly two thousand years old have been unearthed in good preservation in various parts of Europe; and great indeed must be the lapse of time which reduced the skeletons found in our mounds to so evanescent a stage of decay. Fragments of bones have, however, been preserved sufficiently entire to take casts from, including several portions of skulls. These remains speak ill for the intelligence and physiognomical attributes of the race. Perhaps the best preserved skull yet found in an American mound was discovered at Kenton, Illinois. It is hideous, revolting. The frontal bones are strangely abnormal, the superciliary arches stand out in enormous ridges, the skull-face actually frowns. All the frontal bones are prodigiously thick and strong. A modern human being could hardly gaze into a living face similar to that which once clothed this skull without experiencing such a feeling of terror as the aspect of the most ferocious beast of prey could not produce. But it is not reasonable to suppose that this frightful skull, with its inch-thick brows of frowning bone, is by any means a fair specimen of the Mound-builders' cranial development.

The study of American archaeology is annually obtaining greater attention from scientists, and may yet result in the elucidation of some highly important ethnological problems. The antiquities of Mississippi, Missouri, Illinois, Iowa, Michigan, Kentucky and Ohio are perhaps being quite as earnestly discussed in Europe as they have yet been in this country, and the mounds of Miamisburg and Adams County are probably better known in London than they are in Cincinnati. In every county throughout this State plows daily turn up the wondrously hewn flints which formed the agricultural implements or battle weapons of this extinct people.

III

MYTHOLOGY

***

The Shining Pyramid
By *Arthur Machen*

The Call of Cthulhu
By *H. P. Lovecraft*

The creation of mythological races has been a popular theme in fantasy fiction for many years. A great number of such tales have only the slightest connection with scientific knowledge; of the remainder, a few have advanced hypotheses firmly rooted in old traditions and legends, and thereby excite the imaginations of all who read them. Two writers have perhaps contributed most substantially to this genre, and their influence has been felt in a multitude of novels and stories—the Welshman Arthur Machen, and the American H. P. Lovecraft. Machen must certainly take priority of the two, for his writing undoubtedly inspired much of Lovecraft's work, although it is the American who enjoys the greater fame and readership. *Arthur Llewellyan Machen* (1863–1947), who was born and brought up in the legend-haunted district of Caerleon (King Arthur is thought to have held his famous court there), propounded a simple but dramatically exciting theory that the "Little People" of legend were not, in fact, imaginary, but the descendants of the prehistoric people who inhabited Europe before the arrival of the Celts from the North. Machen drew on facts, collected by anthropologists, that supported belief in a race of small, Mongoloid people who were workers in flint and flourished during the Neolithic, or polished stone, Age. They were known variously as Turanians, Picts and Mediterraneans, and the relics of their time, which scientific research brought to light, showed them to have reached a comparatively high stage of primitive culture by the beginning of the Bronze Age. It was then that the Celts moved south and destroyed or enslaved the diminutive inhabitants—until they, too, were ousted by the Teutonic tribes. From this time onward, stories were occasionally rumored that not all the "Little People" had been slaughtered, but that some had hidden themselves away in caverns from which they emerged only at night to steal their food and carry off children for their sacrificial rites. Such was the history which so intrigued Arthur Machen and which he embellished into a whole new concept of an ancient tradition. He visualized how the original tales could have been varied to take on supernatural significance—becoming the fairy tales so beloved of children—and discovered that traces of a small, dark people were still to be found in certain areas of Europe, such as his own native Wales, in Ireland and Scotland, central France and the Basque provinces of Spain. He appreciated that many people might argue that folklore had no place in a sophisticated modern society, but he knew from personal experience that its traditions still flourished in the wilder regions of most nations. So why shouldn't remnants of these small, malign people still exist in secret conclaves? This subject, then, became one of the most enduring of his literary themes, and, as his biographer Wesley D. Sweetser has noted: "his romanticism, his bent for fantasy, and his symbolic and mystical concepts of the nature of the universe, gave him unusual qualifications for the creation of believable and fascinating tales." Although Machen was a modest and idiosyncratic man about his work (he called many of his stories "highly ingenious rubbish"), he did believe unshakably in his hypothesis about the "Little People" and that remnants of their race still existed in certain places. "They are horribly evil," he wrote, "and they are something more—or something less—than human." As is now well known, Machen enjoyed little acclaim, and even less financial reward, during his lifetime; yet today he is acknowledged as one of the masters of *outré* literature. "The Shining Pyramid" was published in a privately circulated occult journal in 1895; it did not see book publication until 1925. His appreciation undoubtedly owes much to the man who took his hypothesis still further and wrote so enthusiastically of his work, the strange and retiring H. P. Lovecraft. A story by Lovecraft follows after "The Shining Pyramid," which is perhaps the best of all Machen's stories of the "Little People" and seems to be endowed with a special kind of personal knowledge.

THE SHINING PYRAMID
Arthur Machen

1

"Haunted, you said?"

"Yes, haunted. Don't you remember, when I saw you three years ago, you told me about your place in the west with the ancient woods hanging all about it, and the wild, domed hills, and the ragged land? It has always remained a sort of enchanted picture in my mind as I sit at my desk and hear the traffic rattling in the street in the midst of whirling London. But when did you come up?"

"The fact is, Dyson, I have only just got out of the train. I drove to the station early this morning and caught the 10.45."

"Well, I am very glad you looked in on me. How have you been getting on since we last met? There is no Mrs. Vaughan, I suppose?"

"No," said Vaughan, "I am still a hermit, like yourself. I have done nothing but loaf about."

Vaughan had lit his pipe and sat in the elbow chair, fidgeting and glancing about him in a somewhat dazed and restless manner. Dyson had wheeled round his chair when his visitor entered and sat with one arm fondly reclining on the desk of his bureau, and touching the litter of manuscript.

"And you are still engaged in the old task?" said Vaughan, pointing to the pile of papers and the teeming pigeon-holes.

"Yes, the vain pursuit of literature, as idle as alchemy, and as entrancing. But you have come to town for some time, I suppose; what shall we do to-night?"

"Well, I rather wanted you to try a few days with me down in the west. It would do you a lot of good, I'm sure."

"You are very kind, Vaughan, but London in September is hard to leave. Doré could not have designed anything more wonderful and mystic than Oxford Street as I saw it the other evening; the sunset flaming, the blue haze transmuting the plain street into a road 'far in the spiritual city'."

"I should like you to come down though. You would enjoy roaming over our hills. Does this racket go on all day and all night? It quite bewilders me; I wonder how you can work through it. I am sure you would revel in the great peace of my old home among the woods."

Vaughan lit his pipe again, and looked anxiously at Dyson to see if his inducements had had any effect, but the man of letters shook his head, smiling, and vowed in his heart a firm allegiance to the streets.

"You cannot tempt me," he said.

"Well, you may be right. Perhaps, after all, I was wrong to speak of the peace of the country. There, when a tragedy does occur, it is like a stone thrown into a pond; the circles of disturbance keep on widening, and it seems as if the water would never be still again."

"Have you ever any tragedies where you are?"

"I can hardly say that. But I was a good deal disturbed about a month ago by something that happened; it may or may not have been a tragedy in the usual sense of the word."

"What was the occurrence?"

"Well, the fact is a girl disappeared in a way which seems highly mysterious. Her parents, people of the name of Trevor, are well-to-do farmers, and their eldest daughter Annie was a sort of village beauty; she was really remarkably handsome. One afternoon she thought she would go and see her aunt, a widow who farms her own land, and as the two houses are only about five or six miles apart, she started off, telling her parents she would take the short cut over the hills. She never got to her aunt's. She's still missing. That's putting it in a few words."

"What an extraordinary thing! I suppose there are no disused mines, are there, on the hills? I don't think you quite run to anything so formidable as a precipice?"

"No; the path the girl must have taken had no pitfalls of any description; it is just a track over wild, bare hillside, far, even, from a by-road. One may walk for miles without meeting a soul, but it is all perfectly safe."

"And what do people say about it?"

"Oh, they talk nonsense—among themselves. You have no notion as to how superstitious cottagers are in out-of-the-way parts like mine. They are as bad as the Irish, every whit, and even more secretive."

"But what do they say?"

"Oh, the poor girl is supposed to have 'gone with the fairies', or to have been 'taken by the fairies'. Such stuff!" he went on, "one would laugh if it were not for the real tragedy of the case."

Dyson looked somewhat interested.

"Yes," he said, " 'fairies' certainly strike a little curiously on the ear in these days. But what do the police say? I presume they do not accept the fairytale hypothesis?"

"No; but they seem quite at fault. What I am afraid of is that Annie Trevor must have fallen in with some scoundrels on her way. Castletown is a large seaport, you know, and some of the worst of the foreign sailors occasionally desert their ships and go on the tramp up and down the country. Not many years ago a Spanish sailor named Garcia murdered a whole family for the sake of plunder that was not worth sixpence. They are hardly human, some of these fellows, and I am dreadfully afraid the poor girl must have come to an awful end."

"But no foreign sailor was seen by anyone about the country?"

"No; there is certainly that; and of course country people are quick to notice anyone whose appearance and dress are a little out of the common. Still it seems as if my theory were the only possible explanation."

"There are no data to go upon," said Dyson, thoughtfully. "There was no question of a love affair, or anything of the kind, I suppose?"

"Oh, no, not a hint of such a thing. I am sure if Annie were alive she would have contrived to let her mother know of her safety."

"No doubt, no doubt. Still it is barely possible that she is alive and yet unable to communicate with her friends. But all this must have disturbed you a good deal."

"Yes, it did; I hate a mystery, and especially a mystery which is probably the veil of horror. But frankly, Dyson, I want to make a clean breast of it; I did not come here to tell you all this."

"Of course not," said Dyson, a little surprised at Vaughan's uneasy manner. "You came to have a chat on more cheerful topics."

"No, I did not. What I have been telling you about happened a month ago, but something which seems likely to affect me more personally has happened within the last few days, and to be quite plain, I came up to town with the idea that you might be able to help me. You recollect that curious case you spoke to me about at our last meeting; something about a spectacle-maker."

"Oh, yes, I remember that. I know I was quite proud of my acumen at the time; even to this day the police have no idea why those peculiar yellow spectacles were wanted. But, Vaughan, you really look quite put out; I hope there is nothing serious?"

"No, I think I have been exaggerating, and I want you to reassure me. But what has happened is very odd."

"And what has happened?"

"I am sure that you will laugh at me, but this is the story. You must know there is a path, a right of way, that goes through my land, and to be precise, close to the wall of the kitchen garden. It is not used by many people; a woodman now and again finds it useful, and five or six children who go to school in the village pass twice a day. Well, a few days ago I was taking a walk about the place before breakfast, and I happened to stop to fill my pipe just by the large doors in the garden wall. The wood, I must tell you, comes to within a few feet of the wall, and the track I spoke of runs right in the shadow of the trees. I thought the shelter from a brisk wind that was blowing rather pleasant, and I stood there smoking with my eyes on the ground. Then something caught my attention. Just under the wall, on the short grass, a number of small flints were arranged in a pattern; something like this": and

Mr. Vaughan caught at a pencil and piece of paper, and dotted down a few strokes.

"You see," he went on, "there were, I should think, twelve little stones neatly arranged in lines, and spaced at equal distances as I have shewn it on the paper. They were pointed stones and the points were very carefully directed one way."

"Yes," said Dyson, without much interest, "no doubt the children you have mentioned had been playing there on their way from school. Children, as you know, are very fond of making such devices with oyster shells or flints or flowers, or with whatever comes in their way."

"So I thought; I just noticed these flints were arranged in a sort of pattern and then went on. But the next morning I was taking the same round, which, as a matter of fact, is habitual with me, and again I saw at the same spot a device in flints. This time it was really a curious pattern; something like the spokes of a wheel, all meeting at a common centre, and this centre formed by a device which looked like a bowl; all, you understand, done in flints."

"You are right," said Dyson, "that seems odd enough. Still it is reasonable that your half a dozen school children are responsible for these fantasies in stone."

"Well, I thought I would set the matter at rest. The children pass the gate every evening at half-past five, and I walked by at six, and found the device just as I had left it in the morning. The next day I was up and about at a quarter to seven, and I found the whole thing had been changed. There was a pyramid outlined in flints upon the grass. The children I saw going by an hour and a half later, and they ran past the spot without glancing to right or left. In the evening I watched them going home, and this morning when I got to the gate at six o'clock there was a thing like a half-moon waiting for me."

"So then the series runs thus: firstly ordered lines, then the device of the spokes and the bowl, then the pyramid, and finally, this morning, the half-moon. That is the order, isn't it?"

"Yes; that is right. But do you know it has made me feel very uneasy? I suppose it seems absurd, but I can't help thinking that some kind of signalling is going on under my nose, and that sort of thing is disquieting."

"But what have you to dread? You have no enemies?"

"No; but I have some very valuable old plate."

"You are thinking of burglars then?" said Dyson, with an accent of considerable interest, "but you must know your neighbours. Are there any suspicious characters about?"

"Not that I am aware of. But you remember what I told you of the sailors."

"Can you trust your servants?"

"Oh, perfectly. The plate is preserved in a strong-room; the butler, an old family servant, alone knows where the key is kept. There is nothing wrong there. Still, everybody is aware that I have a lot of old silver, and all country folks are given to gossip. In that way information may have got abroad in very undesirable quarters."

"Yes, but I confess there seems something a little unsatisfactory in the burglar theory. Who is signalling to whom? I cannot see my way to accepting such an explanation. What put the plate into your head in connection with these flint signs, or whatever one may call them?"

"It was the figure of the bowl," said Vaughan. "I happen to possess a very large and very valuable Charles II punch-bowl. The chasing is really exquisite, and the thing is worth a lot of money. The sign I described to you was exactly the same shape as my punch-bowl."

"A queer coincidence certainly. But the other figures or devices: you have nothing shaped like a pyramid?"

"Ah, you will think that queerer. As it happens, this punch-bowl of mine, together with a set of rare old ladles, is kept in a mahogany chest of a pyramidal shape. The four sides slope upwards, the narrow towards the top."

"I confess all this interests me a good deal," said Dyson. "Let us go on then. What about the other figures; how about the Army, as we may call the first sign, and the Crescent or Half-moon?"

"Ah, there is no reference that I can make out of these two. Still, you see I have some excuse for curiosity at all events. I should be very vexed to lose any of the old plate; nearly all the pieces have been in the family for generations. And I cannot get it out of my head that some scoundrels mean to rob me, and are communicating with one another every night."

"Frankly," said Dyson, "I can make nothing of it; I am as much in the dark as yourself. Your theory seems certainly the only possible explanation, and yet the difficulties are immense."

He leaned back in his chair, and the two men faced each other, frowning, and perplexed by so bizarre a problem.

"By the way," said Dyson, after a long pause, "what is your geological formation down there?"

Mr. Vaughan looked up, a good deal surprised by the question.

"Old red sandstone and limestone, I believe," he said. "We are just beyond the coal measures, you know."

"But surely there are no flints either in the sandstone or the limestone?"

"No, I never see any flints in the fields. I confess that did strike me as a little curious."

"I should think so! It is very important. By the way, what size were the flints used in making these devices?"

"I happen to have brought one with me; I took it this morning."

"From the Half-moon?"

"Exactly. Here it is."

He handed over a small flint, tapering to a point, and about three inches in length.

Dyson's face blazed up with excitement as he took the thing from Vaughan.

"Certainly," he said, after a moment's pause, "you have some curious neighbours in your country. I hardly think they can harbour any designs on your punch-bowl. Do you know this is a flint arrow-head of vast antiquity, and not only that, but an arrow-head of a unique kind? I have seen specimens from all parts of the world, but there are features about this thing that are quite peculiar."

He laid down his pipe, and took out a book from a drawer.

"We shall just have time to catch the 5.45 to Castletown," he said.

2

Mr. Dyson drew in a long breath of the air of the hills and felt all the enchantment of the scene about him. It was very early morning, and he stood on the terrace in the front of the house. Vaughan's ancestor had built on the lower slope of a great hill, in the shelter of a deep and ancient wood that gathered on three sides about the house, and on the fourth side, the south-west, the land fell gently away and sank to the valley, where a brook wound in and out in mystic esses, and the dark and gleaming alders tracked the stream's course to the eye. On the terrace in that sheltered place no wind blew, and far beyond the trees were still. Only one sound broke in upon the silence, and Dyson heard the noise of the brook singing far below, the song of clear and shining water rippling over the stones, whispering and murmuring as it sank to dark deep pools. Across the stream, just below the house, rose a grey stone bridge, vaulted and buttressed, a fragment of the Middle Ages, and then beyond the bridge the hills rose again, vast and rounded like bastions, covered here and there with dark woods and thickets of undergrowth, but the heights were all bare of trees, showing only grey turf and patches of bracken, touched here and there with the gold of fading fronds. Dyson looked to the north and south, and still he saw the wall of the hills, and the ancient woods, and the stream drawn in and out between them; all grey and dim with morning mist beneath a grey sky in a hushed and haunted air.

Mr. Vaughan's voice broke in upon the silence.

"I thought you would be too tired to be about so early," he said. "I see you are admiring the view. It is very pretty, isn't it, though I suppose old Meyrick Vaughan didn't think much about the scenery when he built the house. A queer grey, old place, isn't it?"

"Yes, and how it fits into the surroundings; it seems of a piece with the grey hills and the grey bridge below."

"I am afraid I have brought you down on false pretences, Dyson," said Vaughan, as they began to walk up and down the terrace. "I have been to the place, and there is not a sign of anything this morning."

"Ah, indeed. Well, suppose we go round together."

They walked across the lawn and went by a path through the ilex shrubbery to the back of the house. There Vaughan pointed out the track leading down to the valley and up to the heights above the wood, and presently they stood beneath the garden wall, by the door.

"Here, you see, it was," said Vaughan, pointing to a spot on the turf. "I was standing just where you are now that morning I first saw the flints."

"Yes, quite so. That morning it was the Army, as I call it; then the Bowl, then the Pyramid, and, yesterday, the Half-moon. What a queer old stone that is," he went on, pointing to a block of limestone rising out of the turf just beneath the wall. "It looks like a sort of dwarf pillar, but I suppose it is natural."

"Oh, yes, I think so. I imagine it was brought here, though, as we stand on the red sandstone. No doubt it was used as a foundation stone for some older building."

"Very likely." Dyson was peering about him attentively, looking from the ground to the wall, and from the wall to the deep wood that hung almost over the garden and made the place dark even in the morning.

"Look here," said Dyson at length, "it is certainly a case of children this time. Look at that."

He was bending down and staring at the dull red surface of the mellowed bricks of the wall. Vaughan came up and looked hard where Dyson's finger was pointing, and could scarcely distinguish a faint mark in deeper red.

"What is it?" he said. "I can make nothing of it."

"Look a little more closely. Don't you see it is an attempt to draw the human eye?"

"Ah, now I see what you mean. My sight is not very sharp. Yes, so it is, it is meant for an eye, no doubt, as you say. I thought the children learnt drawing at school."

"Well, it is an odd eye enough. Do you notice the peculiar almond shape; almost like the eye of a Chinaman?"

Dyson looked meditatively at the work of the undeveloped artist, and scanned the wall again, going down on his knees in the minuteness of his inquisition.

"I should like very much," he said at length, "to know how a child in this out-of-the-way place could have any idea of the shape of the Mongolian eye. You see the average child has a very distinct impression of the subject; he draws a circle, or something like a circle, and puts a dot in the centre. I don't think any child imagines that the eye is really made like that; it's just a convention of infantile art. But this almond-shaped thing puzzles me extremely. Perhaps it may be derived from a gilt Chinaman on a tea-canister in the grocer's shop. Still that's hardly likely."

"But why are you so sure it was done by a child?"

"Why! Look at the height. These old-fashioned bricks are little more than two inches thick; there are twenty courses from the ground to the sketch if we call it so; that gives a height of three and a half feet. Now, just imagine you are going to draw something on this wall. Exactly; your pencil, if you had one, would touch the wall somewhere on the level with your eyes, that is, more than five feet from the ground. It seems, therefore, a very simple deduction to conclude that this eye on the wall was drawn by a child about ten years old."

"Yes, I had not thought of that. Of course one of the children must have done it."

"I suppose so; and yet as I said, there is something singularly unchildlike about those two lines, and the eyeball itself, you see, is almost an oval. To my mind, the thing has an odd, ancient air; and a touch that is not altogether pleasant. I cannot help fancying that if we could see a whole face from the same hand it would not be altogether agreeable. However, that is nonsense, after all, and we are not getting further in our investigations. It is odd that the flint series has come to such an abrupt end."

The two men walked away towards the house, and as they went in at the porch there was a break in the grey sky, and a gleam of sunshine on the grey hill before them.

All the day Dyson prowled meditatively about the fields and woods surrounding the house. He was thoroughly and completely puzzled by the trivial circumstances he proposed to elucidate, and now he again took the flint arrow-head from his pocket, turning it over and examining it with deep attention. There was something about the thing that was altogether different from the specimens he had seen at the museums and private collections; the shape was of a distinct type, and around the edge there was a line of little punctured dots, apparently a suggestion of ornament. Who, thought Dyson, could possess such things in so remote a place; and who, possessing the flints, could have put them to the fantastic use of designing meaningless figures under Vaughan's garden wall? The rank absurdity of the whole affair offended him unutterably; and as one theory after another rose in his mind only to be rejected, he felt strongly tempted to take the next train back to town. He had seen the silver plate which Vaughan treasured, and had inspected the punch-bowl, the gem of the collection, with close attention; and what he saw and his interview with the butler convinced him that a plot to rob the strong-box was out of the limits of enquiry. The chest in which the bowl was kept, a heavy piece of mahogany, evidently dating from the beginning of the century, was certainly strongly suggestive of a pyramid, and Dyson was at first inclined to the inept manoeuvres of the detective, but a little sober thought convinced him of the impossibility of the burglary hypothesis, and he cast wildly about for something more satisfying. He asked Vaughan if there were any gypsies in the neighbourhood, and heard that the Romany had not been seen for years. This dashed him a good deal, as he knew the gypsy habit of leaving queer hieroglyphics on the line of march, and had been much elated when the thought occurred to him. He was facing Vaughan by the old-fashioned hearth when he put the question, and leaned back in his chair in disgust at the destruction of his theory.

"It is odd," said Vaughan, "but the gypsies never trouble us here.

Now and then the farmers find traces of fires in the wildest part of the hills, but nobody seems to know who the fire-lighters are."

"Surely that looks like gypsies?"

"No, not in such places as those. Tinkers and gypsies and wanderers of all sorts stick to the roads and don't go very far from the farmhouses."

"Well, I can make nothing of it. I saw the children going by this afternoon, and, as you say, they ran straight on. So we shall have no more eyes on the wall at all events."

"No, I must waylay them one of these days and find out who is the artist."

The next morning when Vaughan strolled in his usual course from the lawn to the back of the house he found Dyson already awaiting him by the garden door, and evidently in a state of high excitement, for he beckoned furiously with his hand, and gesticulated violently.

"What is it?" asked Vaughan. "The flints again?"

"No; but look here, look at the wall. There; don't you see it?"

"There's another of those eyes!"

"Exactly. Drawn, you see, at a little distance from the first, almost on the same level, but slightly lower."

"What on earth is one to make of it? It couldn't have been done by the children; it wasn't there last night, and they won't pass for another hour. What can it mean?"

"I think the very devil is at the bottom of all this," said Dyson. "Of course, one cannot resist the conclusion that these infernal almond eyes are to be set down to the same agency as the devices in the arrowheads; and where that conclusion is to lead us is more than I can tell. For my part, I have to put a strong check on my imagination or it would run wild."

"Vaughan," he said, as they turned away from the wall, "has it struck you that there is one point—a very curious point—in common between the figures done in flints and the eyes drawn on the wall?"

"What is that?" asked Vaughan, on whose face there had fallen a certain shadow of indefinite dread.

"It is this. We know that the signs of the Army, the Bowl, the Pyramid, and the Half-moon must have been done at night. Presumably they were meant to be seen at night. Well, precisely the same reasoning applies to those eyes on the wall."

"I do not quite see your point."

"Oh, surely. The nights are dark just now, and have been very cloudy, I know, since I came down. Moreover, those overhanging trees would throw that wall into deep shadow even on a clear night."

"Well?"

"What struck me was this. What very peculiarly sharp eyesight they, whoever 'they' are, must have to be able to arrange arrow-heads in intricate order in the blackest shadow of the wood, and then draw the eyes on the wall without a trace of bungling, or a false line."

"I have read of persons confined in dungeons for many years who have been able to see quite well in the dark," said Vaughan.

"Yes," said Dyson, "there was the abbé in *Monte Cristo*. But it is a singular point."

3

"Who was that old man that touched his hat to you just now?" said Dyson, as they came to the bend of the lane near the house.

"Oh, that was old Trevor. He looks very broken, poor old fellow."

"Who is Trevor?"

"Don't you remember? I told you the story that afternoon I came to your rooms—about a girl named Annie Trevor, who disappeared in the most inexplicable manner about five weeks ago. That was her father."

"Yes, yes, I recollect now. To tell the truth I had forgotten all about it. And nothing has been heard of the girl?"

"Nothing whatever. The police are quite at fault."

"I am afraid I did not pay very much attention to the details you gave me. Which way did the girl go?"

"Her path would take her right across those wild hills above the house; the nearest point in the track must be about two miles from here."

"Is it near that little hamlet I saw yesterday?"

"You mean Croesyceiliog, where the children come from? No; it goes more to the north."

"Ah, I have never been that way."

They went into the house, and Dyson shut himself up in his room, sunk deep in doubtful thought, but yet with the shadow of a suspicion growing within him that for a while haunted his brain, all vague and fantastic, refusing to take definite form. He was sitting by the open window and looking out on the valley and saw, as if in a picture, the intricate winding of the brook, the grey bridge, and the vast hills rising beyond; all still and without a breath of wind to stir the mystic hanging woods, and the evening sunshine glowed warm on the bracken, and down below a faint mist, pure white, began to rise from the stream. Dyson sat by the window as the day darkened and the huge bastioned hills loomed vast and vague, and the woods became dim and more shadowy; and the fancy that had seized him no longer appeared altogether impossible. He passed the rest of the evening in a reverie, hardly hearing what Vaughan said; and when he took his candle in the hall, he paused a moment before bidding his friend good night.

"I want a good rest," he said. "I have got some work to do tomorrow."

"Some writing, you mean?"

"No. I am going to look for the Bowl."

"The Bowl! If you mean my punch-bowl, that is safe in the chest."

"I don't mean the punch-bowl. You may take my word for it that your plate has never been threatened. No; I will not bother you with any suppositions. We shall in all probability have something much stronger than suppositions before long. Good night, Vaughan."

The next morning Dyson set off after breakfast. He took the path by the garden wall, and noted that there were now eight of the weird almond eyes dimly outlined on the brick.

"Six days more," he said to himself, but as he thought over the theory he had formed, he shrank, in spite of strong conviction, from such a wildly incredible fancy. He struck up through the dense shadows of the wood, and at length came out on the bare hillside, and climbed higher and higher over the slippery turf, keeping well to the north, and following the indications given him by Vaughan. As he went on, he seemed to mount ever higher above the world of human life and customary things; to his right he looked at a fringe of orchard and saw a faint blue smoke rising like a pillar; there was the hamlet from which the children came to school, and there the only sign of life, for the woods embowered and concealed Vaughan's old grey house. As he reached what seemed the summit of the hill, he realized for the first time the desolate loneliness and strangeness of the land; there was nothing but grey sky and grey hill, a high, vast plain that seemed to stretch on for ever and ever, and a faint glimpse of a blue peaked mountain far away and to the north. At length he came to the path, a slight track scarcely noticeable, and from its position and by what Vaughan had told him he knew that it was the way the lost girl, Annie Trevor, must have taken. He followed the path on the bare hill-top, noticing the great limestone rocks that cropped out of the turf, grim and hideous, and of an aspect as forbidding as an idol of the South Seas; and suddenly he halted, astonished, although he had found what he searched for. Almost without warning the ground shelved suddenly away on all sides and Dyson looked down into a circular depression, which might well have been a Roman amphitheatre, and the ugly crags of limestone rimmed it round as if with a broken wall. Dyson walked round the hollow, and noted the position of the stones, and then turned on his way home.

"This," he thought to himself, "is more than curious. The Bowl is discovered, but where is the Pyramid?"

"My dear Vaughan," he said, when he got back, "I may tell you that I have found the Bowl, and that is all I shall tell you for the present. We have six days of absolute inaction before us; there is really nothing to be done."

4

"I have just been round the garden," said Vaughan one morning. "I have been counting those infernal eyes, and I find there are fourteen of them. For heaven's sake, Dyson, tell me what the meaning of it all is."

"I should be very sorry to attempt to do so. I may have guessed this or that, but I always make it a principle to keep my guesses to myself. Besides, it is really not worth while anticipating events; you will remember my telling you that we had six days of inaction before us? Well, this is the sixth day, and the last of idleness. To-night I propose we take a stroll."

"A stroll! Is that all the action you mean to take?"

"Well, it may show you some very curious things. To be plain, I want you to start with me at nine o'clock this evening for the hills. We may have to be out all night, so you had better wrap up well, and bring some of that brandy."

"Is it a joke?" asked Vaughan, who was bewildered with strange events and strange surmises.

"No, I don't think there is much joke in it. Unless I am much mistaken we shall find a very serious explanation of the puzzle. You will come with me, I am sure?"

"Very good. Which way do you want to go?"

"By the path you told me of; the path Annie Trevor is supposed to have taken."

Vaughan looked white at the mention of the girl's name.

"I did not think you were on that track," he said. "I thought it was the affair of those devices in flint and of the eyes on the wall that you were engaged on. It's no good saying any more, but I will go with you."

At a quarter to nine that evening the two men set out, taking the path through the wood, and up the hillside. It was a dark and heavy night, the sky was thick with clouds, and the valley full of mist, and all the way they seemed to walk in a world of shadow and gloom, hardly speaking, and afraid to break the haunted silence. They came out at last on the steep hillside, and instead of the oppression of the wood there was the long, dim sweep of the turf, and higher, the fantastic limestone rocks hinted horror through the darkness, and the wind sighed as it passed across the mountain to the sea, and in its passage beat chill about their hearts. They seemed to walk on and on for hours, and the dim outline of the hill still stretched before them, and the haggard rocks still loomed through the darkness, when suddenly Dyson whispered, drawing his breath quickly, and coming close to his companion.

"Here," he said, "we will lie down. I do not think there is anything yet."

"I know the place," said Vaughan, after a moment. "I have often been by in the daytime. The country people are afraid to come here, I believe; it is supposed to be a fairies' castle, or something of the kind. But why on earth have we come here?"

"Speak a little lower," said Dyson. "It might not do us any good if we are overheard."

"Overheard here! There is not a soul within three miles of us."

"Possibly not; indeed, I should say certainly not. But there might be a body somewhat nearer."

"I don't understand you in the least," said Vaughan, whispering to humour Dyson, "but why have we come here?"

"Well, you see this hollow before us is the Bowl. I think we had better not talk even in whispers."

They lay full length upon the turf; the rock between their faces and the Bowl, and now and again, Dyson, slouching his dark, soft hat over his forehead, put out the glint of an eye, and in a moment drew back, not daring to take a prolonged view. Again he laid an ear to the ground and listened, and the hours went by, and the darkness seemed to blacken, and the faint sigh of the wind was the only sound.

Vaughan grew impatient with this heaviness of silence, this watching for indefinite terror; for to him there was no shape or form of apprehension, and he began to think the whole vigil a dreary farce.

"How much longer is this to last?" he whispered to Dyson, and Dyson who had been holding his breath in the agony of attention put his mouth to Vaughan's ear and said:

"Will you listen?" with pauses between each syllable, and in the voice with which the priest pronounces the awful words.

Vaughan caught the ground with his hands, and stretched forward, wondering what he was to hear. At first there was nothing, and then a low and gentle noise came very softly from the Bowl, a faint sound, almost indescribable, but as if one held the tongue against the roof of the mouth and expelled the breath. He listened eagerly and presently the noise grew louder, and became a strident and horrible hissing as if the pit beneath boiled with fervent heat, and Vaughan, unable to remain in suspense any longer, drew his cap half over his face in imitation of Dyson, and looked down to the hollow below.

It did, in truth, stir and seethe like an infernal cauldron. The whole of the sides and bottom tossed and writhed with vague and restless forms that passed to and fro without the sound of feet, and gathered thick here and there and seemed to speak to one another in those tones of horrible sibilance, like the hissing of snakes, that he had heard. It was as if the sweet turf and the cleanly earth had suddenly become quickened with some foul writhing growth. Vaughan could not draw back his face, though he felt Dyson's finger touch him, but he peered into the quaking mass and saw faintly that there were things like faces and human limbs, and yet he felt his inmost soul chill with the sure belief that no fellow soul or human thing stirred in all that tossing and hissing host. He looked aghast, choking back sobs of horror, and at length the loathsome forms gathered thickest about some vague object in the middle of the hollow and the hissing of their speech grew more venomous, and he saw in the uncertain light the abominable limbs, vague and yet too plainly seen, writhe and intertwine, and he thought he heard, very faint, a low human moan striking through the noise of speech that was not of man. At his heart something seemed to whisper ever "the worm of corruption, the worm that dieth not," and grotesquely the image was pictured to his imagination of a piece of putrid offal stirring through and through with bloated and horrible creeping things. The writhing of the dusky limbs continued, they seemed clustered round the dark form in the middle of the hollow, and the sweat dripped and poured off Vaughan's forehead, and fell cold on his hand beneath his face.

Then, it seemed done in an instant, the loathsome mass melted and fell away to the sides of the Bowl, and for a moment Vaughan saw in the middle of the hollow the tossing of human arms. But a spark gleamed beneath, a fire kindled, and as the voice of a woman cried out loud in a shrill scream of utter anguish and terror, a great pyramid of flame spired up like a bursting of a pent fountain, and threw a blaze of light upon the whole mountain. In that instant Vaughan saw the myriads beneath; the things made in the form of men but stunted like children hideously deformed, the faces with the almond eyes burning with evil and unspeakable lusts; the ghastly yellow of the mass of naked flesh; and then as if by magic the place was empty, while the fire roared and crackled, and the flames shone abroad.

"You have seen the Pyramid," said Dyson in his ear, "the Pyramid of fire."

5

"Then you recognize the thing?"

"Certainly. It is a brooch that Annie Trevor used to wear on Sundays; I remember the pattern. But where did you find it? You don't mean to say that you have discovered the girl?"

"My dear Vaughan, I wonder you have not guessed where I found the brooch. You have not forgotten last night already?"

"Dyson," said the other, speaking very seriously, "I have been turning it over in my mind this morning while you have been out. I have thought about what I saw, or perhaps I should say about what I thought I saw, and the only conclusion I can come to is this, that the thing won't bear recollection. As men live, I have lived soberly and honestly, in the fear of God, all my days, and all I can do is believe that I suffered from some monstrous delusion, from some phantasmagoria of the bewildered senses. You know we went home together in silence, not a word passed between us as to what I fancied I saw; had we not better agree to keep silence on the subject? When I took my walk in the peaceful morning sunshine, I thought all the earth seemed full of praise, and passing by that wall I noticed there were no more signs recorded, and I blotted out those that remained. The mystery is over, and we can live quietly again. I think some poison has been working for the last few weeks; I have trodden on the verge of madness, but I am sane now."

Mr. Vaughan had spoken earnestly, and bent forward in his chair and glanced at Dyson with something of entreaty.

"My dear Vaughan," said the other, after a pause, "what's the use of this? it is much too late to take that tone; we have gone too deep. Besides you know as well as I that there is no delusion in the case; I wish there were with all my heart. No, in justice to myself I must tell you the whole story, so far as I know it."

"Very good," said Vaughan with a sigh, "if you must, you must."

"Then," said Dyson, "we will begin with the end if you please. I found this brooch you have just identified in the place we have called the Bowl. There was a heap of grey ashes, as if a fire had been burning, indeed, the embers were still hot, and this brooch was lying on the ground, just outside the range of the flame. It must have dropped accidentally from the dress of the person who was wearing it. No, don't interrupt me; we can pass now to the beginning, as we have had the end. Let us go back to that day you came to see me in my rooms in London. So far as I can remember, soon after you came in you mentioned, in a somewhat casual manner, that an unfortunate and mysterious incident had occurred in your part of the country; a girl named Annie Trevor had gone to see a relative, and had disappeared. I confess freely that what you said did not greatly interest me; there are so many reasons which may make it extremely convenient for a man and more expecially a woman to vanish from the circle of their relations and friends. I suppose, if we were to consult the police, one would find that in London somebody disappears mysteriously every other week, and the officers would no doubt shrug their shoulders, and tell you that by the law of averages it could not be otherwise. So I was very culpably careless to your story, and besides, there is another reason for my lack of interest; your tale was inexplicable. You could only suggest a blackguard sailor on the tramp, but I discarded the explanation immediately. For many reasons, but chiefly because the occasional criminal, the amateur in brutal crime, is always found out, especially if he selects the country as the scene of his operations. You will remember the case of that Garcia you mentioned; he strolled into a railway station the day after the murder, his trousers covered with blood, and the works of the Dutch clock, his loot, tied in a neat parcel. So rejecting this, your only suggestion, the whole tale became, as I say, inexplicable, and, therefore, profoundly uninteresting. Yes, *therefore,* it is a perfectly valid conclusion. Do you ever trouble your head about problems which you know to be insoluble? Did you ever bestow much thought on the old puzzle of Achilles and the Tortoise? Of course not, because you knew it was a hopeless quest, and so when you told me the story of a country girl who had disappeared I simply placed the whole thing down in the category of the insoluble, and thought no more about the matter. I was mistaken, so it has turned out; but if you remember, you immediately passed on to an affair which interested you more intensely, because personally. I need not go over the very singular narrative of the flint signs; at first I thought it all trivial, probably some children's game, and if not that a hoax of some sort; but your showing me the arrow-head awoke my acute interest. Here, I saw, there was something widely removed from the commonplace, and matter of real curiosity; and as soon as I came here I set to work to find the solution, repeating to myself again and again the signs you had described. First came the sign we have agreed to call the Army; a number of serried lines of flints, all pointing in the same way. Then the lines, like the spokes of a wheel, all converging towards the figure of a Bowl, then the triangle or Pyramid, and last of all the Half-moon. I confess that I exhausted conjecture in my efforts to unveil this mystery, and as you will understand it was a duplex or rather triplex problem. For I had not merely to ask myself: what do these figures mean? but also, who can possibly be responsible for the designing of them? And again, who can possibly possess such valuable things, and knowing their value thus throw them down by the wayside? This line of thought led me to suppose that the person or persons in question did not know the value of unique flint arrow-heads, and yet this did not lead me far, for a well-educated man might easily be ignorant on such a subject. Then came the complication of the eye on the wall, and you remember that we could not avoid the conclusion that in the two cases the same agency was at work. The peculiar position of these eyes on the wall made me enquire if there was such a thing as a dwarf anywhere in the neighbourhood, but I found that there was not, and I knew that the children who pass by every day had nothing to do with the matter. Yet I felt convinced that whoever drew the eyes must be from three and a half to four feet high, since, as I pointed out at the time, anyone who draws on a perpendicular surface chooses by instinct a spot about level with his face. Then again, there was the question of the peculiar shape of the eyes; that marked Mongolian character of which the English countryman could have no conception, and for a final cause of confusion the obvious fact that the designer or designers must be able practically to see in the dark. As you remarked, a man who has been confined for many years in an extremely dark cell or dungeon might acquire that power; but since the days of Edmond Dantés, where would such a prison be found in Europe? A sailor, who had been immured for a considerable period in some horrible Chinese *oubliette*, seemed the individual I was in search of, and though it looked improbable, it was not absolutely impossible that a sailor or, let us say, a man employed on shipboard, should be a dwarf. But how to account for my imaginary sailor being in possession of prehistoric arrow-heads? And the possession granted, what was the meaning and object of these mysterious signs of flint, and the almond-shaped eyes? Your theory of a contemplated burglary I saw, nearly from the first, to be quite untenable, and I confess I was utterly at a loss for a working hypothesis. It was a mere accident which put me on the track; we passed poor old Trevor, and your mention of his name and of the disappearance of his daughter, recalled the story which I had forgotten, or which remained unheeded. Here, then, I said to myself, is another problem, uninteresting, it is true, by itself; but what if it prove to be in relation with all these enigmas which torture me? I shut myself in my room, and endeavoured to dismiss all prejudice from my mind, and I went over everything *de novo*, assuming for theory's sake that the disappearance of Annie Trevor had some connection with the flint signs and the eyes on the wall. This assumption did not lead me very far, and I was on the point of giving the whole problem up in despair, when a possible significance of the Bowl struck me. As you know there is a 'Devil's Punch-bowl' in Surrey, and I saw that the symbol might refer to some feature in the country. Putting the two extremes together, I determined to look for the Bowl near the path which the lost girl had taken, and you know how I found it. I interpreted the signs by what I knew, and read the first, the Army, thus: 'there is to be a gathering or assembly at the Bowl in a fortnight (that is the Half-moon) to see the Pyramid, or to build the Pyramid.' The eyes, drawn one by one, day by day, evidently checked off the days, and I knew that there would be fourteen and no more. Thus far the way seemed pretty plain; I would not trouble myself to enquire as to the nature of the assembly, or as to who was to assemble in the loneliest and most dreaded place among these lonely hills. In Ireland or China or the west of America the question would have been easily answered; a muster of the disaffected, the meeting of a secret society, Vigilantes summoned to report: the thing would be simplicity itself; but in this quiet corner of Wales, inhabited by quiet folk, no such suppositions were possible for a moment. But I knew that I should have an opportunity of seeing and watching the assembly, and I did not care to perplex myself with hopeless research; and in place of reasoning a wild fancy entered into judgment; I remembered what people had said about Annie Trevor's disappearance, that she had been 'taken by the fairies'. I tell you, Vaughan, I am a sane man as you are, my brain is not, I trust, mere vacant space to let to any wild improbability, and I tried my best to thrust the fantasy away. And the hint came of the old name of fairies, 'the little people', and the very probable belief that they represent a tradition of the prehistoric Turanian inhabitants of the country, who were cave dwellers: and then I realized with a shock that I was looking for a being under four feet in height, accustomed to live in darkness, possessing stone instruments, and familiar with the Mongolian cast of features! I say this, Vaughan, that I should be ashamed to hint at such visionary stuff to you, if it were not for that which you saw with your very eyes last night, and I say that I might doubt the evidence of my senses, if they were not confirmed by yours. But you and I cannot look each other in the face and pretend delusion; as you lay on the turf beside me I felt your flesh shrink and quiver, and I saw your eyes in the light of the flame. And so I tell you without any shame what was in my mind last night as we went through the wood and climbed the hill, and lay hidden beneath the rock.

There was one thing that should have been most evident that puzzled me to the very last. I told you how I read the sign of the Pyramid; the assembly was to see a pyramid, and the true meaning of the symbol escaped me to the last moment. The old derivation from πυρ, fire, though false, should have set me on the track, but it never occurred to me.

I think I need say very little more. You know we were quite helpless, even if we had foreseen what was to come. Ah, the particular place where these signs were displayed? Yes, that is a curious question. But this house is, so far as I can judge, in a pretty central situation amongst the hills; and possibly, who can say yes or no, that queer, old limestone pillar by your garden wall was a place of meeting before the Celt set foot in Britain. But there is one thing I must add: I don't regret our inability to rescue the wretched girl. You saw the appearance of those things that gathered thick and writhed in the Bowl; you may be sure that what lay bound in the midst of them was no longer fit for earth."

"So?" said Vaughan.

"So she passed in the Pyramid of Fire," said Dyson, "and they passed again to the underworld, to the places beneath the hills."

6

"All my stories, unconnected as they may be, are based on the fundamental lore or legend that this world was inhabited at one time by another race who, in practicing black magic, lost their foothold and were expelled, yet live on outside ever ready to take possession of this earth again." In these words H. P. Lovecraft summarized the fictional obsession of his life—an obsession which had been initiated by reading the works of Arthur Machen, whom he considered the creator of stories "few if any can hope to equal." In them, he said, "the elements of hidden horror and brooding fright attain an almost incomparable substance and realistic acuteness." *Howard Phillips Lovecraft* (1890–1937), like Machen, was a lonely, brooding figure who spent much of his life in isolation and became deeply immersed in the occult legends and traditions of prehistory. So deeply immersed, in fact, that some modern scholars believe his fiction half-hides a terrible truth he was on the verge of discovering. As the occult authority Kenneth Grant put it recently: "The myth-cycle which he initiated now raises the question whether it was a mere fiction engendered in the haunted mind of an obscure New England writer, or whether it foreshadows a particularly sinister kind of occult invasion." Lovecraft, like his mentor, believed in the malevolent "Little People"—"Prior to the Druids," he wrote, "Western Europe was undoubtedly inhabited by a squat Mongoloid race"—but he took the concept further and presented the idea that these creatures had learned their evil creed not from beings of this world, but from outcast entities who lurked on the edge of human consciousness waiting to be summoned again by those who believed in them. He theorized that these creatures had, over the centuries, been responsible for the formation of many cults to worship them—citing witches and warlocks as just one instance. To affirm the factual elements of his stories he introduced local archaeological knowledge and relevant literary material. He lived most of his life in Rhode Island and from there drew knowledge of the megaliths which dotted the countryside and seemed mute witnesses to ancient races and dead religions. He shared with archaeologists the belief that the builders were probably of Celtic or northwest European origin. But did these people come to America "in the fabulous years before history" (as Lovecraft wrote)? Or were they the handiwork of some secret order of new colonists practicing strange rites during the birth of modern America? Salem, with its terrible witchcraft history, was the site of several such stories and became the model for Lovecraft's town of Arkham, where many of his tales of the Cthulhu Mythos—as he called his ancient race—are set. He further made use of real works of scholarship, such as Sir James Frazer's *The Golden Bough* and Doctor Margaret Murray's books on the origin of witchcraft, to strengthen his case, skillfully adding to them totally fictitious works such as "the abhorred *Necronomicon* of the mad Arab Abdul Alhazred," Ludwig Prinn's *De Vermis Mysteriis,* and the "infamous" *Cultes des Goules* of the Comte d'Erlette. (So vividly and carefully did Lovecraft describe these books that some readers of the stories actually believed they existed and scoured old bookshops all over America in search of copies!) On this premise he created his series of tales about the Mythos and those who attempted to propitiate its gods (designated with bizarre names such as Azathoth, Yog-Sothoth, Nyarlathotep, Greath Cthulhu, and so on), and those who unwittingly and horrifyingly came into knowledge of them and were hounded to awful deaths. Like Machen before him, Lovecraft enjoyed little success during his lifetime, but thanks mainly to the work of the late August Derleth, a fellow author and also a publisher, his stories were republished in volume form, and thereafter began the widespread appreciation of his work which has now reached cult proportions. "The Cthulhu Mythos," August Derleth wrote in 1963, "took hold of the public fancy in precisely the same way that Sherlock Holmes captured it at the turn of the century." Since the growth of their popularity, tales continuing the theme of the Cthulhu Mythos have been written by numerous writers in both America and Europe, and there is every indication that this will continue in the future. Of all the stories Lovecraft wrote on this theme, "The Call of Cthulhu" —one of the first, which appeared in 1928 in *Weird Tales*—is perhaps among the very best and also the most perfectly self-contained for the reader new to his work. It originated partly in a dream—as did so many of this author's stories—and is infused with his belief that fragments of ancient lore are transmitted to the mind during sleep. (Lovecraft wrote on one occasion that "nightmares are the punishment meted out to the soul for sins committed in previous incarnations—perhaps millions of years ago!") It is of further interest because of the quote by Algernon Blackwood which introduces it—Blackwood was another of Lovecraft's influences and similarly believed in the continuing presence in this world of ancient beings from other places and other times.

THE CALL OF CTHULHU
H. P. Lovecraft

*Of such great powers or beings there may be conceivably a survival
. . . a survival of a hugely remote period when . . . consciousness
was manifested, perhaps, in shapes and forms long since withdrawn
before the tide of advancing humanity . . . forms of which poetry and
legend alone have caught a flying memory and called them gods,
monsters, mythical beings of all sorts and kinds . . .*

—ALGERNON BLACKWOOD

1.
The Horror in Clay

The most merciful thing in the world, I think, is the inability of the
human mind to correlate all its contents. We live on a placid island of
ignorance in the midst of black seas of infinity, and it was not meant
that we should voyage far. The sciences, each straining in its own direction, have hitherto harmed us little; but some day the piecing together of dissociated knowledge will open up such terrifying vistas of
reality, and of our frightful position therein, that we shall either go
mad from the revelation or flee from the deadly light into the peace
and safety of a new dark age.

Theosophists have guessed at the awesome grandeur of the cosmic
cycle wherein our world and human race form transient incidents.
They have hinted at strange survivals in terms which would freeze the
blood if not masked by a bland optimism. But it is not from them
that there came the single glimpse of forbidden eons which chills me
when I think of it and maddens me when I dream of it. That glimpse,
like all dread glimpses of truth, flashed out from an accidental piecing
together of separated things—in this case an old newspaper item and
the notes of a dead professor. I hope that no one else will accomplish
this piecing out; certainly, if I live, I shall never knowingly supply a
link in so hideous a chain. I think that the professor, too, intended to
keep silent regarding the part he knew, and that he would have destroyed his notes had not sudden death seized him.

My knowledge of the thing began in the winter of 1926–27 with the
death of my granduncle, George Gammell Angell, Professor Emeritus

of Semitic Languages in Brown University, Providence, Rhode Island. Professor Angell was widely known as an authority on ancient inscriptions, and had frequently been resorted to by the heads of prominent museums; so that his passing at the age of ninety-two may be recalled by many. Locally, interest was intensified by the obscurity of the cause of death. The professor had been stricken whilst returning from the Newport boat; falling suddenly, as witnesses said, after having been jostled by a nautical-looking negro who had come from one of the queer dark courts on the precipitous hillside which formed a short cut from the waterfront to the deceased's home in Williams Street. Physicians were unable to find any visible disorder, but concluded after perplexed debate that some obscure lesion of the heart, induced by the brisk ascent of so steep a hill by so elderly a man, was responsible for the end. At the time I saw no reason to dissent from this dictum, but latterly I am inclined to wonder—and more than wonder.

As my granduncle's heir and executor, for he died a childless widower, I was expected to go over his papers with some thoroughness; and for that purpose moved his entire set of files and boxes to my quarters in Boston. Much of the material which I correlated will be later published by the American Archaeological Society, but there was one box which I found exceedingly puzzling, and which I felt much averse from showing to other eyes. It had been locked, and I did not find the key till it occurred to me to examine the personal ring which the professor carried always in his pocket. Then, indeed, I succeeded in opening it, but when I did so seemed only to be confronted by a greater and more closely locked barrier. For what could be the meaning of the queer clay bas-relief and the disjointed jottings, ramblings, and cuttings which I found? Had my uncle, in his latter years become credulous of the most superficial impostures? I resolved to search out the eccentric sculptor responsible for this apparent disturbance of an old man's peace of mind.

The bas-relief was a rough rectangle less than an inch thick and about five by six inches in area; obviously of modern origin. Its designs, however, were far from modern in atmosphere and suggestion; for, although the vagaries of cubism and futurism are many and wild, they do not often reproduce that cryptic regularity which lurks in prehistoric writing. And writing of some kind the bulk of these designs seemed certainly to be; though my memory, despite much familiarity with the papers and collections of my uncle, failed in any way to identify this particular species, or even hint at its remotest affiliations.

Above these apparent hieroglyphics was a figure of evidently pictorial intent, though its impressionistic execution forbade a very clear idea of its nature. It seemed to be a sort of monster, or symbol representing a monster, of a form which only a diseased fancy could conceive. If I say that my somewhat extravagant imagination yielded simultaneous pictures of an octopus, a dragon, and a human caricature, I shall not be unfaithful to the spirit of the thing. A pulpy, tentacled head surmounted a grotesque and scaly body with rudimentary wings; but it was the *general outline* of the whole which made it most shockingly frightful. Behind the figure was a vague suggestion of a Cyclopean architectural background.

The writing accompanying this oddity was, aside from a stack of press cuttings, in Professor Angell's most recent hand; and made no pretense to literary style. What seemed to be the main document was headed "CTHULHU CULT" in characters painstakingly printed to avoid the erroneous reading of a word so unheard-of. This manuscript was divided into two sections, the first of which was headed "1925—Dream and Dream Work of H. A. Wilcox, 7 Thomas St., Providence, R. I.," and the second, "Narrative of Inspector John R. Legrasse, 121 Bienville St., New Orleans, La., at 1908 A. A. S. Mtg.—Notes on Same, & Prof. Webb's Acct." The other manuscript papers were all brief notes, some of them accounts of the queer dreams of different persons, some of them citations from theosophical books and magazines (notably W. Scott-Elliott's *Atlantis and the Lost Lemuria*), and the rest comments on long-surviving secret societies and hidden cults, with references to passages in such mythological and anthropological source-books as Frazer's *Golden Bough* and Miss Murray's *Witch-Cult in Western Europe*. The cuttings largely alluded to outré mental illness and outbreaks of group folly or mania in the spring of 1925.

The first half of the principal manuscript told a very peculiar tale. It appears that on March 1st, 1925, a thin, dark young man of neurotic and excited aspect had called upon Professor Angell bearing the singular clay bas-relief, which was then exceedingly damp and fresh. His card bore the name of Henry Anthony Wilcox, and my uncle had recognized him as the youngest son of an excellent family slightly known to him, who had latterly been studying sculpture at the Rhode Island School of Design and living alone at the Fleur-de-Lys Building near that institution. Wilcox was a precocious youth of known genius but great eccentricity, and had from childhood excited attention through the strange stories and odd dreams he was in the habit of relating. He called himself "psychically hypersensitive," but the staid folk of the ancient commercial city dismissed him as merely "queer." Never mingling much with his kind, he had dropped gradually from social visibility, and was now known only to a small group of esthetes from other towns. Even the Providence Art Club, anxious to preserve its conservatism, had found him quite hopeless.

On the occasion of the visit, ran the professor's manuscript, the sculptor abruptly asked for the benefit of his host's archaeological knowledge in identifying the hieroglyphics on the bas-relief. He spoke in a dreamy, stilted manner which suggested pose and alienated sympathy; and my uncle showed some sharpness in replying, for the conspicuous freshness of the tablet implied kinship with anything but archaeology. Young Wilcox's rejoinder, which impressed my uncle enough to make him recall and record it verbatim, was of a fantastically poetic cast which must have typified his whole conversation, and which I have since found highly characteristic of him. He said, "It is new, indeed, for I made it last night in a dream of strange cities; and dreams are older than brooding Tyre, or the contemplative Sphinx, or garden-girdled Babylon."

It was then that he began that rambling tale which suddenly played upon a sleeping memory and won the fevered interest of my uncle. There had been a slight earthquake tremor the night before, the most considerable felt in New England for some years; and Wilcox's imagination had been keenly affected. Upon retiring, he had had an unprecedented dream of great Cyclopean cities of titan blocks and sky-flung monoliths, all dripping with green ooze and sinister with latent horror. Hieroglyphics had covered the walls and pillars, and from some undetermined point below had come a voice that was not a voice; a chaotic sensation which only fancy could transmute into sound, but which he attempted to render by the almost unpronounceable jumble of letters, "*Cthulhu fhtagn.*"

This verbal jumble was the key to the recollection which excited and disturbed Professor Angell. He questioned the sculptor with scientific minuteness; and studied with almost frantic intensity the bas-relief on which the youth had found himself working, chilled and clad only in his nightclothes, when waking had stolen bewilderingly over him. My uncle blamed his old age, Wilcox afterward said, for his slowness in recognizing both hieroglyphics and pictorial design. Many of his questions seemed highly out of place to his visitor, especially those which tried to connect the latter with strange cults or societies; and Wilcox could not understand the repeated promises of silence which he was offered in exchange for an admission of membership in some wide-spread mystical or paganly religious body. When Professor Angell became convinced that the sculptor was indeed ignorant of any cult or system of cryptic lore, he besieged his visitor with demands for future reports of dreams. This bore regular fruit, for after the first interview the manuscript records daily calls of the young man, during which he related startling fragments of nocturnal imagery whose burden was always some terrible Cyclopean vista of dark and dripping stone, with a subterrene voice or intelligence shouting monotonously in enigmatical sense-impacts uninscribable save as gibberish. The two sounds most frequently repeated are those rendered by the letters *"Cthulhu"* and *"R'lyeh."*

On March 23, the manuscript continued, Wilcox failed to appear; and inquiries at his quarters revealed that he had been stricken with an obscure sort of fever and taken to the home of his family in Waterman Street. He had cried out in the night, arousing several other artists in the building, and had manifested since then only alternations of unconsciousness and delirium. My uncle at once telephoned the family, and from that time forward kept close watch of the case; calling often at the Thayer Street office of Dr. Tobey, whom he learned to be in charge. The youth's febrile mind, apparently, was dwelling on strange things; and the doctor shuddered now and then as he spoke of them. They included not only a repetition of what he had formerly dreamed, but touched wildly on a gigantic thing "miles high" which walked or lumbered about. He at no time fully described this object but occasional frantic words, as repeated by Dr. Tobey, convinced the professor that it must be identical with the nameless monstrosity he had sought to depict in his dream-sculpture. Reference to this object, the doctor added, was invariably a prelude to the young man's subsidence into lethargy. His temperature, oddly enough, was not greatly above normal; but the whole condition was otherwise such as to suggest true fever rather than mental disorder.

On April 2 at about 3 P.M. every trace of Wilcox's malady suddenly ceased. He sat upright in bed, astonished to find himself at home and completely ignorant of what had happened in dream or reality since the night of March 22. Pronounced well by his physician, he returned to his quarters in three days; but to Professor Angell he was of no further assistance. All traces of strange dreaming had vanished with his recovery, and my uncle kept no record of his night-thoughts after a week of pointless and irrelevant accounts of thoroughly usual visions.

Here the first part of the manuscript ended, but references to certain of the scattered notes gave me much material for thought—so much, in fact, that only the ingrained skepticism then forming my philosophy can account for my continued distrust of the artist. The notes in question were those descriptive of the dreams of various persons covering the same period as that in which young Wilcox had had his strange visitations. My uncle, it seems, had quickly instituted a prodigiously far-flung body of inquiries amongst nearly all the friends whom he could question without impertinence, asking for nightly reports of their dreams, and the dates of any notable visions for some time past. The reception of his request seems to have been varied; but he must, at the very least, have received more responses than any ordinary man could have handled without a secretary. This original correspondence was not preserved, but his notes formed a thorough and really significant digest. Average people in society and business—New England's traditional "salt of the earth"—gave an almost completely negative result, though scattered cases of uneasy but formless nocturnal impressions appear here and there, always between March 23 and April 2—the period of young Wilcox's delirium. Scientific men were little more affected, though four cases of vague description suggest fugitive glimpses of strange landscapes, and in one case there is mentioned a dread of something abnormal.

It was from the artists and poets that the pertinent answers came, and I know that panic would have broken loose had they been able to compare notes. As it was, lacking their original letters, I half suspected the compiler of having asked leading questions, or of having edited the correspondence in corroboration of what he had latently resolved to see. That is why I continued to feel that Wilcox, somehow cognizant of the old data which my uncle had possessed, had been imposing on the veteran scientist. These responses from esthetes told a disturbing tale. From February 28 to April 2 a large proportion of them had dreamed very bizarre things, the intensity of the dreams being immeasurably the stronger during the period of the sculptor's delirium. Over a fourth of those who reported anything, reported scenes and half-sounds not unlike those which Wilcox had described; and some of the dreamers confessed acute fear of the gigantic nameless thing visible toward the last. One case, which the note describes with emphasis, was very sad. The subject, a widely known architect with leanings toward theosophy and occultism, went violently insane on the date of young Wilcox's seizure, and expired several months later after incessant screamings to be saved from some escaped denizen of hell. Had my uncle referred to these cases by name instead of merely by number, I should have attempted some corroboration and personal investigation; but as it was, I succeeded in tracing down only a few. All of these, however, bore out the notes in full. I have often wondered if all the objects of the professor's questioning felt as puzzled as did this fraction. It is well that no explanation shall ever reach them.

The press cuttings, as I have intimated, touched on cases of panic, mania, and eccentricity during the given period. Professor Angell must have employed a cutting bureau, for the number of extracts was tremendous, and the sources scattered throughout the globe. Here was a nocturnal suicide in London, where a lone sleeper had leaped from a window after a shocking cry. Here likewise a rambling letter to the editor of a paper in South America, where a fanatic deduces a dire future from visions he has seen. A dispatch from California describes a theosophist colony as donning white robes en masse for some "glorious fulfilment" which never arrives, whilst items from India speak guardedly of serious native unrest toward the end of March. Voodoo orgies multiply in Haiti, and African outposts report ominous mutterings. American officers in the Philippines find certain tribes bothersome about this time, and New York policemen are mobbed by hysterical Levantines on the night of March 22-23. The west of Ireland, too, is full of wild rumour and legendry, and a fantastic painter named Ardois-Bonnot hangs a blasphemous *Dream Landscape* in the Paris spring salon of 1926. And so numerous are the recorded troubles in insane asylums that only a miracle can have stopped the medical fraternity from noting strange parallelisms and drawing mystified conclusions. A weird bunch of cuttings, all told; and I can at this date scarcely envisage the callous rationalism with which I set them aside. But I was then convinced that young Wilcox had known of the older matters mentioned by the professor.

2.

The Tale of Inspector Legrasse

The older matters which had made the sculptor's dream and bas-relief so significant to my uncle formed the subject of the second half of his long manuscript. Once before, it appears, Professor Angell had seen the hellish outlines of the nameless monstrosity, puzzled over the unknown hieroglyphics, and heard the ominous syllables which can be rendered only as *"Cthulhu";* and all this in so stirring and horrible a connection that it is small wonder he pursued young Wilcox with queries and demands for data.

This earlier experience had come in 1908, seventeen years before, when the American Archaeological Society held its annual meeting in St. Louis. Professor Angell, as befitted one of his authority and attainments, had had a prominent part in all the deliberations; and was one of the first to be approached by the several outsiders who took advantage of the convocation to offer questions for correct answering and problems for expert solution.

The chief of these outsiders, and in a short time the focus of interest for the entire meeting, was a commonplace-looking middle-aged man who had travelled all the way from New Orleans for certain special information unobtainable from any local source. His name was John Raymond Legrasse, and he was by profession an inspector of police. With him he bore the subject of his visit, a grotesque, repulsive, and apparently very ancient stone statuette whose origin he was at a loss to determine.

It must not be fancied that Inspector Legrasse had the least interest in archaeology. On the contrary, his wish for enlightenment was prompted by purely professional considerations. The statuette, idol, fetish, or whatever it was, had been captured some months before in the wooded swamps south of New Orleans during a raid on a supposed voodoo meeting; and so singular and hideous were the rites connected with it, that the police could not but realize that they had stumbled on a dark cult totally unknown to them, and infinitely more diabolic than even the blackest of the African voodoo circles. Of its origin, apart from the erratic and unbelievable tales extorted from the captured members, absolutely nothing was to be discovered; hence the anxiety of the police for any antiquarian lore which might help them to place the frightful symbol, and through it track down the cult to its fountainhead.

Inspector Legrasse was scarcely prepared for the sensation which his offering created. One sight of the thing had been enough to throw the assembled men of science into a state of tense excitement, and they lost no time in crowding around him to gaze at the diminutive figure whose utter strangeness and air of genuinely abysmal antiquity hinted so potently at unopened and archaic vistas. No recognized school of sculpture had animated this terrible object, yet centuries and even thousands of years seemed recorded in its dim and greenish surface of unplaceable stone.

The figure, which was finally passed slowly from man to man for close and careful study, was between seven and eight inches in height, and of exquisitely artistic workmanship. It represented a monster of vaguely anthropoid outline, but with an octopuslike head whose face was a mass of feelers, a scaly, rubbery-looking body, prodigious claws on hind and fore feet, and long, narrow wings behind. This thing, which seemed instinct with a fearsome and unnatural malignancy, was of a somewhat bloated corpulence, and squatted evilly on a rectangular block or pedestal covered with undecipherable characters. The tips of the wings touched the back edge of the block, the seat occupied the center, whilst the long, curved claws of the doubled-up, crouching hind legs gripped the front edge and extended a quarter of the way down toward the bottom of the pedestal. The cephalopod head was bent forward, so that the ends of the facial feelers brushed the backs of huge forepaws which clasped the croucher's elevated knees. The aspect of the whole was abnormally lifelike, and the more subtly fearful because its source was so totally unknown. Its vast, awesome, and incalculable age was unmistakable; yet not one link did it show with any known type of art belonging to civilization's youth—or indeed to any other time.

Totally separate and apart, its very material was a mystery; for the soapy, greenish-black stone with its golden or iridescent flecks and striations resembled nothing familiar to geology or mineralogy. The characters along the base were equally baffling; and no member present, despite a representation of half the world's expert learning in this field, could form the least notion of even their remotest linguistic kinship. They, like the subject and material, belonged to something horribly remote and distinct from mankind as we know it; something frightfully suggestive of old and unhallowed cycles of life in which our world and our conceptions have no part.

And yet, as the members severally shook their heads and confessed defeat at the inspector's problem, there was one man in that gathering who suspected a touch of bizarre familiarity in the monstrous shape and writing, and who presently told with some diffidence of the odd trifle he knew. This person was the late William Channing Webb, professor of anthropology in Princeton University, and an explorer of no slight note.

Professor Webb had been engaged, forty-eight years before, in a tour of Greenland and Iceland in search of some Runic inscriptions which he failed to unearth; and whilst high up on the West Greenland coast had encountered a singular tribe or cult of degenerate Eskimos whose religion, a curious form of devil-worship, chilled him with its deliberate bloodthirstiness and repulsiveness. It was a faith of which other Eskimos knew little, and which they mentioned only with shudders, saying that it had come down from horribly ancient eons before ever the world was made. Besides nameless rites and human sacrifices there were certain queer hereditary rituals addressed to a supreme elder devil or *tornasuk;* and of this Professor Webb had taken a careful phonetic copy from an aged *angekok* or wizard-priest, expressing the sounds in Roman letters as best he knew how. But just now of prime significance was the fetish which this cult had cherished, and around which they danced when the aurora leaped high over the ice cliffs. It was, the professor stated, a very crude bas-relief of stone, comprising a hideous picture and some cryptic writing. And as far as he could tell, it was a rough parallel in all essential features of the bestial thing now lying before the meeting.

These data, received with suspense and astonishment by the assembled members, proved doubly exciting to Inspector Legrasse; and he began at once to ply his informant with questions. Having noted and copied an oral ritual among the swamp cult-worshipers his men had arrested, he besought the professor to remember as best he might the syllables taken down amongst the diabolist Eskimos. There then followed an exhaustive comparison of details, and a moment of really awed silence when both detective and scientist agreed on the virtual identity of the phrase common to two hellish rituals so many worlds of distance apart. What, in substance, both the Eskimo wizards and the Louisiana swamp-priests had chanted to their kindred idols was something very like this—the word-divisions being guessed at from traditional breaks in the phrase as chanted aloud:

"Ph'nglui mglw'nafh Cthulhu R'lyeh wgah'nagl fhtagn."

Legrasse had one point in advance of Professor Webb, for several among his mongrel prisoners had repeated to him what older celebrants had told them the words meant. This text, as given, ran something like this:

"In his house at R'lyeh dead Cthulhu waits dreaming."

And now, in response to a general urgent demand, Inspector Le-

grasse related as fully as possible his experience with the swamp worshipers; telling a story to which I could see my uncle attached profound significance. It savored of the wildest dreams of mythmaker and
theosophist, and disclosed an astonishing degree of cosmic imagination
among such half-castes and pariahs as might be least expected to
possess it.

On November 1, 1907, there had come to New Orleans police a
frantic summons from the swamp and lagoon country to the south.
The squatters there, mostly primitive but good-natured descendants of
Lafitte's men, were in the grip of stark terror from an unknown thing
which had stolen upon them in the night. It was voodoo, apparently,
but voodoo of a more terrible sort than they had ever known; and
some of their women and children had disappeared since the malevolent tom-tom had begun its incessant beating far within the black
haunted woods where no dweller ventured. There were insane shouts
and harrowing screams, soul-chilling chants and dancing devil-flames;
and, the frightened messenger added, the people could stand it no
more.

So a body of twenty police, filling two carriages and an automobile,
had set out in the late afternoon with the shivering squatter as a guide.
At the end of the passable road they alighted, and for miles splashed
on in silence through the terrible cypress woods where day never
came. Ugly roots and malignant hanging nooses of Spanish moss beset
them, and now and then a pile of dank stones or fragments of a rotting
wall intensified by its hint of morbid habitation a depression which
every malformed tree and every fungous islet combined to create. At
length the squatter settlement, a miserable huddle of huts, hove in
sight; and hysterical dwellers ran out to cluster around the group of
bobbing lanterns. The muffled beat of tom-toms was now faintly audible far, far ahead; and a curdling shriek came at infrequent intervals
when the wind shifted. A reddish glare, too, seemed to filter through
the pale undergrowth beyond endless avenues of forest night. Reluctant even to be left alone again, each one of the cowed squatters
refused point-blank to advance another inch toward the scene of unholy worship, so Inspector Legrasse and his nineteen colleagues
plunged on unguided into black arcades of horror that none of them
had ever trod before.

The region now entered by the police was one of traditionally evil
repute, substantially unknown and untraversed by white men. There
were legends of a hidden lake unglimpsed by mortal sight, in which

dwelt a huge, formless white polypous thing with luminous eyes; and squatters whispered that bat-winged devils flew up out of caverns in inner earth to worship it at midnight. They said it had been there before D'Iberville, before La Salle, before the Indians, and before even the wholesome beasts and birds of the woods. It was nightmare itself, and to see it was to die. But it made men dream, and so they knew enough to keep away. The present voodoo orgy was, indeed, on the merest fringe of this abhorred area, but that location was bad enough; hence perhaps the very place of the worship had terrified the squatters more than the shocking sounds and incidents.

Only poetry or madness could do justice to the noises heard by Legrasse's men as they plowed on through the black morass toward the red glare and the muffled tom-toms. There are vocal qualities peculiar to men, and vocal qualities peculiar to beasts; and it is terrible to hear the one when the source should yield the other. Animal fury and orgiastic license here whipped themselves to demoniac heights by howls and squawking ecstasies that tore and reverberated through those nighted woods like pestilential tempests from the gulfs of hell. Now and then the less organized ululations would cease, and from what seemed a well-drilled chorus of hoarse voices would rise in singsong chant that hideous phrase or ritual:

"Ph'nglui mglw'nafh Cthulhu R'lyeh wgah'nagl fhtagn."

Then the men, having reached a spot where the trees were thinner, came suddenly in sight of the spectacle itself. Four of them reeled, one fainted, and two were shaken into a frantic cry which the mad cacophony of the orgy fortunately deadened. Legrasse dashed swamp water on the face of the fainting man, and all stood trembling and nearly hypnotized with horror.

In a natural glade of the swamp stood a grassy island of perhaps an acre's extent, clear of trees and tolerably dry. On this now leaped and twisted a more indescribable horde of human abnormality than any but a Sime or an Angarola could paint. Void of clothing, this hybrid spawn were braying, bellowing and writhing about a monstrous ring-shaped bonfire; in the center of which, revealed by occasional rifts in the curtain of flame, stood a great granite monolith some eight feet in height; on top of which, incongruous in its diminutiveness, rested the noxious carven statuette. From a wide circle of ten scaffolds set up at regular intervals with the flame-girt monolith as a center hung, head downward, the oddly marred bodies of the helpless squatters who had disappeared. It was inside this circle that the ring of worshipers jumped and roared, the general direction of the mass motion being from left to right in endless bacchanale between the ring of bodies and the ring of fire.

It may have been only imagination and it may have been only echoes which induced one of the men, an excitable Spaniard, to fancy he heard antiphonal responses to the ritual from some far and unillu-mined spot deeper within the wood of ancient legendry and horror. This man, Joseph D. Galvez, I later met and questioned; and he proved distractingly imaginative. He indeed went so far as to hint of the faint beating of great wings, and of a glimpse of shining eyes and mountainous white bulk beyond the remotest trees—but I suppose he had been hearing too much native superstition.

Actually, the horrified pause of the men was of comparatively brief duration. Duty came first; and although there must have been nearly a hundred mongrel celebrants in the throng, the police relied on their firearms and plunged determinedly into the nauseous rout. For five minutes the resultant din and chaos were beyond description. Wild blows were struck, shots were fired, and escapes were made; but in the end Legrasse was able to count some forty-seven sullen prisoners, whom he forced to dress in haste and fall into line between two rows of policemen. Five of the worshipers lay dead, and two severely wounded ones were carried away on improvised stretchers by their fellow-prisoners. The image on the monolith, of course, was carefully re-moved and carried back by Legrasse.

Examined at headquarters after a trip of intense strain and weari-ness, the prisoners all proved to be men of a very low, mixed-blooded, and mentally aberrant type. Most were seamen, and a sprinkling of negroes and mulattoes, largely West Indians or Brava Portuguese from the Cape Verde Islands, gave a coloring of voodooism to the het-erogeneous cult. But before many questions were asked, it became manifest that something far deeper and older than negro fetishism was involved. Degraded and ignorant as they were, the creatures held with surprising consistency to the central idea of their loathsome faith.

They worshiped, so they said, the Great Old Ones who lived ages before there were any men, and who came to the young world out of the sky. These Old Ones were gone now, inside the earth and under the sea; but their dead bodies had told their secrets in dreams to the first man, who formed a cult which had never died. This was that cult, and the prisoners said it had always existed and always would exist, hidden in distant wastes and dark places all over the world until the time when the great priest Cthulhu, from his dark house in the mighty city of R'lyeh under the waters, should rise and bring the earth again beneath his sway. Some day he would call, when the stars were ready, and the secret cult would always be waiting to liberate him.

Meanwhile no more must be told. There was a secret which even torture could not extract. Mankind was not absolutely alone among the conscious things of earth, for shapes came out of the dark to visit the faithful few. But these were not the Great Old Ones. No man had ever seen the Old Ones. The carven idol was great Cthulhu, but none might say whether or not the others were precisely like him. No one could read the old writing now, but things were told by word of mouth. The chanted ritual was not the secret—that was never spoken aloud, only whispered. The chant meant only this: "In his house at R'lyeh dead Cthulhu waits dreaming."

Only two of the prisoners were found sane enough to be hanged, and the rest were committed to various institutions. All denied a part in the ritual murders, and averred that the killing had been done by Black-winged Ones which had come to them from their immemorial meeting-place in the haunted wood. But of those mysterious allies no coherent account could ever be gained. What the police did extract came mainly from an immensely aged mestizo named Castro, who claimed to have sailed to strange ports and talked with undying leaders of the cult in the mountains of China.

Old Castro remembered bits of hideous legend that paled the speculations of theosophists and made man and the world seem recent and transient indeed. There had been eons when other Things ruled on the earth, and They had had great cities. Remains of Them, he said the deathless Chinamen had told him, were still to be found as Cyclopean stones on islands in the Pacific. They all died vast epochs of time before man came, but there were arts which could revive Them when the stars had come round again to the right positions in the cycle of eternity. They had, indeed, come themselves from the stars, and brought Their images with them.

These Great Old Ones, Castro continued, were not composed altogether of flesh and blood. They had shape—for did not this star-fashioned image prove it?—but that shape was not made of matter. When the stars were right, They could plunge from world to world through the sky; but when the stars were wrong, They could not live. But although They no longer lived, They would never really die. They all lay in stone houses in Their great city of R'lyeh, preserved by the spells of mighty Cthulhu for a glorious resurrection when the stars and the earth might once more be ready for Them. But at that time some force from outside must serve to liberate Their bodies. The spells that preserved Them intact likewise prevented Them from making an initial move, and They could only lie awake in the dark and think whilst uncounted millions of years rolled by. They knew all that was occurring in the universe, for Their mode of speech was transmitted thought. Even now They talked in Their tombs. When, after infinities of chaos, the first men came, the Great Old Ones spoke to the sensitive among them by molding their dreams; for only thus could Their language reach the fleshy minds of mammals.

Then, whispered Castro, those first men formed the cult around small idols which the Great Ones showed them; idols brought in dim eras from dark stars. That cult would never die till the stars came right again, and the secret priests would take great Cthulhu from His tomb to revive His subjects and resume His rule of earth. The time would be easy to know, for then mankind would have become as the Great Old Ones; free and wild and beyond good and evil, with laws and morals thrown aside and all men shouting and killing and reveling in joy. Then the liberated Old Ones would teach them new ways to shout and kill and revel and enjoy themselves, and all the earth would flame with a holocaust of ecstasy and freedom. Meanwhile the cult, by appropriate rites, must keep alive the memory of those ancient ways and shadow forth the prophecy of their return.

In the elder time chosen men had talked with the entombed Old Ones in dreams, but then something had happened. The great stone city R'lyeh, with its monoliths and sepulchers, had sunk beneath the waves; and the deep waters, full of the one primal mystery through which not even thought can pass, had cut off the spectral intercourse. But memory never died, and high priests said that the city would rise again when the stars were right. Then came out of the earth the black spirits of earth, moldy and shadowy, and full of dim rumors picked up in caverns beneath forgotten sea-bottoms. But of them old Castro dared not speak much. He cut himself off hurriedly, and no amount of persuasion or subtlety could elicit more in this direction. The *size* of the Old Ones, too, he curiously declined to mention. Of the cult, he said that he thought the center lay amid the pathless deserts of Arabia, where Irem, the City of Pillars, dreams hidden and untouched. It was not allied to the European witch-cult, and was virtually unknown beyond its members. No book had ever really hinted of it, though the deathless Chinamen said that there were double meanings in the *Necronomicon* of the mad Arab Abdul Alhazred which the initiated might read as they chose, especially the much-discussed couplet:

> That is not dead which can eternal lie,
> And with strange eons even death may die.

Legrasse, deeply impressed and not a little bewildered, had inquired in vain concerning the historic affiliations of the cult. Castro, apparently, had told the truth when he said that it was wholly secret. The authorities at Tulane University could shed no light upon either cult or image, and now the detective had come to the highest authorities in the country and met with no more than the Greenland tale of Professor Webb.

The feverish interest aroused at the meeting by Legrasse's tale, corroborated as it was by the statuette, is echoed in the subsequent correspondence of those who attended; although scant mention occurs in the formal publication of the society. Caution is the first care of those accustomed to face occasional charlatanry and imposture. Legrasse for some time lent the image to Professor Webb, but at the latter's death it was returned to him and remains in his possession, where I viewed it not long ago. It is truly a terrible thing, and unmistakably akin to the dream-sculpture of young Wilcox.

That my uncle was excited by the tale of the sculptor I did not wonder, for what thoughts must arise upon hearing, after a knowledge of what Legrasse had learned of the cult, of a sensitive young man who had *dreamed* not only the figure and exact hieroglyphics of the swamp-found image and the Greenland devil tablet, but had come *in his dreams* upon at least three of the precise words of the formula uttered alike by Eskimo diabolists and mongrel Louisianans? Professor Angell's instant start on an investigation of the utmost thoroughness was eminently natural; though privately I suspected young Wilcox of having heard of the cult in some indirect way, and of having invented a series of dreams to heighten and continue the mystery at my uncle's expense. The dream-narratives and cuttings collected by the professor were, of course, strong corroboration; but the rationalism of my mind and the extravagance of the whole subject led me to adopt what I thought the most sensible conclusions. So, after thoroughly studying the manuscript again and correlating the theosophical and anthropological notes with the cult narrative of Legrasse, I made a trip to Providence to see the sculptor and give him the rebuke I thought proper for so boldly imposing upon a learned and aged man.

Wilcox still lived alone in the Fleur-de-Lys Building in Thomas Street, a hideous Victorian imitation of Seventeenth Century Breton architecture which flaunts its stuccoed front amidst the lovely Colonial houses on the ancient hill, and under the very shadow of the finest Georgian steeple in America. I found him at work in his rooms, and at once conceded from the specimens scattered about that his genius is indeed profound and authentic. He will, I believe, be heard from sometime as one of the great decadents; for he has crystallized in clay and will one day mirror in marble those nightmares and fantasies which Arthur Machen evokes in prose, and Clark Ashton Smith makes visible in verse and in painting.

Dark, frail, and somewhat unkempt in aspect, he turned languidly at my knock and asked me my business without rising. When I told him who I was, he displayed some interest; for my uncle had excited his curiosity in probing his strange dreams, yet had never explained the reason for the study. I did not enlarge his knowledge in this regard, but sought with some subtlety to draw him out.

In a short time I became convinced of his absolute sincerity for he spoke of the dreams in a manner none could mistake. They and their subconscious residuum had influenced his art profoundly, and he showed me a morbid statue whose contours almost made me shake with the potency of its black suggestion. He could not recall having seen the original of this thing except in his own dream bas-relief, but the outlines had formed themselves insensibly under his hands. It was, no doubt, the giant shape he had raved of in delirium. That he really knew nothing of the hidden cult, save from what my uncle's relentless catechism had let fall, he soon made clear; and again I strove to think of some way in which he could possibly have received the weird impressions.

He talked of his dreams in a strangely poetic fashion; making me see with terrible vividness the damp Cyclopean city of slimy green stone—whose *geometry*, he oddly said, was *all wrong*—and hear with frightened expectancy the ceaseless, half-mental calling from underground: *"Cthulhu fhtagn," "Cthulhu fhtagn."*

These words had formed part of that dread ritual which told of dead Cthulhu's dream-vigil in his stone vault at R'lyeh, and I felt deeply moved despite my rational beliefs. Wilcox, I was sure, had heard of the cult in some casual way, and had soon forgotten it amidst the mass of his equally weird reading and imagining. Later, by virtue of its sheer impressiveness, it had found subconscious expression in dreams, in the bas-relief, and in the terrible statue I now beheld; so that his imposture upon my uncle had been a very innocent one. The youth was of a type, at once slightly affected and slightly ill-mannered, which I could never like; but I was willing enough now to admit both his genius and his honesty. I took leave of him amicably, and wish him all the success his talent promises.

The matter of the cult still remained to fascinate me, and at times I had visions of personal fame from researches into its origin and connections. I visited New Orleans, talked with Legrasse and others of that old-time raiding-party, saw the frightful image, and even questioned such of the mongrel prisoners as still survived. Old Castro, unfortunately, had been dead for some years. What I now heard so graphically at first hand, though it was really no more than a detailed confirmation of what my uncle had written, excited me afresh; for I felt sure that I was on the track of a very real, very secret, and very ancient religion whose discovery would make me an anthropologist of note. My attitude was still one of absolute materialism *as I wish it still were,* and I discounted with a most inexplicable perversity the coincidence of the dream notes and odd cuttings collected by Professor Angell.

One thing which I began to suspect, and which I now fear I *know,* is that my uncle's death was far from natural. He fell on a narrow hill street leading up from an ancient waterfront swarming with foreign mongrels, after a careless push from a negro sailor. I did not forget the mixed blood and marine pursuits of the cult-members in Louisiana, and would not be surprised to learn of secret methods and poison needles as ruthless and as anciently known as the cryptic rites and beliefs. Legrasse and his men, it is true, have been let alone; but in Norway a certain seaman who saw things is dead. Might not the deeper inquiries of my uncle after encountering the sculptor's data have come to sinister ears? I think Professor Angell died because he knew too much, or because he was likely to learn too much. Whether I shall go as he did remains to be seen, for I have learned much now.

3.
The Madness from the Sea

If heaven ever wishes to grant me a boon, it will be a total effacing of the results of a mere chance which fixed my eye on a certain stray piece of shelf-paper. It was nothing on which I would naturally have stumbled in the course of my daily round, for it was an old number of an Australian journal, *Sydney Bulletin* for April 18, 1925. It had escaped even the cutting bureau which had at the time of its issuance been avidly collecting material for my uncle's research.

I had largely given over my inquiries into what Professor Angell called the "Cthulhu Cult," and was visiting a learned friend of Paterson, New Jersey, the curator of a local museum and a mineralogist of note. Examining one day the reserve specimens roughly set on the storage shelves in a rear room of the museum, my eye was caught by an odd picture in one of the old papers spread beneath the stones. It was the *Sydney Bulletin* I have mentioned, for my friend has wide affiliations in all conceivable foreign parts; and the picture was a half-tone cut of a hideous stone image almost identical with that which Legrasse had found in the swamp.

Eagerly clearing the sheet of its precious contents, I scanned the item in detail; and was disappointed to find it of only moderate length. What it suggested, however, was of portentous significance to my flagging quest; and I carefully tore it out for immediate action. It read as follows:

MYSTERY DERELICT FOUND AT SEA

Vigilant Arrives with Helpless Armed New Zealand Yacht in Tow. One Survivor and Dead Man Found Aboard. Tale of Desperate Battle and Deaths at Sea. Rescued Seaman Refuses Particulars of Strange Experience. Odd Idol Found in His Possession. Inquiry to Follow.

The Morrison Co.'s freighter *Vigilant,* bound from Valparaiso, arrived this morning at its wharf in Darling Harbour, having in tow the battled and disabled but heavily armed steam yacht *Alert* of Dunedin, N. Z., which was sighted April 12th in S. Latitude 34° 21′, W. Longitude 152° 17′, with one living and one dead man aboard.

The *Vigilant* left Valparaiso March 25th, and on April 2d was driven considerably south of her course by exceptionally heavy storms and monster waves. On April 12th the derelict was sighted; and though apparently deserted, was found upon boarding to contain one survivor in a half-delirious condition and one man who had evidently been dead for more than a week.

The living man was clutching a horrible stone idol of unknown origin, about a foot in height, regarding whose nature authorities at Sydney University, the Royal Society, and the Museum in College Street all profess complete bafflement, and which the survivor says he found in the cabin of the yacht, in a small carved shrine of common pattern.

This man, after recovering his senses, told an exceedingly strange story of piracy and slaughter. He is Gustaf Johansen, a Norwegian of some intelligence, and had been second mate of the two-masted schooner *Emma* of Auckland, which sailed for Callao February 20th, with a complement of eleven men.

The *Emma,* he says, was delayed and thrown widely south of her course by the great storm of March 1st, and on March 22d, in S. Latitude 49° 51', W. Longitude 128° 34', encountered the *Alert,* manned by a queer and evil-looking crew of Kanakas and half-castes. Being ordered peremptorily to turn back, Capt. Collins refused; whereupon the strange crew began to fire savagely and without warning upon the schooner with a peculiarly heavy battery of brass cannon forming part of the yacht's equipment.

The *Emma*'s men showed fight, says the survivor, and though the schooner began to sink from shots beneath the waterline they managed to heave alongside their enemy and board her, grappling with the savage crew on the yacht's deck, and being forced to kill them all, the number being slightly superior, because of their particularly abhorrent and desperate though rather clumsy mode of fighting.

Three of the *Emma*'s men, including Capt. Collins and First Mate Green, were killed; and the remaining eight under Second Mate Johansen proceeded to navigate the captured yacht, going ahead in their original direction to see if any reason for their ordering back had existed.

The next day, it appears, they raised and landed on a small island, although none is known to exist in that part of the ocean; and six of the men somehow died ashore, though Johansen is queerly reticent about this part of his story and speaks only of their falling into a rock chasm.

Later, it seems, he and one companion boarded the yacht and tried to manage her, but were beaten about by the storm of April 2d.

From that time till his rescue on the 12th, the man remembers little, and he does not even recall when William Briden, his companion, died. Briden's death reveals no apparent cause, and was probably due to excitement or exposure.

Cable advices from Dunedin report that the *Alert* was well known there as an island trader, and bore an evil reputation along the waterfront. It was owned by a curious group of half-castes whose frequent meetings and night trips to the woods attracted no little curiosity; and it had set sail in great haste just after the storm and earth tremors of March 1st.

Our Auckland correspondent gives the *Emma* and her crew an excellent reputation, and Johansen is described as a sober and worthy man.

The admiralty will institute an inquiry on the whole matter beginning tomorrow, at which every effort will be made to induce Johansen to speak more freely than he has done hitherto.

This was all, together with the picture of the hellish image; but what a train of ideas it started in my mind! Here were new treasuries of data on the Cthulhu Cult, and evidence that it had strange interests at sea as well as on land. What motive prompted the hybrid crew to order back the *Emma* as they sailed about with their hideous idol? What was the unknown island on which six of the *Emma*'s crew had died, and about which the mate Johansen was so secretive? What had the vice-admiralty's investigation brought out, and what was known of the noxious cult in Dunedin? And most marvelous of all, what deep and more than natural linkage of dates was this which gave a malign and now undeniable significance to the various turns of event so carefully noted by my uncle?

March 1st—our February 28th according to the International Date Line—the earthquake and storm had come. From Dunedin the *Alert* and her noisome crew had darted eagerly forth as if imperiously summoned, and on the other side of the earth poets and artists had begun to dream of a strange, dank Cyclopean city whilst a young sculptor had molded in his sleep the form of the dreaded Cthulhu. March 23rd the crew of the *Emma* landed on an unknown island and left six men dead; and on that date the dreams of sensitive men assumed a heightened vividness and darkened with dread of a giant monster's malign pursuit, whilst an architect had gone mad and a sculptor had lapsed suddenly into delirium! And what of this storm of April 2nd—the date on which all dreams of the dank city ceased, and Wilcox emerged unharmed from the bondage of strange fever? What of all this—and of those hints of old Castro about the sunken, star-born Old Ones and their coming reign; their faithful cult *and their mastery of dreams?* Was I tottering on the brink of cosmic horrors beyond man's power to bear? If so, they must be horrors of the mind alone, for in some way the second of April had put a stop to whatever monstrous menace had begun its siege of mankind's soul.

That evening, after a day of hurried cabling and arranging, I bade my host adieu and took a train for San Francisco. In less than a month I was in Dunedin: where, however, I found that little was known of the strange cult-members who had lingered in the old sea taverns. Waterfront scum was far too common for special mention; though there was vague talk about one inland trip these mongrels had made, during which faint drumming and red flame were noted on the distant hills.

In Auckland I learned that Johansen had returned *with yellow hair turned white* after a perfunctory and inconclusive questioning at Sydney, and had thereafter sold his cottage in West Street and sailed with his wife to his old home in Oslo. Of his stirring experience he would tell his friends no more than he had told the admiralty officials, and all they could do was to give me his Oslo address.

After that I went to Sydney and talked profitlessly with seamen and members of the vice-admiralty court. I saw the *Alert,* now sold and in commercial use, at Circular Quay in Sydney Cove, but gained nothing from its noncommittal bulk. The crouching image with its cuttlefish head, dragon body, scaly wings, and hieroglyphed pedestal, was preserved in the Museum at Hyde Park; and I studied it long and well, finding it a thing of balefully exquisite workmanship, and with the same utter mystery, terrible antiquity, and unearthly strangeness of material which I had noted in Legrasse's smaller specimen. Geologists, the curator told me, had found it a monstrous puzzle; for they vowed that the world held no rock like it. Then I thought with a shudder of what old Castro had told Legrasse about the primal Great Ones: "They had come from the stars, and had brought Their images with them."

Shaken with such a mental revolution as I had never before known, I now resolved to visit Mate Johansen in Oslo. Sailing for London, I re-embarked at once for the Norwegian capital; and one autumn day landed at the trim wharves in the shadow of the Egeberg.

Johansen's address, I discovered, lay in the Old Town of King Harold Haardrada, which kept alive the name of Oslo during all the centuries that the greater city masqueraded as "Christiania." I made the brief trip by taxicab, and knocked with palpitant heart at the door of a neat and ancient building with plastered front. A sad-faced woman in black answered my summons, and I was stung with disappointment when she told me in halting English that Gustaf Johansen was no more.

He had not long survived his return, said his wife, for the doings at sea in 1925 had broken him. He had told her no more than he had told the public, but had left a long manuscript—of "technical matters" as he said—written in English evidently in order to safeguard her from the peril of casual perusal. During a walk through a narrow lane near the Gothenburg dock, a bundle of papers falling from an attic window had knocked him down. Two Lascar sailors at once helped him to his feet, but before the ambulance could reach him he was dead. Physicians found no adequate cause for the end, and laid it to heart trouble and a weakened constitution.

I now felt gnawing at my vitals that dark terror which will never leave me till I, too, am at rest; "accidentally" or otherwise. Persuading the widow that my connection with her husband's "technical matters" was sufficient to entitle me to his manuscript, I bore the document away and began to read it on the London boat.

It was a simple, rambling thing—a naïve sailor's effort at a post-facto diary—and strove to recall day by day that last awful voyage. I can not attempt to transcribe it verbatim in all its cloudiness and redundance, but I will tell its gist enough to show why the sound of the water against the vessel's sides became so unendurable to me that I stopped my ears with cotton.

Johansen, thank God, did not know quite all, even though he saw the city and the Thing, but I shall never sleep calmly again when I think of the horrors that lurk ceaselessly behind life in time and in space, and of those unhallowed blasphemies from elder stars which dream beneath the sea, known and favored by a nightmare cult ready and eager to loose them on the world whenever another earthquake shall heave their monstrous stone city again to the sun and air.

Johansen's voyage had begun just as he told it to the vice-admiralty. The *Emma,* in ballast, had cleared Auckland on February 20th, and had felt the full force of that earthquake-born tempest which must have heaved up from the sea-bottom the horrors that filled men's dreams. Once more under control, the ship was making good progress when held up by the *Alert* on March 22nd, and I could feel the mate's regret as he wrote of her bombardment and sinking. Of the swarthy cult-fiends on the *Alert* he speaks with significant horror. There was some peculiarly abominable quality about them which made their destruction seem almost a duty, and Johansen shows ingenuous wonder at the charge of ruthlessness brought against his party during the proceedings of the court of inquiry. Then, driven ahead by curiosity in their captured yacht under Johansen's command, the men sight a great stone pillar sticking out of the sea, and in S. Latitude 47° 9′, W. Longitude 126° 43', come upon a coastline of mingled mud, ooze, and weedy Cyclopean masonry which can be nothing less than the tangible substance of earth's supreme terror—the nightmare corpse-city of R'lyeh, that was built in measureless eons behind history by the vast, loathsome shapes that seeped down from the dark stars. There lay great Cthulhu and his hordes, hidden in green slimy vaults and sending out at last, after cycles incalculable, the thoughts that spread fear to the dreams of the sensitive and called imperiously to the faithful to come on a pilgrimage of liberation and restoration. All this Johansen did not suspect, but God knows he soon saw enough!

I suppose that only a single mountain-top, the hideous monolith-crowned citadel whereon great Cthulhu was buried, actually emerged from the waters. When I think of the *extent* of all that may be brooding down there I almost wish to kill myself forthwith. Johansen and his men were awed by the cosmic majesty of this dripping Babylon of elder demons, and must have guessed without guidance that it was nothing of this or of any sane planet. Awe at the unbelievable size of the greenish stone blocks, at the dizzying height of the great carven monolith, and at the stupefying identity of the colossal statues and bas-reliefs with the queer image found in the shrine on the *Alert*, is poignantly visible in every line of the mate's frightened description.

Without knowing what futurism is like, Johansen achieved something very close to it when he spoke of the city; for instead of describing any definite structure or building, he dwells only on the broad impressions of vast angles and stone surfaces—surfaces too great to belong to any thing right or proper for this earth, and impious with horrible images and hieroglyphs. I mention his talk about *angles* because it suggests something Wilcox had told me of his awful dreams. He had said that the *geometry* of the dream-place he saw was abnormal, non-Euclidean, and loathsomely redolent of spheres and dimensions apart from ours. Now an unlettered seaman felt the same thing whilst gazing at the terrible reality.

Johansen and his men landed at a sloping mud-bank on this monstrous acropolis, and clambered slipperily up over titan oozy blocks which could have been no mortal staircase. The very sun of heaven seemed distorted when viewed through the polarizing miasma welling out from this sea-soaked perversion, and twisted menace and suspense lurked leeringly in those crazily elusive angles of carven rock where a second glance showed concavity after the first showed convexity.

Something very like fright had come over all the explorers before anything more definite than rock and ooze and weed was seen. Each would have fled had he not feared the scorn of the others, and it was only half-heartedly that they searched—vainly, as it proved—for some portable souvenir to bear away.

It was Rodriguez the Portuguese who climbed up the foot of the monolith and shouted of what he had found. The rest followed him, and looked curiously at the immense carved door with the now familiar squid-dragon bas-relief. It was, Johansen said, like a great barndoor; and they all felt that it was a door because of the ornate lintel, threshold, and jambs around it, though they could not decide whether it lay flat like a trap door or slantwise like an outside cellar-door. As Wilcox would have said, the geometry of the place was all wrong. One could not be sure that the sea and the ground were horizontal, hence the relative position of everything else seemed phantasmally variable.

Briden pushed at the stone in several places without result. Then Donovan felt over it delicately around the edge, pressing each point separately as he went. He climbed interminably along the grotesque stone molding—that is, one would call it climbing if the thing was not after all horizontal—and the men wondered how any door in the universe could be so vast. Then, very softly and slowly, the acre-great panel began to give inward at the top; and they saw that it was balanced.

Donovan slid or somehow propelled himself down or along the jamb and rejoined his fellows, and everyone watched the queer recession of the monstrously carven portal. In this fantasy of prismatic distortion it moved anomalously in a diagonal way, so that all the rules of matter and perspective seemed upset.

The aperture was black with a darkness almost material. That tenebrousness was indeed a *positive quality;* for it obscured such parts of the inner walls as ought to have been revealed, and actually burst forth like smoke from its eon-long imprisonment, visibly darkening the sun as it slunk away into the shrunken and gibbous sky on flapping membranous wings. The odor arising from the newly opened depths was intolerable, and at length the quick-eared Hawkins thought he heard a nasty, slopping sound down there. Everyone listened, and everyone was listening still when It lumbered slobberingly into sight and gropingly squeezed Its gelatinous green immensity through the black doorway into the tainted outside air of that poison city of madness.

Poor Johansen's handwriting almost gave out when he wrote of this. Of the six men who never reached the ship, he thinks two perished of pure fright in that accursed instant. The Thing can not be described—there is no language for such abysms of shrieking and immemorial lunacy, such eldritch contradictions of all matter, force, and cosmic order. A mountain walked or stumbled. God! What wonder that across the earth a great architect went mad, and poor Wilcox raved with fever in that telepathic instant? The Thing of the idols, the green, sticky spawn of the stars, had awaked to claim his own. The stars were right again, and what an age-old cult had failed to do by design, a band of innocent sailors had done by accident. After vigintillions of years great Cthulhu was loose again, and ravening for delight.

Three men were swept up by the flabby claws before anybody turned. God rest them, if there be any rest in the universe. They were Donovan, Guerrera and Angstrom. Parker slipped as the other three were plunging frenziedly over endless vistas of green-crusted rock to the boat, and Johansen swears he was swallowed up by an angle of masonry which shouldn't have been there; an angle which was acute, but behaved as if it were obtuse. So only Briden and Johansen reached the boat, and pulled desperately for the *Alert* as the mountainous monstrosity flopped down the slimy stones and hesitated, floundering at the edge of the water.

Steam had not been suffered to go down entirely, despite the departure of all hands for the shore; and it was the work of only a few moments of feverish rushing up and down between wheels and engines to get the *Alert* under way. Slowly, amidst the distorted horrors of that indescribable scene, she began to churn the lethal waters; whilst on the masonry of that charnel shore that was not of earth the titan Thing from the stars slavered and gibbered like Polypheme cursing the fleeing ship of Odysseus. Then, bolder than the storied Cyclops, great Cthulhu slid greasily into the water and began to pursue with vast wave-raising strokes of cosmic potency. Briden looked back and went mad, laughing at intervals till death found him one night in the cabin whilst Johansen was wandering deliriously.

But Johansen had not given out yet. Knowing that the Thing could surely overtake the *Alert* until steam was fully up, he resolved on a desperate chance; and, setting the engine for full speed, ran lightning-like on deck and reversed the wheel. There was a mighty eddying and foaming in the noisome brine, and as the steam mounted higher and higher the brave Norwegian drove his vessel head on against the pursuing jelly which rose above the unclean froth like the stern of a demon galleon. The awful squid-head with writhing feelers came nearly up to the bowsprit of the sturdy yacht, but Johansen drove on relentlessly.

There was a bursting as of an exploding bladder, a slushy nastiness as of a cloven sunfish, a stench as of a thousand opened graves, and a sound that the chronicler would not put on paper. For an instant the ship was befouled by an acrid and blinding green cloud, and then there was only a venomous seething astern; where—God in heaven!—the scattered plasticity of that nameless sky-spawn was nebulously *recombining* in its hateful original form, whilst its distance widened every second as the *Alert* gained impetus from its mounting steam.

That was all. After that Johansen only brooded over the idol in the cabin and attended to a few matters of food for himself and the laughing maniac by his side. He did not try to navigate after the first bold flight; for the reaction had taken something out of his soul. Then came the storm of April 2nd, and a gathering of the clouds about his consciousness. There is a sense of spectral whirling through liquid gulfs of infinity, of dizzying rides through reeling universes on a comet's tail, and of hysterical plunges from the pit to the moon and from the moon back again to the pit, all livened by a cachinnating chorus of the distorted, hilarious elder gods and the green, bat-winged mocking imps of Tartarus.

Out of that dream came rescue—the *Vigilant*, the vice-admiralty court, the streets of Dunedin, and the long voyage back home to the old house by the Egeberg. He could not tell—they would think him mad. He would write of what he knew before death came, but his wife must not guess. Death would be a boon if only it could blot out the memories.

That was the document I read, and now I have placed it in the tin box beside the bas-relief and the papers of Professor Angell. With it shall go this record of mine—this test of my own sanity, wherein is pieced together that which I hope may never be pieced together again. I have looked upon all that the universe has to hold of horror, and even the skies of spring and the flowers of summer must ever afterward be poison to me. But I do not think my life will be long. As my uncle went, as poor Johansen went, so I shall go. I know too much, and the cult still lives.

Cthulhu still lives, too, I suppose, again in that chasm of stone which has shielded him since the sun was young. His accursed city is sunken once more, for the *Vigilant* sailed over the spot after the April storm; but his ministers on earth still bellow and prance and slay around idol-capped monoliths in lonely places. He must have been trapped by the sinking whilst within his black abyss, or else the world would by now be screaming with fright and frenzy. Who knows the end? What has risen may sink, and what has sunk may rise. Loathsomeness waits and dreams in the deep, and decay spreads over the tottering cities of men. A time will come—but I must not and can not think! Let me pray that, if I do not survive this manuscript, my executors may put caution before audacity and see that it meets no other eye.

IV

LOST RACES

***

The Moon Pool
By A. Merritt

The Terror of Blue John Gap
By Sir Arthur Conan Doyle

7

After considering the origins of mankind, one naturally progresses into the fascinating realm of lost races and secret worlds. These depend not so much on conjecture and theory, but evidence of places where man once lived—in some cases, might still live—far from the eyes of the rest of humanity. The evidence may consist of as little as a recurring legend and the whispered tales of travelers, or as much as ruined buildings standing like mute witnesses on some far-flung corner of the earth. In the realms of fantasy fiction it is a topic which has attracted the talents of some of the most famous writers in the genre. Rider Haggard, for instance, built a whole series of novels around legends of lost races as far apart as the Arctic and the inferno of Central Africa; Talbot Mundy similarly took his experience of world travel to portray hitherto undiscovered or long-separated communities in India and the Far East; while Edgar Rice Burroughs was as likely to place his civilizations in the jungles of Africa or on remote islands of the Pacific. Great though the contributions of all these men have been, the "lost race" story probably owes its tremendous popularity mainly to the American author *Abraham Merritt* (1884–1943). Only those who lived in America during the quarter of a century when Merritt dominated the ranks of fantasy-fiction storytellers can fully appreciate his importance. A new story by Merritt could quadruple sales of a magazine overnight, and when a serial reached its conclusion, almost created hysteria among readers. At a time when the market was packed with talented and ingenious writers, Merritt stood head and shoulders above the rest, and the measure of his success has been the continued reprinting of most of his novels and stories. Although he spent much of his later life as the editor of a popular magazine, *The American Weekly*, he could draw on an exciting and adventurous youth for his spare-time writing. He had traveled extensively in Mexico and Central America, explored Mayan cities and hunted for buried treasure in Yucatan, and even been initiated by secret rites into an Indian tribe. He was also a voracious reader of books on folklore and strange phenomena, and came to fantasy fiction with wide-ranging qualifications. Merritt's popularity with readers was instantly won, just as his influence became quickly noticeable in the work of other writers. The story that did most to establish his reputation is undoubtedly "The Moon Pool," which appeared in 1918 and opened the floodgates of "lost race" stories which Rider Haggard and Edgar Rice Burroughs had already been promoting. The tale is set around the island of Ponape in the Caroline Islands. Here, on the East Coast, in the tribal district of Metalanim, lies the Nam-Matal, "the place of the Waterways," nine square miles of lagoon sprinkled with almost sixty rectangular artificial islands intersected by a network of canals. Who built this "veritable Venice from a forgotten age," as one observer has called it, has puzzled scientists and explorers alike. Study on the island, however, has revealed enclosures and vaults very similar to mysterious stone constructions on Easter Island, seven thousand miles away. Excavation has also brought to light strange axes made from the shells of giant

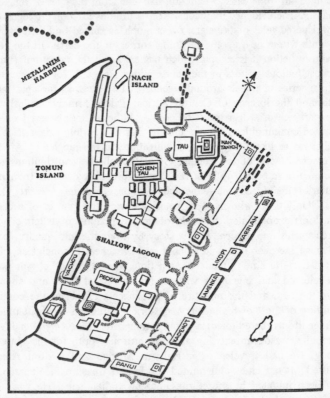

An old map from the Geographical Journal *was used by A. Merritt as the model for his map of the Moon Pool Island. It was made by F. W. Christian, the first explorer to map the baffling maze.*

clams, together with pearl-shell beads and the shanks of fishhooks. The island is populated, and although Christianized, there is still widespread belief in the *Ani,* or deified ancestors, who reside in many places and things. Merritt took all these elements and wove them into the tapestry of his short story—a tale he later enlarged, in response to public demand, into a full-length novel, *The Conquest of the Moon Pool.* Here, the magazine story, original from 1918, appears again, complete with its "introductory letter"—omitted from the only other two reprints of the story I have ever seen.

THE MOON POOL
A. Merritt

To the Editor:
The International Association of Science has directed me to place before you the following narrative with the view, if you are agreeable, of publication as soon as possible. Because of your extraordinarily large circulation and its diffusion not only throughout the United States, but throughout the reading world, it was felt that yours was the ideal medium to bring the facts before the greatest audience and so enable the association to right a wrong which, but for Dr. Goodwin's very understandable and perhaps entirely human hesitation, would never have gained headway.

The association, in selecting you as the subject of this request, took into consideration the fact that the space limitations of newspapers are such that the complete narrative of Dr. Goodwin could not be published therein, whereas with you this handicap does not exist. It was also convinced that so important and unusual a document could not communicate its unique impression of truth and sincerity unless read in its entirety exactly as it was before the International Association of Science, April 18, 1918.

I have been authorized to announce that we have discovered that Dr. Goodwin is now actually on his way to the Caroline Islands, and that the association is preparing an expedition to follow him speedily; to save him if it can arrive in time; at least to investigate and to destroy if possible, and if necessary, the cause of his journey.

The maps which Dr. Goodwin received from Dr. Throckmartin accompany this manuscript. It is our desire that they be published with it for the guidance of other scientists or courageous men who may be impelled on reading it to follow us with another expedition. For it is not at all certain that the human expedients planned by the association can cope with phenomena so clearly beyond the range of present human knowledge as that which Dr. Throckmartin describes as emanating from what he calls "the moon pool," and that which Dr. Goodwin saw on board the *Southern Queen.*

Again it may be that this unearthly dweller in the prehistoric island ruins of the South Seas is only one of many. Further, there is the hint conveyed by the underground chanting heard by Dr. Throckmartin; raising the question of the existence of considerable other forces or creatures possessing powers of knowledge of which we are densely ignorant, and in the exercise of which the world must be deeply concerned.

It is unnecessary to say to you that Dr. Walter T. Goodwin, Ph.D., F.R.G.S., *et cetera,* though in his early thirties, is known as the foremost of American botanists, and that Dr. David Throckmartin's scientific reputation is so great that even the cloud that has gathered about his memory could not blacken his achievements.

For those who would follow us, full information as to the methods of the expedition can be secured at the office of the president of the association.

Our foremost purpose in asking publication is, however, as I have said, to remove the shadow from the name of Dr. Throckmartin, of his young wife, and of his brilliant young associate, Dr. Charles Stanton, who accompanied him on his ill-fated journey.

The association has entrusted this explanation and the narrative of Dr. Goodwin to Mr. A. Merritt, who has courteously volunteered to set it before you together with other facts which we have asked him to communicate to you verbally.

Respectfully yours,
The International Association of Science,
Per J. B. K., President.

1

I break a silence of three years to clear the name of Dr. David Throckmartin and to lift the shadow of scandal from that of his wife and of Dr. Charles Stanton, his assistant. That I have not found the courage to do so before, all men who are jealous of their scientific reputations will understand when they have heard what I have written. How strongly I attest to my belief in the truth of what I am about to lay before you will be equally clear as you listen and realize, as I do, the storm of ridicule and disbelief it is sure to bring upon me. Yet I hope that you will also believe before this narrative is finished.

Let me recapitulate what, until now, has actually been known of the Throckmartin expedition to the island of Ponape in the Carolines—the Throckmartin Mystery, as it is called.

Dr. Throckmartin set forth early in 1915 to make detailed observations of Nan-Matal, that extraordinary group of island ruins, remains of a high and prehistoric civilization, that are clustered along the eastern shore of Ponape. With him went his wife to whom he had been wedded less than half a year. The daughter of Professor Fraizier-Smith, she was as deeply interested and almost as well informed as he, upon these relics of a vanished race that titanically strew certain islands of the Pacific and form the basis for the theory of a submerged Pacific continent.

Mrs. Throckmartin, it will be recalled, was much younger, fifteen years at least, than her husband. Dr. Charles Stanton, who accompanied them as Dr. Throckmartin's assistant, was about her age. These three and a Swedish woman, Thora Helversen, who had been Edith Throckmartin's nurse in babyhood and who was entirely devoted to her, made up the expedition.

Dr. Throckmartin planned to spend a year among the ruins, not only of Ponape, but of Lele—the twin centers of that colossal riddle of humanity whose answer has its roots in immeasurable antiquity; a weird flower of man-made civilization that blossomed ages before the seeds of Egypt were sown; of whose arts we know little and of whose science and secret knowledge and nature nothing.

He carried with him complete equipment for his work and gathered at Ponape a dozen or so natives for laborers. They went straight to Metalanim harbor and set up their camp on the island called Uschen-Tau in the group known as the Nan-Matal. You will remember that these islands are entirely uninhabited and are shunned by the people on the main island.

Three months later Dr. Throckmartin appeared at Port Moresby, Papua. He came on a schooner manned by Solomon Islanders and commanded by a Chinese half-breed captain. He reported that he was on his way to Melbourne for additional scientific equipment and whites to help him in his excavations, saying that the superstition of the natives made their aid negligible. He went immediately on board the steamer *Southern Queen* which was sailing that same morning. Three nights later he disappeared from the *Southern Queen* and it was officially reported that he had met death either by being swept overboard or by casting himself into the sea.

A relief-boat sent with the news to Ponape found the Throckmartin camp on the island Uschen-Tau and a smaller camp on the island called Nan-Tanach. All the equipment, clothing, supplies were intact. But of Mrs. Throckmartin, or Dr. Stanton or of Thora Helversen they could not find a single trace!

The natives who had been employed by the archaeologist were questioned. They said that the ruins were the abode of great spirits—*ani*—who were particularly powerful when the moon was at the full. On these nights all the islanders were doubly careful to give the ruins wide berth. Upon being employed, they had demanded leave from the day before full moon until it was on the wane and this had been granted them by Dr. Throckmartin. Thrice they had left the expedition alone on these nights. On their third return they had found the four white people gone and they "knew that the *ani* had eaten them." They were afraid and had fled.

That was all.

The Chinese half caste was found and reluctantly testified at last that he had picked Dr. Throckmartin up from a small boat about fifty miles off Ponape. The scientist had seemed half mad, but he had given the seaman a large sum of money to bring him to Port Moresby and to say, if questioned, that he had boarded the boat at Ponape harbor.

That, gentlemen, is all that has been known of the fate of the Throckmartin expedition.

Why, you will ask, do I break silence now? And how came I in possession of the facts I am about to set forth?

To the first I answer: I was at the Geographical Club last evening and overheard two members talking. They mentioned the name of Throckmartin and I became, frankly, eavesdropper. One said:

"Of course what probably happened was that Throckmartin killed them all. It's a dangerous thing for a man to marry a woman so much younger than himself and then throw her into the necessarily close company of exploration with a man as young and as agreeable as Stan-

THE ANCIENT MYSTERIES READER

ton was. The inevitable happened, no doubt. Throckmartin discovered; avenged himself. Then followed remorse and suicide."

"Throckmartin didn't seem to be that kind," said the other thoughtfully.

"No, he didn't," agreed the first.

"Isn't there another story?" went on the second speaker. "Something about Mrs. Throckmartin running away with Stanton and taking the woman, Thora, with her? Somebody told me they had been recognized in Singapore recently."

"You can take your pick of the two stories," replied his *vis-à-vis*. "It's one or the other I suppose."

It was neither one nor the other, gentlemen. I know—and I answer now the second question—because I was with Throckmartin when he—vanished. I know what he told me and I know what my own eyes saw. Incredible, abnormal, against all the known facts of our science as it was, I testify to it. And it is my intention, after sending you this, to sail to Ponape, to go to the Nan-Matal and to the islet beneath whose frowning walls dwells the mystery that Throckmartin sought and found—and at the last sought and found Throckmartin!

I attach herewith a copy of the map of the islands that he gave me. I attach also his sketch of the great courtyard of Nan-Tanach, the location of the moon door, his recollection of the probable location of the moon pool and the passage to it and his approximation of the position of the shining globes. If I do not return and there are any with enough belief, scientific curiosity and courage to follow, I leave them in these a plain trail.

I will now proceed straightforwardly with my narrative.

For six months I had been on the d'Entrecasteaux Islands gathering data for the concluding chapters of my book upon "Flora of the Volcanic Islands of the South Pacific." The day before, I had reached Port Moresby and had seen my specimens safely stored on board the *Southern Queen*. As I sat on the upper deck that morning I thought, with homesick mind, of the long leagues between me and Melbourne and New York.

It was one of Papua's yellow mornings, when she shows herself in her most somber, most baleful mood. The sky was a smouldering ocher. Over the islands brooded a spirit sullen, implacable and alien; filled with the threat of latent, malefic forces waiting to be unleashed. It seemed an emanation from the untamed, sinister heart of Papua herself—sinister even when she smiles. And now and then, on the wind, came a breath from unexplored jungles, filled with unfamiliar odors, mysterious, and menacing.

It is on such mornings that Papua speaks to you of her immemorial ancientness and of her power. I am not unduly imaginative but it is a mood that makes me shrink—I mention it because it bears directly upon Dr. Throckmartin's fate. Nor is the mood Papua's alone. I have felt it in New Guinea, in Australia, in the Solomons and in the Carolines. But it is in Papua that it seems most articulate. It is as though she said, "I am the ancient of days; I have seen the earth in the throes of its shaping; I am the primeval; I have seen races born and die and, lo, in my breast are secrets that would blast you by the telling, you pale babes of a puling age. You and I ought not to be in the same world yet I am and I shall be! Never will you fathom me and you I hate though I tolerate! I tolerate—but how long?"

And then I seem to see a giant paw that reaches from Papua toward the outer world, stretching and sheathing monstrous claws.

All feel this mood of hers. Her own people have it woven in them, part of their web and woof flashing into light unexpectedly like a soul from another universe; masking itself as swiftly.

I have fought against Papua as every white man must on one of her yellow mornings. And as I fought I saw a tall figure come striding down the pier. Behind him came a Kapa-Kapa boy swinging a new valise. There was something familiar about the tall man. As he reached the gangplank he looked up straight into my eyes, stared at me for a moment and waved his hand. It was Dr. Throckmartin!

Coincident with my recognition of him there came a shock of surprise that was definitely—unpleasant. It was Throckmartin—but there was something disturbingly different about him and the man I had known so well and had bidden farewell less than a year before. He was then, as you know, just turned forty, lithe, erect, muscular; the face of a student and of a seeker. His controlling expression was one of enthusiasm, of intellectual keenness, of—what shall I say?—expectant search. His ever eagerly questioning brain had stamped itself upon his face.

I sought in my mind for an explanation of that which I had felt on the flash of his greeting. Hurrying down to the lower deck I found him with the purser. As I spoke he turned and held out to me an eager hand—and then I saw what the change was that had come over him!

He knew, of course, by my face, the uncontrollable shock that my closer look had given me. His eyes filled and he turned bruskly to the purser; then hurried off to his stateroom, leaving me standing, half dazed.

At the stair he half turned.

"Oh, Goodwin," he said. "I'd like to see you later. Just now—there's something I must write before we start—"

He went up swiftly.

" 'E looks rather queer—eh?" said the purser. "Know 'im well, sir? Seems to 'ave given you quite a start, sir."

I made some reply and went slowly to my chair. I tried to analyze what it was that had disturbed me so; what profound change in Throckmartin that had so shaken me. Now it came to me. It was as though the man had suffered some terrific soul searing shock of rapture and horror combined; some soul cataclysm that in its climax had remolded his face deep from within, setting on it the seal of wedded joy and fear. As though indeed ecstasy supernal and terror infernal had once come to him hand in hand, taken possession of him, looked out of his eyes and, departing, left behind upon him ineradicably their shadow.

Gone was Throckmartin's old eager look, utterly gone, and in its place was this—something—I had never seen before on any face. I caught myself wondering what his face must have been when the seal was stamped freshly upon it. And what in the name of all knowledge was the agency that had done this thing! For it came to me suddenly that the true reason for the distress, the deep perturbation and amaze that he stirred in me was that the two expressions were mingled, inextricably, lay side by side, not contending but in some frightful fashion— harmonious! That was what shocked. For how could hate and love, ecstasy and horror, heaven and hell mix, join hands—kiss? Yet these were what, close embraced, lay on his face.

If I seem to dwell on this, have patience; it is necessary indeed.

Alternately I looked out over the port and paced about the deck, striving to read the riddle; to banish it from my mind. And all the time still over Papua brooded its baleful spirit of ancient evil, unfathomable, not to be understood; nor had it lifted when the *Southern Queen* lifted anchor and steamed out into the gulf.

2

I watched with relief the shores sink down behind us; welcomed the touch of the free sea wind. We seemed to be drawing away from something malefic; something that lurked with the island spell I have described, and the thought crept into my mind, spoke—whispered rather —from Throckmartin's face.

I had hoped—and within the hope was an inexplicable shrinking, an unexpressed dread—that I would meet Throckmartin at lunch. He did not come down and I was sensible of a distinct relief within my disappointment. All that afternoon I lounged about uneasily but still he kept to his cabin. Nor did he appear at dinner.

Dusk and night fell swiftly. I was warm and went back to my deckchair. The *Southern Queen* was rolling to a disquieting swell and I had the place to myself. I had looked my fellow passengers over while we were at table. They were a scant dozen. A couple of English officials and their wives, engrossed in "shop" and bulwarked by the English unapproachableness of the first night out; a clerk or two; a shoe salesman from Brisbane; a scattering of others—none of them worth breaking my solitude for, I decided.

Over the heavens was a canopy of cloud, glowing faintly and testifying to the moon riding behind it. There was much phosphorescence. Now and then, before the ship and at the sides, arose those strange little swirls of mist that stream up from the Southern Ocean like the breath of sea monsters, whirl for a moment and disappear. I lighted a cigarette and tried once more to banish from my mind Throckmartin's face—and unsuccessfully as ever.

Suddenly the deck door opened and through it came Throckmartin himself. He paused uncertainly, looked up at the sky with a curiously eager, intent gaze, hesitated, then closed the door behind him.

"Throckmartin," I called. "Come sit with me. It's Goodwin."

Immediately he made his way to me, sitting beside me with a gasp of relief that I noted curiously. His hand touched mine and gripped it with a tenseness that hurt. His hand was icelike. I puffed up my cigarette and by its glow scanned him closely. He was watching a large swirl of the mist that was passing before the ship. The phosphorescence beneath it illumined it with a fitful opalescence. I saw fear in his eyes. The swirl passed; he sighed; his grip relaxed and he sank back.

"Throckmartin," I said, wasting no time in preliminaries. "What's wrong? Can I help you?"

He was silent.

"Is your wife all right and what are you doing here when I heard you had gone to the Carolines for a year?" I went on.

I felt his body grow tense again. He did not speak for a moment and then:

"I'm going to Melbourne, Goodwin," he said. "I need a few things—need them urgently. And more men—white men."

His voice was low, preoccupied. It was as though the brain that dictated the words did so perfunctorily, half impatiently; aloof, watching, strained to catch the first hint of approach of something dreaded.

"You are making progress then?" I asked. It was a banal question, put forth in a blind effort to claim his attention.

"Progress?" he repeated. "Progress—"

He stopped abruptly; rose from his chair, gazed intently toward the north. I followed his gaze. Far, far away the moon had broken through the clouds. Almost on the horizon, you could see the faint luminescence of it upon the quiet sea. The distant patch of light quivered and shook. The clouds thickened again and it was gone. The ship raced southward, swiftly.

Throckmartin dropped into his chair. He lighted a cigarette with a hand that trembled. The flash of the match fell on his face and I noted with a queer thrill of apprehension that its unfamiliar expression had deepened; become curiously intensified as though a faint acid had passed over it, etching its lines faintly deeper.

"It's the full moon tonight, isn't it?" he asked, palpably with studied inconsequence.

"The first night of the full mooon," I answered. He was silent again. I sat silent too, waiting for him to make up his mind to speak. He turned to me as though he had made a sudden resolution.

"Goodwin," he said. "I do need help. If ever man needed it, I do. Goodwin—can you imagine yourself in another world, alien, unfamiliar, a world of terror, whose unknown joy is its greatest terror of all; you all alone there; a stranger! As such a man would need help, so I need—"

He paused abruptly and arose to his feet stiffly; the cigarette dropped from his fingers. I saw that the moon had again broken through the clouds, and this time much nearer. Now a mile away was the patch of light that it threw upon the waves. Back of it, to the rim of the sea was a lane of moonlight; it was a gigantic serpent racing over the rim of the world straight and surely toward the ship.

Throckmartin gazed at it as though turned to stone. He stiffened to it as a pointer does to a hidden covey. To me from him pulsed a thrill of terror—but terror tinged with an unfamiliar, an infernal joy. It came to me and passed away—leaving me trembling with its shock of bitter sweet.

He bent forward, all his soul in his eyes. The moon path swept closer, closer still. It was now less than half a mile away. From it the ship fled; almost it came to me, as though pursued. Down upon it, swift and straight, a radiant torrent cleaving the waves, raced the moon stream. And then—

"Good God!" breathed Throckmartin, and if ever the words were a prayer and an invocation, they were.

And then, for the first time—I saw—*it!*

The moon path, as I have said, stretched to the horizon and was bordered by darkness. It was as though the clouds above had been parted to form a lane—drawn aside like curtains or as the waters of the Red Sea were held back to let the hosts of Israel through. On each side of the stream was the black shadow cast by the folds of the high canopies. And straight as a road between the opaque walls gleamed, shimmered and danced the shining, racing rapids of the moonlight.

Far, it seemed immeasurably far, along this stream of silver fire I sensed, rather than saw, something coming. It drew into sight as a deeper glow within the light. On and on it sped toward us—an opalescent mistiness that swept on with the suggestion of some winged creature in darting flight. Dimly there crept into my mind memory of the Dyak legend of the winged messenger of Buddha—the Akla bird whose feathers are woven of the moon rays, whose heart is a living opal, whose wings in flight echo the crystal clear music of the white stars—but whose beak is of frozen flame and shreds the souls of unbelievers. Still it sped on, and now there came to me sweet, insistent tinklings—like a pizzicati on violins of glass, crystalline, as purest, clearest glass transformed to sound. And again the myth of the Akla bird came to me.

But now it was close to the end of the white path; close up to the barrier of darkness still between the ship and the sparkling head of the moon stream. And now it beat up against that barrier as a bird against the bars of its cage. And I knew that this was no mist born of sea and air. It whirled with shimmering plumes, with swirls of lacy light, with spirals of living vapor. It held within it odd, unfamiliar gleams as of shifting mother-of-pearl. Coruscations and glittering atoms drifted through it as though it drew them from the rays that bathed it.

Nearer and nearer it came, borne on the sparkling waves, and less and less grew the protecting wall of shadow between it and us. The crystalline sounds were louder—rhythmic as music from another planet.

Now I saw that within the mistiness was a core, a nucleus of intenser light—veined, opaline, effulgent, intensely alive. And above it, tangled in the plumes and spirals that throbbed and whirled, were seven glowing lights.

Through all the incessant but strangely ordered movement of the—*thing*—these lights held firm and steady. They were seven—like seven little moons. One was of a pearly pink, one of delicate nacreous blue, one of lambent saffron, one of the emerald you see in the shallow waters of tropic isles; a deathly white; a ghostly amethyst; and one of the silver that is seen only when the flying fish leap beneath the moon. There they shone—these seven little varicolored orbs within the opaline mistiness of whatever it was that, poised and expectant, waited to be drawn to us on the light filled waves.

The tinkling music was louder still. It pierced the ears with a shower of tiny lances; it made the heart beat jubilantly—and checked it dolorously. It closed your throat with a throb of rapture and gripped it tight like the hand of infinite sorrow!

Came to me now a murmuring cry, stilling the crystal clear notes, it was articulate—but as though from something utterly foreign to this world. The ear took the cry and translated it with conscious labor into the sounds of earth. And even as it compassed, the brain shrank from it irresistibly and simultaneously it seemed, reached toward it with irresistible eagerness.

"Av-o-lo-ha! Av-o-lo-ha!" So the cry seemed to throb.

The grip of Throckmartin's hand relaxed. He walked stiffly toward the front of the deck, straight toward the vision, now but a few yards away from the bow. I ran toward him and gripped him—and fell back. For now his face had lost all human semblance. Utter agony and utter ecstasy—there they were side by side, not resisting each other; unholy inhuman companions blending into a look that none of God's creatures should wear—and deep, deep as his soul! A devil and a God dwelling harmoniously side by side! So must Satan, newly fallen, still divine, seeing heaven and contemplating hell, have looked.

And then—swiftly the moon path faded! The clouds swept over the sky as though a hand had drawn them together. Up from the south came a roaring squall. As the moon vanished, what I had seen vanished with it—blotted out as an image on a magic lantern; the tinkling ceased abruptly—leaving a silence like that which follows an abrupt and stupendous thunder clap. There was nothing about us but silence and blackness!

Through me there passed a great trembling as one who had stood on the very verge of the gulf wherein the men of the Louisades say lurks the fisher of the souls of men, and has been plucked back by sheerest chance.

Throckmartin passed an arm around me. "It is as I thought," he said. In his voice was a new note; of the calm certainty that has swept aside a waiting terror of the unknown. "Now I know! Come with me to my cabin, old friend. For now that you too have seen I can tell you"— he hesitated—"what it was you saw," he ended.

As we passed through the door we came face to face with the ship's first officer. Throckmartin turned quickly, but not soon enough for the mate to see and to stare at him with amazement. His eyes went questioningly to me.

With a strong effort of will Throckmartin composed his face into at least a semblance of normality.

"Are we going to have much of a storm?" he asked.

"Yes," said the mate. Then the seaman, getting the better of his curiosity, added, profanely, "We'll probably have it all the way to Melbourne."

Throckmartin straightened as though with a new thought. He gripped the officer's sleeve eagerly.

"You mean at least cloudy weather—for" —he hesitated— "for the next three nights, say?"

"And for three more," replied the mate.

"Thank God!" cried Throckmartin, and I think I never heard such relief and hope as was in his voice.

The sailor stood amazed. "Thank God?" he repeated. "Thank— what d'ye mean?"

But Throckmartin was moving onward to his cabin. I started to follow. The first officer stopped me.

"Your friend," he said, "is he ill?"

"The sea!" I answered hurriedly. "He's not used to it. I am going to look after him."

I saw doubt and disbelief in the seaman's eyes, but I hurried on. For I knew now that Throckmartin was ill indeed—but that it was not a sickness the ship's doctor nor any other could heal.

Throckmartin was sitting on the side of his berth as I entered. He had taken off his coat. He was leaning over, face in hands.

"Lock the door," he said quietly, not raising his head. "Close the port-holes and draw the curtains—and—have you an electric flash in your pocket—a good, strong one?"

He glanced at the small pocket flash I handed him and clocked it on. "Not big enough I'm afraid," he said. "And after all"—he hesitated—"it's only a theory."

"What's only a theory?" I asked in astonishment.

"Thinking of it as a weapon against—what you saw," he said with a little wry smile.

"Throckmartin," I cried. "What was it? Did I really see—that thing—there in the moon path? Did I really hear—"

"This, for instance," he interrupted.

Softly he whispered: "Av-o-lo-ha!" With the murmur I seemed to hear again the crystalline unearthly music; an echo of it, faint, sinister, mocking, jubilant.

"Throckmartin," I said. "What was it? What are you flying from, man? Where is your wife—and Stanton?"

"Dead!" he said monotonously. "Dead! All dead!" Then as I recoiled in horror—"All dead. Edith, Stanton, Thora—dead—or worse. And Edith in the moon pool—with them—drawn by what you saw on the moon path—and that wants me—and that has put its brand upon me—and pursues me."

With a vicious movement he ripped open his shirt.

"Look at this," he said. I gazed. Around his chest, an inch above his heart, the skin was white as pearl. This whiteness was sharply defined against the healthy tint of the body. He turned and I saw it ran around his back. It circled him. The band made a perfect cincture about two inches wide.

"Burn it!" he said, and offered me his cigarette. I drew back. He gestured—peremptorily. I pressed the glowing end of the cigarette into the ribbon of white flesh. He did not flinch nor was there odor of burning nor, as I drew the little cylinder away, any mark upon the whiteness.

"Feel it!" he commanded again. I placed my fingers upon the band. It was cold—like frozen marble.

He handed me a small penknife.

"Cut!" he ordered. This time, my scientific interest fully aroused, I did so without reluctance. The blade cut into flesh. I waited for the blood to come. None appeared. I drew out the knife and thrust it in again, fully a quarter of an inch deep. I might have been cutting paper so far as any evidence followed that what I was piercing was human skin and muscle.

Another thought came to me and I drew back, revolted.

"Throckmartin," I whispered. "Not leprosy!"

"Nothing so easy," he said. "Look again and find the places you cut."

I looked, as he bade me, and in the white ring there was not a single mark. Where I had pressed the blade there was no trace. It was as though the skin had parted to make way for the blade and then had quietly closed again.

Throckmartin arose and drew his shirt about him.

"Two things you have seen," he said. "*It*—and its mark—the seal it placed on me that gives it, I think, the power to follow me. Seeing, you must believe my story. Goodwin, I tell you again that my wife is dead—or worse—I do not know; the prey of—what you saw; so, too, is Stanton; so Thora. How—" He stopped for a moment. Then continued:

"And I am going to Melbourne for the things to empty its den and its shrine; for dynamite to destroy it and its lair—if anything made on earth will destroy it; and for white men with courage to use them. Perhaps—perhaps after you have heard, you will be one of these men?" He looked at me a bit wistfully. "And now—do not interrupt, I beg of you, till I am through—for" —he smiled wanly— "the mate may be wrong. And if he is" —he arose and paced twice about the room— "if he is I may not have time to tell you."

"Throckmartin," I answered, "I have no closed mind. Tell me—and if I can I will help."

He took my hand and pressed it.

"Goodwin," he began, "if I have seemed to take the death of my wife lightly—or rather" —his face contorted— "or rather—if I have seemed to pass it by as something not of first importance to me—believe me it is not so. If the rope is long enough—if what the mate says is so—if there is cloudy weather until the moon begins to wane—I can conquer—that I know. But if it does not—if the dweller in the moon pool gets me—then must you or someone avenge my wife—and me—and Stanton. Yet I cannot believe that God would let a thing like that conquer! But why did He then let it take my Edith? And why does He allow it to exist? Are there things stronger than God, do you think, Goodwin?"

He turned to me feverishly. I hesitated.

"I do not know just how you define God," I said. "If you mean the will to know, working through science—"

He waved me aside impatiently.

"Science," he said. "What is our science against—that? Or against the science of whatever cursed, vanished race that made it—or made the way for it to enter this world of ours?"

With an effort he regained control of himself.

"Goodwin," he said, "do you know at all of the ruins on the Carolines; the cyclopean, megolithic cities and harbors of Ponape and Lele, of Kusaie, of Ruk and Hogolu, and a score of other islets there? Particularly, do you know of the Nan-Matal and Metalanim?"

"Of the Metalanim I have heard and seen photographs," I said. "They call it, don't they, the lost Venice of the Pacific?"

"Look at this map," said Throckmartin. He handed me the map. "That," he went on, "is Christian's map of Metalanim harbor and the Nan-Matal. Do you see the rectangles marked Nan-Tanach?"

"Yes," I said.

"There," he said, "under those walls is the moon pool and the seven gleaming lights that raise the dweller in the pool and the altar and shrine of the dweller. And there in the moon pool with it lie Edith and Stanton and Thora."

"The dweller in the moon pool?" I repeated half-incredulously.

"The thing you saw," said Throckmartin solemnly.

A solid sheet of rain swept the ports, and the *Southern Queen* began to roll on the rising swells. Throckmartin drew another deep breath as of relief, and drawing aside a curtain peered out into the night. Its blackness seemed to reassure him. At any rate, when he sat again he was calm.

"There are no more wonderful ruins in the world than those of the island Venice of Metalanim on the east shore of Ponape," he said almost casually. "They take in some fifty islets and cover with their intersecting canals and lagoons about twelve square miles. Who built them? None knows. When were they built? Ages before the memory of present man, that is sure. Ten thousand, twenty thousand, a hundred thousand years ago—the last more likely.

"All these islets, Goodwin, are squared, and their shores are frowning sea-walls of gigantic basalt blocks hewn and put in place by the hands of ancient man. Each inner waterfront is faced with a terrace of those basalt blocks which stand out six feet above the shallow canals that meander between them. On the islets behind these walls are cyclopean and time shattered fortresses, palaces, terraces, pyramids; immense courtyards strewn with ruins—and all so old that they seem to wither the eyes of those who look on them.

"There has been a great subsidence. You can stand out of Metalanim harbor for three miles and look down upon the tops of similar monolithic structures and walls twenty feet below you in the water.

"And all about strung on their canals, are the bulwarked islets with their enigmatic giant walls peering through the dense growths of mangroves—dead, deserted for incalculable ages; shunned by those who live near.

"You as a botanist are familiar with the evidence that a vast shadowy continent existed in the Pacific—a continent that was not rent asunder by volcanic forces as was that legendary one of Atlantis in the Eastern Ocean. My work in Java, in Papua, and in the Ladrones had set my mind upon this Pacific lost land. Just as the Azores are believed to be the last high peaks of Atlantis, so evidence came to me steadily that Ponape and Lele and their basalt bulwarked islets were the last points of the slowly sunken western land clinging still to the sunlight, and had been the last refuge and sacred places of the rulers of that race which had lost their immemorial home under the rising waters of the Pacific.

"I believed that under these ruins I might find the evidence of what I sought. Time and again I had encountered legends of subterranean networks beneath the Nan-Matal, of passages running back into the main island itself; basalt corridors that followed the lines of the shallow canals and ran under them to islet after islet, linking them in mysterious chains.

"My—my wife and I had talked before we were married of making this our great work. After the honeymoon we prepared for the expedition. It was to be my monument. Stanton was as enthusiastic as ourselves. We sailed, as you know, last May in fulfillment of our dreams.

"At Ponape we selected, not without difficulty, workmen to help us —diggers. I had to make extraordinary inducements before I could get together my force. Their beliefs are gloomy, these Ponapeans. They people their swamps, their forests, their mountains and shores with malignant spirits—*ani* they call them. And they are afraid—bitterly afraid of the isles of ruins and what they think the ruins hide. I do not wonder—now! For their fear has come down to them through the ages, from the people 'before their fathers,' as they call them, who, they say, made these mighty spirits their slaves and messengers.

"When they were told where they were to go, and how long we expected to stay, they murmured. Those who, at last, were tempted made what I thought then merely a superstitious proviso, that they were to be allowed to go away on the three nights of the full moon. Would to God I had heeded them and gone too!"

He stopped and again over his face the lines etched deep.

"We passed," he went on, "into Metalanim harbor. Off to our left—a mile away—arose a massive quadrangle. Its walls were all of forty feet high and hundreds of feet on each side. As we passed it our natives grew very silent; watched it furtively, fearfully. I knew it for the ruins that are called Nan-Tanach, the 'place of frowning walls.' And at the silence of my men I recalled what Christian had written of this place; of how he had come upon its 'ancient platforms and tetragonal enclosures of stone-work; its wonder of tortuous alleyways and labyrinth of shallow canals; grim masses of stone-work peering out from behind verdant screens; cyclopean barricades,' and of how, when we had turned into its ghostly shadows, straightway the merriment of our guides was hushed and conversation died down to whispers. For we were close to Nan-Tanach—the place of lofty walls, the most remarkable of all the Metalanim ruins." He arose and stood over me.

"Nan-Tanach, Goodwin," he said solemnly— "a place where merriment is hushed indeed and words are stifled. Nan-Tanach—where the moon pool lies hidden—lies hidden behind the moon rock, but sends its diabolic soul out—even through the prisoning stone." He raised clenched hands. "Oh, God," he breathed, "grant me that I may blast it from earth!"

He was silent for a little time.

"Of course I wanted to pitch our camp there," he began again quietly, "but I soon gave up that idea. The natives were panic-stricken —threatened to turn back. 'No,' they said, 'too great *ani* there. We go to any other place—but not there.' Although, even then, I felt that the secret of the place was in Nan-Tanach, I found it necessary to give in. The laborers were essential to the success of the expedition, and I told myself that after a little time had passed and I had persuaded them that there was nothing anywhere that could molest them, we would move our tents to it. We finally picked for our base the islet called Uschen-Tau—you see it here—" He pointed to the map. "It was close to the isle of desire, but far enough away from it to satisfy our men.

There was an excellent camping-place there and a spring of fresh water. It offered, besides, an excellent field for preliminary work before attacking the larger ruins. We pitched our tents, and in a couple of days the work was in full swing.

"I do not intend to tell you now," Throckmartin continued, "the results of the next two weeks, Goodwin, nor of what we found. Later—if I am allowed, I will lay all that before you. It is sufficient to say that at the end of those two weeks I had found confirmation for many of my theories, and we were well under way to solve a mystery of humanity's youth—so we thought. But enough. I must hurry on to the first stirrings of the inexplicable thing that is in store for us.

"The place, for all its decay and desolation, had not infected us with any touch of morbidity—that is, not Edith, Stanton or myself. My wife was happy—never had she been happier. Stanton and she, while engrossed in the work as much as I, were of the same age, and they frankly enjoyed the companionship that only youth can give youth. I was glad—never jealous.

"But Thora was very unhappy. She was a Swede, as you know, and in her blood ran the beliefs and superstitions of the Northland—some of them so strangely akin to those of this far southern land; beliefs of spirits of mountain and forest and water—werewolves and beings malign. From the first she showed a curious sensitivity to what, I suppose, may be called the 'influences' of the place. She said it 'smelled' of ghosts and warlocks.

"I laughed at her then—but now I believe this sensitivity of what we call primitive people is perhaps only a clearer perception of the unknown which we, who deny the unknown, had lost. It is a *rapprochement* toward an acknowledgment of other forces which, no doubt, betrays them to the very forces they sense and fear. It was what made Thora first to feel—what was to happen. A prey to these fears, she followed my wife about like a shadow; carried with her always a little sharp hand-ax, and although we twitted her about the futility of chopping fantoms with such a weapon she would not relinquish it.

"Two weeks slipped by, and at their end the spokesman for our natives came to us. The next night was the full of the moon, he said. He reminded me of my promise. They would go back to their village next morning; they would return after the third night, as at that time the power of the *ani* would begin to wane with the moon. They left us sundry charms for our 'protection', and solemnly cautioned us to keep

as far away as possible from Nan-Tanach during their absence—
although their leader politely informed us that, no doubt, we were
stronger than the spirits. Half-exasperated, half-amused, I watched
them go.

"No work could be done without them, of course, so we decided to
spend the days of their absence junketing about the southern islets of
the group. Under the moon the ruins were inexpressibly weird and
beautiful. We marked down several spots for subsequent exploration,
and on the morning of the third day set forth along the east face of the
breakwater for our camp on Uschen-Tau, planning to have everything
in readiness for the return of our men the next day.

"We landed just before dusk, tired and ready for our cots. It was
only a little after ten o'clock that Edith awakened me.

" 'Listen!' she said. 'Lean over with your ear close to the ground!' I
did so, and seemed to hear, far, far below, as though coming up from
great distances, a faint chanting. It gathered strength, died down,
ended; began, gathered volume, faded away into silence.

" 'It's the waves rolling on rocks somewhere,' I said. 'We're probably over some ledge of rock that carries the sound.'

" 'It's the first time I've heard it,' replied my wife doubtfully. We listened again. Then through the dim rhythms, deep beneath us, another
sound came. It drifted across the lagoon that lay between us and Nan-
Tanach in little tinkling waves. It was music—of a sort; I won't describe the strange effect it had upon me. You've felt it—"

"You mean on the deck?" I asked. Throckmartin nodded.

"I went to the flap of the tent," he continued, "and peered out. As I
did so Stanton lifted his flap and walked out into the moonlight, looking over to the other islet and listening. I called to him.

" 'That's the queerest sound!' he said. He listened again. 'Crystalline! Like little notes of translucent glass. Like the bells of crystal on
the sistrums of Isis at Dendarah Temple,' he added half-dreamily. We
gazed intently at the island. Suddenly, on the gigantic sea-wall, moving
slowly, rhythmically, we saw a little group of lights. Stanton laughed.

" 'The beggars!' he exclaimed. 'That's why they wanted to get away,
is it? Don't you see, Dave, it's some sort of festival—rites of some kind
that they hold during the full moon! That's why they were so eager to
have us *keep* away, too.'

"I felt a curious sense of relief, although I had not been sensible of
any oppression. The explanation seemed good. It explained the tinkling music and also the chanting—worshipers, no doubt, in the ruins—

their voices carried along passages I now knew honeycombed the whole Nan-Matal.

"'Let's slip over,' suggested Stanton—but I would not.

"'They're a difficult lot as it is,' I said. 'If we break into one of their religious ceremonies they'll probably never forgive us. Let's keep out of any family party where we haven't been invited.'

"'That's so,' agreed Stanton.

"The strange tinkling music, if music it can be called, rose and fell, rose and fell—now laden with sorrow, now filled with joy.

"'There's something—something very unsettling about it,' said Edith at last soberly. 'I wonder what they make those sounds with. They frighten me half to death, and, at the same time, they make me feel as though some enormous rapture was just around the corner.'

"I had noted this effect, too, although I had said nothing of it. And at the same time there came to me a clear perception that the chanting which had preceded it had seemed to come from a vast multitude— thousands more than the place we were contemplating could possibly have held. Of course, I thought, this might be due to some acoustic property of the basalt; an amplification of sound by some gigantic sounding-board of rock; still—

"'It's devilish uncanny!' broke in Stanton, answering my thought.

"And as he spoke the flap of Thora's tent was raised and out into the moonlight strode the old Swede. She was the great Norse type—tall, deep-breasted, molded on the old Viking lines. Her sixty years had slipped from her. She looked like some ancient princess of Odin." He hesitated. "She knew," he said slowly. "Something more far-seeing than my science had given her sight. She warned me—she warned me! Fools and mad that we are to pass such things by without heed!" He brushed a hand over his eyes.

"She stood there," he went on. "Her eyes were wide, brilliant, star- ing. She thrust her head toward Nan-Tanach, regarding the moving lights; she listened. Suddenly she raised her arms and made a curi- ous gesture to the moon. It was—an archaic—movement; she seemed to drag it from remote antiquity—yet in it was a strange sugges- tion of power. Twice she repeated this gesture and—the tinklings died away! She waited a moment longer and then turned to us.

"'Go!' she said, and her voice seemed to come from far distances. 'Go from here—and quickly! Go while you may. They have called—' She pointed to the islet. 'They know you are here. They wait.' Her eyes widened further. 'It is there,' she wailed. 'It beckons—the—the—'

"She fell at Edith's feet, and as she fell over the lagoon came again the tinklings, now with a quicker note of jubilance—almost of triumph.

"We ran to Thora, Stanton and I, and picked her up. Her head rolled and her face, eyes closed, turned as though drawn full into the moonlight. I felt in my heart a throb of unfamiliar fear—for her face had changed again. Stamped upon it was a look of mingled transport and horror—alien, terrifying, strangely revolting. It was" —he thrust his face close to my eyes— "what you see in mine!"

For a dozen heart-beats I stared at him, fascinated; then he sank back again into the half-shadow of the berth.

"I managed to hide her face from Edith," he went on. "I thought she had suffered some sort of a nervous seizure. We carried her into her tent. Once within, the unholy mask dropped from her, and she was again only the kindly, rugged old woman. I watched her throughout the night. The sounds from Nan-Tanach continued until about an hour before moonset. In the morning Thora awoke, none the worse, apparently. She had had bad dreams, she said. She could not remember what they were—except that they had warned her of danger. She was oddly sullen, and I noted that throughout the morning her gaze returned again half-fascinatedly, half-wonderingly to the neighboring isles.

"That afternoon the natives returned. They were so exuberant in their apparent relief to find us well and intact that Stanton's suspicions of them were confirmed. He slyly told their leader that 'from the noise they had made on Nan-Tanach the night before they must have thoroughly enjoyed themselves.'

"I think I never saw such stark-terror as the Ponapean manifested at the remark! Stanton himself was so plainly startled that he tried to pass it over as a jest. He met poor success! The men seemed panic-stricken, and for a time I thought they were about to abandon us—but they did not. They pitched their camp at the western side of the island —out of sight of Nan-Tanach. I noticed that they built large fires, and whenever I awoke that night I heard their voices in slow, minor chant —one of their song 'charms,' I thought drowsily, against evil *ani*. I heard nothing else; the place of frowning walls was wrapped in silence —no lights showed. The next morning the men were quiet, a little depressed, but as the hours wore on they regained their spirits, and soon life at the camp was going on just as it had before.

"You will understand, Goodwin, how the occurrences I have

related would excite the scientific curiosity. We rejected immediately, of course, any explanation admitting the supernatural. Why not? Except the curiously disquieting effects of the tinkling music and Thora's behavior there was nothing to warrant any such fantastic theories—even if our minds had been the kind to harbor them.

"Our—symptoms let me call them—could all very easily be accounted for. It is unquestionable that the vibrations created by certain musical instruments have definite and sometimes extraordinary effect upon the nervous system. We accepted this as the explanation of the reactions we had experienced in hearing the unfamiliar sounds. Thora's nervousness, her superstitious apprehensions, had wrought her up to a condition of semisomnambulistic hysteria. Science would readily explain her part in the night's scene.

"We came to the conclusion that there must be a passageway between Ponape and Nan-Tanach, known to the natives—and used by them during their rites. Ceremonies were probably held in great vaults or caverns beneath the ruins—for certainly a race which could have cut and set into place the enormous basalt blocks that formed them would have had little difficulty in hollowing out caverns, even had none existed before. Evidence of such subterranean passages we had already discovered. We decided at last that on the next departure of our laborers we would set forth immediately to Nan-Tanach. We would investigate during the day, and at evening my wife and Thora would go back to camp, leaving Stanton and me to spend the night on the island, observing from some safe hiding-place what might occur.

"The moon waned; appeared to crescent in the west; waxed slowly toward the full. Before the men left us they literally prayed us to accompany them. Their importunities only made us more eager to see what it was that, we were now convinced, they wanted to conceal from us. At least that was true of Stanton and myself. It was not true of Edith. She was thoughtful, abstracted—reluctant. Thora, on the other hand, showed an unusual restlessness, almost an eagerness to go. Goodwin" —he paused— "Goodwin, I know now that the poison was working in Thora—and that women have perceptions that we men lack —forebodings, sensings. Would to God I had known it then—Edith!" he cried suddenly. "Edith—come back to me! Forgive me!"

I stretched the decanter out to him. He drank deeply. Soon he had regained control of himself.

"When the men were out of sight around the turn of the harbor," he went on, "we took our boat and made straight for Nan-Tanach. Soon its mighty sea-wall towered above us. We passed through the water-gate with its gigantic hewn prisms of basalt and landed beside a half-submerged pier. In front of us stretched a series of giant steps leading into a vast court strewn with fragments of fallen pillars. In the center of the court, beyond the shattered pillars, rose another terrace of basalt blocks, concealing, I knew, still another enclosure.

"And now, Goodwin, for the better understanding of what follows and to guide you, should I—not be able—to accompany you when you go there, listen carefully to my description of this place: Nan-Tanach is literally three rectangles. The first rectangle is the sea-wall, built up of monoliths—hewn and squared, twenty feet wide at the top. To get to the gateway in the sea-wall you pass along the canal marked on the map between Nan-Tanach and the islet named Tau. The entrance to the canal is hidden by dense thickets of mangroves; once through these the way is clear. The gigantic steps lead up from the landing of the sea-gate through the entrance to the courtyard.

"This courtyard is surrounded by another basalt wall, rectangular, following with mathematical exactness the march of the outer barricades. The sea-wall is from thirty to forty feet high—originally it must have been much higher, but there has been subsidence in parts. The wall of the first enclosure is fifteen feet across the top and its height varies from twenty to fifty feet—here, too, the gradual sinking of the land has caused portions of it to fall.

"Between the terrace of this enclosure and the sea-wall is, on each side, a considerable space. It is covered with little thickets of fern, of eucalyptus, shrubs; hibiscus vines run riot, covering the fragments with their flowers.

"Within this courtyard is the second enclosure. Its terrace, of the same basalt as the outer walls, is about twenty feet high. Entrance is gained to it by many breaches which time has made in its stone-work. This is the inner court, the heart of Nan-Tanach! There lies the great central vault with which is associated the one name of living being that has come to us out of the mists of the past. The natives say it was the treasure-house of Chau-te-leur, a mighty king who reigned long 'before their fathers.' As Chau is the ancient Ponapean word both for sun and king, the name means, without doubt, 'place of the sun king.' It is a memory of a dynastic name of the race that ruled the Pacific continent, now vanished—just as the rulers of ancient Crete took the name of Minos and the rulers of Egypt the name of Pharaoh.

"And opposite this place of the sun king is the moon rock that hides the moon pool.

"It was Stanton who first found what I call the moon rock. We had been inspecting the inner courtyard; Edith and Thora were getting together our lunch. I forgot to say that we had previously gone all over the islet and had found not a trace of living thing. I came out of the vault of Chau-te-leur to find Stanton before a part of the terrace studying it wonderingly.

" 'What do you make of this?' he asked me as I came up. He pointed to the wall. I followed his finger and saw a slab of stone about fifteen feet high and ten wide. At first all I noticed was the exquisite nicety with which its edges joined the blocks about it. Then I realized that its color was subtly different—tinged with gray and of a smooth, peculiar—deadness.

" 'Looks more like calcite than basalt,' I said. I touched it and withdrew my hand quickly, for at the contact every nerve in my arm tingled as though a shock of frozen electricity had passed through it. It was not as cold as we know cold that I felt. It was a chill force—the phrase I have used—frozen electricity—describes it better than anything else. Stanton looked at me oddly.

" 'So you felt it too,' he said. 'I was wondering whether I was developing hallucinations like Thora. Notice, by the way, that the blocks beside it are quite warm beneath the sun.'

"I felt them and touched the grayish stone again. The same faint shock ran through my hand—a tingling chill that had in it a suggestion of substance, of force. We examined the slab more closely. Its edges were cut as though by an engraver of jewels. They fitted against the neighboring blocks in almost a hair-line. Its base, we saw, was slightly curved, and fitted as closely as top and sides upon the huge stones on which it rested. And then we noted that these stones had been hollowed along the line of the gray stone's foot.

"There was a semi-circular depression running from one side of the slab to the other. It was as though the gray rock stood in the center of a shallow cup—revealing half, covering half. Something about this hollow attracted me. I reached down and felt it. Goodwin, although the balance of the stones that formed it, like all the stones of the courtyard, were rough and age-worn—this was as smooth, as even surfaced as though it had just left the hands of the polisher.

" 'It's a door!' exclaimed Stanton. 'It swings around in that little cup. That's what makes the hollow of the cup so smooth.'

" 'Maybe you're right,' I replied. 'But how the devil can we open it?'

"We went over the slab again—pressing upon its edges, thrusting against its sides. During one of these efforts I happened to look up—and cried out. For a foot above and on each side of the corner of the gray rock's lintel I had seen a slight convexity, visible only from the angle at which my gaze struck it. These bosses on the basalt were circular, eighteen inches in diameter, as we learned later, and at the center extended two inches only beyond the face of the terrace. Unless one looked directly up at them while leaning against the moon rock—for this slab, Goodwin, *is* the moon rock—they were invisible. And none would dare stand there!

"We carried with us a small scaling-ladder, and up this I went. The bosses were apparently nothing more than chiseled curvatures in the stone. I laid my hand on the one I was examining, and drew it back so sharply I almost threw myself from the ladder. In my palm, at the base of my thumb, I had felt the same shock that I had in touching the slab below. I put my hand back. The impression came from a spot not more than an inch wide. I went carefully over the entire convexity, and six times more the chill ran through my arm. There were, Goodwin, seven circles an inch wide in the curved place, each of which communicated the precise sensation I have described. The convexity on the opposite side of the slab gave precisely the same results. But no amount of touching or of pressing these spots singly or in any combination gave the slightest promise of motion to the slab itself.

" 'And yet—they're what open it,' said Stanton positively.

" 'Why do you say that?' I asked.

" 'I—don't know,' he answered hesitatingly. 'But something tells me so, Throck,' he went on half earnestly, half laughingly, 'the purely scientific part of me is fighting the purely human part of me. The scientific part is urging me to find some way to get that slab either down or open. The human part is just as strongly urging me to do nothing of the sort and get away while I can!'

"He laughed again—a little shamefacedly.

" 'Which will it be?' he asked—and I thought that in his stare the human side of him was ascendent.

" 'It will probably stay as it is—unless we blow it to bits,' I said.

" 'I thought of that,' he answered, 'and—I wouldn't dare,' he added soberly enough. And even as I had spoken there came to me the same feeling that he had expressed. It was as though something passed out of the gray rock that struck my heart as a hand strikes an impious lip. We turned away—uneasily, and faced Thora, who was coming through a breach in the terrace.

" 'Miss Edith wants you quick,' she began—and stopped. I saw her eyes go past me and widen. She was looking at the gray rock.

"Her body grew suddenly rigid; she took a few stiff steps forward and then ran straight to it. We saw her cast herself upon its breast, hands and face pressed against it; heard her scream as though her very soul were being drawn from her—and watched her fall at its foot. As we picked her up I saw steal from her face the look I had observed when first we heard the crystal music of Nan-Tanach—that unhuman and weird mingling of opposites!

3

"We carried Thora back, down to where Edith was waiting. We told her what had happened and what we had found. She listened gravely, and as we finished Thora sighed and opened her eyes.

" 'I would like to see the stone,' she said. 'Charles, you stay here with Thora.' We passed through the outer court silently—and stood before the rock. She touched it, drew back her hand as I had; thrust it forward again resolutely and held it there. She seemed to be listening. Then she turned to me.

" 'David,' said my wife, and the wistfulness in her voice hurt me— 'David, would you be very, very disappointed if we went from here— without trying to find out any more about it—would you?'

"Goodwin, I never wanted anything so much in my life as I wanted to learn what that rock concealed. You will understand—the cumulative curiosity that all the happenings had caused; the certainty that before me was an entrance to a place that, while known to the natives —for I still clung to that theory—was utterly unknown to any man of my race; that within, ready for my finding, was the answer to the stupendous riddle of these islands and a lost chapter of the history of humanity. There before me—and was I asked to turn away, leaving it unread!

"Nevertheless, I tried to master my desire, and I answered— 'Edith, not a bit if you want us to do it.'

"She read my struggle in my eyes. She looked at me searchingly for a moment and then turned back toward the gray rock. I saw a shiver pass through her. I felt a tinge of remorse and then of pity!

" 'Edith,' I exclaimed, 'we'll go!'

"She looked at me again. 'Science is a jealous mistress,' she quoted. 'No, after all it may be just fancy. At any rate, you can't run away. No! But, Dave, I'm going to stay too!'

" 'You are not!' I exclaimed. 'You're going back to the camp with Thora. Stanton and I will be all right.'

" 'I'm going to stay,' she repeated. And there was no changing her decision. As we neared the others she laid a hand on my arm.

" 'Dave,' she said, 'if there should be something—well—inexplicable tonight—something that seems—too dangerous—will you promise to go back to our own islet tomorrow, or, while we can, and wait until the natives return?'

"I promised eagerly—for the desire to stay and see what came with the night was like a fire within me.

"And would to God that I had not waited another moment, Goodwin; would to God that I had gathered them all together then and sailed back on the instant through the mangroves to Uschen-Tau!

"We found Thora on her feet again and singularly composed. She claimed to have no more recollection of what had happened after she had spoken to Stanton and to me in front of the gray rock than she had after the seizure on Uschen-Tau. She grew sullen under our questioning, precisely as she had before. But to my astonishment, when she heard of our arrangements for the night, she betrayed a febrile excitement that had in it something of exultance.

"We had picked a place about five hundred feet away from the steps leading into the outer court. I would have preferred going into the inner enclosure, but I feared for Edith. Besides, it was better to go slowly until we knew what was opposed to us. And there was no place in the heart of the ruins where we could hide—except in the vault, and none of us liked to think of that. The spot we had selected was well hidden. We could not be seen, and yet we had a clear view of the stairs and the gateway. We settled down just before dusk to wait for whatever might come. I was nearest the giant steps; next me Edith; then Thora, and last Stanton. Each of us had with us automatic pistols, and all, except Thora, had rifles.

"Night fell. After a time the eastern sky began to lighten, and we knew that the moon was rising; grew lighter still, and the orb peeped over the sea; swam suddenly into full sight. Edith gripped my hand, for, as though the full emergence into the heavens had been a signal, we heard begin beneath us the deep chanting. It came from illimitable depths.

"The moon poured her rays down upon us, and I saw Stanton start. On the instant I caught the sound that had roused him. It came from the inner enclosure. It was like a long, soft sighing. It was not human; seemed in some way—mechanical. I glanced at Edith and then at Thora. My wife was intently listening. Thora sat, as she had since we had placed ourselves, elbows on knees, her hands covering her face.

"And then suddenly from the moonlight flooding us there came to me a great drowsiness. Sleep seemed to drip from the rays and fall upon my eyes, closing them—closing them inexorably. I felt Edith's hand relax in mine, and under my own heavy lids saw her nodding. I saw Stanton's head fall upon his breast and his body sway drunkenly. I tried to rise—to fight against the profound desire for slumber that pressed in on me.

"And as I fought I saw Thora raise her head as though listening; saw her rise and turn her face toward the gateway. For a moment she gazed, and my drugged eyes seemed to perceive within it a deeper, stronger radiance. Thora looked at us. There was infinite despair in her face—and expectancy. I tried again to rise—and a surge of sleep rushed over me. Dimly, as I sank within it, I heard a crystalline chiming; raised my lids once more with a supreme effort, saw Thora, bathed in light, standing at the top of the stairs, and then—sleep took me for its very own—swept me into the very heart of oblivion!

"Dawn was breaking when I wakened. Recollection rushed back on me and I thrust a panic-stricken hand out toward Edith; touched her and felt my heart give a great leap of thankfulness. She stirred, sat up, rubbing dazed eyes. I glanced toward Stanton. He lay on his side, back toward us, head in arms.

"Edith looked at me laughingly. 'Heavens! What sleep!' she said. Memory came to her. Her face paled. 'What happened?' she whispered. 'What made us sleep like that?' She looked over to Stanton, sprang to her feet, ran to him, shook him. He turned over with a mighty yawn, and I saw relief lighten her face as it had lightened my heart.

"Stanton raised himself stiffly. He looked at us. 'What's the matter?' he exclaimed. 'You look as though you've seen ghosts!'

"Edith caught my hands. 'Where's Thora?' she cried. Before I could answer she ran out into the open calling, 'Thora! Thora!'

"Stanton stared at me. 'Taken!' was all I could say. Together we went to my wife, now standing beside the great stone steps, looking up fearfully at the gateway into the terraces. There I told them what I had seen before sleep had drowned me. And together then we ran up the stairs, through the court and up the gray rock.

"The gray rock was closed as it had been the day before, nor was there trace of its having opened. No trace! Even as I thought this Edith dropped to her knees before it and reached toward something lying at its foot. It was a little piece of gay silk. I knew it for part of the kerchief Thora wore about her hair. She lifted the fragment; hesitated. I saw then that it had been *cut* from the kerchief as though by a razor-edge; I saw, too, that a few threads ran from it—down toward the base of the slab; ran to the base of the gray rock and—under it! The gray rock was a door! And it had opened and Thora had passed through it!

"I think, Goodwin, that for the next few minutes we were all a little insane. We beat upon that diabolic entrance with our hands, with stones and clubs. At last reason came back to us. Stanton set forth for the camp to bring back blasting powder and tools. While he was gone Edith and I searched the whole islet for any other clue. We found not a trace of Thora nor any indication of any living being save ourselves. We went back to the gateway to find Stanton returned.

"Goodwin, during the next two hours we tried every way in our power to force entrance through the slab. The rock within effective blasting radius of the cursed door resisted our drills. We tried explosions at the base of the slab with charges covered by rock. They made not the slightest impression on the surface beneath, expending their force, of course, upon the slighter resistance of their coverings.

"Afternoon found us hopeless, so far as breaking through the rock was concerned. Night was coming on and before it came we would have to decide our course of action. I wanted to go to Ponape for help. But Edith objected that this would take hours and after we had reached there it would be impossible to persuade our men to return with us that night, if at all. What then was left? Clearly only one of two choices: to go back to our camp and wait for our men to return and on their return try to persuade them to go with us to Nan-Tanach. But this would mean the abandonment of Thora for at least two days. We could not do it; it would have been too cowardly.

"The other choice was to wait where we were for night to come; to wait for the rock to open as it had the night before, and to make a sortie through it for Thora before it could close again. With the sun had come confidence; at least a shattering of the mephitic mists of superstition with which the strangeness of the things that had befallen us had clouded for a time our minds. In that brilliant light there seemed no place for fantoms.

"The evidence that the slab had opened was unmistakable, but might not Thora simply have *found* it open through some mechanism, still working after ages, and dependent for its action upon laws of physics unknown to us upon the full light of the moon? The assertion of the natives that the *ani* had greatest power at this time might be a far-flung reflection of knowledge which had found ways to use forces contained in moonlight, as we have found ways to utilize the forces in the sun's rays. If so, Thora was probably behind the slab, sending out prayers to us for help.

"But how explain the sleep that had descended upon us? Might it not have been some emanation from plants or gaseous emanations from the island itself? Such things were far from uncommon, we agreed. In some way the period of their greatest activity might coincide with the period of the moon, but if this were so why had not Thora also slept?

"There, indeed, we faced an impasse. It might be, of course, that Thora had been resistant to such emanations, as certain of us are resistant and immune from various bacteria. It was possible. And it might still be that our first theory was correct and that Nan-Tanach was a sacred place; a gathering point for priests possessing fragments of the ancient secrets, vanished knowledge, and they resented intruders. We knew the command certain primitive folk have of sleep sounds and vapors. It might be that here was the explanation.

"But whatever the truth, our path lay clear before us. We had to spend that night on Nan-Tanach!

"As dusk fell we looked over our weapons. Edith was an excellent shot with both rifle and pistol. With the idea that the impulse toward sleep was the result either of emanations such as I have described or man made, we constructed rough-and-ready but effective neutralizers, which we placed over our mouths and nostrils. We had decided that my wife was to remain in the hiding-place. Stanton would take up a station on the far side of the stairway and I would place myself opposite him on the side near Edith. The place I picked out was less than five hundred feet from her, and I could reassure myself now, as to her safety, as it looked down upon the hollow wherein she crouched. As the phenomena had previously synchronized with the rising of the moon, we had no reason to think they would occur any earlier this night. From our respective stations Stanton and I could command the gateway entrance. His position gave him also a glimpse of the outer courtyard.

"A faint glow in the sky heralded the moon. I kissed Edith, and Stanton and I took our places. The moon dawn increased rapidly; the disk swam up, and in a moment it seemed was shining in full radiance upon ruins and sea.

"As it rose there came as on the night before the curious little sighing sound from the inner terrace. I saw Stanton straighten up and stare intently through the gateway, rifle ready. Even at the distance he was from me, I discerned amazement in his eyes. The moonlight within the gateway thickened, grew stronger.

"I watched his amazement grow into sheer wonder.

"I arose.

"'Stanton, what do you see?' I called cautiously. He waved a silencing hand. I turned my head to look at Edith. A shock ran through me. She lay upon her side. Her face was turned full toward the moon. She was in deepest sleep!

"As I turned again to call to Stanton, my eyes swept the head of the steps and stopped, fascinated. For the moonlight had thickened more. It seemed to be—curdled—there; and through it ran little gleams and veins of shimmering white fire. A languor passed through me. It was not the ineffable drowsiness of the preceding night. It was a sapping of all will to move. I tore my eyes away and forced them upon Stanton. I tried to call out to him. I had not the will to make my lips move! I had struggled against this paralysis and as I did so I felt through me a sharp shock. It was like a blow. And with it came utter inability to make a single motion. Goodwin, I could not even move my eyes!

"I saw Stanton leap upon the steps and move toward the gateway. As he did so the light in the courtyard grew dazzlingly brilliant. Through it rained tiny tinklings that set the heart to racing with pure joy and stilled it with terror.

"And now for the first time I heard that cry 'Av-o-lo-ha! Av-o-lo-ha!' the cry you heard on deck. It murmured with the strange effect of a sound only partly in our own space—as though it were a part of a fuller phrase passing through from another dimension and losing much as it came; infinitely caressing, infinitely cruel!

"On Stanton's face I saw come the look I dreaded—and yet knew would appear; that mingled expression of delight and fear. The two lay side by side as they had on Thora, but were intensified. He walked on up the stairs; disappeared beyond the range of my fixed gaze. Again I heard the murmur—'*Av-o-lo-ha!*' There was triumph in it now and triumph in the storm of tinklings that swept over it.

"For another heart-beat there was silence. Then a louder burst of sound and ringing through it Stanton's voice from the courtyard—a great cry—a scream—filled with ecstasy insupportable and horror unimaginable! And again there was silence. I strove to burst the invisible bonds that held me. I could not. Even my eyelids were fixed. Within them my eyes burned.

"Then, Goodwin—I first saw the inexplicable! The crystalline music swelled. Where I sat I could take in the gateway and its basalt portals, rough and broken, rising to the top of the wall forty feet above, shattered, ruined portals—unclimbable. From this gateway an intenser light began to flow. It grew, it gushed, and into it, into my sight, walked Stanton.

"Stanton! But—God! What a vision!"

He ceased. I waited—waited.

"Goodwin," Throckmartin said at last, "I can describe him only as a thing of living light. He radiated light; was filled with light; overflowed with it. Around him was a shining cloud that whirled through and around him in radiant swirls, shimmering tentacles, luminescent, coruscating spirals.

"I saw his face. It shone with a rapture too great to be borne by living men, and was shadowed with insuperable misery. It was as though his face had been remolded by the hand of God and the hand of Satan, working together and in harmony. You have seen it on my face. But you have never seen it in the degree that Stanton bore it. The eyes were wide open and fixed, as though upon some inward vision of hell and heaven! He walked like the corpse of a man damned who carried within him an angel of light!

"The music swelled again. I heard again the murmuring—'*Av-o-lo-ha!*' Stanton turned, facing the ragged side of the portal. And then I saw that the light that filled and surrounded him had a nucleus, a core —something shiftingly human shaped—that dissolved and changed, gathered itself, whirled through and beyond him and back again. And as this shining nucleus passed through him Stanton's whole body pulsed with light. As the luminescence moved, there moved with it, still and serene always, seven tiny globes of light like seven little moons.

"So much I saw and then swiftly Stanton seemed to be lifted—levitated—up the unscalable wall and to its top. The glow faded from the moonlight, the tingling music grew fainter. I tried again to move. The spell still held me fast. The tears were running down now from my rigid lids and they brought relief to my tortured eyes.

"I have said my gaze was fixed. It was. But from the side, peripherally, they took in a part of the far wall of the outer enclosure. Ages seemed to pass and I saw a radiance stealing along it. Soon there came into sight the figure that was Stanton. Far away he was—on the gigantic wall. But still I could see the shining spirals whirling jubilantly around and through him; felt rather than saw his tranced face beneath the seven lights. A swirl of crystal notes, and he had passed. And all the time, as though from some opened well of light, the courtyard gleamed and sent out silver fires that dimmed the moon-rays, yet seemed strangely to be a part of them.

"Ten times he passed before me so. The luminescence came with the music; swam for a while along the man-made cliff of basalt and passed away. Between times eternities rolled and still I crouched there, a helpless thing of stone with eyes that would not close!

"At last the moon neared the horizon. There came a louder burst of sound; the second, and last, cry of Stanton, like an echo of his first! Again the soft sigh from the inner terrace. Then—utter silence. The light faded; the moon was setting and with a rush life and power to move returned to me. I made a leap for the steps, rushed up them, through the gateway and straight to the gray rock. It was closed—as I knew it would be. But did I dream it or did I hear, echoing through it as though from distances a triumphant shouting—'*Av-o-lo-ha! Av-o-lo-ha!*'

"I remembered Edith. I ran back to her. At my touch she wakened; looked at me wanderingly; raised herself slightly on a hand.

" 'Dave!' she said, 'I slept—after all.' She saw the despair on my face and leaped to her feet. 'Dave!' she cried. 'What is it? Where's Charles?'

"I lighted a fire before I spoke. Then I told her. And for the balance of that night we sat before the flames, arms around each other—like two frightened children."

Suddenly Throckmartin held his hands out to me appealingly.

"Goodwin, old friend!" he cried. "Don't look at me as though I were mad. It's truth, absolute truth. Wait—" I comforted him as well as I could. After a little time he took up his story.

"Never," he said, "did man welcome the sun as we did that morning. As soon as it was light we went back to the courtyard. The basalt walls whereon I had seen Stanton were black and silent. The terraces were as they had been. The gray slab was in its place. In the shallow hollow at its base was—nothing. Nothing—nothing was there anywhere on the islet of Stanton—not a trace, not a sign on Nan-Tanach to show that he had ever lived.

"What were we to do? Precisely the same arguments that had kept us there the night before held good now—and doubly good. We could not abandon these two; could not go as long as there was the faintest hope of finding them—and yet for love of each other how could we remain? I loved my wife, Goodwin—how much I never knew until that day; and she loved me as deeply.

" 'It takes only one each night,' she said. 'Beloved, let it take me.'

"I wept, Goodwin. We both wept.

" 'We will meet it together,' she said. And it was thus at last that we arranged it."

"That took great courage indeed, Throckmartin," I interrupted. He looked at me eagerly.

"You do believe, then?" he exclaimed.

"I believe," I said. He pressed my hand with a grip that nearly crushed it.

"Now," he told me, "I do not fear. If I—fail, you will prepare and carry on the work."

I promised. And—God forgive me—that was three years ago.

"It did take courage," he went on, again quietly. "More than courage. For we knew it was renunciation. Each of us in our hearts felt that one of us would not be there to see the sun rise. And each of us prayed that the death, if death it was, would not come first to the other.

"We talked it all over carefully, bringing to bear all our power of analysis and habit of calm, scientific thought. We considered minutely the time element in the phenomena. Although the deep chanting began at the very moment of moonrise, fully five minutes had passed between its full lifting and the strange sighing sound from the inner terrace. I went back in memory over the happenings of the night before. At least fifteen minutes had intervened between the first heralding sigh and the intensification of the moonlight in the courtyard. And this glow grew for at least ten minutes more before the first burst of the crystal notes. Indeed, more than half an hour must have elapsed, I calculated, between the moment the moon showed above the horizon and the first delicate onslaught of the tinklings.

"The sighing sound—of what had it reminded me? Of course—of a door revolving and swishing softly along its base.

" 'Edith!' I cried. 'I think I have it! The gray rock opens five minutes after the moonrise. But whoever or whatever it is that comes through it must wait until the moon has risen higher, or else it must come from a distance. The thing to do is not to wait for it, but to surprise it before it passes out the door. We will go into the inner court early. You will take your rifle and pistol and hide yourself where you can command the opening—if the slab does open. The instant it moves I will enter. It's our best chance, Edith. I think it's our only one.'

"My wife demurred strongly. She wanted to go with me. But I convinced her that it was better for her to stand guard without, prepared to help me if I were forced from what lay behind the rock again in the open.

"The day passed too swiftly. In the face of what we feared our love seemed stronger than ever. Was it the flare of the spark before extinguishment? I wondered. We prepared and ate a good dinner. We tried to keep our minds from anything but the scientific aspect of the phenomena. We agreed that whatever it was its cause must be human, and that we must keep that fact in mind every second. But what kind of men could create such prodigies? We thrilled at the thought of finding perhaps the remnants of a vanished race, living perhaps in cities over whose rocky skies the Pacific rolled; exercising there the lost wisdom of the half-gods of earth's youth.

"At the half-hour before moonrise we two went into the inner courtyard. I took my place at the side of the gray rock. Edith crouched behind a broken pillar twenty feet away, slipped her rifle-barrel over it so that it would cover the opening.

"The minutes crept by. The courtyard was very quiet. The darkness lessened and through the breaches of the terrace I watched the far sky softly lighten. With the first pale flush the stillness became intensified. It deepened—became unbearably—expectant. The moon rose, showed the quarter, the half, then swam up into full sight like a great bubble.

"Its rays fell upon the wall before me and suddenly upon the convexities I have described seven little circles of light sprang out. They gleamed, glimmered, grew brighter—shone. The gigantic slab before me turned as though on a pivot, sighing softly as it moved.

"For a moment I gasped in amazement. It was like a conjuror's trick. And the moving slab I noticed was also glowing, becoming opalescent like the little shining circles above.

"Only for a second I gazed and then with a word to Edith flung myself through the opening which the slab had uncovered. Before me was a platform and from the platform steps led downward into a smooth corridor. This passage was not dark; it glowed with the same faint silvery radiance as the door. Down it I raced. As I ran, plainer than ever before, I heard the chanting. The passage turned abruptly, passed parallel to the walls of the outer courtyard and then once more led abruptly downward. Still I ran, and as I ran I looked at the watch on my wrist. Less than three minutes had elapsed.

"The passage ended. Before me was a high vaulted arch. For a moment I paused. It seemed to open into space; a space filled with lambent, coruscating, many-colored mist whose brightness grew even as I watched. I passed through the arch and stopped in sheer awe!

"In front of me was a pool. It was circular, perhaps twenty feet wide. Around it ran a low, softly curved lip of glimmering silvery stone. Its water was palest blue. The pool with its silvery rim was like a great blue eye staring upward.

"Upon it streamed seven shafts of radiance. They poured down upon the blue eye like cylindrical torrents; they were like shining pillars of light rising from a sapphire floor.

"One was the tender pink of the pearl; one of the aurora's green; a third a deathly white; the fourth the blue in mother-of-pearl; a shimmering column of pale amber; a beam of amethyst; a shaft of molten silver. Such are the colors of the seven lights that stream upon the moon pool. I drew closer, awestricken. The shafts did not illumine the depths. They played upon the surface and seemed there to diffuse, to melt into it. The pool drank them!

"Through the water tiny gleams of phosphorescence began to dart, sparkles and coruscations of pale incandescence. And far, far below I sensed a movement, a shifting glow as of something slowly rising.

"I looked upward, following the radiant pillars, to their source. Far above were seven shining globes, and it was from these that the rays poured. Even as I watched their brightness grew. They were like seven moons set high in some caverned heaven. Slowly their splendor increased, and with it the splendor of the seven beams streaming from them. It came to me that they were crystals of some unknown kind set in the roof of the moon pool's vault and that their light was drawn from the moon shining high above them. They were wonderful, those lights—and what must have been the knowledge of those who set them there!

"Brighter and brighter they grew as the moon climbed higher, sending its full radiance down through them. I tore my gaze away and stared at the pool. It had grown milky, opalescent. The rays gushing into it seemed to be filling it; it was alive with sparklings, scintillations, glimmerings. And the luminescence I had seen rising from its depths was larger, nearer!

"A swirl of mist floated up from its surface. It drifted within the embrace of the rosy beam and hung there for a moment. The beam seemed to embrace it, sending through it little shining corpuscles, tiny rosy spiralings. The mist absorbed the rays, was strengthened by it, gained substance. Another swirl sprang into the amber shaft, clung and fed there, moved swiftly toward the first and mingled with it. And now other swirls arose, here and there, too fast to be counted, hung poised in the embrace of the light streams; flashed and pulsed into each other.

"Thicker and thicker still they arose until the surface of the pool was a pulsating pillar of opalescent mist; steadily growing stronger; drawing within it life from the seven beams falling upon it; drawing to it from below the darting, red atoms of the pool. Into its center was passing the luminescence I had sensed rising from the far depths. And the center glowed, throbbed—began to send out questing swirls and tendrils—

"There forming before me was *that* which had walked with Stanton, which had taken Thora—the thing I had come to find!

"With the shock of realization my brain sprang into action. My hand fell to my pistol and I fired shot after shot into its radiance. The place rang with the explosions and there came to me a sense of unforgivable profanation. Devilish as I knew it to be, that chamber of the moon pool seemed also—in some way—holy. As though a god and a demon dwelt there, inextricably commingled.

"As I shot the pillar wavered; the water grew more disturbed. The mist swayed and shook; gathered itself again. I slipped a second clip into the automatic and another idea coming to me took careful aim at one of the globes in the roof. From thence I knew came the force that shaped the dweller in the pool. From the pouring rays came its strength. If I could destroy them I could check its forming. I fired again and again. If I hit the globes I did no damage. The little motes in their beams danced with the motes in the mist, troubled. That was all.

"Up from the pool like little bells, like bubbles of crystal notes, rose the tinklings. Their notes were higher, had lost their sweetness, were angry, as it were, with themselves.

"And then out from the Inexplicable, hovering over the pool, swept a shining swirl. It caught me above the heart; wrapped itself around me. I felt an icy coldness and then there rushed over me a mingled ecstasy and horror. Every atom of me quivered with delight and at the same time shrank with despair. There was nothing loathsome in it. But it was as though the icy soul of evil and the fiery soul of good had stepped together within me. The pistol dropped from my hand.

"So I stood while the pool gleamed and sparkled; the streams of light grew more intense and the mist glowed and strengthened. I saw that its shining core had shape—but a shape that my eyes and brain could not define. It was as though a being of another sphere should assume what it might of human semblance, but was not able to conceal that what human eyes saw was but a part of it. It was neither man nor woman; it was unearthly and androgynous. Even as I found its human semblance it changed. And still the mingled rapture and terror held me. Only in a little corner of my brain dwelt something untouched; something that held itself apart and watched. Was it the soul? I have never believed—and yet—

"Over the head of the misty body there sprang suddenly out seven little lights. Each was the color of the beam beneath which it rested. I knew now that the dweller was—complete!

"And then—behind me I heard a scream. It was Edith's voice. It came to me that she had heard the shots and followed me. I felt every faculty concentrate into a mighty effort. I wrenched myself free from the gripping tentacle and it slipped back. I turned to catch Edith, and as I did so slipped—fell. As I dropped I saw the radiant shape above the pool leap swiftly for me!

"There was the rush past me and as the dweller paused, straight into it raced Edith, arms outstretched to shield me from it! God!"

He trembled.

"She threw herself squarely within its diabolic splendor," he whispered. "She stopped and reeled as though she had encountered solidity. And as she faltered it wrapped its shining self around her. The crystal tinklings burst forth jubilantly. The light filled her, ran through and around her as it had with Stanton, and I saw drop upon her face—the look. From the pillar came the murmur—'*Av-o-lo-ha!*' The vault echoed it.

" 'Edith!' I cried. 'Edith!' I was in agony. She must have heard me, even through the—thing. I saw her try to free herself. Her rush had taken her to the very verge of the moon pool. She tottered; and in an instant—she fell—with the radiance still holding her, still swirling and winding around and through her—into the moon pool! She sank, Goodwin, and with her went—the dweller!

"I dragged myself to the brink. Far down I saw a shining, many-colored nebulous cloud descending; caught a glimpse of Edith's face, disappearing; her eyes stared up to me filled with supernal ecstasy and horror. And—vanished!

"I looked about me stupidly. The seven globes still poured their radiance upon the pool. It was pale blue again. Its sparklings and coruscations were gone. From far below there came a muffled outburst of triumphant chanting!

" 'Edith!' I cried again. 'Edith, come back to me!' And then a darkness fell upon me. I remember running back through the shimmering corridors and out into the courtyard. Reason had left me. When it returned I was far out at sea in our boat wholly estranged from civilization. A day later I was picked up by the schooner in which I came to Port Moresby.

"I have formed a plan; you must hear it, Goodwin—" He fell upon his berth. I bent over him. Exhaustion and the relief of telling his story had been too much for him. He slept like the dead.

4

All that night I watched over him. When dawn broke I went to my room to get a little sleep myself. But my slumber was haunted.

The next day the storm was unabated. Throckmartin came to me at lunch. He looked better. His strange expression had waned. He had regained his alertness.

"Come to my cabin," he said. There, he stripped his shirt from him. "Something is happening," he said. "The mark is smaller." It was as he said.

"I'm escaping," he whispered jubilantly. "Just let me get to Melbourne safely, and then we'll see who'll win! For, Goodwin, I'm not at all sure that Edith is dead—as we know death—nor that the others are. There was something outside experience there—some great mystery.

"There's a natural explanation, of course," he said. "My theory is that the moon rock is of some composition sensitive to the action of moon rays; somewhat as the metal selenium is to sun rays. There is a powerful quality in moonlight, as both science and legends can attest. We know of its effect upon the mentality, the nervous system, even upon certain diseases.

"The moon slab is of some material that reacts to moonlight. The little circles over the top are, without doubt, its operating agency. When the light strikes them they release the mechanism that opens the slab, just as you can open doors with sunlight by an ingenious arrangement of selenium-cells. Apparently it takes the strength of the full moon to do this. We will first try a concentration of the rays of the *nearly* full moon upon these circles to see whether that will open the rock. If it does we will be able to investigate the pool without interruption from—from—what emanates.

"Look, here on the chart are their locations.

"Here," he said, "is where I believe the seven great globes to be. They are probably hidden somewhere in the ruins of the islet called Tau, where they can catch the first moon rays.

"They are certainly cleverly concealed, but they must be open to the air to get the light. They should not be too hard to find. They must be found." He hesitated again. "I suppose it would be safer to destroy them, for it is clearly through them that the phenomena of the pool is manifested; and yet, to destroy so wonderful a thing! Perhaps the better way would be to have some men up by them, and if it were necessary, to protect those below, to destroy them on signal. Or they might simply be covered. That would neutralize them. To destroy them—" He hesitated again. "No, the phenomena is too important to be destroyed without fullest investigation." His face clouded again. "But it is *not* human; it can't be!"

Again— "We need half a dozen diving-suits. The pool must be entered and searched to its depths. That will indeed take courage, yet in the time of the new moon it should be safe, or perhaps better after the dweller is destroyed or made safe."

We went over plans, accepted them, rejected them, and still the storm raged—and all that day and all that night.

I hurry to the end. That afternoon there came a steady lightening of the clouds which Throckmartin watched with deep uneasiness. Toward dusk they broke away suddenly and soon the sky was clear. The stars came twinkling out.

"It will be tonight," Throckmartin said to me. "Goodwin, friend, stand by me. Tonight it will come, and I must fight."

I could say nothing. About an hour before moonrise we went to his cabin. We fastened the port-holes tightly and turned on the electrics. Throckmartin had some queer theory that the electric rays would be a bar to his pursuer. I don't know why. A little later he complained of sleepiness.

"But it's just weariness," he said. "Not at all like that other drowsiness. It's an hour till moonrise still," he yawned at last. "Wake me up a good fifteen minutes before."

He lay upon the berth. I sat thinking. I came to myself with a start. What time was it? I looked at my watch and jumped to the port-hole. It was full moonlight; the orb had been up for fully half an hour. I strode over to Throckmartin and shook him by the shoulder.

"Up, quick, man!" I cried. He rose sleepily. His shirt fell open at the neck and I looked, in amazement, at the white band around his chest. Even under the electric light it shone softly, as though little flecks of light were in it.

"Oh, yes," he said drowsily, "it's coming—to take me back to Edith! Well, I'm glad."

"Throckmartin!" I cried. "Wake up! Fight."

"Fight!" he said. "No use; keep the maps; come after us."

He went to the port and drowsily drew aside the curtain. The moon traced a broad path of light straight to the ship. Under its rays the band around his chest gleamed brighter and brighter; shot forth little rays; seemed to move.

He peered out intently and, suddenly, before I could stop him, threw open the port. I saw a glimmering presence moving swiftly along the moon path toward us, skimming over the waters.

And with it raced little crystal tinklings and far off I heard a long-drawn murmuring cry.

On the instant the lights went out in the cabin, evidently throughout the ship, for I heard shoutings above. I sprang back into a corner and crouched there. At the porthole was a radiance; swirls and spirals of living white cold fire. It poured into the cabin and it was filled with dancing motes of light, and over the radiant core of it shone seven little lights like tiny moons. It gathered Throckmartin to it. Light pulsed through and from him. I saw his skin turn to a translucent, shimmering whiteness like illumined porcelain. His face became unrecognizable, inhuman with the monstrous twin expressions. So he stood for a moment. The pillar of light seemed to hesitate and the seven lights to contemplate me. I shrank further down into the corner. I saw Throckmartin drawn to the port. The room filled with murmuring. I fainted.

When I awakened the lights were on.

But of Throckmartin there was no trace!

Gentlemen, there are some things we are doomed to regret all our life. Born in me then was a great fear. I suppose I was unbalanced by what I had seen. I could not think clearly. But there came to me the sheer impossibility of telling the ship's officers what I had seen; what Throckmartin had told me. They would accuse me, I felt, of his murder. At neither appearance of the phenomena had any save our two selves witnessed it. I was certain of this because they would surely have discussed it.

The next morning when Throckmartin's absence was noted, I merely said that I had left him early in the evening. It occurred to no one to doubt me, or to question me further. And so it was officially reported that he had fallen or jumped from the ship during the failure of the lights.

Afterward, the same inhibition held me back from making his and my story known to my fellow scientists.

But this inhibition is suddenly dead, and I am not sure that its death is not a summons from Throckmartin.

I go to Nan-Tanach, gentlemen, to make amends for my cowardice by seeking out the dweller.

And, gentlemen, I stake all my reputation, all my faith, all that I hold sacred and dear that what I have written here is absolute truth.

8

It is not only human beings that popular conjecture has visualized in strange worlds beyond normal experience, but animals as well. Over the years many dense jungles and high, unscalable plateaux in the vast reaches of Africa, South America and Asia have been rumored to be the homes of strange animal survivals from the past—creatures unchanged since prehistoric times. The most famous novel embodying this theme is, of course, Conan Doyle's *The Lost World* (1912), which is perhaps more firmly based in fact than any other similar tale—although only as recently as November 1973 a group of British explorers set foot for the first time on the alleged site—the plateau of Roraima in Guiana—and reported, rather sadly, that "there were no pterodactyls, but plenty of 'nasties,' five-inch-high spiders, huge poisonous centipedes and enormous snakes." The men did report, however, that during their brief stay they had found a new species of scorpion and believed that there might be several other unknown varieties of large insects. *Sir Arthur Conan Doyle* (1859–1930) based his novel on an ancient tradition about a "lost world" in the mountain range on the border of Venezuela, Brazil and Guiana, and got his inspiration from reading Jules Verne's *A Journey to the Center of the Earth*. The central character in *The Lost World* is Professor Challenger, who has become known as "The Sherlock Holmes of Science Fiction" and was regarded by Doyle as his finest literary creation. For his book, Doyle devised special maps and plans and even simulated photographs of the "lost world"—all executed with an eye for authenticity. In the story, Professor Challenger leads an expedition to find the "lost world" and returns to confound all those skeptical of his mission by producing a huge pterodactyl, which escapes during his explanatory lecture and causes much panic! On its publication, the novel became an instant sensation and revealed yet another facet of Conan Doyle's amazing talent. He later produced other scientific adventures featuring Professor Challenger, including *The Poison Belt* (1913), *The Land of the Mist* (1925), and some ingenious short stories such as "When the World Screamed," in which the Professor sought to determine the actual composition of the Earth by drilling to its core and being greeted with an agonized cry of pain! Despite the demands of Sherlock Holmes—and his time-consuming, obsessive

The location of "The Lost World" as immortalized by Sir Arthur Conan Doyle. A British expedition reached this site of myth and legend in 1973.

devotion to the cause of spiritualism—Conan Doyle wrote several more stories of science fiction: among them, "The Captain of the Polestar" (inspired by Poe's "The Narrative of A. Gordon Pym"), "The Maracot Deep" (in which Atlantis is discovered) and "The Horror of the Heights," published in 1913, which science-fiction authority Sam Moskowitz believes "may be the source from which Flying Saucer enthusiasts have derived the imaginative concept that alien and incredible life forms dwell in the upper atmosphere of the earth." One of the least known of all Conan Doyle's short stories, however, is "The Terror of Blue John Gap," which is considered by some experts to be not only the best written but also the most ingenious in concept. It appeared in 1910 in *The Strand Magazine* and demonstrates the flowering of Conan Doyle's interest in "lost worlds," which was to culminate in the great novel of that title. The short story is set in his native England, and postulated the idea of giant creatures living in old caverns in the more remote districts of the North. Doyle's creature resembled the "bearlike thing" which was featured in a legend from the county of Derbyshire, but with his consummate skill he managed to give the story a relevance to just about any similar tale from anywhere in the world. The story now makes its first appearance again in an anthology after many years . . .

THE TERROR OF BLUE JOHN GAP
Sir Arthur Conan Doyle

The following narrative was found among the papers of Dr. James Hardcastle, who died of phthisis on February 4, 1908, at 36, Upper Coventry Flats, South Kensington. Those who knew him best, while refusing to express an opinion upon this particular statement, are unanimous in asserting that he was a man of a sober and scientific turn of mind, absolutely devoid of imagination, and most unlikely to invent any abnormal series of events. The paper was contained in an envelope, which was docketed, "A Short Account of the Circumstances which occurred near Miss Allerton's Farm in North-West Derbyshire in the Spring of Last Year." The envelope was sealed, and on the other side was written in pencil—

"DEAR SEATON,—

"It may interest, and perhaps pain you, to know that the incredulity with which you met my story has prevented me from ever opening my mouth upon the subject again. I leave this record after my death, and perhaps strangers may be found to have more confidence in me than my friend."

Inquiry has failed to elicit who this Seaton may have been. I may add that the visit of the deceased to Allerton's Farm, and the general nature of the alarm there, apart from his particular explanation, have been absolutely established. With this foreword I append his account

exactly as he left it. It is in the form of a diary, some entries in which
have been expanded, while a few have been erased.

April 17.—Already I feel the benefit of this wonderful upland air.
The farm of the Allertons lies fourteen hundred and twenty feet above
sea-level, so it may well be a bracing climate. Beyond the usual morning cough I have very little discomfort, and, what with the fresh milk
and the home-grown mutton, I have every chance of putting on
weight. I think Saunderson will be pleased.

The two Miss Allertons are charmingly quaint and kind, two dear
little hard-working old maids, who are ready to lavish all the heart
which might have gone out to husband and to children upon an invalid
stranger. Truly, the old maid is a most useful person, one of the reserve forces of the community. They talk of the superfluous woman,
but what would the poor superfluous man do without her kindly presence? By the way, in their simplicity they very quickly let out the
reason why Saunderson recommended their farm. The Professor rose
from the ranks himself, and I believe that in his youth he was not
above scaring crows in these very fields.

It is a most lonely spot, and the walks are picturesque in the extreme. The farm consists of grazing land lying at the bottom of an irregular valley. On each side are the fantastic limestone hills, formed of
rock so soft that you can break it away with your hands. All this
country is hollow. Could you strike it with some gigantic hammer it
would boom like a drum, or possibly cave in altogether and expose
some huge subterranean sea. A great sea there must surely be, for on
all sides the streams run into the mountain itself, never to reappear.
There are gaps everywhere amid the rocks, and when you pass through
them you find yourself in great caverns, which wind down into the
bowels of the earth. I have a small bicycle lamp, and it is a perpetual
joy to me to carry it into these weird solitudes, and to see the wonderful silver and black effects when I throw its light upon the stalactites
which drape the lofty roofs. Shut off the lamp, and you are in the
blackest darkness. Turn it on, and it is a scene from the Arabian
Nights.

But there is one of these strange openings in the earth which has a
special interest, for it is the handiwork, not of nature, but of man. I
had never heard of Blue John when I came to these parts. It is the
name given to a peculiar mineral of a beautiful purple shade, which is
only found at one or two places in the world. It is so rare that an ordi-

nary vase of Blue John would be valued at a great price. The Romans, with that extraordinary instinct of theirs, discovered that it was to be found in this valley, and sank a horizontal shaft deep into the mountain side. The opening of their mine has been called Blue John Gap, a clean-cut arch in the rock, the mouth all overgrown with bushes. It is a goodly passage which the Roman miners have cut, and it intersects some of the great water-worn caves, so that if you enter Blue John Gap you would do well to mark your steps and to have a good store of candles, or you may never make your way back to the daylight again. I have not yet gone deeply into it, but this very day I stood at the mouth of the arched tunnel, and peering down into the black recesses beyond, I vowed that when my health returned I would devote some holiday to exploring those mysterious depths and finding out for myself how far the Roman had penetrated into the Derbyshire hills.

Strange how superstitious these country men are! I should have thought better of young Armitage, for he is a man of some education and character, and a very fine fellow for his station in life. I was standing at the Blue John Gap when he came across the field to me.

"Well, doctor," said he, "you're not afraid, anyhow."

"Afraid!" I answered. "Afraid of what?"

"Of it," said he, with a jerk of this thumb toward the black vault, "of the Terror that lives in the Blue John Cave."

How absurdly easy it is for a legend to arise in a lonely countryside! I examined him as to the reasons for his weird belief. It seems that from time to time sheep have been missing from the fields, carried bodily away, according to Armitage. That they could have wandered away of their own accord and disappeared among the mountains was an explanation to which he would not listen. On one occasion a pool of blood had been found, and some tufts of wool. That also, I pointed out, could be explained in a perfectly natural way. Further, the nights upon which sheep disappeared were invariably very dark, cloudy nights with no moon. This I met with the obvious retort that those were the nights which a commonplace sheep-stealer would naturally choose for his work. On one occasion a gap had been made in a wall, and some of the stones scattered for a considerable distance. Human agency again, in my opinion. Finally, Armitage clinched all his arguments by telling me that he had actually heard the Creature—indeed, that anyone could hear it who remained long enough at the Gap. It was a distant roaring of an immense volume. I could not but smile at this, knowing, as I do, the strange reverberations which come out of an underground water system running amid the chasms of a limestone formation. My incredulity annoyed Armitage so that he turned and left me with some abruptness.

And now comes the queer point about the whole business. I was still standing near the mouth of the cave turning over in my mind the various statements of Armitage, and reflecting how readily they could be explained away, when suddenly, from the depth of the tunnel beside me, there issued a most extraordinary sound. How shall I describe it? First of all, it seemed to be a great distance away, far down in the bowels of the earth. Secondly, in spite of this suggestion of distance, it was very loud. Lastly, it was not a boom, nor a crash, such as one would associate with falling water or tumbling rock, but it was a high whine, tremulous and vibrating, almost like the whinnying of a horse. It was certainly a most remarkable experience, and one which for a moment, I must admit, gave a new significance to Armitage's words. I waited by the Blue John Gap for half an hour or more, but there was no return of the sound, so at last I wandered back to the farm-house, rather mystified by what had occurred. Decidedly I shall explore that cavern when my strength is restored. Of course, Armitage's explanation is too absurd for discussion, and yet that sound was certainly very strange. It still rings in my ears as I write.

April 20.—In the last three days I have made several expeditions to the Blue John Gap, and have even penetrated some short distance, but my bicycle lantern is so small and weak that I dare not trust myself very far. I shall do the thing more systematically. I have heard no sound at all, and could almost believe that I had been the victim of some hallucination suggested, perhaps, by Armitage's conversation. Of course, the whole idea is absurd, and yet I must confess that those bushes at the entrance of the cave do present an appearance as if some heavy creature had forced its way through them. I begin to be keenly interested. I have said nothing to the Miss Allertons, for they are quite superstitious enough already, but I have bought some candles, and mean to investigate for myself.

I observed this morning that among the numerous tufts of sheep's wool which lay among the bushes near the cavern there was one which was smeared with blood. Of course, my reason tells me that if sheep wander into such rocky places they are likely to injure themselves, and yet somehow that splash of crimson gave me a sudden shock, and for a moment I found myself shrinking back in horror from the old Roman arch. A fetid breath seemed to ooze from the black depths into which I peered. Could it indeed be possible that some nameless thing, some dreadful presence, was lurking down yonder? I should have been incapable of such feelings in the days of my strength, but one grows more nervous and fanciful when one's health is shaken.

For the moment I weakened in my resolution, and was ready to leave the secret of the old mine, if one exists, for ever unsolved. But tonight my interest has returned and my nerves grown more steady. Tomorrow I trust that I shall have gone more deeply into this matter.

April 22.—Let me try and set down as accurately as I can my extraordinary experience of yesterday. I started in the afternoon, and made my way to the Blue John Gap. I confess that my misgivings returned as I gazed into its depths, and I wished that I had brought a companion to share my exploration. Finally, with a return of resolution, I lit my candle, pushed my way through the briars, and descended into the rocky shaft.

It went down at an acute angle for some fifty feet, the floor being covered with broken stone. Thence there extended a long, straight passage cut in the solid rock. I am no geologist, but the lining of this corridor was certainly of some harder material than limestone, for there were points where I could actually see the tool-marks which the old miners had left in their excavation, as fresh as if they had been done yesterday. Down this strange, old-world corridor I stumbled, my feeble flame throwing a dim circle of light around me, which made the shadows beyond the more threatening and obscure. Finally, I came to a spot where the Roman tunnel opened into a water-worn cavern—a huge hall, hung with long white icicles of lime deposit. From this central chamber I could dimly perceive that a number of passages worn by the subterranean streams wound away into the depths of the earth. I was standing there wondering whether I had better return, or whether I dare venture farther into this dangerous labyrinth, when my eyes fell upon something at my feet which strongly arrested my attention.

The greater part of the floor of the cavern was covered with boulders of rock or with hard incrustations of lime, but at this particular point there had been a drip from the distant roof, which had left a patch of soft mud. In the very centre of this there was a huge mark—an ill-defined blotch, deep, broad and irregular, as if a great boulder had fallen upon it. No loose stone lay near, however, nor was there anything to account for the impression. It was far too large to be caused by any possible animal, and besides, there was only the one, and the patch of mud was of such a size that no reasonable stride could have covered it. As I rose from the examination of that singular mark and then looked round into the black shadows which hemmed me in, I must confess that I felt for a moment a most unpleasant sinking of my heart, and that, do what I could, the candle trembled in my outstretched hand.

I soon recovered my nerve, however, when I reflected how absurd it was to associate so huge and shapeless a mark with the track of any known animal. Even an elephant could not have produced it. I determined, therefore, that I would not be scared by vague and senseless fears from carrying out my exploration. Before proceeding, I took good note of a curious rock formation in the wall by which I could recognise the entrance of the Roman tunnel. The precaution was very necessary, for the great cave, so far as I could see it, was intersected by passages. Having made sure of my position, and reassured myself by examining my spare candles and my matches, I advanced slowly over the rocky and uneven surface of the cavern.

And now I come to the point where I met with such sudden and desperate disaster. A stream, some twenty feet broad, ran across my path, and I walked for some little distance along the bank to find a spot where I could cross dry-shod. Finally, I came to a place where a single flat boulder lay near the centre, which I could reach in a stride. As it chanced, however, the rock had been cut away and made top-heavy by the rush of the stream, so that it tilted over as I landed on it and shot me into the ice-cold water. My candle went out, and I found myself floundering about in utter and absolute darkness.

I staggered to my feet again, more amused than alarmed by my adventure. The candle had fallen from my hand, and was lost in the stream, but I had two others in my pocket, so that it was of no importance. I got one of them ready, and drew out my box of matches to light it. Only then did I realise my position. The box had been soaked in my fall into the river. It was impossible to strike the matches.

A cold hand seemed to close round my heart as I realised my position. The darkness was opaque and horrible. It was so utter that one put one's hand up to one's face as if to press off something solid. I stood still, and by an effort I steadied myself. I tried to reconstruct in my mind a map of the floor of the cavern as I had last seen it. Alas! the bearings which had impressed themselves upon my mind were high on the wall, and not to be found by touch. Still, I remembered in a general way how the sides were situated, and I hoped that by groping my way along them I should at last come to the opening of the Roman tunnel.

Moving very slowly, and continually striking against the rocks, I set out on this desperate quest.

But I very soon realized how impossible it was. In that black, velvety darkness one lost all one's bearings in an instant. Before I had made a dozen paces, I was utterly bewildered as to my whereabouts. The rippling of the stream, which was the one sound audible, showed me where it lay, but the moment that I left its bank I was utterly lost. The idea of finding my way back in absolute darkness through that limestone labyrinth was clearly an impossible one.

I sat down upon a boulder and reflected upon my unfortunate plight. I had not told anyone that I proposed to come to the Blue John mine, and it was unlikely that a search party would come after me. Therefore I must trust to my own resources to get clear of the danger. There was only one hope, and that was that the matches might dry. When I fell into the river, only half of me had got thoroughly wet. My left shoulder had remained above the water. I took the box of matches, therefore, and put it into my left armpit. The moist air of the cavern might possibly be counteracted by the heat of my body, but even so, I knew that I could not hope to get a light for many hours. Meanwhile there was nothing for it but to wait.

By good luck I had slipped several biscuits into my pocket before I left the farm-house. These I now devoured, and washed them down with a draught from that wretched stream which had been the cause of all my misfortunes. Then I felt about for a comfortable seat among the rocks, and, having discovered a place where I could get a support for my back, I stretched out my legs and settled myself down to wait. I was wretchedly damp and cold, but I tried to cheer myself with the reflection that modern science prescribed open windows and walks in all weather for my disease. Gradually, lulled by the monotonous gurgle of the stream, and by the absolute darkness, I sank into an uneasy slumber.

How long this lasted I cannot say. It may have been for an hour, it may have been for several. Suddenly I sat up on my rock couch, with every nerve thrilling and every sense acutely on the alert. Beyond all doubt I had heard a sound—some sound very distinct from the gurgling of the waters. It had passed, but the reverberation of it still lingered in my ear. Was it a search party? They would most certainly have shouted, and vague as this sound was which had wakened me, it was very distinct from the human voice. I sat palpitating and hardly daring to breathe. There it was again! And again! Now it had become continuous. It was a tread—yes, surely it was the tread of some living creature. But what a tread it was! It gave one the impression of enormous weight carried upon spongelike feet, which gave forth a muffled but ear-filling sound. The darkness was as complete as ever, but the tread was regular and decisive. And it was coming beyond all question in my direction.

My skin grew cold, and my hair stood on end as I listened to that steady and ponderous footfall. There was some creature there, and surely by the speed of its advance, it was one which could see in the dark. I crouched low on my rock and tried to blend myself into it. The steps grew nearer still, then stopped, and presently I was aware of a loud lapping and gurgling. The creature was drinking at the stream. Then again there was silence, broken by a succession of long sniffs and snorts of tremendous volume and energy. Had it caught the scent of me? My own nostrils were filled by a low fetid odour, mephitic and abominable. Then I heard the steps again. They were on my side of the stream now. The stones rattled within a few yards of where I lay. Hardly daring to breathe, I crouched upon my rock. Then the steps drew away. I heard the splash as it returned across the river, and the sound died away into the distance in the direction from which it had come.

For a long time I lay upon the rock, too much horrified to move. I thought of the sound which I had heard coming from the depths of the cave, of Armitage's fears, of the strange impression in the mud, and now came this final and absolute proof that there was indeed some inconceivable monster, something utterly unearthly and dreadful, which lurked in the hollow of the mountain. Of its nature or form I could frame no conception, save that it was both light-footed and gigantic. The combat between my reason, which told me that such things could not be, and my senses, which told me that they were, raged within me as I lay. Finally, I was almost ready to persuade myself that this experience had been part of some evil dream, and that my abnormal condition might have conjured up an hallucination. But there remained one final experience which removed the last possibility of doubt from my mind.

I had taken my matches from my armpit and felt them. They seemed perfectly hard and dry. Stooping down into a crevice of the rocks, I tried one of them. To my delight it took fire at once. I lit the candle, and, with a terrified backward glance into the obscure depths of the cavern, I hurried in the direction of the Roman passage. As I did so I passed the patch of mud on which I had seen the huge imprint. Now I stood astonished before it, for there were three similar imprints upon its surface, enormous in size, irregular in outline, of a depth which indicated the ponderous weight which had left them. Then a great terror surged over me. Stooping and shading my candle with my hand, I ran in a frenzy of fear to the rocky archway, hastened up it, and never stopped until, with weary feet and panting lungs, I rushed up the final slope of stones, broke through the tangle of briars, and flung myself exhausted upon the soft grass under the peaceful light of the stars. It was three in the morning when I reached the farmhouse, and to-day I am all unstrung and quivering after my terrific adventure. As yet I have told no one. I must move warily in the matter. What would the poor lonely women, or the uneducated yokels here think of it if I were to tell them my experience? Let me go to someone who can understand and advise.

April 25.—I was laid up in bed for two days after my incredible adventure in the cavern. I use the adjective with a very definite meaning, for I have had an experience since which has shocked me almost as much as the other. I have said that I was looking round for someone who could advise me. There is a Dr. Mark Johnson who practises some few miles away, to whom I had a note of recommendation from Professor Saunderson. To him I drove, when I was strong enough to get about, and I recounted to him my whole strange experience. He listened intently, and then carefully examined me, paying special attention to my reflexes and to the pupils of my eyes. When he had finished, he refused to discuss my adventure, saying that it was entirely beyond him, but he gave me the card of a Mr. Picton at Castleton, with the advice that I should instantly go to him and tell him the story exactly as I had done to himself. He was, according to my adviser, the very man who was pre-eminently suited to help me. I went on to the station, therefore, and made my way to the little town, which is some ten miles away. Mr. Picton appeared to be a man of importance, as his brass plate was displayed upon the door of a considerable building on the outskirts of the town. I was about to ring his bell, when some misgiving came into my mind, and, crossing to a neighbouring shop, I asked the man behind the counter if he could tell me anything of Mr. Picton. "Why," said he, "he is the best mad doctor in Derbyshire, and yonder is his asylum." You can imagine that it was not long before I had shaken the dust of Castleton from my feet and returned to the farm, cursing all unimaginative pedants who cannot conceive that there may be things in creation which have never yet chanced to come across their mole's vision. After all, now that I am cooler, I can afford to admit that I have been no more sympathetic to Armitage than Dr. Johnson has been to me.

April 27.—When I was a student I had the reputation of being a man of courage and enterprise. I remember that when there was a ghost-hunt at Coltbridge it was I who sat up in the haunted house. Is it advancing years (after all, I am only thirty-five), or is it this physical malady which has caused degeneration? Certainly my heart quails when I think of that horrible cavern in the hill, and the certainty that it has some monstrous occupant. What shall I do? There is not an hour in the day that I do not debate the question. If I say nothing, then the mystery remains unsolved. If I do say anything, then I have the alternative of mad alarm over the whole countryside, or of absolute incredulity which may end in consigning me to an asylum. On the whole, I think that my best course is to wait, and to prepare for some expedition which shall be more deliberate and better thought out than the last. As a first step I have been to Castleton and obtained a few essentials—a large acetylene lantern for one thing, and a good double-barrelled sporting rifle for another. The latter I have hired, but I have bought a dozen heavy game cartridges, which would bring down a rhinoceros. Now I am ready for my troglodyte friend. Give me better health and a little spate of energy, and I shall try conclusions with him yet. But who and what is he? Ah! there is the question which stands between me and my sleep. How many theories do I form, only to discard each in turn! It is all so utterly unthinkable. And yet the cry, the footmark, the tread in the cavern—no reasoning can get past these. I think of the old-world legends of dragons and of other monsters. Were they, perhaps, not such fairy-tales as we have thought? Can it be that there is some fact which underlies them, and am I, of all mortals, the one who is chosen to expose it?

May 3.—For several days I have been laid up by the vagaries of an English spring, and during those days there have been developments, the true and sinister meaning of which no one can appreciate save myself. I may say that we have had cloudy and moonless nights of late, which according to my information were the seasons upon which sheep disappeared. Well, sheep *have* disappeared. Two of Miss Allerton's, one of old Pearson's of the Cat Walk, and one of Mrs. Moulton's. Four in all during three nights. No trace is left of them at all, and the countryside is buzzing with rumours of gipsies and of sheep-stealers.

But there is something more serious than that. Young Armitage has disappeared also. He left his moorland cottage early on Wednesday night and has never been heard of since. He was an unattached man, so there is less sensation than would otherwise be the case. The popular explanation is that he owes money, and has found a situation in some other part of the country, whence he will presently write for his belongings. But I have grave misgivings. Is it not much more likely that the recent tragedy of the sheep has caused him to take some steps which may have ended in his own destruction? He may, for example, have lain in wait for the creature and been carried off by it into the recesses of the mountains. What an inconceivable fate for a civilized Englishman of the twentieth century! And yet I feel that it is possible and even probable. But in that case, how far am I answerable both for his death and for any other mishap which may occur? Surely with the knowledge I already possess it must be my duty to see that something is done, or if necessary to do it myself. It must be the latter, for this morning I went down to the local police-station and told my story. The inspector entered it all in a large book and bowed me out with commendable gravity, but I heard a burst of laughter before I had got down his garden path. No doubt he was recounting my adventure to his family.

June 10.—I am writing this, propped up in bed, six weeks after my last entry in this journal. I have gone through a terrible shock both to mind and body, arising from such an experience as has seldom befallen a human being before. But I have attained my end. The danger from the Terror which dwells in the Blue John Gap has passed never to return. Thus much at least I, a broken invalid, have done for the common good. Let me now recount what occurred as clearly as I may.

The night of Friday, May 3, was dark and cloudy—the very night for the monster to walk. About eleven o'clock I went from the farm-house with my lantern and my rifle, having first left a note upon the table of my bedroom in which I said that, if I were missing, search should be made for me in the direction of the Gap. I made my way to the mouth of the Roman shaft, and, having perched myself among the rocks close to the opening, I shut off my lantern and waited patiently with my loaded rifle ready to my hand.

It was a melancholy vigil. All down the winding valley I could see the scattered lights of the farm-houses, and the church clock of Chapel-le-Dale tolling the hours came faintly to my ears. These tokens of my fellowmen served only to make my own position seem the more lonely, and to call for a greater effort to overcome the terror which tempted me continually to get back to the farm, and abandon for ever this dangerous quest. And yet there lies deep in every man a rooted self-respect which makes it hard for him to turn back from that which he has once undertaken. This feeling of personal pride was my salvation now, and it was that alone which held me fast when every instinct of my nature was dragging me away. I am glad now that I had the strength. In spite of all that it has cost me, my manhood is at least above reproach.

Twelve o'clock struck in the distant church, then one, then two. It was the darkest hour of the night. The clouds were drifting low, and there was not a star in the sky. An owl was hooting somewhere among the rocks, but no other sound, save the gentle sough of the wind, came to my ears. And then suddenly I heard it! From far away down the tunnel came those muffled steps, so soft and yet so ponderous. I heard also the rattle of stones as they gave way under that giant tread. They drew nearer. They were close upon me. I heard the crashing of the bushes round the entrance, and then dimly through the darkness I was conscious of the loom of some enormous shape, some monstrous inchoate creature, passing swiftly and very silently out from the tunnel. I was paralysed with fear and amazement. Long as I had waited, now that it had actually come I was unprepared for the shock. I lay motionless and breathless, whilst the great dark mass whisked by me and was swallowed up in the night.

But now I nerved myself for its return. No sound came from the sleeping countryside to tell of the horror which was loose. In no way could I judge how far off it was, what it was doing, or when it might be back. But not a second time should my nerve fail me, not a second time should it pass unchallenged. I swore it between my clenched teeth as I laid my cocked rifle across the rock.

And yet it nearly happened. There was no warning of approach now as the creature passed over the grass. Suddenly, like a dark, drifting shadow, the huge bulk loomed up once more before me, making for the entrance of the cave. Again came that paralysis of volition which held my crooked forefinger impotent upon the trigger. But with a desperate effort I shook it off. Even as the brushwood rustled, and the monstrous beast blended with the shadow of the Gap, I fired at the retreating form. In the blaze of the gun I caught a glimpse of a great shaggy mass, something with rough and bristling hair of a withered grey colour, fading away to white in its lower parts, the huge body supported upon short, thick, curving legs. I had just that glance, and then I heard the rattle of the stones as the creature tore down into its burrow. In an instant, with a triumphant revulsion of feeling, I had cast my fears to the wind, and uncovering my powerful lantern, with my rifle in my hand, I sprang down from my rock and rushed after the monster down the old Roman shaft.

My splendid lamp cast a brilliant flood of vivid light in front of me, very different from the yellow glimmer which had aided me down the same passage only twelve days before. As I ran, I saw the great beast lurching along before me, its huge bulk filling up the whole space from wall to wall. Its hair looked like coarse faded oakum, and hung down in long, dense masses which swayed as it moved. It was like an enormous unclipped sheep in its fleece, but in size it was far larger than the largest elephant, and its breadth seemed to be nearly as great as its height. It fills me with amazement now to think that I should have dared to follow such a horror into the bowels of the earth, but when one's blood is up, and when one's quarry seems to be flying, the old primeval hunting-spirit awakes and prudence is cast to the wind. Rifle in hand, I ran at the top of my speed upon the trail of the monster.

I had seen that the creature was swift. Now I was to find out to my cost that it was also very cunning. I had imagined that it was in panic flight, and that I had only to pursue it. The idea that it might turn upon me never entered my excited brain. I have already explained that the passage down which I was racing opened into a great central cave. Into this I rushed, fearful lest I should lose all trace of the beast. But he had turned upon his own traces, and in a moment we were face to face.

That picture, seen in the brilliant white light of the lantern, is etched for ever upon my brain. He had reared up on his hind legs as a bear would do, and stood above me, enormous, menacing—such a creature as no nightmare had ever brought to my imagination. I have said that he reared like a bear, and there was something bear-like—if one could conceive a bear which was tenfold the bulk of any bear seen upon earth—in his whole pose and attitude, in his great crooked forelegs with their ivory-white claws, in his rugged skin, and in his red, gaping mouth, fringed with monstrous fangs. Only in one point did he differ from the bear, or from any other creature which walks the earth, and even at that supreme moment a shudder of horror passed over me as I observed that the eyes which glistened in the glow of my lantern were huge, projecting bulbs, white and sightless. For a moment his great paws swung over my head. The next he fell forward upon me, I and my broken lantern crashed to the earth, and I remember no more.

When I came to myself I was back in the farm-house of the Allertons. Two days had passed since my terrible adventure in the Blue John Gap. It seems that I had lain all night in the cave insensible from concussion of the brain, with my left arm and two ribs badly fractured. In the morning my note had been found, a search party of a dozen farmers assembled, and I had been tracked down and carried back to my bedroom, where I had lain in high delirium ever since. There was, it seems, no sign of the creature, and no bloodstain which would show that my bullet had found him as he passed. Save for my own plight and the marks upon the mud, there was nothing to prove that what I said was true.

Six weeks have now elapsed, and I am able to sit out once more in the sunshine. Just opposite me is the steep hillside, grey with shaly rock, and yonder on its flank is the dark cleft which marks the opening of the Blue John Gap. But it is no longer a source of terror. Never again through that ill-omened tunnel shall any strange shape flit out into the world of men. The educated and the scientific, the Dr. Johnsons and the like, may smile at my narrative, but the poorer folk of the countryside had never a doubt as to its truth. On the day after my recovering consciousness they assembled in their hundreds round the Blue John Gap. As the *Castleton Courier* said:

"It was useless for our correspondent, or for any of the adventurous gentlemen who had come from Matlock, Buxton, and other parts, to offer to descend, to explore the cave to the end, and to finally test the extraordinary narrative of Dr. James Hardcastle. The country people had taken the matter into their own hands, and from an early hour of the morning they had worked hard in stopping up the entrance of the tunnel. There is a sharp slope where the shaft begins, and great boulders, rolled along by many willing hands, were thrust down it until the Gap was absolutely sealed. So ends the episode which has caused such excitement throughout the country. Local opinion is fiercely divided upon the subject. On the one hand are those who point to Dr. Hardcastle's impaired health, and to the possibility of cerebral lesions of tubercular origin giving rise to strange hallucinations. Some *idée fixe,* according to these gentlemen, caused the doctor to wander down the tunnel, and a fall among the rocks was sufficient to account for his injuries. On the other hand, a legend of a strange creature in the Gap has existed for some months back, and the farmers look upon Dr. Hardcastle's narrative and his personal injuries as a final corroboration. So the matter stands, and so the matter will continue to stand, for no definite solution seems to us to be now possible. It transcends human wit to give any scientific explanation which could cover the alleged facts."

Perhaps before the *Courier* published these words they would have been wise to send their representative to me. I have thought the matter out, as no one else has occasion to do, and it is possible that I might have removed some of the more obvious difficulties of the narrative and brought it one degree nearer to scientific acceptance. Let me then write down the only explanation which seems to me to elucidate what I know to my cost to have been a series of facts. My theory may seem to be wildly improbable, but at least no one can venture to say that it is impossible.

My view is—and it was formed, as is shown by my diary, before my personal adventure—that in this part of England there is a vast subterranean lake or sea, which is fed by the great number of streams which pass down through the limestone. Where there is a large collection of water there must also be some evaporation, mists or rain, and a possibility of vegetation. This in turn suggests that there may be animal life, arising, as the vegetable life would also do, from those seeds and types which had been introduced at an early period of the world's history, when communication with the outer air was more easy. This place had then developed a fauna and flora of its own, including such monsters as the one which I had seen, which may well have been the old cave-bear, enormously enlarged and modified by its new environment. For countless æons the internal and the external creation had kept apart, growing steadily away from each other. Then there had come some rift in the depths of the mountain which had enabled one creature to wander up and, by means of the Roman tunnel, to reach the open air. Like all subterranean life, it had lost the power of sight, but this had no doubt been compensated for by nature in other directions. Certainly it had some means of finding its way about, and of hunting down the sheep upon the hillside. As to its choice of dark nights, it is part of my theory that light was painful to those great white eyeballs, and that it was only a pitch-black world which it could tolerate. Perhaps, indeed, it was the glare of my lantern which saved my life at that awful moment when we were face to face. So I read the riddle. I leave these facts behind me, and if you can explain them, do so; or if you choose to doubt them, do so. Neither your belief nor your incredulity can alter them, nor affect one whose task is nearly over.

So ended the strange narrative of Dr. James Hardcastle.

V

ANCIENT CIVILIZATIONS

***

The Valley of the Sorceress
By Sax Rohmer

A New God Was Born
By B. Traven

9

Perhaps the greatest of all the early recorded civilizations—certainly in terms of mystery and legend—was Egypt, with its amazing dynasties of Pharaohs, the worship of totemic animals, and the creation of monuments and pyramids which are still among the great wonders of the world. Egyptian history begins in the mists of time, but the state itself was founded about 5200 B.C. by the semilegendary figure Menes, and thereafter enjoyed periods of magnificence and power interrupted by anarchy and disillusion. Of all Egypt's many rulers, few were more powerful or mysterious than Queen Hatshepsut, who ruled during the eighteenth dynasty (1580–1350 B.C.) and almost immediately preceded the legendary Pharaohs Amenhotep and Tutankhamen. She is doubly remarkable in that she managed to govern Egypt at all—the nation was traditionally opposed to rule by women—and that after her death all traces of her existence were painstakingly removed from monuments and public records for reasons which still puzzle Egyptologists today. Hatshepsut was the daughter of the Pharaoh Thutmose I, and married her half-brother Thutmose III in a bid for power. Thereafter, by a mixture of cunning, ability and her undoubted beauty, she made him install her as Queen on his accession—overcoming his desire to call her merely "great or chief wife" in the tradition of the day. Despite Thutmose's claims that he had received his divinity in a personal meeting with the Sun God, he could do little to stop the spread of his wife's influence in court and governmental circles. In time, so strong did this influence become, that she had the constitution changed so that she could, in effect, become ruler, and was thereafter called "the female Horuse." Much of her power was based on the unquestioning support she received from the priests, but there were apparently rumors that she was also in league with the forces of evil. Once in command, however, she made full use of her power and set about an ambitious program of building magnificent works and monuments, developing the resources of her empire, and instituted an age of great achievements in the arts. "This aggressive career," the renowned Egyptologist Professor James Breasted has informed us, "made her the first great woman in history of whom we are informed." She also built a temple for her own mortuary service at Thebes, had her tomb excavated in the desolate Valley of the Kings, and began the erection of "two obelisks of electrum, whose points mingle with heaven to do honor to him who fashioned me." Two gigantic shafts were sunk to take the obelisks, which were the tallest ever erected in Egypt up to that time—being ninety-seven-and-a-half-feet tall and weighing nearly three-hundred-and-fifty tons each. Sadly, the obelisks were barely in place before Queen Hatshepsut died and the strange campaign to obliterate all traces of her memory began. "Everywhere her name was erased," says Professor Breasted, "and in the temple on all the walls both her figure and her name were hacked out." The blame for some of this desecration must certainly be apportioned to the Queen's frustrated and vengeful husband, Thutmose, but many of the ordinary people were also said to have taken part in the work, as they were afraid that the Queen's remarkable powers might reach out to them from beyond the tomb. To this day, students have puzzled over the story of Hatshepsut and it remains one of the great mysteries of Egypt. Apart from the many studies of the period, one modern short story stands out from the body of literature with an imaginative interpretation of the personality of the Queen, "The Valley of the Sorceress", written in 1924 by Sax Rohmer, creator of the famed Fu Manchu. Rohmer, or *Arthur Sarsfield Ward* (1886–1959), knew Egypt intimately and was deeply read in its traditions. "My earliest interests centered in Ancient Egypt," he wrote, "and I cannot doubt that I spent at least one incarnation beside the Nile. I studied hieroglyphics and collected books on my pet subject—in this way forming the basis of a considerable library of Ancient Egypt and occult literature." From all this knowledge and experience he presented his answer to the riddle of the first great lady of history.

THE VALLEY OF THE SORCERESS
Sax Rohmer

1

Condor wrote to me three times before the end (said Neville, Assistant-Inspector of Antiquities, staring vaguely from his open window at a squad drilling before the Kasr-en-Nîl Barracks). He dated his letters from the camp at Deir-el-Bahari. Judging from these, success appeared to be almost within his grasp. He shared my theories, of course, respecting Queen Hatshepsut, and was devoting the whole of his energies to the task of clearing up the great mystery of Ancient Egypt which centers around that queen.

For him, as for me, there was a strange fascination about those defaced walls and roughly obliterated inscriptions. That the queen under whom Egyptian art came to the apogee of perfection should thus have been treated by her successors; that no perfect figure of the wise, famous, and beautiful Hatshepsut should have been spared to posterity; that her very cartouche should have been ruthlessly removed from every inscription upon which it appeared, presented to Condor's mind a problem only second in interest to the immortal riddle of Gîzeh.

You know my own views upon the matter? My monograph, "Hatshepsut, the Sorceress," embodies my opinion. In short, upon certain evidences, some adduced by Theodore Davis, some by poor Condor, and some resulting from my own inquiries, I have come to the conclusion that the source—real or imaginary—of this queen's power was an intimate acquaintance with what nowadays we term, vaguely, magic. Pursuing her studies beyond the limit which is lawful, she met with a certain end, not uncommon, if the old writings are to be believed, in the case of those who penetrate too far into the realms of the Borderland.

For this reason—the practice of black magic—her statues were dishonored, and her name erased from the monuments. Now, I do not propose to enter into any discussion respecting the reality of such practices; in my monograph I have merely endeavored to show that, according to contemporary belief, the queen was a sorceress. Condor was seeking to prove the same thing; and when I took up the inquiry, it was in the hope of completing his interrupted work.

He wrote to me early in the winter of 1908, from his camp by the Rock Temple. Davis's tomb, at Bibân el-Mulûk, with its long, narrow passage, apparently had little interest for him; he was at work on the high ground behind the temple, at a point one hundred yards or so due west of the upper platform. He had an idea that he should find there the mummies of Hatshepsut—and another; the latter, a certain Sen-Mût, who appears in the inscriptions of the reign as an architect high in the queen's favor. The archaeological points of the letter do not concern us in the least, but there was one odd little paragraph which I had cause to remember afterwards.

"A girl belonging to some Arab tribe," wrote Condor, "came racing to the camp two nights ago to claim my protection. What crime she had committed, and what punishment she feared, were far from clear; but she clung to me, trembling like a leaf, and positively refused to depart. It was a difficult situation, for a camp of fifty native excavators, and one highly respectable European enthusiast, affords no suitable quarters for an Arab girl—and a very personable Arab girl. At any rate, she is still here; I have had a sort of lean-to rigged up in a little valley east of my own tent, but it is very embarrassing."

Nearly a month passed before I heard from Condor again; then came a second letter, with the news that on the eve of a great discovery —as he believed—his entire native staff—the whole fifty—had deserted one night in a body! "Two days' work," he wrote, "would have seen the tomb opened—for I am more than ever certain that my plans are accurate. Then I woke up one morning to find every man jack of my fellows missing! I went down into the village where a lot of them live, in a towering rage, but not one of the brutes was to be found, and their relations professed entire ignorance respecting their whereabouts. What caused me almost as much anxiety as the check in my work was the fact that Mahâra—the Arab girl—had vanished also. I am wondering if the thing has any sinister significance."

Condor finished with the statement that he was making tremendous efforts to secure a new gang. "But," said he, "I shall finish the excavation, if I have to do it with my own hands."

His third and last letter contained even stranger matters than the two preceding it. He had succeeded in borrowing a few men from the British Archaeological Camp in the Fáyûm. Then, just as the work was restarting, the Arab girl, Mahâra, turned up again, and entreated him to bring her down the Nile, "at least as far as Dendera. For the vengeance of her tribesmen," stated Condor, "otherwise would result not only in her own death, but in mine! At the moment of writing I am in two minds what to do. If Mahâra is to go upon this journey, I do not feel justified in sending her alone, and there is no one here who could perform the duty," etc.

I began to wonder, of course; and I had it in mind to take the train to Luxor merely in order to see this Arab maiden, who seemed to occupy so prominent a place in Condor's mind. However, Fate would have it otherwise; and the next thing I heard was that Condor had been brought into Cairo, and was at the English hospital.

He had been bitten by a cat—presumably from the neighboring village; and although the doctor at Luxor dealt with the bite at once, traveled down with him, and placed him in the hand of the Pasteur man at the hospital, he died, as you remember, in the night of his arrival, raving mad; the Pasteur treatment failed entirely.

I never saw him before the end, but they told me that his howls were horribly like those of a cat. His eyes changed in some way, too, I understand; and, with his fingers all contracted, he tried to *scratch* everyone and everything within reach.

They had to strap the poor beggar down, and even then he tore the sheets into ribbons.

Well, as soon as possible, I made the necessary arrangements to finish Condor's inquiry. I had access to his papers, plans, etc., and in the spring of the same year I took up my quarters near Deir-el-Bahari, roped off the approaches to the camp, stuck up the usual notices, and prepared to finish the excavation, which, I gathered, was in a fairly advanced state.

My first surprise came very soon after my arrival, for when, with the plan before me, I started out to find the shaft, I found it, certainly, but only with great difficulty.

It had been filled in again with sand and loose rock right to the very top!

2

All my inquiries availed me nothing. With what object the excavation had been thus closed I was unable to conjecture. That Condor had not reclosed it I was quite certain, for at the time of his mishap he had actually been at work at the bottom of the shaft, as inquiries from a native of Suefee, in the Fáyûm, who was his only companion at the time, had revealed.

In his eagerness to complete the inquiry, Condor, by lantern light, had been engaged upon a solitary night-shift below, and the rabid cat had apparently fallen into the pit; probably in a frenzy of fear, it had attacked Condor, after which it had escaped.

Only this one man was with him, and he, for some reason that I could not make out, had apparently been sleeping in the temple—quite a considerable distance from Condor's camp. The poor fellow's cries had aroused him, and he had met Condor running down the path and away from the shaft.

This, however, was good evidence of the existence of the shaft at the time, and as I stood contemplating the tightly packed rubble which alone marked its site, I grew more and more mystified, for this task of reclosing the cutting represented much hard labor.

Beyond perfecting my plans in one or two particulars, I did little on the day of my arrival. I had only a handful of men with me, all of whom I knew, having worked with them before, and beyond clearing Condor's shaft I did not intend to excavate further.

Hatshepsut's Temple presents a lively enough scene in the daytime during the winter and early spring months, with the streams of tourists constantly passing from the white causeway to Cook's Rest House on the edge of the desert. There had been a goodly number of visitors that day to the temple below, and one or two of the more curious and venturesome had scrambled up the steep path to the little plateau which was the scene of my operations. None had penetrated beyond the notice boards, however, and now, with the evening sky passing through those innumerable shades which defy palette and brush, which can only be distinguished by the trained eye, but which, from palest blue melt into exquisite pink, and by some magical combination form that deep violet which does not exist to perfection elsewhere than in the skies of Egypt, I found myself in the silence and the solitude of "the Holy Valley."

I stood at the edge of the plateau, looking out at the rosy belt which marked the course of the distant Nile, with the Arabian hills vaguely sketched beyond. The rocks stood up against that prospect as great black smudges, and what I could see of the causeway looked like a gray smear upon a drab canvas. Beneath me were the chambers of the Rock Temple, with those wall paintings depicting events in the reign of Hatasu which rank among the wonders of Egypt.

Not a sound disturbed my reverie, save a faint clatter of cooking utensils from the camp behind me—a desecration of that sacred solitude. Then a dog began to howl in the neighboring village. The dog ceased, and faintly to my ears came the note of a reed pipe. The breeze died away, and with it the piping.

I turned back to the camp and, having partaken of a frugal supper, turned in upon my campaigner's bed, thoroughly enjoying my freedom from the routine of official life in Cairo, and looking forward to the morrow's work pleasurably.

Under such circumstances a man sleeps well; and when, in an uncanny gray half-light, which probably heralded the dawn, I awoke with a start, I knew that something of an unusual nature alone could have disturbed my slumbers.

Firstly, then, I identified this with a concerted howling of the village dogs. They seemed to have conspired to make night hideous; I have never heard such an eerie din in my life. Then it gradually began to die away, and I realized, secondly, that the howling of the dogs and my own awakening might be due to some common cause. This idea grew upon me and, as the howling subsided, a sort of disquiet possessed me and, despite my efforts to shake it off, grew more urgent with the passing of every moment.

In short, I fancied that the thing which had alarmed or enraged the dogs was passing from the village through the Holy Valley, upward to the Temple, upward to the plateau, and was approaching *me*.

I have never experienced an identical sensation since, but I seemed to be audient of a sort of psychic patrol, which, from a remote *pianissimo,* swelled *fortissimo,* to an intimate but silent clamor, which beat in some way upon my brain, but not through the faculty of hearing, for now the night was deathly still.

Yet I was persuaded of some *approach*—of the coming of something sinister, and the suspense of waiting had become almost insupportable, so that I began to accuse my Spartan supper of having given me nightmare, when the tent-flap was suddenly raised and, outlined against the paling blue of the sky, with a sort of reflected elfin light playing upon her face, I saw an Arab girl looking in at me!

By dint of exerting all my self-control I managed to restrain the cry and upward start which this apparition prompted. Quite still, with my fists tightly clenched, I lay and looked into the eyes which were looking into mine.

The style of literary work which it has been my lot to cultivate fails me in describing that beautiful and evil face. The features were severely classical and small, something of the Bisharîn type, with a cruel little mouth and a rounded chin, firm to hardness. In the eyes alone lay the languor of the Orient; they were exceedingly—indeed, excessively—long and narrow. The ordinary ragged, picturesque finery of a desert girl bedecked this midnight visitant, who, motionless, stood there watching me.

I once read a work by Pierre de l'Ancre, dealing with the Black Sabbaths of the Middle Ages, and now the evil beauty of this Arab face threw my memory back to those singular pages, for, perhaps owing to the reflected light which I have mentioned, although the explanation scarcely seemed adequate, those long, narrow eyes shone catlike in the gloom.

Suddenly I made up my mind. Throwing the blanket from me, I leaped to the ground, and in a flash had gripped the girl by the wrists. Confuting some lingering doubts, she proved to be substantial enough. My electric torch lay upon a box at the foot of the bed and, stooping, I caught it up and turned its searching rays upon the face of my captive.

She fell back from me, panting like a wild creature trapped, then dropped upon her knees and began to plead—began to plead in a voice and with a manner which touched some chord of consciousness that I could swear had never spoken before, and has never spoken since.

She spoke in Arabic, of course, but the words fell from her lips as liquid music in which lay all the beauty and all the deviltry of the "Siren's Song." Fully opening her astonishing eyes, she looked up at me and, with her free hand pressed to her bosom, told me how she had fled from an unwelcome marriage; how, an outcast and a pariah, she had hidden in the desert places for three days and three nights, sustaining life only by means of a few dates which she had brought with her, and quenching her thirst with stolen watermelons.

"I can bear it no longer, *effendi*. Another night out in the desert, with the cruel moon beating, beating, beating upon my brain, with creeping things coming out from the rocks, wriggling, wriggling, their many feet making whisperings in the sand—ah, it will kill me! And I am for ever outcast from my tribe, from my people. No tent of all the Arabs, though I fly to the gates of Damascus, is open to me, save I enter in shame, as a slave, as a plaything, as a toy. My heart"—furiously she beat upon her breast—"is empty and desolate, *effendi*. I am meaner than the lowliest thing that creeps upon the sand; yet the God that made that creeping thing made me also—and you, you, who are merciful and strong, would not crush any creature because it was weak and helpless."

I had released her wrist now, and was looking down at her in a sort of stupor. The evil which at first I had seemed to perceive in her was effaced, wiped out as an artist wipes out an error in his drawing. Her dark beauty was speaking to me in a language of its own; a strange language, yet one so intelligible that I struggled in vain to disregard it. And her voice, her gestures, and the witch-fire of her eyes were whipping up my blood to a fever heat of passionate sorrow—of despair. Yes, incredible as it sounds, despair!

In short, as I see it now, this siren of the wilderness was playing upon me as an accomplished musician might play upon a harp, striking this string and that at will, and sounding each with such full notes as they had rarely, if ever, emitted before.

Most damnable anomaly of all, I—Edward Neville, archaeologist, most prosy and matter-of-fact man in Cairo, perhaps—*knew* that this nomad who had burst into my tent, upon whom I had set eyes for the first time scarce three minutes before, held me enthralled; and yet, with her wondrous eyes upon me, I could summon up no resentment, and could offer but poor resistance.

"In the Little Oasis, *effendi,* I have a sister who will admit me into her household, if only as a servant. There I can be safe, there I can rest. O *Inglisi,* at home in England you have a sister of your own! Would you see her pursued, a hunted thing from rock to rock, crouching for shelter in the lair of some jackal, stealing that she might live— and flying always, never resting, her heart leaping for fear, flying, flying, with nothing but dishonor before her?"

She shuddered and clasped my left hand in both her own convulsively, pulling it down to her bosom.

"There can be only one thing, *effendi,*" she whispered. "Do you not see the white bones bleaching in the sun?"

Throwing all my resolution into the act, I released my hand from her clasp and, turning aside, sat down upon the box which served me as chair and table, too.

A thought had come to my assistance, had strengthened me in the moment of my greatest weakness; it was the thought of that Arab girl mentioned in Condor's letters. And a scheme of things, an incredible scheme, that embraced and explained some, if not all, of the horrible circumstances attendant upon his death, began to form in my brain.

Bizarre it was, stretching out beyond the realm of things natural and proper, yet I clung to it, for there, in the solitude, with this wildly beautiful creature kneeling at my feet, and with her uncanny powers of fascination yet enveloping me like a cloak, I found it not so improbable as inevitably it must have seemed at another time.

I turned my head, and through the gloom sought to look into the long eyes. As I did so they closed and appeared as two darkly luminous slits in the perfect oval of the face.

"You are an impostor!" I said in Arabic, speaking firmly and deliberately. "To Mr. Condor"—I could have sworn that she started slightly at sound of the name—"you called yourself Mahâra. I know you, and I will have nothing to do with you."

But in saying it I had to turn my head aside, for the strangest, maddest impulses were bubbling up in my brain in response to the glances of those half-shut eyes.

I reached for my coat, which lay upon the foot of the bed, and, taking out some loose money, I placed fifty piastres in the nerveless brown hand.

"That will enable you to reach the Little Oasis, if such is your desire," I said. "It is all I can do for you, and now—you must go."

The light of the dawn was growing stronger momentarily, so that I could see my visitor quite clearly. She rose to her feet, and stood before me, a straight, slim figure, sweeping me from head to foot with such a glance of passionate contempt as I had never known or suffered.

She threw back her head magnificently, dashed the money on the ground at my feet and, turning, leaped out of the tent.

For a moment I hesitated, doubting, questioning my humanity, testing my fears; then I took a step forward, and peered out across the plateau. Not a soul was in sight. The rocks stood up gray and eerie, and beneath lay the carpet of the desert stretching unbroken to the shadows of the Nile Valley.

3

We commenced the work of clearing the shaft at an early hour that morning. The strangest ideas were now playing in my mind, and in some way I felt myself to be in opposition to definite enmity. My excavators labored with a will and, once we had penetrated below the first three feet or so of tightly packed stone, it became a mere matter of shoveling, for apparently the lower part of the shaft had been filled up principally with sand.

I calculated that four days' work at the outside would see the shaft clear to the base of Condor's excavation. There remained, according to his own notes, only another six feet or so; but it was solid limestone— the roof of the passage, if his plans were correct, communicating with the tomb of Hatshepsut.

With the approach of night, tired as I was, I felt little inclination for sleep. I lay down on my bed with a small Browning pistol under the pillow, but after an hour or so of nervous listening drifted off into slumber. As on the night before, I awoke shortly before the coming of dawn.

Again the village dogs were raising a hideous outcry, and again I was keenly conscious of some ever-nearing menace. This consciousness grew stronger as the howling of the dogs grew fainter, and the sense of *approach* assailed me as on the previous occasion.

I sat up immediately with the pistol in my hand and, gently raising the tent flap, looked out over the darksome plateau. For a long time I could perceive nothing; then, vaguely outlined against the sky, I detected something that moved above the rocky edge.

It was so indefinite in form that for a time I was unable to identify it, but as it slowly rose higher and higher, two luminous eyes—obviously feline eyes, since they glittered greenly in the darkness—came into view. In character and in shape they were the eyes of a cat, but in point of size they were larger than the eyes of any cat I had ever seen. Nor were they jackal eyes. It occurred to me that some predatory beast from the Sûdan might conceivably have strayed thus far north.

The presence of such a creature would account for the nightly disturbance amongst the village dogs; and, dismissing the superstitious notions which had led me to associate the mysterious Arab girl with the phenomenon of the howling dogs, I seized upon this new idea with a sort of gladness.

Stepping boldly out of the tent, I strode in the direction of the gleaming eyes. Although my only weapon was the Browning pistol, it was a weapon of considerable power and, moreover, I counted upon the well-known cowardice of nocturnal animals. I was not disappointed in the result.

The eyes dropped out of sight, and as I leaped to the edge of rock overhanging the Temple a lithe shape went streaking off in the grayness beneath me. Its coloring appeared to be black, but this appearance may have been due to the bad light. Certainly it was no cat, was no jackal; and once, twice, thrice my Browning spat into the darkness.

Apparently I had not scored a hit, but the loud reports of the weapon aroused the men sleeping in the camp, and soon I was surrounded by a ring of inquiring faces.

But there I stood on the rock-edge, looking out across the desert in silence. Something in the long, luminous eyes, something in the sinuous, flying shape had spoken to me intimately, horribly.

Hassan es-Sugra, the headman, touched my arm, and I knew that I must offer some explanation.

"Jackals," I said shortly. And with no other word I walked back to my tent.

The night passed without further event, and in the morning we addressed ourselves to the work with such a will that I saw, to my satisfaction, that by noon of the following day the labor of clearing the loose sand would be completed.

During the preparation of the evening meal I became aware of a certain disquiet in the camp, and I noted a disinclination on the part of the native laborers to stray far from the tents. They hung together in a group, and whilst individually they seemed to avoid meeting my eye, collectively they watched me in a furtive fashion.

A gang of Moslem workmen calls for delicate handling, and I wondered if, inadvertently, I had transgressed in some way their ironbound code of conduct. I called Hassan es-Sugra aside.

"What ails the men?" I asked him. "Have they some grievance?"

Hassan spread his palms eloquently.

"If they have," he replied, "they are secret about it, and I am not in their confidence. Shall I thrash three or four of them in order to learn the nature of this grievance?"

"No, thanks all the same," I said, laughing at this characteristic proposal. "If they refuse to work to-morrow, there will be time enough for you to adopt those measures."

On this, the third night of my sojourn in the Holy Valley by the Temple of Hatshepsut, I slept soundly and uninterruptedly. I had been looking forward with the keenest zest to the morrow's work, which promised to bring me within sight of my goal, and when Hassan came to awaken me, I leaped out of bed immediately.

Hassan es-Sugra, having performed his duty, did not, as was his custom, retire; he stood there, a tall, angular figure looking at me strangely.

"Well?" I said.

"There is trouble," was his simple reply. "Follow me, Neville Effendi."

Wondering greatly, I followed him across the plateau and down the slip to the excavation. There I pulled up short with a cry of amazement.

Condor's shaft was filled in to the very top, and presented, to my astonished gaze, much the same aspect that had greeted me upon my first arrival!

"The men——" I began.

Hassan es-Sugra spread wide his palms.

"Gone!" he replied. "Those Coptic dogs, those eaters of carrion, have fled in the night."

"And this"—I pointed to the little mound of broken granite and sand—"is their work?"

"So it would seem," was the reply; and Hassan sniffed his sublime contempt.

I stood looking bitterly at this destruction of my toils. The strangeness of the thing at the moment did not strike me, in my anger; I was only concerned with the outrageous impudence of the missing workmen, and if I could have laid hands upon one of them it had surely gone hard with him.

As for Hassan es-Sugra, I believe he would cheerfully have broken the necks of the entire gang. But he was a man of resource.

"It is so newly filled in," he said, "that you and I, in three days, or in four, can restore it to the state it had reached when those nameless dogs, who regularly prayed with their shoes on, those devourers of pork, began their dirty work."

His example was stimulating. *I* was not going to be beaten, either.

After a hasty breakfast, the pair of us set to work with pick and shovel and basket. We worked as those slaves must have worked whose toil was directed by the lash of the Pharaoh's overseer. My back acquired an almost permanent crook, and every muscle in my body seemed to be on fire. Not even in the midday heat did we slacken or stay our toils; and when dusk fell that night a great mound had arisen beside Condor's shaft, and we had excavated to a depth it had taken our gang double the time to reach.

When at last we threw down our tools in utter exhaustion, I held out my hand to Hassan, and wrung his brown fist enthusiastically. His eyes sparkled as he met my glance.

"Neville Effendi," he said, "you are a true Moslem!"

And only the initiated can know how high was the compliment conveyed.

That night I slept the sleep of utter weariness, yet it was not a dreamless sleep, or perhaps it was not so deep as I supposed, for blazing cat-eyes encircled me in my dreams, and a constant feline howling seemed to fill the night.

When I awoke the sun was blazing down upon the rock outside my tent and, springing out of bed, I perceived, with amazement, that the morning was far advanced. Indeed, I could hear the distant voices of the donkey-boys and other harbingers of the coming tourists.

Why had Hassan es-Sugra not awakened me?

I stepped out of the tent and called him in a loud voice. There was no reply. I ran across the plateau to the edge of the hollow.

Condor's shaft had been reclosed to the top!

Language fails me to convey the wave of anger, amazement, incredulity, which swept over me. I looked across to the deserted camp and back to my own tent; I looked down at the mound, where but a few hours before had been a pit, and seriously I began to question whether I was mad or whether madness had seized upon all who had been with me. Then, pegged down upon the heap of broken stones, I perceived, fluttering, a small piece of paper.

Dully I walked across and picked it up. Hassan, a man of some education, clearly was the writer. It was a pencil scrawl in doubtful Arabic and, not without difficulty, I deciphered it as follows:

"Fly, Neville Effendi! This is a haunted place!"

Standing there by the mound, I tore the scrap of paper into minute fragments, bitterly casting them from me upon the ground. It was incredible; it was insane.

The man who had written that absurd message, the man who had undone his own work, had the reputation of being fearless and honorable. He had been with me before a score of times, and had quelled petty mutinies in the camp in a manner which marked him a born overseer. I could not understand; I could scarcely believe the evidence of my own senses.

What did I do?

I suppose there are some who would have abandoned the thing at once and for always, but I take it that the national traits are strong within me. I went over to the camp and prepared my own breakfast; then, shouldering pick and shovel, I went down into the valley and set to work. What ten men could not do, what two men had failed to do, one man was determined to do.

It was about half an hour after commencing my toils, and when, I suppose, the surprise and rage occasioned by the discovery had begun to wear off, that I found myself making comparisons between my own case and that of Condor. It became more and more evident to me that events—mysterious events—were repeating themselves.

The frightful happenings attendant upon Condor's death were marshaling in my mind. The sun was blazing down upon me, and distant voices could be heard in the desert stillness. I knew that the plain below was dotted with pleasure-seeking tourists, yet nervous tremors shook me. Frankly, I dreaded the coming of the night.

Well, tenacity or pugnacity conquered, and I worked on until dusk. My supper despatched, I sat down on my bed and toyed with the Browning.

I realized already that sleep, under existing conditions, was impossible. I perceived that on the morrow I must abandon my one-man enterprise, pocket my pride, in a sense, and seek new assistants, new companions.

The fact was coming home to me conclusively that a menace, real and not mythical, hung over that valley. Although, in the morning sunlight and filled with indignation, I had thought contemptuously of Hassan es-Sugra, now, in the mysterious violet dusk so conducive to calm consideration, I was forced to admit that he was at least as brave a man as I. And he had fled! What did that night hold in keeping for me?

*   *   *

I will tell you what occurred, and it is the only explanation I have to give of why Condor's shaft, said to communicate with the real tomb of Hatshepsut, to this day remains unopened.

There, on the edge of my bed, I sat far into the night, not daring to close my eyes. But physical weariness conquered in the end and, although I have no recollection of its coming, I must have succumbed to sleep, since I remember—can never forget—a repetition of the dream, or what I had assumed to be a dream, of the night before.

A ring of blazing green eyes surrounded me. At one point this ring was broken, and in a kind of nightmare panic I leaped at that promise of safety, and found myself outside the tent.

Lithe, slinking shapes hemmed me in—cat shapes, ghoul shapes, veritable figures of the pit. And the eyes, the shapes, although they were the eyes and shapes of cats, sometimes changed elusively, and became the wicked eyes and the sinuous, writhing shapes of women. Always the ring was incomplete, and always I retreated in the only direction by which retreat was possible. I retreated from those cat-things.

In this fashion I came at last to the shaft, and there I saw the tools which I had left at the end of my day's toil.

Looking around me, I saw also, with such a pang of horror as I cannot hope to convey to you, that the ring of green eyes was now unbroken about me.

And it was closing in.

Nameless feline creatures were crowding silently to the edge of the pit, some preparing to spring down upon me where I stood. A voice seemed to speak in my brain; it spoke of capitulation, telling me to accept defeat lest, resisting, my fate be the fate of Condor.

Peals of shrill laughter rose upon the silence. The laughter was mine.

Filling the night with this hideous, hysterical merriment, I was working feverishly with pick and with shovel filling in the shaft.

The end? The end is that I awoke, in the morning, lying, not on my bed, but outside on the plateau, my hands torn and bleeding and every muscle in my body throbbing agonizingly. Remembering my dream—for even in that moment of awakening I thought I had dreamed—I staggered across to the valley of the excavation.

Condor's shaft was reclosed to the top.

10

If Egypt has the distinction of being the most mysterious nation of the Old World, the regions of Mexico and Peru must qualify for this designation in the New World. The Americas were, of course, peopled long before the arrival of Columbus, and Mexico and Peru particularly were the centers of high civilizations with exalted rulers and magnificent cities. The origins of these people are still subject to much argument, but the most widely held viewpoint is that the whole of the pre-Columbian population was descended from hunting people who had crossed from Asia into Alaska more than twelve thousand years ago. (Another intriguing theory attributes the development to a series of voyagers of Sumerian, Phoenician and Mycenaean origin, who settled in various parts of the continent and thereby evolved the different cultures and achievements found by explorers.) It was Hernando Cortes in the sixteenth century who first opened up the world's vision of this new land, and he and his soldiers were quite unprepared, not to say amazed, by what they saw. As his companion Bernard Diaz recorded in *The Conquest of New Spain:* "We were staggered and said it was like the enchantments they tell of in the legend of Amadis on account of the great towns and cities, and the buildings arising from the water, and all built of masonry." Far from the primitive savages they had expected to find, the Conquistadors met with a civilization not unlike the one they had left behind in Renaissance Europe. Contact with these people was to show that they were, in fact, the descendants of still more advanced civilizations which had probably flourished—and enjoyed similar standards—as the Egyptians when they had their great epoch of achievement. Unfortunately, the ravaging of the people by the Spaniards, and the pillaging of so much that was rare and precious, has made conjectures which might be advanced about links between the earliest civilizations of mankind—separated as they were by the wide gulf of the Atlantic—now almost impossible to prove. Nevertheless, mysteries by the dozen have developed, a fascinating puzzle for the historian and archaeologist and a challenge to the story writer. One particular man who has chosen this area of the world as his theme and utilized its past and present in a series of superb books and stories, is almost as mysterious as the subject itself. He is *B. Traven* (1890–   ), an American author who has lived in almost total seclusion in Mexico for nearly half a century. Little is known of the man other than his work, although one writer, Charles Miller, believes his real name is Berick Traven Torsvan, and that he was born in poverty in Chicago. Miller maintains that Traven had an adventurous youth mainly spent at sea, before settling in the state of Tamaulipas in Mexico and making the oppressed Indians who lived there one of his main literary topics. What is indisputable is that since 1920 he has gripped the reading public with novels like *The Death Ship* (1925), *The Treasure of Sierra Madre* (1926) and *March to the Monteria* (1934), not to mention several collections of short stories, the latest of which was published in 1966, *Collected Stories of B. Traven,* which contained "A New God Was Born." Understandably, legends about this strange man have proliferated. Some have maintained that no such person exists—Traven being merely the pen name for a group of writers —while among the wilder rumors was one that he was actually the President of Mexico, Lopez Mateos. (President Mateos, in fact, had to call a special press conference to dispel this rumor, so persistent did it become at one time!) Whatever the truth, Traven refuses to be drawn into comment, and has now assuredly become Mexico's most famous, if least known, storyteller. Here, drawing on the nation's history, he retells the story of the strange monument inspired by Cortes which, without one crucial piece of evidence, "would have remained one of the greatest mysteries of mankind," to quote the author himself.

A NEW GOD WAS BORN
B. Traven

A few years after Hernando Cortes had conquered Mexico, he formed an expedition with the idea of discovering a seaway from the Atlantic to the Pacific. For in that period of history the Americas were believed to be huge islands and not one continental land mass extending from the Arctic to the Antarctic.

Cortes' expedition marched south with the hope of coming upon a strait connecting the two great oceans. The farther south they marched the more difficult became their situation, and they were close to complete exhaustion when they arrived at the great Lake of Peten, situated in what is today the Republic of Guatemala.

On the islands of that lake and along the shores the expedition found many villages inhabited by Indians of the most hospitable and peaceful nature. They were the first human beings Cortes had met for weeks on his arduous march through the immense jungle, which stretched out for hundreds of miles to the west and to the east of the mighty Usumacinta River.

After its tedious march through tropical areas, where the trail had to be hacked out by Indian auxiliaries brought from Tlaxcala, the Cortes army was suffering from hunger and from all kinds of fevers and jungle diseases. The soldiers' bodies were covered with infected wounds caused by bites and stings of reptiles and insects. The expedition was considered even by its most optimistic officers to be a total loss. In its helpless condition, had it not come upon the hospitable natives of Peten, the so gloriously initiated enterprise would have ended in a huge disaster with no hope for any member of it ever to return to Mexico. Those Indians, had they been a warlike tribe, could have cornered and massacred the whole Cortes army.

(The expedition, by the way, was looked upon as a complete failure when it returned. It added little knowledge to what was known already. Its only achievement was its proof that, as far as it had ventured, there was no navigable strait between the Atlantic and the Pacific.)

The natives of Peten fed Cortes' men as they hadn't been fed since leaving the last populated region in Mexico many weeks before. They cured the sick and wounded, and they gave Cortes plenty of provisions so that the army could march without fear of hunger for the next few weeks.

In their fervor to please their uninvited guests even more and make them happier still, the Indian natives cheerfully agreed to be baptized by the visiting army. And so it was that all of them became good Christians.

The monks who accompanied the expedition saw to it that everything was done properly, according to the established rules. The peaceful natives appeared to have no objection to the destruction of their gods and images, to the cleansing of the Indian temples and the installing of new images brought by the strangers—images of the Holy Virgin, of Santiago, of San Antonio, and half a dozen more.

Because the monks hadn't time enough to baptize each native individually, they used another method. The baptismal ceremony was turned into a great fiesta, and all the natives of that region were directed to meet on a vast plain where their foreign guests would offer them a show such as they had never before witnessed.

They came, a thousand or so of them. They were asked to kneel down. Then the monks, with hands raised up as if in prayer, bestowed upon them the benediction and declared them Christians, good and true Catholics, who must obey their superiors in Rome.

Those kneeling near the monks, who had been touched personally upon their heads, were ordered to confer that touch upon any man or woman they were to meet.

Now the real show commenced. And what a show! Bugles and trumpets blared. Cannons and muskets were fired. Horsemen performed tournament feats, as knights used to do centuries ago.

These natives of Peten had never seen or heard cannons fired or trumpets sounded. Nor had they ever seen a horse before. So it was only natural that they believed every rider to be physically united to the steed he straddled. The fiesta was an awesome display of powers and happenings strange to the Indians. Of course they were confused. They saw the whole expedition army on their knees singing the *Te Deum,* the monks chanting and performing strange rites, the trumpets and bugles raised up and blaring, cannons and muskets spitting fire and thundering, and horsemen jousting and riding wildly upon the plain.

That whole show was such that even today anywhere on earth it would attract huge crowds and satisfy their craving for excitement. The natives received an impression which would live forever in their memories.

It was part of the clever policy of the conquistadores to impress natives with their power and make them believe that the white men of the expedition were gods of a kind. It was for that reason that it had been possible for such a ridiculously small number of Spanish soldiers to march on and on, leaving their rear unprotected, because the Indians whom they met on the way would never dare to raise arms against such divine beings.

Fortunately, those peaceful natives of Peten owned no jewelry of gold or silver, possessions which would have made the Spaniards believe the natives knew of gold or silver mines. To discover such mines and deposits had been the second reason—and for most members the first and only reason—that this costly expedition was undertaken. Nor did the Indians have pearls or precious stones. Not even the surrounding land was tempting to the Spaniards, who could lay their hands on better, more fertile properties in Mexico. The lake was the principal source of native income, an income which couldn't be earned just by loafing on the shore and looking dreamily across the water.

It was natural for Cortes to leave that unfertile area as soon as his army was well and on its feet again.

For all the services the Spaniards had received from the natives they paid nothing. Cortes considered them well rewarded in that their sins (of whose existence the Indians formerly had known nothing) had been cleansed by the monks and all obstacles to their admission into heaven had been cleared away. In fact, Cortes left these people in a state of poverty such as they hadn't known for generations. He took full advantage of the Indians' natural generosity. All their stock of fruit, dried fish, dried meat, salt, medicinal herbs and roots, corn, chili, and cocoa beans (which served them for money) was carried off by the army for provisions.

On the day of his departure, however, Cortes decided to show the natives of Peten his gratitude by leaving them a royal gift. He presented them with a horse—which, as he well knew, would be accepted by them as the most precious payment they might have hoped to receive. The horse was of no further use to Cortes, since one leg was so badly injured and swollen that the poor animal would only have been a burden to the soldiers if taken on the return march. So it is a fact that this single sign of gratitude and generosity on the part of Cortes was given exclusively in his own interest.

The natives received the horse with all the excitement which such a kingly gift merited. Then the strange visitors disappeared as mysteriously as they had arrived. Had it not been for the horse they now possessed, and the vanished stock of food and supplies they no longer possessed, the peaceful hosts might have believed the whole adventure was a sort of mass hallucination.

Cortes had left a horse with the natives. What he, that mean trader, hadn't left with them was instructions on how to take care of that strange animal.

Now, every Indian the Spaniards met in peace or in battle since their arrival in America had always professed more fear of horses and horsemen than of cannons and muskets. The Spaniards were soon exploiting this fear and took the utmost care never to let Indians go near the horses in camp or at rest sites. Thus, Indians never got a chance to see horses fed. The Spaniards even spread the story that horses and horsemen were invulnerable. In those days horses and riders were heavily armored when in battle, and the Indians, with their primitive arms, couldn't kill or wound the horses or their riders. For this reason the Indians came to believe horses were war gods of a kind they could never defeat. In the siege of Mexico City, however, this belief was badly shaken when Indians managed to kill several horses and their riders too.

The natives of Peten now had a horse. Word spread, and thousands came to see with their own eyes that strange creature the bearded white men had left behind in payment for services received. Because the exotic animal seemed related not only to the white men but also to the fire and thunder of cannons and muskets, the natives looked at the horse in constant awe. Soon they declared it a god.

They brought it the most beautiful flowers and the choicest fruit for gifts, just as they had brought offerings of flowers and fruit to their gods in the temples. The horse sniffed at the flowers in hopes of finding some fodder among them, for it had become very hungry since the conquerors' army had left.

The Indians noted this gesture of the horse and believed that the animal had graciously accepted the offering. Yet, after sniffing the flowers, it turned around and stared longingly across the plain, where in the near distance a huge patch of the finest grass and fields rich with young green corn could be seen. But to these riches the horse couldn't go because it was firmly tied to a big tree.

The natives grew very sad, thinking they had offended this divine creature who refused to accept the flowers and fruit and turned its head aside in open disgust.

The oldest medicine man of the tribe was now sent for. He came, looked the horse over, and said: "You stupid tribesmen, can't you see that this godly being is very sick? Its leg is terribly wounded. See, it has a horrible looking lump there. Treat its ailments and it will be well again in no time, and then it will bless our lake, our fields, and our hunts."

It was then a custom with Indians, as it still is today in remote regions, to feed a sick person only wild turkey, in the belief, based on ages of observation, that the meat of wild turkey has highly curative properties.

The horse's leg was doctored with mashed herbs and it was bandaged. This done, heaps of roast turkey, spiced with the finest aromatic vegetables, were arranged on large native jícara trays, decorated with flowers and fruit, and placed before the starving horse.

The poor animal, plainly at a loss as to how it was possible for human beings to be so utterly ignorant of what a horse likes to eat, began to trample and shy about, trying harder and still harder to free itself from the rope so that it might reach the green pasture from where a light breeze brought the sweetest of odors to its quivering nostrils.

With every hour the horse grew more restless, started to dance about and neigh unceasingly until it tired itself out. Again the medicine man was called. Said he: "Well, you boneheads, don't you see what he needs?"

The natives understood. A beautiful young maiden was chosen, adorned, and offered to the horse. The horse, though, had no interest in this sacrifice either, and didn't even sniff at such a rare gift.

The poor natives by now couldn't think of anything to do to make the horse happy. It dawned on them that this divine creature was sinking fast, and their gloom turned to terror.

Here was a situation where a horse might have led a life so sweet, so quiet, and so happy, a life such as no horse had ever enjoyed since the time horses were found useful to man. Since the natives had no domesticated animals except a species of dog, all the rich pastures in the whole region would have been at the disposal of that horse, to be shared only by an occasional antelope. But ill luck had it that this horse with the heavenly prospects around it was destined to perish by starvation amidst plenty.

There was no remedy for these misunderstandings between the horse and the Indians. The horse finally could do nothing but lie down and die miserably, with a last hopeless glance of its bursting eyes upon that huge crowd of humans, among whom there was not one individual with horse sense.

Horror and consternation seized the natives when they found the horse stiff and cold and dead. Superstitious as they were, they naturally feared the revenge of that godly being.

What better could they do to protect themselves against the wrath of the foreign gods than to bestow upon the dead horse all the honors which a deity had a right to expect from frightened men?

With great ceremony, the horse was buried, and on top of its resting place a temple was built.

Ninety-three years later, in the year of Our Lord 1618, two monks of the Franciscan order came to Lake Peten carrying the gospel to the natives living there. Since Hernando Cortes had left the region no white man had visited Peten.

The two monks entered a temple with the intention of dethroning heathen gods and setting up in their place the image of the Holy Virgin.

Inside the temple their sight fell upon a huge sculpture in stone, very crudely shaped. No matter which way they looked at it, there wasn't the slightest doubt that it was meant to be a horse. In the opinion of those monks the Indian artist had followed an inexplicable whim in making one of the horse's legs imperfect, exposing an ugly protuberance. Yet, from an artistic point of view, that imperfect horse leg was well done.

The monks had seen, heard, and read about very strange gods, but never had they expected to find a horse elevated to the highest worship, as this one was by the Indians of Lake Peten. That piece of sculpture was not only the natives' highest and most powerful creature god, but it was also their god of thunder and lightning, in whose honor, every year on a certain day, great celebrations took place.

The greatest surprise the monks received in their search of the temple, however, was a wooden cross so weather-beaten and decayed that they believed it to be easily a thousand years old. It was standing behind the stone horse and, according to the native folk tales, a white man with a long beard had either brought the cross or made it from a mahogany tree there in the area.

The monks' report on this strange find reached Spain and the rest of Europe and caused immense excitement among scientists and historians. The most fantastic speculations arose to explain the origin of that cross in such strange connection with the stone image of a horse, on a continent where, to the best knowledge of scholars, no horses had existed and no Indians would know anything of the shape or appearance of horses.

Just as speculations and theories had reached the stage where learned men seriously began to maintain that one of the apostles had come in person to the Americas during the first century, a certain registrar to the crown who was studying the archives of former Spanish kings stumbled upon a short note in one of the letters which Hernando Cortes had written to his sovereign, Emperor Charles the Fifth.

This note, relating the episodes of the so-called Hibneras Expedition, cleared up the event of the horse-god and the cross. Without the note, it would have remained one of the greatest mysteries of mankind.

VI

LEGENDARY CONTINENTS

***

The Lost Continent
By Geoffrey Household

An Offering to the Moon
By Clark Ashton Smith

11

There is probably no more famous or exotic mystery than that of Atlantis, the ancient civilization which is believed to have sunk beneath the waves of the Atlantic. The tradition has been discussed in at least two thousand books and articles, not to mention scores of novels and short stories, and has been an obsession with people from all walks of life for hundreds of years. Stories of the legendary continent go back beyond the recorded history of man, and according to its first chronicler, the Greek philosopher Plato, have their origins in the year 10,000 B.C. Plato tells us, in his dialogue "Timaeus," that it was a Utopian land, inhabited by wise and beautiful people, whose society and technology were far in advance of any known. In his work, he describes the end of this great nation thus: "But there occurred violent earthquakes and floods, and in a single day and night of misfortune all your warlike men in a body sank into the earth, and the island of Atlantis in like manner disappeared in the depths of the sea." Such was the first description of Atlantis, and in the ensuing centuries the legend was enlarged, embellished and enriched with a whole mythology of gods and heroes, until serious doubt about there being any truth in the stories at all was widely voiced. In the face of this there has been much scientific inquiry in recent times, and while sites have been proposed in places as widely separated as the North Atlantic Ocean, Iceland, the British Isles, France, South Africa, Brazil and the West Indies, there is now a general consensus which believes it *did* exist and most probably somewhere off the coast of southwest Spain. Much credit for first assembling the most relevant data from generations of conjecture must go to the American scholar and historian Ignatius Donnelly, whose *Atlantis: The Antediluvian World* (1882) is still the major textbook for all who are interested in the mystery. Donnelly went to great lengths to catalogue the natural disasters which might have caused the end of the continent, and attempted to outline the kind of civilization the Atlanteans might have created in the light of what was happening in other early empires such as those of the Greeks and Egyptians. A year after publication of the book, the terrible earthquake on the island of Krakatoa, which virtually destroyed the land mass and wiped out forty thousand people, lent weight to the theory that Atlantis might also have been sited on an earthquake which similarly erupted causing vast destruction. Over the years, in fact, the mystery as to what might have caused the end of Atlantis has become almost as absorbing a topic as the existence of the continent itself, and speculation has run the gamut from a flood or deluge to self-destruction through internal strife, and from the devastation of the land by a comet to the explosion of some device of war many centuries ahead of its time. (It is also interesting to note that during the great age of exploration some scholars identified Atlantis with America, even though the land was supposed to have sunk!) Writers of fiction, particularly, have found it a theme for endless conjecture, and one

The location of Atlantis as proposed by Ignatius Donnelly in his Atlantis: The Antediluvian World (*1882*).

can dip as deeply into classical literature as Sir Francis Bacon's *The New Atlantis* or reach for the modern occult authority Dennis Wheatley's *They Found Atlantis,* for examples of this. Short-story writers, too, have had their theories, and there are few more convincing interpretations of the legend, I think, than "The Lost Continent" by *Geoffrey Household* (1903–   ), which appeared in 1964 in *The Saturday Evening Post.* The distinguished author of "Rogue Male" (1939), Household has lived and worked in a little coastal village near Malaga in southern Spain for many years, and consequently gained an intimate knowledge of the local legends about Atlantis—from a point not all that far from the alleged site. From this he has distilled a tale sparkling with invention and its own very special answer to the great riddle.

THE LOST CONTINENT
Geoffrey Household

Atlantis? It's of more interest to poets and mystics than to archaeologists. The lost continent is only a fable. We have no proof; you're looking at the best there is. No, not me. In the case behind my desk.

A puma, you think? Have you just been to the zoo? Well, then, why do you call it a puma rather than a lion or a leopard? Yes, you're quite right. One could swear it was dug up in Peru or Ecuador. But an ivory puma is impossible. No pumas in the Old World. No elephants in the New World.

I'll tell you its history, though I warn you it is very unsatisfactory. It has no ending. You go out where you came in. You'll just say to hell with me and Jim Hawkes and all those visionary swordsmen who conquered the Americas and carefully destroyed or displaced every blessed thing they ought to have preserved for us.

But like all good stories it is really that of a man's character—a grubby little man with bad teeth and no education, who cared as little for money and as much for truth as any dedicated scholar rediscovering the past for the wages of a manual worker.

At first Jim Hawkes was not allowed in when he turned up at the side door of the museum and asked to see me. They thought he had samples in his little bag. That was what he looked like—a salesman peddling cheap pens on commission. Yet there was something honest and earthy about him which was hard to distrust. He was a real Cockney too—with the Londoner's genius for summing up doormen and minor officials and getting his own way in spite of them.

While he remembered to be on his best behaviour he addressed me as "sir." When he got excited he called me "guv'nor." At that first interview he sensibly gave a thumbnail sketch of his background before coming to business, but I can't distinguish between what he said then and all I learned about him later. It's enough that he had passed twenty years of peace and war as steward on a tramp steamer, married a Portuguese wife and settled down on her little farm in the Azores. He was one of those Englishmen who consciously loathe industrial civilization. Most of them haven't the enterprise to get out until they are tied to it. But Jim Hawkes knew an opportunity when he saw one. And the sea had already accustomed him to exile.

Introductions over, he asked me if I believed in Atlantis. He used the right word. It's a matter of belief, not scholarship. I told him gently that we believed in nothing without proof.

"Here it is," he said.

He opened his bag, scattering straw all over the room, and put that ivory puma on my desk.

It was like nothing I had ever seen. So far as technique and material went it might have been a superb Persian ivory of the sixth or fifth century B.C., possibly brought to the Azores by the Carthaginians. But the style was wrong. Too realistic.

I remember thinking it odd that such a marvelous craftsman at carving ivory in the round had been unable to reproduce the strength and majesty of the lion. I know lions. In art, that is. Remind me to give you a copy of my monograph, *Treatment of the Conventional Mane*.

"It's not a lion," Jim Hawkes said. "I think it's a puma."

I made no comment. I took him across to the American Section and put his ivory alongside our two pre-Inca pumas—one in stone and one in pottery. Jim Hawkes had a case.

When we were sitting down again in my office I asked him how he had got hold of such a curiosity, rather suspecting that he would tell me some unbelievable yarn to cover up the fact that he hadn't any right to it. But, no. He was eager, falling over himself to invite questions. That was why he had come.

He told me that on the island of Graciosa he had discovered a shallow cave with its entrance nearly hidden beneath subtropical vegetation. The floor—part earth, part fine, dry dust—was completely undisturbed. On a rock ledge at the back of the cave was standing the ivory puma.

He thought at first that it was a child's toy. For all I know, it may have been—though an ivory as large as a half-grown kitten argues a very high level of civilization in the nursery. Then he realized that it did not belong to our day at all, and his mind at once jumped to Atlantis.

But it would be wrong to think of him as just one of those lost-continent-cum-flying-saucer sort of cranks. His hobby—and I can't think of a better for anyone living in the Azores—was Atlantis. He knew all the usual arguments for and against. Like so many seamen he was a great reader, though he had left school at the age of twelve. And he had a passion for facts. I tell you; he saw the difference between fact and conjecture much more clearly than some of my colleagues.

"What I want, Mr. Penkivel, sir," he said, "is to 'ave that cave excavated proper like. Not treasure 'unting! Every cupful of soil sifted by them as knows what's what. And I don't want nothink out of it for meself—and I'll pay the labor."

I asked him why me. Simple. He had turned up at the museum and demanded the bloke who knew most about ivories. Just possibly I am. But I also happened to be the bloke whom the porter was most annoyed with at the moment.

Now I really must repeat that there is no conclusive evidence for the existence of Atlantis. But as well as a so-called expert in ancient art, I am also a Cornishman. Part of us always dips into the ocean with the sun. So when I had taken Jim out to lunch next day and again convinced myself that he was dead straight, I decided I might as well spend the six weeks' holiday, which was coming to me, in running a trial trench through that cave. I did not tell my colleagues what I intended. They would have thought I needed a holiday even more than I really did.

Like all islanders Jim knew how to travel cheaply. When he returned to the Azores on a Portuguese cargo boat, I went with him—feeling self-consciously precious and wondering to what sort of society I had condemned myself.

I needn't have worried. Jim's background was in keeping with the man—simple and satisfying. He had a white, single-storied, peasant house, three acres of wheat and pasture and some terraces of fruit and vine, which wandered up the hillside. It was one of the highest farms on Graciosa, blazing with sun or hidden under blowing mist half a dozen times a day and looking out over a full semicircle of empty, secretive Atlantic.

All this he had married, together with *Senhora* Hawkes. It was certainly a love match, though it wouldn't have been possible without her inheritance. Maria Hawkes was a peasant poppet, with the face of an angel and the body of Humpty Dumpty. She, too, had got a bargain by her marriage. Her energetic little ex-steward, always wanting to know why, had doubled the value of her land. They had as yet no children. That allowed Jim his luxury of Atlantis. His excuse for the journey to London had been a visit to his brother, but the *senhora* knew as well as I did that his true motive was to explain the ivory.

His cave was on a steep, overgrown hillside, high above their land. The entrance was a horizontal cleft under an overhang of rock, so that it could be seen only by a man climbing up from below, and even then he might not spot it through the bushes for what it was. Beyond the cleft was a roomy, low-roofed chamber which ran back into the hill for seventy feet, narrowing all the way, until the passage ended at a fallen boulder.

It was just the sort of place to have sheltered early man. But the islands were uninhabited when the Portuguese discovered them; so I could not expect to find traces of anything larger than a rabbit. If I did, the historians and geographers would have a good deal of rewriting to do. That was a fascinating thought for a holiday, let alone the fact that I might come across another inexplicable ivory.

I don't normally dig; it's my job to give my opinion of what others have dug. But the cave would have been easy even for an amateur. Right inside, where Jim had made his find, there was only a layer of dust over the bedrock. We sifted all of this. It was quite sterile. I could trust him absolutely with the sieve. When I tell you that he managed to spot a rat's tooth you can imagine how keen he was.

Over the rock at the entrance were eight feet of soil, shallowing rapidly, of course, as one got farther into the cave. Through this we drove our trench with the help of two laborers whom Jim had hired. Meanwhile Maria Hawkes brought up enormous meals of fish and wine on a donkey and loaded the panniers with earth from our dig to put on her pineapples. She couldn't understand our professionally slow, patient progress. But if that was how her man wished to amuse himself she did not complain. Other wives had to put up with drink or gambling.

For the first week I was as happy as any fellow let out of an office can be. At the end of the second week I began to get bored. So did the onlookers, who left us for good. We found not a trace of man. The authorities are always right. A pity—except when I am the authority myself.

The only excitement came when one of our cross trenches hit charcoal only two feet above the bedrock. Jim Hawkes was bursting with expectancy and quite silent. He saw what it could mean. So did the laborers. But I had to tell them there was no evidence of a human hearth; it was undoubtedly blown debris from a forest fire. I think I shall go out and look at it again.

Jim wouldn't let me pay for anything, and I knew he could not afford to go on. The farm was being neglected; ready money was short after his trip to London; and dear Maria Hawkes had added to the expense by considering it her duty to feed the spectators as well as us. At the end of the third week I persuaded Jim to give up and dismiss the laborers. I felt like—well, like a doctor telling him he must lose his leg. But it had become quite obvious that excavation was not going to tell us anything of the ivory puma.

When the first idle day was over—idle for me—I scrambled up to the cave and, of course, found Jim already there. He had been up before dawn and hoeing ever since, but now he was chipping away with a cold chisel at the boulder which blocked the end of the passage.

"Know anything about explosives, guv'?" he asked.

I said I did. Not a very likely trade for an antiquarian. But in the war I was a sapper.

"Then 'ow about it? Think we'd be muckin' up the evidence?"

Yes. That was what he said. He had the instincts of a born archaeologist.

I told him I was sure there was no evidence to muck up, but that the boulder would take some smashing. It had fallen from the roof recently. Say, two or three hundred years ago. To judge by the narrowing of the cave walls, I decided nothing much could be behind it, except a cleft or vent. That had to be there, for an occasional draft or warmish air could be felt at floor level. The air had removed my last, faint doubt of Jim's story. It accounted for the preservation of the ivory—otherwise rather unlikely in the moist climate of the Azores.

There was a wide crack down the middle of the boulder and a useful cavity below it. Doubtfully I told Jim my requirements. They didn't bother him. He spoke very serviceable Portuguese and was popular everywhere. He was back the next evening with a keg of old-fashioned gunpowder—excellent stuff for shifting rock—from the island's general stores, this time on my bill, and had got fuse and detonators free from the whalers.

He did not mention what we were doing, even to Maria—most women are inclined to be excitable in the presence of explosives—so we had complete privacy. I made a good job of it, although my main length of fuse turned out to be a lot faster than the sample I had cut. I'm not sure whether I shot out of that cave together with the blast or just before it.

When the smoke had cleared Jim and I opened up the passage. Fortunately, as it turned out, the whole force of the explosion had been directed outward, showering debris onto our working floor, cracking the rock, but disturbing nothing beyond it. We had still a couple of hours of work with pick and crowbar before we could reduce it to rubble and climb over.

To my surprise the cave had done all the narrowing it was going to do and continued as a very rough v-shaped passage. I am not enough of a geologist to be sure of its origin. A combination of earthquake and steam pressure, I think.

Keeping the beams of our flashlights as much on the untrustworthy roof as on the ground, we cautiously followed the tunnel until it ended at an appalling abyss in the volcanic rock. That was where the warm air came from. A steam-heated hell fed by the tricklings-in at sea level or below. We threw down boulders and heard not the faintest sound. The gap was too wide to jump but fairly easy to bridge.

While I was wondering if I could ever pluck up enough courage to cross the homemade bridge which Jim—I knew it—was going to insist on constructing, he gave a shout. He was lying on his stomach examining from a respectful distance the sheer edge of that terrifying drop. He pointed to what he had found. Two shallow grooves for the beams of a bridge had been chiseled out of the rock. Our flashlights showed two corresponding grooves on the opposite side of the chasm.

I have never been nearer to believing in a drowned continent. Who wouldn't in a place like that? I had quite unjustifiable visions of the very last of the inhabitants clinging to a barren peak which later became the green island of Graciosa and using the cave as their temple or treasure house. Nothing impossible about the rock cutting. Atlanteans, if they existed, presumably had chisels of bronze or obsidian.

Oh, yes, I thought of that! I took some scrapings and dust home in an envelope. No trace of bronze or any metal at all. Not conclusive, but in favor of steel. Particles so tiny as those from a steel chisel would have been oxidized and blown away on a breath. The microscope did show a glassy dust like a form of obsidian, but even my Cornish blood refuses to build on that. A thousand to one that it was a natural component of the rock.

Farm work went overboard again. Serious, this time. There was a sudden squall from the south which laid the heavy, overripe wheat. Maria wept, but Jim damned the weather and continued to square the ends of two twenty-foot lengths of pine sapling with a ship-builder's adz so that they would fit the channels. On to these spars we nailed planks from the bottom of an old farm cart. The donkey was busy all day hauling timber up the slope.

By the next evening our bridge was ready. I don't believe we would ever have thrown it across the gap if not for Maria. She had a marvelous head for heights and just laughed at her husband, whose distaste for this beastly brink of nothingness was just as great as mine. But he was far more determined.

The roof of the passage was not high enough for us to stand the spars of the bridge in the grooves and lower the far end by ropes. So we mounted the near end on a pair of wheels and kept up the far end at an angle of forty-five degrees by pulling on a rope. Maria pushed this contraption forward, or acted as brake if we raised it too high. When we finally dropped the bridge into position, axle and wheels went over the edge. We never heard a sound after the first bounce.

Maria greeted the accident with a merry laugh. She was perfectly happy standing a foot from the edge—and after all, the old wheels weren't worth anything. She strolled about on the bridge with plump unconcern. Jim and I went over it on our hands and knees.

After a few yards the passage opened out into an irregular rock chamber too large for the beams of our flashlights to explore. The *senhora,* becoming the weaker sex again, remained at the entrance with a flashlight of her own. She didn't like that place at all.

Working our way round the walls, we had just decided that this was the end of the cave with no way out of it, when Maria let out a piercing scream. She had sat down with her back against the rock and a pool of light in front of her to keep off the bogeys. She stretched out her left hand to make herself more comfortable and placed it on the face of a corpse.

We rushed across to her. The dead man was a Spaniard or Portuguese of the early sixteenth century. Body, clothes and weapons were well preserved in the still, dry air. He was on his back, with arms crossed on his chest. He knew he had had it and laid himself down to die with dignity, trusting in the mercy of God. And there in the dust, undisturbed since his last unsteady steps, were the marks of his loose boots.

He had taken a sword or dagger thrust low down on the side of the throat. I should not have noticed the perforation of the mummified skin if the linen of his shirt had not been dark with dried blood.

It wasn't the expert, the scholar trained to facts and nothing but facts, who saw the vital bearing of a four-hundred-year-old murder on the problem of the ivory puma. It was Jim, of course—Jim with his passion for never destroying the record of the past through avoidable carelessness.

"We can find aht what 'appened, Mr. Penkivel, guv'," he said. "Spend a bit of time on it and we don't 'ave to be Sherlock 'Olmeses."

He was right. The pointed, rather feminine tracks, though the edges were blurred, were utterly unlike our own and told the story. Two men had crossed the chasm. Side by side they walked to the far right-hand corner of the cave. There the dust was thoroughly trampled and disturbed as if they had been removing something which they carried away. On their way back to the bridge the man walking a little behind had stabbed the other.

The murderer's footprints had been overlaid by ours, and were muddled anyway; but a set of clean impressions which we found pointing to the gap seemed unexpectedly deep and firm. My astonishing collaborator was not content with a "seemed." He measured the depth of the heel prints. No doubt about it at all. The murderer when he left the inner cave was weighed down by his comrade's burden as well as his own.

The movements of the other were equally clear. When he fell forward he left impressions of his knees and body. About where his neck would have been, a patch of dust was caked by blood. Badly wounded or dying, he had then risen to his feet, staggered to where Maria nearly sat on him and crossed his hands on his breast.

You see why. Because the trusted companion who had stabbed him from behind made doubly sure of him by destroying the bridge. So he lay down to wait for the end. No weeping and cursing on the edge of that uncrossable abyss for him. His simple act made me understand the contemporaries of Cortes and Pizarro as no books could. Probably he had the sense to see that the sword had been merciful, that he hadn't long to live. Even so I think that if the corpse had been mine it would have been found on the brink of the chasm with arms out-stretched and mouth open.

I could now make a plausible guess at how the ivory puma came to be in the outer cave. The murderer, repacking his loot, had got rid of it as an object of no value and inconvenient bulk. But it pleased him. He was a man of the Renaissance. I like to think of him as an Italian. So he stood it on the rock ledge instead of just throwing it away.

We found no concrete evidence of what the valuables had been. Maria with her quick fingers helped us to sift the dust. Nothing. Not even a spilt coin. But there was no need to drag in Atlantis. Boxes of gold and silver must often have gone astray in those days when the treasure fleets called at the Azores on their homeward voyage from the Spanish Main. The two adventurers, I suggested, could have been removing from the cave a hoard of stolen loot.

Jim did not deny it. He didn't stick to his lost continent. He merely pointed out, as modestly as the more courteous type of Oxford don, that I was ignoring inconvenient facts without explaining them.

"'Ow about the footprints of the blokes what put it there?" he asked.

I hadn't thought of that. Obviously the prints of the blokes who put it there—whatever "it" was—were not visible at the time of the murder or they would be visible still. So in the sixteenth century they had already been obliterated by slow time. In that case the treasure had been put in the cave long before the Azores were discovered.

By now I was unconsciously treating Jim as an authority. I suspect that my voice echoed through the darkness in a genuine academic falsetto as I tried to answer his question by complicated theories involving drafts of air cut off by the fallen boulder. But I had to admit that the case for Atlantis could not be finally dismissed.

You would have thought he'd have jumped at it and driven home another point, too—that the chiseled footings we had found suggested a permanent bridge, not the casual construction which would have been thrown across the abyss by two fearless conquistadors hiding or seeking a hoard of loot.

Jim stuck to the evidence, however, and nothing but the evidence. He squatted on the floor sucking his teeth—and then he blew his own beloved Atlantis sky high.

"Them two was puttin' somethink in," he said, "not takin' it aht!"

And he fiddled around some more in the marks of the heels with flashlight and foot ruler.

He was on to the truth. The tracks which led from the entrance to the disturbed corner were deeper than the tracks which led back to the site of the murder. So there it was. The two men *were* putting something in. They did not find a treasure in the inner cave at all. They carried it in across their bridge and dumped it.

So far, so good—but if that was what really happened, the murderer had to return from his victim to the corner in order to pick up the two loads and make off with them. And his tracks must still be there.

They were. Along the wall all the way. That's why we had missed them. Reconstruction was easy. Torch or candle had gone out in the struggle, so the murderer felt his way back to the treasure round the wall. Wounded man also had a pistol—a very fine one for its date—which may have influenced the cautious movements of the other.

"Not what you wanted, Jim," I said. "I'm sorry. But you're a lot better off."

"Fifty-fifty, Mr. Penkivel, sir," he answered sternly.

I knew he must have noticed it. There was nothing his eyes missed, though, of course, he could not know the value of the emerald set in the pommel of the dead man's sword. Nor could I in the beam of a flashlight. But it was worth a lot for its extraordinary size even if flawed, as it almost certainly had to be.

I turned his offer down flat. In proportion to his resources, Jim had contributed to an archaeological expedition more than any millionaire's fund ever dreamed of. He was entitled to the finds, if any.

And then that amazing man reflected doubtfully, "Would yer say we 'ad the right to take it aht, guv'? We're 'ere for knowledge, not treasure 'unting."

I assured him that there were plenty of sixteenth-century swords in the world and that this was of no special value except for the emerald set roughly and strongly into the hilt. Safest place to keep it, I suppose.

Well, yes, I must admit it was a superb weapon. But I wanted Jim to have the emerald; and I didn't know enough about the Portuguese law of treasure trove to be sure that if he produced sword and emerald as they were he would be allowed the value. Take it from me—state museums don't like paying out when they can get something for nothing.

"O.K., guv'nor," he said. "Sell it for me when yer gets 'ome because I wouldn't know 'ow. And you 'ave the ivory puma for the museum."

Why isn't it on exhibition? I've told you. Because the blasted thing is impossible! It asks us to assume a lost culture with affinities to both Old World and New. Yes, naturally, I had it dated by the radiocarbon method. The very large elephant which supplied the ivory died not later than 2000 B.C.

Origin unknown. All we can say. Nothing surprising in that. Every great museum has some lovely thing in the basement waiting for the day when our successors will know enough to be able to label it.

There was nothing else in the cave worth recording. Jim and I decided to leave the body where it was and remove our bridge. Like a couple of idiots we talked of cementing a ring bolt into the roof so that we could support the far end while we pulled it back. Maria's feminine common sense soon dealt with that.

"But why not drop it down the hole?" she asked in her lilting Portuguese. "We can always make another."

It's the end of the story. Unsatisfactory, as I told you, except for Jim. I got him six thousand pounds for the emerald.

The chiseled bridge footings? Oh, those! Well, the romanticist—that's me—finds them so inexplicable that he is re-examining (please keep it to yourself!) the case for Atlantis. The cold-blooded authority —that's Jim—suggested that our two adventurers made a solid bridge because they intended at some later date to bring over a heavy mule train of stuff which they did not want to risk losing.

Possible, but odd. Remember they only entered the inner cavern once. They never explored it at all while they were building their bridge or afterward. They carried in their mysterious loot straightway and dumped it. Doesn't that look as if the bridge was already there?

And doesn't it suggest a sudden, hasty decision, not the behavior of men stacking away valuables in a carefully chosen hiding place? My own guess is that they found the cave and the treasure at the same time. They didn't know what to do with such wealth, how to ship it and dispose of it. So they agreed to carry it into the inner cave for the moment and perhaps break down the bridge.

Where did they find it? In the outer cave, of course, where it had remained untouched ever since it was abandoned by desperate refugees from the sunken cities of the plain on the lost continent of Atlantis.

12

The other great legendary continent which has attracted the attention of students and laymen is Mu, or The Motherland of Man, which, long before the end of Atlantis, had disappeared into the depths of the Pacific Ocean. According to the traditions, Mu had been the original "Garden of Eden," a huge land mass straddling the Equator and richly covered by exotic vegetation and fauna. It had flourished some fifty thousand years ago and supported a population of sixty-four million people who in their civilization and science were vastly superior to modern man. Like Atlantis and Ignatius Donnelly, Mu also found a great champion—in a nineteenth-century British Army officer and archaeologist, Colonel James Churchward. Having spent much of his life in the East, Churchward claimed to have learned the secrets of this lost civilization while on active service in India. He had become friendly with an old Hindu priest, or "rishi," who had told him of some mysterious slates or "Naacal Tablets" which had survived in secret from the days of the ancient continent and contained details of its inhabitants. After much persuasion, Churchward said he was allowed to see the slates, and the old man even helped him in translating them. "From these I discovered that this lost continent had extended from somewhere north of Hawaii to the south as far as the Fijis and Easter Island," Churchward wrote, "and was undoubtedly the original habitat of man. I learned that in this beautiful country there lived a people that over the years had colonized the earth, and that the land had been obliterated by terrific earthquakes and submersion twelve thousand years ago —vanishing in a vortex of fire and water. Also, I learned an original story of the creation of the world. It was on the continent of Mu that man first came into being." Based on his reading of these tablets, Churchward maintained that the peoples of Mu were divided into ten tribes, with all the distinctive races we know today represented, and were governed by a high priest, or Ra, whose monotheistic religion was later to be emulated by Christ. (The Colonel also claimed that the Lord's Prayer was based on certain sacred Mu texts, and that the last words Jesus spoke on the cross were in the language of Mu.) In the 1920s and '30s, Churchward published a string of books outlining and explaining the legend of the lost continent—and in so doing opened up the controversy which has con-

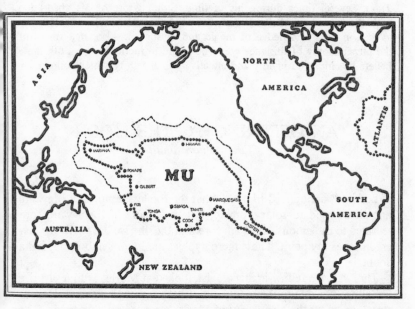

The site of the legendary continent of Mu in the Pacific Ocean, according to James Churchward.

tinued to this day. Some authorities doubted the very existence of the "Naacal Tablets" (one was never seen by anyone other than Churchward, and the second was said by archaeologists to be nothing more than an ancient work of art), while others questioned his interpretation of ancient Greek and Egyptian texts. They also found it hard to believe his contention that man had been created and not evolved biologically, and that the continent itself had been destroyed when "gas belts" in the earth's core had collapsed, leading to vast upheavals in the Pacific. Other archaeologists and students, however, were prepared to give credence to much that he propounded, and it was they who pointed out that there were many similarities in his story of Mu and the tales of Lemuria, the legendary "land bridge" between Africa and Asia, so beloved of biologists. Unlike Atlantis, Mu has not become the basis for a great many books and stories, nor has it attracted theorists in such large numbers as has its legendary companion in the Atlantic. It did appeal, though, to one of America's greatest fantasists, *Clark Ashton Smith* (1893–1961), whose tales of strange lands and even stranger peoples has placed him on a par with H. P. Lovecraft in many opinions. As a matter of fact, "An Offering to the Moon" appeared in 1953 in Lovecraft's favorite magazine, *Weird*

Tales. Several times during his lifetime, Smith wrote of his absorption with the legend of Mu and was convinced that its people were far advanced in their knowledge of magic and mysticism. Also, that traces of the physiognomy of this race could be found in modern man. Both these beliefs he employed vividly and effectively in the story which follows.

AN OFFERING TO THE MOON
Clark Ashton Smith

"I believe," announced Morley, "that the roofless temples of Mu were not all devoted to solar worship, but that many of them were consecrated to the moon. And I am sure that the one we have now discovered proves my point. These hieroglyphics are lunar symbols beyond a doubt."

Thorway, his fellow-archaeologist, looked at Morley with a surprise not altogether due to the boldly authoritative pronouncement. He was struck anew by the singularity of Morley's tones and expression. The dreamy, beardless, olive features, that seemed to repeat some aboriginal Aryan type, were transfigured by a look of ecstatic absorption. Thorway himself was not incapable of enthusiasm when the occasion seemed to warrant it; but this well-nigh religious ardor was beyond his comprehension. He wondered (not for the only time) if his companion's mentality were not a trifle . . . eccentric.

However, he mumbled a rejoinder that was deferential even though non-committal. Morley had not only financed the expedition, but had been paying a liberal stipend to Thorway for more than two years. So Thorway could afford to be respectful, even though he was a little tired of his employer's odd and unauthorized notions, and the interminable series of sojourns they had made on Melanesian isles. From the monstrous and primordial stone images of Easter Island to the truncated pyramidal columns of the Ladrones, they had visited all the far-strewn remains which are held to prove the former existence of a great continent in the mid-Pacific. Now, on one of the lesser Marquesas, hitherto unexplored, they had located the massive walls of a large temple-like edifice. As usual, it had been difficult to find, for such places were universally feared and shunned by the natives, who believed them haunted by the immemorial dead, and could not be hired to visit them or even to reveal their whereabouts. It was Morley who had stumbled upon the place, almost as if he were led by a subconscious instinct.

Truly, they had made a significant discovery, as even Thorway was compelled to admit. Except for a few of the colossal topmost stones, which had fallen or splintered away, the walls were in well-nigh perfect preservation. The place was surrounded by a tangle of palms and jackfruit and various tropical shrubs; but somehow none of them had taken root within the walls. Portions of a paved floor were still extant, amid centurial heaps of rubble. In the center was a huge, square block, rising four feet above the ground-level, which might well have served as an altar. It was carved with rude symbols which appeared to represent the moon in all its digits, and was curiously grooved across the top from the middle to one side with a trough that became deeper toward the edge. Like all other buildings of the sort, it was plain that the temple had never supported a roof.

"Yes, the symbols are undoubtedly lunar," admitted Thorway.

"Also," Morley went on, "I believe that rites of human sacrifice were performed in these temples. Oblations of blood were poured not only to the sun but to the moon."

"The idea is maintainable, of course," rejoined Thorway. "Human sacrifice was pretty widespread at a certain stage of evolution. It may well have been practiced by the people who built this edifice."

Morley did not perceive the dryness and formality of his confrere's assent. He was preoccupied with feelings and ideas, some of which could hardly have been the natural result of his investigations. Even as in visiting many others of the ancient remains, he had been troubled by a nervous agitation which was a compound of irresoluble awe and terror, of nameless, eager fascination and expectancy. Here, among these mighty walls, the feeling became stronger than it had been anywhere else; and it mounted to a pitch that was veritably distracting, and akin to the disturbed awareness that ushers in the illusions of delirium.

His idea, that the temple was a place of lunar worship, had seized him almost with the authority of an actual recollection, rather than a closely reasoned inference. Also, he was troubled by sensory impressions that bordered upon the hallucinative. Though the day was tropically warm, he was conscious of a strange chill that emanated from the walls—a chill as of bygone cycles; and it seemed to him that the narrow shadows wrought by a meridian sun were peopled with unseen faces. More than once, he was prompted to rub his eyes, for ghostly films of color, like flashes of yellow and purple garments, came and went in the most infinitesimal fraction of time. Though the air was utterly still, he had the sense of perpetual movement all around him, of the passing to and fro of intangible throngs. It was many thousand years, in all likelihood, since human feet had trodden these pavements; but Morley could have cried aloud with the imminence of the long-dead ages. It appeared to him, in a brief glimpse, that his whole life, as well as his journeyings and explorations in the South Seas, had been but a devious return to some earlier state of being; and that the resumption of this state was now at hand. All this, however, continued to perplex him mightily: it was as if he had suffered the intrusion of an alien entity.

He heard himself speaking to Thorway, and the words were unfamiliar and remote, as if they had issued from the lips of another.

"They were a joyous and a child-like race, those people of Mu," he was saying; "but not altogether joyous, not wholly child-like. There was a dark side . . . and a dark worship—the cult of death and night, personified by the moon, whose white, implacable, frozen lips were appeased only by the warm blood that flowed upon her altars. They caught the blood in goblets as it ran from the stone grooves . . . they raised it aloft . . . and the goblets were swiftly drained in mid-air by the remote goddess, as if the sacrifice had proven acceptable."

"But how do you know all this?" Thorway was quite amazed, no less by his companion's air than by the actual words. Morley, he thought, was less like a modern, every-day American than ever. He remembered, inconsequently, how all the natives of the various island groups had taken to Morley with an odd friendliness, without the reserve and suspicion often accorded to other white men. They had even warned Morley against the guardian spirits of the ruins—and they did not always trouble to warn others. It was almost as if they regarded him as being in some manner akin to themselves. Thorway wondered . . . though he was essentially unimaginative.

"I tell you, I *know*," Morley said, as he walked up and down beside the altar. "I have seen . . ." his voice trailed off in a frozen whisper, and he seemed to stiffen in every limb, and stood still as with some momentary catalepsy. His face grew deadly pale, his eyes were set and staring. Then, from between rigid lips, he uttered the strange words, *"Rhalu muvasa than,"* in a monotonous, hieratic tone, like a sort of invocation.

Morley could not have told what it was that he felt and saw in that moment. He was no longer his known and wonted self; and the man beside him was an unheeded stranger. But he could remember nothing afterwards—not even the odd vocables he had uttered. Whatever his mental experience may have been, it was like a dream that fades instantly when one awakens. The moment passed, the extreme rigidity left his limbs and features, and he resumed his interrupted pacing.

His confrere was staring at him in astonishment, not unmingled with solicitude.

"Are you ill? The sun is pretty hot today. And one should be careful. Perhaps we had best return to the schooner."

Morley gave a mechanical assent and followed Thorway from the ruins toward the seashore, where the schooner they had used in their voyaging was anchored in a little harbor less than a mile distant. His mind was full of confusion and darkness. He no longer felt the queer emotions that had seized him beside the altar; nor could he recall them otherwise than dimly. All the while he was trying to recollect something which lay just below the rim of memory; something very momentous, which he had forgotten long, long ago.

Lying in a cane couch beneath an awning on the schooner's deck, Morley drifted back to his normal plane of consciousness. He was not unwilling to accept Thorway's suggestion, that he had suffered a touch of sun among the ruins. His ghostly sensations, the delirium-like approach to a state of awareness which had no relation to his daily life, were now unlikely and unreal. In an effort to dismiss them altogether, he went over in his mind the whole of the investigative tour he had undertaken, and the events of the years preceding it.

He remembered his youthful luctations against poverty, his desire for that wealth and leisure which alone makes possible the pursuit of every chimera; and his slow but accelerative progress when once he had acquired a modicum of capital and had gone into business for himself as an importer of Oriental rugs. Then he recalled the chance inception of his archaeological enthusiasm—the reading of an illustrated article which described the ancient remains on Easter Island. The insoluble strangeness of these little-known relics had thrilled him profoundly, though he knew not why; and he had resolved to visit them some day. The theory of a lost continent in the Pacific appealed to him with an almost intimate lure and imaginative charm; it became his own particular chimera, though he could not have traced to their psychal origin the feelings behind his interest. He read everything procurable on the subject; and as soon as his leisure permitted, he made a trip to Easter Island. A year later, he was able to leave his business indefinitely in the hands of an efficient manager. He hired Thorway, a professional archaeologist with much experience in Italy and Asia Minor, to accompany him; and purchasing an old schooner, manned by a Swedish crew and captain, he had set out on his long, devious voyage among the islands.

Going over all this in his thoughts, Morley decided that it was now time to return home. He had learned all that was verifiable regarding the mysterious ruins. The study had fascinated him as nothing else in his life had ever done; but for some reason his health was beginning to suffer. Perhaps he had thrown himself too assiduously into his labors; the ruins had absorbed him too deeply. He must get away from them, must not risk a renewal of the queer, delusory sensations he had experienced. He recalled the superstitions of the natives, and wondered if there were something in them after all; if unwholesome influences were attached to those primeval stones. Did ghosts return or linger from a world that had been buried beneath the waves for unknown ages? Damn it, he had almost felt at times as if he were some sort of *revenant* himself.

He called to Thorway, who was standing beside the rail in conversation with one of the Norse sailors.

"I think we have done enough for one voyage, Thorway," he said. "We will lift anchor in the morning and return to San Francisco."

Thorway made little effort to conceal his relief. He did not consider the Polynesian isles a very fruitful field for research: the ruins were too old and fragmentary, the period to which they belonged was too conjectural, and did not deeply engage his interest.

"I agree," he rejoined. "Also, if you will pardon me for saying it, I don't think the South Sea climate is one of ideal salubriousness. I've noticed occasionally indispositions on your part for some time past."

Morley nodded in a weary acquiescence. It would have been impossible to tell Thorway his actual thoughts and emotions. The man was abysmally unimaginative.

He only hoped that Thorway did not think him a little mad—though, after all, it was quite immaterial.

The day wore on; and the swift, purpureal darkness of eventide was curtailed by the rising of a full moon which inundated sea and land with warm, ethereous quicksilver. At dinner, Morley was lost in a taciturn abstraction; and Thorway was discreetly voluble, but made no reference to the late archaeological find. Svensen, the captain, who ate with them, maintained a monosyllabic reticence, even when he was told of the proposed return to San Francisco. After eating, Morley excused himself and went back to the cane couch. Somewhat to his relief, he was not joined by Thorway.

Moonlight had always aroused in Morley a vague but profound emotion. Even as the ruins had done, it stirred among the shadows of his mind a million ghostly intimations; and the thrill he felt was at times not unalloyed with a cryptic awe and trepidation, akin, perhaps, to the primal fear of darkness itself.

Now, as he gazed at the tropic plenilune, he conceived the sudden and obsessing idea that the orb was somehow larger, and its light more brilliant than usual; even as they might have been in ages when the moon and earth were much younger. Then he was possessed by a troublous doubt, by an inenarrable sense of dislocation, and a dream-like vagueness which attached itself to the world about him. A wave of terror surged upon him, and he felt that he was slipping irretrievably away from all familiar things. Then the terror ebbed; for that which he had lost was far off and incredible; and a world of circumstances long-forgot was assuming, or resuming, the tinge of familiarity.

What, he wondered, was he doing on this queer ship? It was the night of the sacrifice to Rhalu, the selenic goddess; and he, Matla, was to play an essential part in the ceremony. He must reach the temple ere the moon had mounted to her zenith above the altar-stone. And it now lacked only an hour of the appointed time.

He rose and peered about with questioning eyes. The deck was deserted, for it was unnecessary to keep watch in that tranquil harbor. Svensen and the mate were doubtless drinking themselves to sleep as usual; the sailors were playing their eternal whist and pedro; and Thorway was in his cabin, probably writing a no-less-eternal monograph on Etruscan tombs. It was only in the most remote and exiguous manner that Morley recollected their existence.

Somehow, he managed to recall that there was a boat which he and Thorway had used in their visits to the isle; and that this boat was moored to the schooner's side. With a tread as lithe and supple as that of a native, he was over the rail and was rowing silently shoreward. A hundred yards, or little more, and then he stood on the moon-washed sand.

Now he was climbing the palm-clustered hill above the shore, and was heading toward the temple. The air was suffused with a primal, brooding warmth, with the scent of colossal flowers and ferns not known to modern botanists. He could see them towering beside his way with their thick, archaic fronds and petals, though such things have not lifted to the moon for aeons. And mounting the crest of the hill, which had dominated the little isle and had looked down to the sea on two sides, he saw in the mellow light the far, unbounded reaches of a softly rolling plain, and sealess horizons everywhere, that glowed with the golden fires of cities. And he knew the names of these cities, and recalled the opulent life of Mu, whose prosperity had of late years been menaced by Atlantean earthquakes and volcanic upheavals. These, it was believed, were owing to the wrath of Rhalu, the goddess who controlled the planetary forces; and human blood was being poured in all her fanes to placate the mysterious deity.

Morley (or Matla) could have remembered a million things; he could have called to mind the simple but strange events of his entire pre-existence in Mu, and the lore and history of the far-flung continent. But there was little room in his consciousness for anything but the destined drama of the night. Long ago (how long he was not sure) he had been chosen among his people for an awful honor; but his heart had failed him ere the time ordained, and he had fled. Tonight, however, he would not flee. A solemn religious rapture, not untinged with fear, guided his steps toward the temple of the goddess.

As he went on, he noticed his raiment, and was puzzled. Why was he wearing these ugly and unseemly garments? He began to remove them and to cast them aside one by one. Nakedness was ordained by sacerdotal law for the role he was to play.

He heard the soft-vowelled murmur of voices about him, and saw the multi-colored robes or gleaming amber flesh of forms that flitted among the archaic plants. The priests and worshippers were also on their way to the temple.

His excitement rose, it became more mystical and more rhapsodic as he neared his destination. His being was flooded by the superstitious awe of ancient man, by the dreadful reverence due to the unknown powers of nature. He peered with a solemn trepidation at the moon as it rose higher in the heavens, and saw in its rounded orb the features of a divinity both benign and malevolent.

Now he beheld the temple, looming whitely above the tops of titan fronds. The walls were no longer ruinous, their fallen blocks were wholly restored. His visit to the place with Thorway was dim as a fever fantasy; but other visits during his life as Matla, and ceremonials of the priests of Rhalu which he had once beheld, were clear and immediate in his memory. He knew the faces he would see, and the ritual wherein he would participate. He thought mostly in pictures; but the words of a strange vocabulary were ready for his recollection; and phrases drifted through his mind with unconscious ease; phrases that would have seemed unintelligible gibberish an hour before.

Matla was aware of the concentrated gaze of several hundred eyes as he entered the great, roofless fane. The place was thronged with people, whose round features were of a pre-Aryan type; and many of the faces were familiar to him. But at that moment all of them were parcel of a mystic horror, and were awesome and obscure as the night. Nothing was clear before him, save an opening in the throng, which led to the altar-stone around which the priests of Rhalu were gathered, and wherein Rhalu herself looked down in relentless, icy splendor from an almost vertical elevation.

He went forward with firm steps. The priests, who were clad in lunar purple and yellow, received him in an impassive silence. Counting them, he found that there were only six instead of the usual seven. One there was among them who carried a large, shallow goblet of silver; but the seventh, whose hand would lift the long and curving knife of some copperish metal, had not yet arrived.

Thorway had found it curiously hard to apply himself to the half-written monograph on Etruscan tombs. An obscure and exasperating restlessness finally impelled him to abandon his wooing of the reluctant muse of archaeology. In a state of steadily mounting irritation, wishing that the bothersome and unprofitable voyage were over, he went on deck.

The moonlight dazzled him with its preternatural brilliance, and he did not perceive for a few moments that the cane couch was empty. When he saw that Morley was gone, he experienced a peculiar mixture of alarm and irritation. He felt sure that Morley had not returned to his cabin. Stepping to the schooner's shoreward side, he noted with little surprise the absence of the moored boat. Morley must have gone ashore for a moonlight visit to the ruined temple; and Thorway frowned heavily at this new presumptive evidence of his employer's eccentricity and aberration. An unwonted sense of responsibility, deep and solemn, stirred within him. He seemed to hear an inward injunction, a strange half-familiar voice, bidding him to take care of Morley. This unhealthy and exorbitant interest in a more than problematic past should be discouraged or at least supervised.

Very quickly, he made up his mind as to what he should do. Going below, he called two of the Swedish sailors from their game of pedro and had them row him ashore in the ship's dinghy. As they neared the beach the boat used by Morley was plainly visible in the plumy shadow of a clump of seaward-leaning palms.

Thorway, without offering any explanation of his purpose in going ashore, told the sailors to return to the ship. Then, following the well-worn trail toward the temple, he mounted the island-slope.

Step by step, as he went on, he became aware of a strange difference in the vegetation. What were these monstrous ferns and primordial-looking flowers about him? Surely it was some weird trick of the moonlight, distorting the familiar palms and shrubs. He had seen nothing of the sort in his daytime visits, and such forms were impossible, anyway. Then, by degrees, he was beset with terrible doubt and bewilderment. There came to him the ineffably horrifying sensation of passing beyond his proper self, beyond all that he knew as legitimate and verifiable. Fantastic, unspeakable thoughts, alien, abnormal impulses, thronged upon him from the sorcerous glare of the effulgent moon. He shuddered at repellent but insistent memories that were not his own, at the ghastly compulsion of an unbelievable command. What on earth was possessing him? Was he going mad like Morley? The moon-bright isle was like some bottomless abyss of nightmare fantasy, into which he sank with nightmare terror.

He sought to recover his hard, materialistic sanity, his belief in the safe literality of things. Then, suddenly and without surprise, he was no longer Thorway.

He knew the real purpose for which he had come ashore—the solemn rite in which he was to play an awful but necessary part. The ordained hour was near—the worshippers, the sacrifice and the six fellow-priests awaited his coming in the immemorial fane of Rhalu.

Unassisted by any of the priests, Matla had stretched himself on the cold altar. How long he lay there, waiting, he could not tell. But at last, by the rustling stir and murmur of the throng, he knew that the seventh priest had arrived.

All fear had left him, as if he were already beyond the pain and suffering of earth. But he knew with a precision well-nigh real as physical sight and sensation the use which would be made of the copperish knife and the silver goblet.

He lay gazing at the wan heavens, and saw dimly, with far-focused eyes, the leaning face of the seventh priest. The face was doubly familiar . . . but he had forgotten something. He did not try to remember. Already it seemed to him that the white moon was drawing nearer, was stooping from her celestial station to quaff the awaited sacrifice. Her light blinded him with unearthly fulgor; but he saw dimly the flash of the falling knife ere it entered his heart. There was an instant of tearing pain that plunged on and on through his body, as if its tissues were a deep abyss. Then a sudden darkness took the heavens and blotted out the face of Rhalu; and all things, even pain, were erased for Matla by the black mist of an eternal nothing.

In the morning, Svensen and his sailors waited very patiently for the return of Morley and Thorway from the island. When afternoon came and the two were still absent, Svensen decided that it was time to investigate.

He had received orders to lift anchor for San Francisco that day; but he could not very well depart without Thorway and Morley.

With one of the crew, he rowed ashore and climbed the hill to the ruins. The roofless temple was empty, save for the plants that had taken root in the crevices of its pavement. Svensen and the sailor, looking about for the archaeologists, were horrified from their stolidity by the stains of newly dried blood that lined the great groove in the altar-block to its edge.

They summoned the remainder of the crew. A daylong search of the little island, however, was without result. The natives knew nothing of the whereabouts of Morley and Thorway, and were queerly reticent even in avowing their ignorance. There was no place where the two men could have hidden themselves, granting that they had any reason for a procedure so peculiar. Svensen and his men gave it up. If they had been imaginative, it might have seemed to them that the archaeologists had vanished bodily into the past.

VII

MYSTERIOUS
MONUMENTS

***

The Secret of Stonehenge
By Harry Harrison

The Bald-Headed Mirage
By Robert Bloch

13

The circle of rocks which comprises Stonehenge on Salisbury Plain in England is perhaps the most famous ancient monument in the world. The circle, some 320 feet in diameter, consists of a variety of erect and fallen stones, which although of great antiquity, were not actually written about until the twelfth century. Early theories believed the stones to be variously the handiwork of Merlin (as a monument to 460 slain noblemen), the burial place of Queen Boadicea, or a Roman temple. In the main, though, people were for many centuries completely mystified by the rocks, and doubtless the majority felt inclined to agree with the diarist Samuel Pepys, who, after he had studied them, noted they were "as prodigeous as any of the tales I ever heard tell of them . . . God knows what their use was." Perhaps the most plausible theory was that advanced by the antiquarians John Aubrey and William Stukeley, who both believed the monument had Druidic origins. The two men were convinced that the Druids—the Celtic priests who had flourished throughout Europe until their merciless persecution by the Romans—were the builders of the circle. Here, it was maintained, they met in their flowing white robes and golden adornments to worship their ancient gods of nature. For a time this theory enjoyed great popularity, but by the close of the nineteenth century it had become somewhat discredited in a wave of new ideas. Scientific tests, however, have led to some definite conclusions: the stones themselves, for instance, fall into two distinct categories —the large, or "Saracen," stones, and the much smaller "Bluestones." The first of these are known to have come from the nearby site of Marlborough Downs, while the Bluestones must have been transported from at least one hundred and thirty miles away in the Prescelly Mountains in southwest Wales, the nearest source of any such rocks. The rings of holes around the circle—named the Aubrey Holes after their discoverer, John Aubrey—have also been excavated, and burned human bones have been found which suggest that Stonehenge served some ceremonial or ritual purpose. The most recent inquiry, however, has led to perhaps the most remarkable of all the theories. It was proposed by the British astronomer Gerald S. Hawkins, who believes the stones were a sun and moon observatory and a counting device for predicting events such as eclipses. In the simplest terms, he claims Stonehenge to have been a neolithic computer! The Professor's findings and books have, naturally enough, been the subject of fierce controversy and debate, but he has been able to link Stonehenge with the achievements of the ancient Egyptians, the Mayas and the Pacific islanders, to demonstrate heretofore unsuspected abilities in prehistoric man which demand further research. The whole issue of Stonehenge has been a delight to writers of speculative fiction, and a wide variety of theories has resulted. But I doubt whether anyone has captured both the mythical and scientific aspects of the stones better than the science-fiction writer *Harry Harrison* (1921–   ) in his story "The Secret of Stonehenge," which appeared in 1968. Author of numerous short stories and novels—including the impressive "Death World"—Harrison has long been fascinated by ancient traditions, those of Britain in particular. In the tale which follows, he has added a little more mystery—not to mention another question mark—to the legend . . .

THE SECRET OF STONEHENGE
Harry Harrison

Low clouds rushed by overhead in the dusk, and there was a spattering of sleet in the air. When Dr. Lanning opened the cab door of the truck, the wind pounced on him, fresh from the arctic, hurtling unimpeded across Salisbury Plain. He buried his chin in his collar and went around to the rear doors. Barker followed him out and tapped on the door of the little office nearby. There was no answer.

"Not so good," Lanning said, gently sliding the bulky wooden box down to the ground. "We don't leave our national monuments unguarded in the States."

"Really," Barker said, striding to the gate in the wire fence. "Then I presume those initials carved in the base of the Washington Monument are neolithic graffiti. As you see, I brought the key."

He unlocked the gate and threw it open with a squeal of unoiled hinges, then went to help Lanning with the case.

In the evening, under a lowering sky, that is the only way to see Stonehenge, without the ice cream cornets and clambering children. The Plain settles flat upon the Earth, pressed outwards to a distant horizon, and only the gray pillars of the sarsen stones have the strength to push up skywards.

Lanning led the way, bending into the wind, up the broad path of the Avenue. "They're always bigger than you expect them to be," he said, and Barker did not answer him, perhaps because it was true. They stopped next to the Altar Stone and lowered the case. "We'll know soon enough," Lanning said, throwing open the latches.

"Another theory?" Barker asked, interested in spite of himself. "Our megaliths seem to hold a certain fascination for you and your fellow Americans."

"We tackle our problems wherever we find them," Lanning answered, opening the cover and disclosing a chunky and complicated piece of apparatus mounted on an aluminum tripod. "I have no theories at all about these things. I'm here just to find out the truth, why this thing was built."

"Admirable," Barker said, and the coolness of his comment was lost in the colder wind. "Might I ask just what this device is?"

"Chronostasis temporal-recorder." He opened the legs and stood the machine next to the Altar Stone. "My team at MIT worked it up. We found that temporal movement—other than the usual 24 hours into the future every day—is instant death for anything living. At least we killed off roaches, rats, and chickens; there were no human volunteers. But inanimate objects can be moved without damage."

"Time travel?" Barker said in what he hoped was a diffident voice.

"Not really; time stasis would be a better description. The machine stands still and lets everything else move by it. We've penetrated a good ten thousand years into the past this way."

"If the machine stands still—that means that time is running backwards?"

"Perhaps it is; would you be able to tell the difference? Here, I think we're ready to go now."

Lanning adjusted the controls on the side of the machine, pressed a stud, then stepped back. A rapid whirring came from the depths of the device: Barker raised one quizzical eyebrow.

"A timer," Lanning explained. "It's not safe to be close to the thing when it's operating."

The whirring ceased and was followed by a sharp click, immediately after which the entire apparatus vanished.

"This won't take long," Lanning said, and the machine reappeared even as he spoke. A glossy photograph dropped from a slot into his hand when he touched the back. He showed it to Barker.

"Just a trial run, I sent it back 20 minutes."

Although the camera had been pointing at them, the two men were not in the picture. Instead, in darkish pastels due to the failing light, the photograph showed a view down the Avenue, with their parked truck just a tiny square in the distance. From the rear doors of the vehicle the two men could be seen removing the yellow box.

"That's very . . . impressive," Barker said, shocked into admission of the truth. "How far back can you send it?"

"Seems to be no limit, just depends on the power source. This model has nicad batteries and is good back to about 10,000 B.C."

"And the future?"

"A closed book, I'm afraid, but we may lick that problem yet." He extracted a small notebook from his hip pocket and consulted it, then set the dials once again. "These are the optimum dates, about the time we figure Stonehenge was built. I'm making this a multiple shot. This lever records the setting, so now I can feed in another one."

There were over twenty settings to be made, which necessitated a great deal of dial spinning. When it was finally done, Lanning actuated the timer and went to join Barker.

This time the departure of the chronostasis temporal-recorder was much more dramatic. It vanished readily enough, but left a glowing replica of itself behind, a shimmering golden outline easily visible in the growing darkness.

"Is that normal?" Barker asked.

"Yes, but only on the big time jumps. No one is really sure just what it is, but we call it a temporal echo, the theory being that it is sort of a resonance in time caused by the sudden departure of the machine. It fades away in a couple of minutes."

Before the golden glow was completely gone the device itself returned, appearing solidly in place of its spectral echo. Lanning rubbed his hands together, then pressed the print button. The machine clattered in response and extruded a long strip of prints.

"Not as good as I expected," Lanning said. "We hit the daytime all right, but there is nothing much going on."

There was enough going on to almost stop Barker's archaeologist's heart. Picture after picture of the megalith standing strong and *complete,* the menhirs upright and the lintels in place upon all the sarsen stones.

"Lots of rock," Lanning said, "but no sign of the people who built the thing. Looks like someone's theories are wrong. Do you have any idea when it was put up?"

"Sir J. Norman Lockyer believed that it was erected on June 24th, 1680 B.C.," he said abstractedly, still petrified by the photographs.

"Sounds good to me."

The dials were spun and the machine vanished once again. The picture this time was far more dramatic. A group of men in rough home-spun genuflected, arms outstretched, facing towards the camera.

"We've got it now," Lanning chortled, and spun the machine about in a half circle so it faced in the opposite direction. "Whatever they're worshipping is behind the camera. I'll take a shot of it and we'll have a good idea why they built this thing."

The second picture was almost identical with the first, as were two more taken at right angles to the first ones.

"This is crazy," Lanning said, "they're all facing into the camera and bowing. Why—the machine must be sitting on top of whatever they are looking at."

"No, the angle proves that the tripod is on the same level that they are." Sudden realization hit Barker and his jaw sagged. "Could your temporal echo be visible in the past as well?"

"Well . . . I don't see why not. Do you mean . . . ?"

"Correct. The golden glow of the machine caused by all those stops must have been visible on and off for years. It gave me a jolt when I first saw it, and it must have been much more impressive to the people then."

"It fits," Lanning said, smiling happily and beginning to repack the machine. "They built Stonehenge around the image of the device sent back to see why they built Stonehenge. So that's solved."

"Solved! The problem has just begun. It's a paradox. Which of them, the machine or the monument, *came first?*"

Slowly, the smile faded from Dr. Lanning's face.

14

If Stonehenge is the most famous ancient monument in the world, the strangest by far must be the gigantic stone heads which stare out across the South Pacific from lonely Easter Island. There are something like six hundred of these huge sculptures on the island (experts believe there may well have been many more, some having fallen into the sea, others stolen or removed for museums, and the rest destroyed), and they range in height from the smallest, just over three feet, to several which tower well over thirty-six feet. Perhaps equally as mysterious as these statues are the people who shaped them. Because of its almost complete isolation, Easter Island was not discovered by Western man until a Dutch admiral, Jacob Roggeveen, made a landfall there on Easter Sunday, 1722. Finding that the natives had not even given the island a traditional name, the Admiral decided to call it after the day of his arrival. Like many other visitors since, he was much puzzled by the light-skinned features of the people, which seemed to indicate an origin thousands of miles away. But how had they traversed such a distance and evolved skills capable of producing the huge statues—if such was the case? Thor Heyerdahl, organizer of the famous Kon Tiki and Ra expeditions and an expert on the Pacific cultures, has devoted much time and study to Easter Island, and believes the islanders may be the product of the intermingling of the Nordic, Peruvian and Polynesian cultures. He has voyaged across the Pacific in the frail craft known to have been available to these early men and claims it was the people gendered by the interbreeding of the three races who finally settled on Easter Island. Once there, he says, they were unable to repair or rebuild any of their boats because of the lack of vegetation on the island and therefore settled into their existence of isolation until the European voyagers arrived. They were certainly cannibals, practiced sexual promiscuity, and seemingly possessed, for a while at least, the remarkable skills capable of producing the huge statues which adorned the island. Such is one theory. Another claims that Easter Island is the last outpost of the fabled continent of Mu and the statues are the god figures of that civilization. A third theory holds that they were built by hands which may not have been of this world at all. Certainly the islanders have no records or traditions which speak of these stone heads or how they were created—to them, the statues exist, and that is all that matters. Scientific rationality has no meaning for these happy and indolent people whose numbers are now less than one thousand. Unlike most of the other mysteries in this book, the statues of Easter Island have received almost no attention at all in modern fiction—and, indeed, I have only been able to find one story which has a theory about the heads, albeit set in a totally different environment. The story is "The Bald-Headed Mirage" by *Robert Bloch* (1917–   ), author of the famous Alfred Hitchcock film *Psycho* and many remarkable stories of fantasy and science fiction. Bloch is a writer of great imagination, and in this tale, written in 1964, he has combined the legend of the statues with the theories of the Russian philosopher Petr Demyanovich Ouspensky, who propounded the idea that time might function in a different way in what seem to be inanimate objects. Although the other stories in this collection have been set in the localities of the mysteries they discuss, here we must make an exception. But such is the ingenuity and skill with which Robert Bloch unfolds his tale on a far-off planet—which is just as isolated in its way, however, as Easter Island—that I think the reader will find it both acceptable within our terms of reference and more than a little unnerving in its conclusions.

THE BALD-HEADED MIRAGE
Robert Bloch

The asteroid didn't have a name, unless one wanted to count the four-letter word which Chuck had used to designate it as he set the ship down.

Barwell didn't like the word, or any of the words Chuck used. Back in the old days, before space-travel, people with Chuck's limited and unsavory vocabulary were often described as "earthy." Barwell wondered what they should be called today. "Planetary"? Or "asteroidy"?

It didn't matter. What mattered was that Chuck happened to be a typical space frontiersman. Some day he and his fellows would probably be transfigured in legend as heroic interplanetary pioneers, just as the early settlers of the old American west had been transfigured. Songs and sagas would be written of their fearless exploits, their bold vision, their thirst for freedom, their struggle to shake down the stars.

But men like Barwell, who had to live with them now, knew that the space frontiersmen were probably no different than their historic counterparts back on Earth. They were misfits, antisocial aberrants who fled the responsibilities of organized society and the punishment of its laws. They sought the skies not out of poetic yearning but in a desperate attempt to evade bad debts, extortion charges, murder raps, bastardy warrants—and what they hoped to find was not the beauty of nature but the booty. They were led not by light but by loot—and because most of them were uncouth, ignorant men, they teamed up with partners like George Barwell who provided the brain to balance the brawn.

Perhaps, Barwell reasoned, he was being unfair. Chuck, like most of his counterparts, had more than brawn; he had natural coordination, natural comprehension manifesting itself in mechanical aptitudes. He was, in a word, a damned good pilot—just as the stumblebums of the Old West were often damned good horsemen, stagecoach drivers, bullwhackers, hunters and scouts. What he lacked in ratiocination Barwell provided. Together they formed a team—cerebrum and cerebellum, plus a psychic *medulla oblongata* composed of a fusion of component qualities.

Only by the time they landed on the asteroid, Barwell was damned sick of Chuck's four-letter words. Chuck had a four-letter word for everything during their long cruise—to describe the food, the confinement in the tiny cabin of the ship, his need for a sexual outlet. Chuck talked about nothing else, was interested in nothing else.

Barwell's own tastes ran towards poetry; the oldstyle poetry of long ago, complete with rhyme and metre and onomatopoeia. But there was no sense even mentioning the subject to Chuck; give him a title like *The Charge of the Light Brigade* and he'd think it was about the narcotics supply of some regiment. And as for *The Lay of the Last Minstrel*—

No, it was easier for Barwell to keep silent and let Chuck do the talking. About the . . . mineral deposits they were going to find, and the . . . money they'd make so they could go back to that . . . Lunadome City and tell everybody to . . .

It was easier for Barwell to keep silent, but not much easier. And by the time they were approaching the surface of the asteroid he was heartily sick of his partner, and his earthy aspirations. If George Barwell had invested his small inheritance in a second-hand ship in order to conduct a private sky-scan, it wasn't because he wanted wealth to gratify his aggressive drives against society. He knew exactly what he meant to do with his money, if successful. He'd buy himself a little place out past Pluto and set up an interplanetary Walden's Pond. Here he'd settle down to write poetry in the ancient manner; not the intermediate *vers libre* of the first space age or today's soundspeak synthesis which had emerged from what the scholars once called "progressive jazz." He hoped, too, to do some erudite and expensive research with the priceless tapes of forgotten folk-songs.

But there was no time for such speculations now, no time for poesy. They were skimming across the surface of the asteroid, off autopilot, of course, while the instruments tested for grav., ox., density, radiation, temp., and all the rest. Chuck was at the controls, set for a handland any minute.

Barwell got the tape comps and studied them. "We'll do all right," he muttered. "One and one-fourth grav. is no problem. But we'll have to wear our bubbles. And—"

Chuck shook his head.

"Dead," he muttered. That was one of the bad things about a trip like this—both of them had gotten into the habit of muttering; they didn't really converse with one another, just vocalized a *monologue interieur*. "All dead. Desert and mountains. Of course, we want the mountains, but why the . . . does it have to be so dead?"

"Because it's an asteroid." Barwell moved over to within visual range of the scanners. "You seldom find mineral deposits on inhabitable bodies."

His mind played the usual tricks, contradicting his last statement. He thought of the mineral deposits he had seen in the form of gold and diamonds, ornamenting the women of Lunadome City; mineral deposits on *very* inhabitable bodies. And that thought led him to still another; the lying premises of most of the "space romances" he had read, or for that matter, the so-called "factual accounts" of space travel. In almost all of them the emphasis was on the so-called thrill and challenge involved in expeditionary flights. Few were honest enough to present the reality of a spaceman's outlook, which was one of constant physical frustration. When he set up his interplanetary Walden's Pond, he'd make sure to bring along some feminine companionship. *All* spaceships were really powered with sex-drive, he decided. But to satisfy the libido required money. *Libidough.*

"Look!" Chuck wasn't muttering now, he was shouting. And pointing at the starboard scanner.

Barwell gazed out and down.

They were at a half-mile elevation, over the desert, and the white sky shone pitilessly on an endless expanse of nothingness—the flat, monotonous expanse of sand or detritus was like a smooth, unrippled lake. *A lake in which giants bathed, immersed to their necks—*

Barwell saw them now; four giant bald heads in a row. He turned to Chuck. "What do you mean, dead?" he murmured. "There's life here. See for yourself."

"Stones," Chuck grunted. "Just stones."

"Look like heads to me."

"Sure they do, from this angle. Wait, I'll make another run."

The ship obeyed, dipping lower.

"Statues," Barwell decided. "Those *are* heads, you can see that now, can't you?"

". . . !" said Chuck. It wasn't a reply, merely a forceful observation. And now Barwell could see what he observed. The four heads set in sand *were* artificially carved, and in their eyesockets blazed a livid luminance.

"Emeralds," Chuck whispered. "Emeralds as big as wagonwheels!"

"Can't be." Barwell shook his head. "There are no such concentrations of stratification—"

"I see 'em. So do you."

"Mirage. Some kind of igneous deposit."

"Why the . . . can't you talk English, like me?" Chuck demanded. "That's no mirage. It's real. Whoever heard of a bald-headed mirage?"

He began to snort and busied himself at the controls.

"What do you think you're doing?"

"Setting down for a landing, that's what."

"Now wait a minute—"

"What for? Man, those emeralds—"

"All right, hold it." Barwell's tone was subdued, but something about it caused Chuck to hesitate.

"Let's think things through for a minute," he continued. "Grant that there *are* actual stone heads down there. And that they have some kind of ornamentation for eyes."

"Emeralds, dammit!"

"That's beside the point. The point is, statues don't come into existence through spontaneous generation."

"Will you for . . . talk English?"

"Somebody has to *make* statuary. Don't you see, there must be life down there."

"So?"

"So we land a good distance away. *And* come out armed. Armed and cautious."

"All right. Anything that shows its head, I blast."

"You don't blast. Not until you know what it is, and whether or not it shows hostility."

"Blast first, talk later." Chuck repeated the code that was older than the hills. *The only good Indian is a dead Indian.* Is prejudice a survival-mechanism?

Chuck's instantaneous, automatic response to anything new or different would be to lash out at it and destroy it. Barwell's would be to examine it and intellectualize. He wondered which of them was reacting correctly, then decided it would depend upon individual circumstance. But then, one must never generalize, because everything is unique—and this in itself is a generalization.

Barwell unracked the weapons, nevertheless, as Chuck went into reverse landing position. He opened the compartment and extracted the suits and the bubbles. He tested the oxygen-cycle of the containers. He checked the food-belts. He brought out the footwear. And all the while he was drowning in the muddy stream-of-consciousness. Bubbles arose.

Columbus, buckling on his armor before the landing at San Salvador . . . Balboa, that voyaging *voyeur,* peeking at a peak on Darien . . . Henry M. Stanley, being presumptuous with Dr. Livingstone . . . the first footfall on the moon, and the first man to scrawl *Kilroy Was Here* and disfigure the lunar landscape with an obscene injunction . . . a faroff memory of the California hills and a whitewashed message writ on rock: *Help Stamp Out Reality* . . . what was this land worth if those *were* emerald eyes? . . . Emerald Isles . . . when Irish eyes are bloodshot, sure, 'tis like a . . . but the eyes weren't emeralds, it was a mirage . . . a bald-headed mirage . . . a mirage of convenience. *What do you think about when you're preparing to land on a strange and alien world? You think about what a wonderful thing it would be to be back in Lunadome City, settling down to a good meal*

of dehydrated eggs or a bad night with a dehydrated woman. Pow-
dered women. A new recipe. Just add water and stir. Serves two.
That's what you think about, that's all you ever think about.

And Chuck? What was *he* thinking about?

"Better make sure you use the relief tube before you put a suit on
and go out there," Chuck grunted.

That was Chuck, all right—the *practical* one.

And on this high note, the expedition proper started.

On the sweat of opening the locks. On the wrenching effort of lowering the landing-ladder. On the stumbling contact with the hard sand.
On the wheezing accommodation to the oxygen-feeders. On the blinding brilliance of the garish glare, searing into the skull through eyes
long-accustomed to half-darkness. On the trickle of sweat inside the
suit, the tightness of the constricting crotch at every step, the heaviness
of tank and weapon. *O Pioneers—*

"Oh . . . !" said Chuck. Barwell couldn't hear him, but like every
spacer, he'd learned lipreading. He'd also learned to keep his own
mouth shut, but now, as he turned towards the stone heads in the sand
a dozen miles to their right, he broke his own self-imposed rule of
silence.

"They're gone!" he gasped. And then blinked, as the echo of his
own voice rebounded in reverberation from the bubble in which his
head was encased.

Chuck followed his stare and nodded.

The heads were gone.

There was no possibility of miscalculation in landing. Chuck had set
down within ten or twelve miles of the sighting spot. And Barwell
remembered now that he had glanced sidelong through a scanner as
he'd donned his suit and bubble. The heads had been visible then.

But they were gone.

Nothing on every side but an expanse of shimmering sand. And far
beyond, to the left, the mountains.

"Mirage," he whispered. "It *was* a mirage, after all."

Chuck was reading him. His own lips formed a phrase. It wasn't exactly a reply—merely an obscene reaction.

As if by common, unspoken consent, the two men turned and
trudged back to the ship. They clambered up the ladder, closed the
locks, wearily removed their suits.

"We were space-bugged," Chuck muttered. "The two of us." He shook his head. "But I saw 'em. So did you."

"Let's go over the course again, retrace our route." Barwell waited until he saw Chuck nod. Then he sought a position at the starboard scanner.

"Waste a lot of juice taking off," Chuck grumbled. "Damn clumsy old tub!"

"If we find what we're looking for, you can have a new one. A whole fleet," Barwell reminded him.

"Sure." Chuck tested, then busied himself. There was a shuddering lurch.

"Slowly," Barwell cautioned.

Chuck answered with a suggestion as impossible as it was indecent, but he obeyed. The ship skimmed.

"Right about here," Barwell murmured. "Wasn't it?"

"Think so."

The ship hovered and the two men peered down. Peered down at empty wasteland.

"If only Mr. Eliot were alive to see it," Barwell told himself aloud.

"Who?"

"T. S. Eliot." Barwell paused. "A minor poet."

"T. S., huh?" Chuck snorted. Then he sobered. "Well, now what do we do?"

"Keep cruising. We'll head for the mountains. That's where we intended to go, anyway."

Chuck nodded and turned away. The ship rose, picked up speed.

Barwell contemplated the dryness of the desert, then refreshed himself by plunging back into the stream-of-consciousness.

Well, Columbus was disappointed with San Salvador, too; it wasn't really Asia. And Balboa never *really* stood upon a peak of Darien, except in the poem. Actually, he was at the Isthmus of Panama. Henry M. Stanley couldn't persuade Dr. Livingstone to return with him, and the first man to reach the moon was the first man to die there. And there were no dehydrated women, either, or hydrated ones, either. *Water, water, everywhere, and not a drop to drink.*

The feeling of frustration came again, and Barwell thought of the one woman he had truly loved, wishing she were somehow beside him now as she had been beside him once, so long ago.

"There they are!"

Chuck's shout brought him wet and dripping tears of self-pity, from the pool of memory. Barwell stared down and out.

The heads rose from the desert below. The great eyes gleamed.

"We're setting down!" Chuck told him.

Barwell shrugged.

Once again, the interminable routine. But this time, after both men were fully accoutred, they stared through the scanner to reassure themselves the stone heads were still visible, scarcely a mile away.

The heads stared back.

Then the locks swung open, the ladder swung down, and they emerged. Emerged upon the emptiness.

"Gone!"

Both men muttered simultaneously.

Then they walked—walked warily, weapons at the ready, across the barren plain. And walked wearily back again.

In the cabin, interminably, they argued and discussed. "Gone with the wind," sighed Barwell. "Only there is no wind."

"It can't be a mirage. I saw those emeralds just as clear—" Chuck shook his head. "But if it was, why in hell did it have to be stone heads? When it comes to mirages, I'll take—"

And he proceeded to describe his preferences in mirages very graphically. It was Barwell who finally resolved the situation.

"The mountains," he said. "Let's not waste any more time."

So they went to the mountains.

That is, they went *near* the mountains, skimming in low for a drop-landing on the smooth sands before the foothills. They squinted through the shimmering sheen of the scene, but there were no stone heads; only the looming loftiness of the great peaks in the distance.

Leaving the ship, they set forth on foot to clamber and climb and curse. But in the end there were merely the muttered oaths. For there was nothing to climb. The mountains were merely another kind of mirage—palpable, but not solid. Mountains of detritus, mountains of dust into which the two men swiftly sank as they attempted to proceed.

"Volcanic ash," Barwell mouthed, through the bubble. "That's the answer."

Chuck had another answer, but Barwell ignored it. He knew now that their quest was quixotic. There would be no mineral deposits in the non-existent soil of this asteroid; it was merely a gigantic lava-splinter flung forth into space by the eon-old eruption of a volcano on some far-distant planet. Either that or a meteoric byproduct. The actual explanation didn't matter. What mattered was that there would be no way to wealth in this wilderness. They'd have to go back to the ship.

The two men turned, the grippers on the soles of their footwear useless in the shifting sand as they plodded down into the plain once more. Far in the distance they could see the black speck of the ship. It was hard to walk, but they kept moving as the speck became a bulk, the bulk became a recognizable object, the object became a—

Chuck must have seen it first, because he halted. Then Barwell squinted and stared. Even in the lurid luminance his eyes widened as he saw the ship; saw the crushed and crumpled hull that had been squashed and serrated—

Then they were both running across the plain, stumbling and lurching towards the wreckage. Everything seemed to function in slow motion, as in a nightmare, but the nightmare continued. It continued as they peered up at the incredibly battered silver shell; proceeded as they swung up the ladder and found the entry squeezed shut.

They stood below, on the surface of the sand, and there was no need to mouth a word from behind the bubbles. Both of them knew the situation. Food and water for a day, if they dared remove the bubbles long enough to ingest a supply. Oxygen for perhaps another twelve hours at most. And then—

There was no point in considering what had happened, or why, or how. All that seemed important now was the *fait accompli*.

"Fate *accompli*," Barwell told himself. And that's all he could tell himself, or trust himself to tell. Staring up at the shattered sides of the spaceship, he experienced a sensation surpassing horror. For this phenomenon was alien.

Alien. A much-used, misused word, which cannot express the inexpressible. *Alien*—foreign. Foreign to understanding, foreign to human comprehension. Barwell recalled Arthur Machen's definition of true evil—when the roses sing.

When the roses sing.

Perhaps *alien* isn't always synonymous with *evil*—but something had destroyed the ship. There was no wind, and no life; yet they had walked away for a few miles and returned, and the ship was crumpled.

The roses were singing. What is a rose? Barwell thought of a long-dead poetess, Gertrude Stein. *A rose is a rose is a rose.* And added, *is evil.* But do roses live, does evil live, does the impalpable truly exist? *A rose by any other name—*

"Dammit, what happened?" Chuck, and the voice of reality. He wasn't concerned with roses, or neuroses, either. He wanted to name the enemy, locate it, and strike back. And with the realization Barwell (like a rose) wilted.

Here was a situation which didn't call for theory, or for any form of abstruse speculation. The ship was gone. They were stranded, with food and oxygen in short supply. A clear call for Chuck and his pioneer blood—or would his pioneer blood, too, be spilled across the sand?

Barwell hesitated helplessly, waiting for his partner to make the first move. No sceptre changed hands, but both sensed it was a moment of abdication. *The king is dead, long live the king. For another twenty-four hours, anyway.*

Both of them knew better than to waste breath in trying to talk through their bubbles. When Chuck turned back towards the mirage-mountains, Barwell followed without even moving his lips in token assent. At least there would be shadow there, and shelter, and surcease. The desert held nothing for either of them. The desert was all utter emptiness and shimmering mirage. Once more, Barwell thought of a lake.

Lake. As he trudged along behind Chuck's steadily-striding figure, he wondered what would happen if—as in the olden space-romances, the aliens actually invaded Earth. They'd probably send out scouting parties first; perhaps one or two at a time, in small ships. Granted the premise that their sensory organs roughly corresponded to the human and afforded similar impressions, what might they surmise from a skimming expedition over the earth at a height of a few hundred miles?

The first thing they would note was that the Earth's surface is more than three-quarters water and less than one-quarter land. So the logical conclusion; if there is any life on this planet, the chances are better than three to one that it is *marine* life—or at the very best, amphibious. The denizens of the great seas must be the highest and most intelligent life-forms. Conquer the fishes and rule the world. A highly sensible notion, that.

But there are times when high sense does not prevail. And if aliens could not be expected to comprehend humanity's existence offhand, then how could humanity interpret alienity?

In short—was there life on this asteroid which Barwell could not detect?

While there's life, there's hope. But Barwell had no hope. He had merely a premise. Something had crushed the spaceship. Where did it come from, where did it go? How did it link with life as he knew it, how did it differ? And the desert—*was* it a desert? The mountains had not been mountains. And the mirage had been—

Chuck still wasn't wasting words, even obscene ones. He merely turned and gripped his partner's arm with a plasticene-and-metal glove. Gripped it tightly, and turned, and pointed with his free hand. Pointed straight ahead, at the heads in the sand. Yes, they were here.

Barwell could have sworn that the heads hadn't been there a moment ago. But there they were, silhouetted against the searing surface, a scant mile before them. Even at this range the emerald eyes gleamed and glared, gleamed and glared as no mirage was meant to.

Four huge stone heads with emerald eyes. Visible to them both; visible to them *now*.

Chuck's lips formed a sentence beneath the bubble. "Keep looking at them," he said.

Barwell nodded. The two men moved forward, slowly.

Their gaze was intent, focussed upon the lambent, livid flame of the monstrous emeralds. Barwell knew, or thought he knew, what Chuck was seeing. Riches, infinite riches.

But he saw something else.

He saw all the idols of all the legends; the idols with the jewelled eyes, who stirred and moved and walked amongst men to spread destruction with a curse. He saw the massive monoliths of Stonehenge and the great figures of Easter Island and the stone horror beneath the waves in sunken R'lyeh. And the waves reminded him again of the lake, and the lake of the aliens who might misconceive and misconstrue the life-forms of Earth, and this in turn caused a curious concept. There had once been a man named Ouspensky who had speculated upon the possibility of *varieties* of time and different *rates* of duration. Perhaps the rocks also live, but at infinitely slow pace by comparison to flesh, so that flesh is unaware of the sentience of stone.

What form might life take, if forged in fire, if birthed precipitately from a volcano's flaming womb? Those great stone heads with the emerald eyes—

And all the while they were coming closer, approaching slowly. The stone heads stared and did not disappear. The emeralds blazed and burned, and now Barwell could no longer think; he could only stare and he tried the old trick again. The cool stream-of-consciousness was waiting. Little eddies of thought swirled.

Emerald eyes. His love had emerald eyes; sometimes turquoise, sometimes smoky jade, but his love was not stone. And she was worlds away and he was here, alone on the desert. But that's not where he wanted to be—plunge back now into the stream, use the fanciful thoughts to ward off the still more fanciful reality. Think of anything but emeralds, think of longforgotten stars of a longforgotten art-form, the motion pictures; think of Pearl White and Ruby Keeler and Jewel Carmen and of anything but emeralds, think of Diamond Jim Brady and the fabulous stones of history which men wrested from the Earth for love of woman. *Love is just around the Kohinoor.* Faith, the Hope Diamond, and Charity . . .

Emerald eyes . . . Esmeralda, and the *Hunchback of Notre Dame* . . . Hugo's title was *Notre Dame de Paris* . . . the vast cathedral with its stone gargoyles staring . . . but stones do not stare . . . or do they? *The emeralds were staring.*

Barwell blinked, shaking his head. He half-turned, noting that Chuck had broken into a run as he neared the four fantastic monuments in the sand. Wheezing and panting, he followed. Chuck didn't see what *he* saw—that was obvious. Even at the point of death, he wanted the emeralds. Even at the point of death—

Somehow Barwell managed to overtake his companion. He clawed at his arms, halted him. Chuck stared at him as he shook his head and mouthed the words.

"Don't go any closer!"

"Why not?"

"Because they're *alive!*"

"Nonsense." That was not the word Chuck used, but Barwell divined its meaning.

"They *are* alive. Don't you see? Living rock. With their immense weight, the desert is like water, like a lake in which they can immerse at will. Immerse and reappear, up to their necks. That's why they disappeared, because they were swimming beneath the surface—"

Barwell knew he was wasting precious oxygen, but he had to make Chuck understand.

"They must have grabbed our ship, picked it up to examine it, then discarded it."

Chuck scowled and said another word which meant, "Nonsense." He pulled free.

"No—don't—keep away—"

But Chuck had the pioneer spirit. The grab-claw-lunge-loot-rape reflex. He could only see the emeralds; the eyes that were bigger than his stomach.

And he started to run the last five hundred yards, moving across the sand towards the four staring heads which waited, *watched* and waited.

Barwell sprinted after him—or tried to sprint. But he could only flounder forward, noting as he did so that the huge rock heads were pitted and eroded, but not *chiselled*. No man, and no conceivable alien, had sculpted these semblances. For they were not semblances but actualities. The rock *lived,* the stone *sensed.*

And the emerald eyes beckoned . . .

"Come back!" It was worse than useless to shout, for Chuck couldn't see his face behind the bubble. He could only see the great faces before him, and the emeralds above. His own eyes were blinded by hunger, by a greed greater than need.

Panting, Barwell caught up with the running man, whirled him around.

"Keep back," he mouthed. "Don't get any closer—they'll crush you like they crushed the ship—"

"You lie!" Chuck turned, his weapon suddenly poised. "Maybe that was a mirage, too. But the jewels are real. I know your idea, you . . . ! Get rid of me, take the emeralds for yourself, repair the ship and take off. Only I'm way ahead of you, because that's *my* idea, too!"

"No—" gasped Barwell, realizing at the same moment that some poet had once said, "Say *Yes* to life!" and simultaneously aware that now there would be no time for further affirmation.

Because the weapon blazed, and then Barwell was falling; falling into the stream-of-consciousness and beyond, into the bubbling blackness of the stream-of-unconsciousness where there were no stone heads or emerald eyes. Where there was, no longer, any Barwell . . .

So it remained for Chuck to stand over the body of his partner at the base of the great stone head; to stand and grin in triumph as the smoke curled up as if before the altar of a god.

And like a giant god, the stone accepted its sacrifice. Incredulous, Chuck watched the incredible—saw the rock split open, saw the mountainous maw loom large as the head dipped and *gulped*.

Then the sand was smooth again. Barwell's body was gone.

Realization came brutally, belatedly. Chuck turned to run, knowing the heads *were* alive. And as he ran a vision came to him of these cyclopean creatures burrowing through the sand, bathing beneath the surface of the plain—rising at will to survey the silence of their dread domain. He could see a great stone paw emerge to fumble with the ship; knew now what the serrations in its sides meant. They were simply the marks of gigantic *teeth*. Teeth in a mouth that tasted, rejected; a hand had tossed the ship aside like a crumpled toy floating on the lake of sand.

For one moment Chuck thought as Barwell thought, and then the thought was transfigured by reality. A gigantic paw *did* emerge from the sand before him as he ran. It scooped Chuck up and tossed him down into the grinding stone mouth.

There was the sound stone makes when it gulps, and then silence.

The four heads turned to stare once more—stare at nothingness. They would gaze silently for a long, long time through ageless emerald eyes, for what is eternity to a stone.

Sooner or later, in another thousand years—or a million, what did it matter?—another ship would come.

VIII

MONSTERS

***

Creature of the Snows
By William Sambrot

The Convenient Monster
By Leslie Charteris

15

There are a great many tales of strange creatures from the mists of antiquity still surviving in lonely areas of the world. The most famous of these is surely the Yeti, or Abominable Snowman, who is said to live in the mist-shrouded peaks of the Himalayas. The creature has been called the "missing link" in evolution, a towering, shaggy figure, half man and half beast. According to the Sherpa natives, the creature has been part of their tradition for centuries and is described as being about eight feet tall, with a body covered with long, brown hair. He has a thin, pointed head and a hairless face reminiscent of a man's. The Yeti's fame, however, is of comparatively recent date, for it is only during the last half century that his existence has been widely known outside the region of the Himalayas. The report of his presence which so amazed the world was made by Colonel Howard Bury, an English military commander and skilled mountaineer, who led an expedition to scale Mount Everest in 1921. Although the assault failed, Bury made a remarkable discovery on the descent. "We distinguished a number of tracks in the snow," he recorded in his journal, "but one mark, like that of a human foot, was most puzzling. The coolies assured us that it was the track of a wild, hairy man, and these men were occasionally to be found in the wildest and most inaccessible mountains." This simple statement set both the public and the scientific world in a ferment. Inquiries were instituted, expeditions planned, and many claims by local Sherpas of having seen the Yeti were investigated. The Nepalese Government also added considerable fuel to the controversy by reporting that two of these "Snowmen" had actually been captured in the past. The first had been an infant, it was claimed, which was found by Sherpas who disappeared with their prize before any inquiry could be made; the other was an adult male who refused to take any nourishment after being seized, and eventually starved to death. Instead of preserving the carcass, the simple Sherpas dumped it in the snow. In the intervening years the legend has grown enormously and been investigated by distinguished scientists such as Professor A. G. Pronin of Leningrad University and Himalayan experts like Sir John Hunt, the conqueror of Everest, all of whom have found evidence to support the existence of the creatures. (Professor Pronin actually claimed to have seen the Yeti twice in the Pamir Mountains.) Although skepticism has been just as strong, photographs of huge footprints in the snow (taken by the English explorer Eric Shipton and, quite separately, by a party led by the American Tom Slick), and strands of found reddish hair which have defied normal human and animal classification, have only served to sustain and deepen the mystery. Of all the theories that abound about the origins of the Abominable Snowman, perhaps the most remarkable has been advanced by Professor Boris Porshnev of the Soviet Academy of Sciences. Both the human race and the Yeti, he claims, have descended from common ancestors. But while humans developed and became dominant in the world, these erstwhile "cousins" have slipped back toward an animal existence. In his view, the "split" occurred in the Neanderthal stage, which may have lasted from 400,000 to 50,000 years ago. He also contends that the Yeti do not actually live in the snow, but merely cross the mountains on their way from one remote valley to another. Writers of fiction have naturally been able to make much of the legend of the Snowman—some treating it as an elaborate joke or hoax, others utilizing the facts in an attempt to throw new light on another baffling legend. Such has been the approach of the distinguished American short-story writer, essayist and novelist *William Sambrot* (1927–   ), who in "Creature of the Snows" created one of the most thought-provoking short stories ever to appear in *The Saturday Evening Post*. Written in 1960, it makes its first appearance here in volume form.

CREATURE OF THE SNOWS
William Sambrot

Ed McKale straightened up under his load of cameras and equipment, squinting against the blasting wind, peering, staring, sweeping the jagged, unending expanse of snow and wind-scoured rock. Looking, searching, as he'd been doing now for two months, cameras at the ready.

Nothing. Nothing but the towering Himalayas, thrusting miles high on all sides, stretching in awesome grandeur from horizon to horizon, each pinnacle tipped with immense banners of snow plumes, streaming out in the wind, vivid against the darkly blue sky. The vista was one of surpassing beauty; viewing it, Ed automatically thought of light settings, focal length, color filters—then just as automatically rejected the thought. He was here, on top of the world, to photograph something infinitely more newsworthy—if only he could find it.

The expedition paused, strung out along a ridge of blue snow, with shadows falling away to the right and left into terrifying abysses, and Ed sucked for air. Twenty thousand feet is really quite high, although many of the peaks beyond rose nearly ten thousand feet above him.

Up ahead, the Sherpa porters—each a marvelous shot, gap-toothed, ebullient grins, seamed faces, leathery brown—bowed under stupendous loads for this altitude, leaning on their coolie crutches, waiting for Doctor Schenk to make up his mind. Schenk, the expedition leader, was arguing with the guides again, his breath spurting little puffs of vapor, waving his arms, pointing—down.

Obviously Schenk was calling it quits. He was within his rights, Ed knew; two months was all Schenk had contracted for. Two months of probing snow and ice; scrambling over crevasses, up rotten rock cliffs, wind-ravaged, bleak, stretching endlessly toward Tibet and the never-never lands beyond. Two months of searching for footprints where none should be. Searching for odors, for droppings, anything to disclose the presence of creatures other than themselves. Without success.

Two months of nothing. Big, fat nothing.

The expedition was a bust. The goofiest assignment of this or any other century, as Ed felt it would be from the moment he'd sat across a desk from the big boss in the picture-magazine's New York office, two months ago, looking at the blurred photograph, while the boss filled him in on the weird details:

The photograph, his boss had told him gravely, had been taken in the Himalayan mountains, at an altitude of twenty-one thousand feet, by a man soaring overhead in a motorless glider.

"A glider," Ed had said noncommittally, staring at the fuzzy enlarged snapshot of a great expanse of snow and rocky ledges, full of harsh light and shadows, a sort of roughly bowl-shaped plateau apparently, and in the middle of it a group of indistinct figures, tiny, lost against the immensity of great ice pinnacles. Ed looked closer. Were the figures people? If so—what had happened to their clothes?

"A glider," his boss reiterated firmly. The glider pilot, the boss said, was maneuvering in an updraft, attempting to do the incredible—soar over Mount Everest in a homemade glider. The wide-winged glider had been unable to achieve the flight over Everest, but, flitting silently about seeking updrafts, it cleared a jagged pinnacle and there, less than a thousand feet below, the pilot saw movement where none should have been. And dropping lower, startled, he'd seen, the boss said dryly, "creatures—creatures that looked exactly like a group of naked men and women and kids, playing in the snow, at an altitude of twenty thousand five hundred feet." He'd had the presence of mind to take a few hasty snapshots before the group disappeared. Only one of the pictures had developed.

Looking at the snapshot with professional scorn, Ed had said, "These things are indistinct. I think he's selling you a bill of goods."

"No," the boss said, "we checked on the guy. He really did make the glider flight. We've had experts go over that blowup. The picture's genuine. Those are naked biped, erect-walking creatures." He flipped the picture irritably. "I can't publish this thing; I want close-ups, action shots, the sort of thing our subscribers have come to expect of us."

He'd lighted a cigar slowly. "Bring me back some pictures I can publish, Ed, and you can write your own ticket."

"You're asking me to climb Mount Everest," Ed said, carefully keeping the sarcasm out of his voice. "To search for this plateau here," he tapped the shoddy photograph, "and take pix of—what are they, biped, erect-walking creatures, you say?"

The boss cleared his throat. "Not Mount Everest, Ed. It's Gauri Sankar, one of the peaks near Mount Everest. Roughly, it's only about twenty-three thousand feet or so high."

"That's pretty rough," Ed said.

The boss looked pained. "Actually it's not Gauri Sankar either. Just one of the lesser peaks of the Gauri Sankar massif. Well under twenty-three thousand. Certainly nothing to bother a hot-shot exparatrooper like you, Ed."

Ed winced, and the boss continued, "This guy—this glider pilot—wasn't able to pin-point the spot, but he did come up with a pretty fair map of the terrain—for a pretty fair price. We've checked it out with the American Alpine Club; it conforms well with their own charts of the general area. Several expeditions have been in the vicinity, but not this exact spot, they tell me. It's not a piece of cake by any means, but it's far from being another Annapurna, or K-Two, for accessibility."

He sucked at his cigar thoughtfully. "The Alpine Club says we've got only about two months of good weather before the inevitable monsoons hit that area—so time, as they say, is of the essence, Ed. But two months for this kind of thing ought to be plenty. Everything will be first class; we're even including these new gas guns that shoot hypodermic needles, or something similar. We'll fly the essentials into Katmandu and air-drop everything possible along the route up to your base at"—he squinted at a map—"Namche Bazar. A Sherpa village which is twelve thousand feet high."

He smiled amiably at Ed. "That's a couple of weeks' march up from the nearest railroad, and ought to get you acclimatized nicely. Plenty of experienced porters at Namche, all Sherpas. We've lined up a couple of expert mountain climbers with Himalayan background. And expedition leader will be Doctor Schenk—top man in his field."

"What is his field?" Ed asked gloomily.

"Zoology. Whatever these things are in this picture, they're animal, which is his field. Everyone will be sworn to secrecy; you'll be the only one permitted to use a camera, Ed. This could be the biggest thing you'll ever cover, if these things are what I think they are."

"What do you think they are?"

"An unknown species of man—or sub-man," his boss said, and prudently Ed remained silent. Two months would tell the tale.

But two months didn't tell. Oh, there were plenty of wild rumors by the Nepalese all along the upper route. Hushed stories of the two-legged creature that walked like a man. A monster the Sherpas called Yeti. Legends. Strange encounters; drums sounding from snow-swept heights; wild snatches of song drifting down from peaks that were inaccessible to ordinary men. And one concrete fact: a ban, laid on by the Buddhist monks, against the taking of any life in the high Himalayas. What life? Ed wondered.

Stories, legends—but nothing else.

Two months of it. Starting from the tropical flatlands, up through the lush, exotic rain forest, where sun struggled through immense trees festooned with orchids. Two months, moving up into the arid foothills, where foliage abruptly ceased and the rocks and wind took over. Up and ever up, to where the first heavy snow pack lay. And higher still, following the trail laid out by the glider pilot—and what impelled a man, Ed wondered, to soar over Mount Everest in a homemade glider?

Two months, during which Ed had come to dislike Doctor Schenk intensely. Tall, saturnine, smelling strongly of formaldehyde, Schenk classified everything into terms of vertebrate, invertebrate.

So now, standing on this wind-scoured ridge with the shadows falling into the abysses on either side, Ed peered through ice-encrusted goggles, watching Schenk arguing with the guides. He motioned to the ledge above, and obediently the Sherpas moved toward it. Obviously that would be the final camping spot. The two months were over by several days; Schenk was within his rights to call it quits. It was only Ed's assurances that the plateau they were seeking lay just ahead that had kept Schenk from bowing out exactly on the appointed time; that and the burning desire to secure his niche in zoology forever with a new specimen: biped, erect-walking—what?

But the plateau just ahead, and the one after that, and all the rest beyond had proved just as empty as those behind.

A bust. Whatever the unknown creatures were the glider pilot had photographed, they would remain just that—unknown.

And yet, as Ed slogged slowly up toward where the porters were setting up the bright blue-and-yellow nylon tents, he was nagged by a feeling that that odd-shaped pinnacle ahead looked awfully much like the one in the blurred photograph. With his unfailing memory for pictures, Ed remembered the tall, jagged cone that had cast a black shadow across a snowy plateau, pointing directly toward the little group that was in the center of the picture.

But Schenk wasn't having any more plateaus. He shook his head vehemently, white-daubed lips a grim line on his sun-blistered face. "Last camp, Ed," he said firmly. "We agreed this would be the final plateau. I'm already a week behind schedule. If the monsoons hit us, we could be in serious trouble below. We have to get started back. I know exactly how you feel, but—I'm afraid this is it."

Later that night, while the wind moved ceaselessly, sucking at the tent, they burrowed in sleeping bags, talking.

"There must be some basis of fact in those stories," Ed said to Doctor Schenk. "I've given them a lot of thought. Has it occurred to you that every one of the sightings, the few face-to-face meetings of the natives and these—these unknowns, has generally been just around dawn, and usually when the native was alone?"

Schenk smiled dubiously. "Whatever this creature may be—and I'm convinced that it's either a species of large bear, or one of the great anthropoids—it certainly must keep off the well-traveled routes. There are very few passes through these peaks, of course, and it would be quite simple for them to avoid these locales."

"But we're not on any known trail," Ed said thoughtfully. "I believe our methods have been all wrong—stringing out a bunch of men, looking for trails in the snow. All we've done is announce our presence to anything with ears for miles around. That glider pilot made no sound; he came on them without warning."

Ed looked intently at Schenk. "I'd like to try that peak up ahead— and the plateau beyond." When Schenk uttered a protesting cry, Ed said, "Wait; this time I'll go alone—with just one Sherpa guide. We could leave several hours before daybreak. No equipment, other than oxygen, food for one meal—and my cameras, of course. Maintain a strict silence. We could be back before noon. Will you wait long enough for this one last try?" Schenk hesitated. "Only a few hours more," Ed urged.

Schenk stared at him, then he nodded slowly. "Agreed. But aren't you forgetting the most important item of all?" When Ed looked blank, Schenk smiled. "The gas gun. If you should run across one, we'll need more proof than just your word for it."

There was very little wind, no moon, but cold, the cold approaching that of outer space, as Ed and one Sherpa porter started away from the sleeping camp, up the shattered floor of an ice river that swept down from the jagged peak ahead.

They moved up, hearing only the squeak of equipment, the peculiar gritty sound of crampons biting into packed snow, an occasional hollow crash of falling ice blocks. To the east already a faint line of gray was visible; daylight was hours away, but at this tremendous height sunrise came early. They moved slowly, the thin air cutting cruelly into their lungs, moving up, up.

They stopped once for hot chocolate from a vacuum bottle, and Ed slapped the Sherpa's shoulder, grinning, pointing ahead to where the jagged peak glowed pink and gold in the first slanting rays of the sun. The Sherpa looked at the peak and quickly shifted his glance to the sky. He gave a long, careful look at the gathering clouds in the east, then muttered something, shaking his head, pointing back, back down to where the camp was hidden in the inky shadows of enormous boulders.

When Ed resumed the climb, the Sherpa removed the long nylon line which had joined them. The route was now comparatively level, on a huge sweeping expanse of snow-covered glacier that flowed about at the base of the peak. The Sherpa, no longer in the lead, began dropping behind as Ed pressed eagerly forward.

The sun was up, and with it the wind began keening again, bitterly sharp, bringing with it a scent of coming snow. In the east, beyond the jagged peak just ahead, the immense escarpment of the Himalayas was lost in approaching cloud. Ed hurried as best he could; it would snow, and soon. He'd have to make better time.

But above, the sky was blue, infinitely blue, and behind, the sun was well up, although the camp was still lost in night below. The peak thrust up ahead, near, with what appeared to be a natural pass skirting its flank. Ed made for it. As he circled an upthrust ridge of reddish, rotten rock, he glanced ahead. The plateau spread out before him, gently sloping, a natural amphitheater full of deep, smooth snow, with peaks surrounding it, and the central peak thrusting a long black shadow directly across the center. He paused, glancing back. The Sherpa had stopped, well below him, his face a dark blur, looking up, gesticulating frantically, pointing to the clouds. Ed motioned, then moved around, leaning against the rock, peering ahead.

That great shadow against the snow was certainly similar to the one in the photo—only, of course, the shadow pointed west now, when, later, it would point northwest, as the sun swung to the south. And when it did, most certainly it was the precise— He sucked in a sharp, lung-piercing breath.

He stared, squinting against the rising wind that seemed to blow from earth's outermost reaches. Three figures stirred slightly, and suddenly leaped into focus, almost perfectly camouflaged against the snow and wind-blasted rock. Three figures, not more than a hundred feet below him. Two small, one larger.

He leaned forward, his heart thudding terribly at this twenty-thousand-foot height. A tremor of excitement shook him. My Lord—it was true. They existed. He was looking at what was undeniably a female and two smaller—what? Apes?

They were covered with downy hair, nearly white, resembling nothing so much as tight-fitting leotards. The female was exactly like any woman on earth—except for the hair. No larger than most women, with arms slightly longer, more muscular. Thighs heavier, legs out of proportion to the trunk—shorter. Breasts full and firm. Not apes.

Hardly breathing, Ed squinted, staring, motionless. Not apes. Not standing so erectly. Not with those broad, high brows. Not with the undeniable intelligence of the two young capering about their mother. Not—and seeing this, Ed trembled against the freezing rock—not with the sudden affectionate sweep of the female as she lifted the smaller and pressed it to her breast, smoothing back hair from its face with a motion common to every human mother on earth. A wonderfully tender gesture.

What were they? Less than human? Perhaps. He couldn't be certain, but he thought he heard a faint gurgle of laughter from the female, fondling the small one, and the sound stirred him strangely. Doctor Schenk had assured him that no animal was capable of genuine laughter; only man.

But they laughed, those three, and, hearing it, watching the mother tickling the younger one, watching its delighted squirming, Ed knew that in that marvelous little grouping below, perfectly lighted, perfectly staged, he was privileged to observe one of the earth's most guarded secrets.

He should get started, shooting his pictures; afterward he should stun the group into unconsciousness with the gas gun and then send the Sherpa back down for Doctor Schenk and the others. Clouds were massing, immensities of blue-black. Already the first few flakes of snow, huge and wet, drifted against his face.

But for a long moment more he remained motionless, oddly unwilling to do anything to destroy the harmony, the aching purity of the scene below, so vividly etched in brilliant light and shadow. The female, child slung casually on one hip, stood erect, hand shading her eyes, and Ed grinned. Artless, but perfectly posed. She was looking carefully about and above, scanning the great outcroppings of rock, obviously searching for something.

Then she paused. She was staring directly at him.

Ed froze, even though he knew he was perfectly concealed by the deep shadows of the high cliff behind him. She was still looking directly at him, and then, slowly her hand came up. She waved.

He shivered uncontrollably in the biting wind, trying to remain motionless. The two young ones suddenly began to jump up and down and show every evidence of joy. And suddenly Ed knew.

He turned slowly, very slowly, and with the sensation of a freezing knife plunging deeply into his chest, he saw the male less than five yards away.

It was huge, easily twice the size of the female below. And, crazily, Ed thought of Schenk's little lecture, given what seemed like eons ago, in the incredible tropical grove far below, and six weeks before, where rhododendrons grew in wild profusion and enormous butterflies flitted about: "In primitive man," Schenk had said, "as in the great apes today, the male was far larger than the female."

The gas gun was hopelessly out of reach, securely strapped to his shoulder pack. Ed stared, knowing there was absolutely nothing he could do to protect himself before this creature, fully eight feet tall, with arms as big as Ed's own thighs, and eyes (*My Lord—blue eyes!*) boring into his. There was a light of savage intelligence there—and something else.

The creature made no move against him, and Ed stared at it, breathing rapidly, shallowly and with difficulty, noting with his photographer's eyes the immense chest span, the easy rise and fall of his breathing, the large, square, white teeth, the somber cast of his face. There was long, sandy fur on the shoulders, chest and back, shortening to off-white over the rest of the magnificent torso. Ears rather small and close to the head. Short, thick neck, rising up from the broad shoulders to the back of the head in a straight line. Toes long and definitely prehensile.

They looked intently at each other across the abyss of time and mystery. Man and—what? How long, Ed wondered, had it stood there, observing him? Why hadn't it attacked? Had it been waiting for Ed to make a single threatening gesture—such as pointing a gun or camera? Seeing the calm awareness in those long, slanting, blue eyes, Ed sped a silent prayer of thanks upward; most certainly if he had made a move for camera or gun, that move would have been his last.

They looked at each other through the falling snow, and suddenly there was a perfect instantaneous understanding between them. Ed made an awkward, half-frozen little bow, moving backward. The great creature stood motionless, merely watching, and then Ed did a strange thing: He held out his hands, palms up, gave a wry grin—and ducked quickly around the outcropping of rock and began a plunging, sliding return down the way he'd come. In spite of the harsh, snow-laden wind, bitterly cold, he was perspiring.

Ed glanced back once. Nothing. Only the thickening veil of swift-blowing snow, blanking out the pinnacle, erasing every trace—every proof that anyone, anything, had stood there moments before. Only the snow, only the rocks, only the unending wind-filled silence of the top of the world. Nothing else.

The Sherpa was struggling up to him from below, terribly anxious to get started back; the storm was rising. Without a word they hooked up and began the groping, stumbling descent back to the last camp. They found the camp already broken, Sherpas already moving out. Schenk paused only long enough to give Ed a questioning look.

What could Ed say? Schenk was a scientist, demanding material proof: If not a corpse, at the very least a photograph. The only photographs Ed had were etched in his mind—not on film. And even if he could persuade Schenk to wait, when the storm cleared, the giant, forewarned, would be gone. Some farther peak, some remoter plateau would echo to his young ones' laughter.

Feeling not a bit bad about it, Ed gave Schenk a barely perceptible negative nod. Instantly Schenk shrugged, turned and went plunging down, into the thickening snow, back into the world of littler men. Ed trailed behind.

On the arduous trek back, through that first great storm, through the snow line, through the rain forest, hot and humid, Ed thought of the giant, back up there where the air was thin and pure.

Who, what was he, and his race? Castaways on this planet, forever marooned, yearning for a distant, never-to-be-reached home?

Or did they date in unbroken descent from the Pleistocene—man's first beginning—when all the races of not-quite-man were giants; unable, or unwilling, to take the fork in the road that led to smaller, cleverer man, forced to retreat higher and higher, to more remote areas, until finally there was only one corner of earth left to them—the high Himalayas?

Or were he and his kind earth's last reserves: not-yet-men, waiting for the opening of still another chapter in earth's unending mystery story?

Whatever the giant was, his secret was safe with him, Ed thought. For who would believe it—even if he chose to tell?

16

Like the Abominable Snowman, the Loch Ness Monster is believed to date from prehistoric times, yet it has only been the subject of intensive study in the twentieth century. A mysterious lake creature, it has been immortalized in books, films and cartoons and has produced a thriving tourist industry for one of Scotland's most beautiful lochs. Written records of the monster date back as far as A.D. 565 when St. Columba, the Abbot of Iona, was said to have been confronted by a "water monster" which he drove off by prayer. Throughout the Middle Ages there were similar reports of local inhabitants seeing a "water horse" or "dark monster" rearing up from the waves of the loch. However, it was not until 1933 that the sighting took place which attracted headlines around the world. On the evening of May 22, John McKay and his wife were driving in their car along the north shore of Loch Ness when suddenly "a huge and terrifying creature loomed out of the water and traveled across the surface at great speed before disappearing under the waves," according to Mr. McKay. No explanation could at first be offered for the dramatic reappearance of the monster who had apparently remained unseen for several centuries—then someone thought of the construction work for a

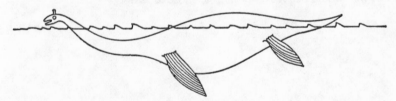

The Loch Ness Monster, based on a sketch made by the Cambridge biologist Bruce Ing in 1960.

new road which was being built around Loch Ness. Could the noise and vibrations of demolition have attracted the monster's attention? It certainly seemed a possibility, for during the remainder of 1933 over one hundred and fifty more sightings were recorded before the work was completed. From these reports it was possible to reconstruct a picture of the creature, which appeared to have a huge humped back and tail, four webbed flippers, and a long, swanlike neck surmounted by a tiny head. The monster's dimensions were estimated to be about forty feet long and fourteen feet high, with an arched neck and strong tail. Although some reports described him as "terrifyingly powerful," he seemingly disappeared at the first movement or sound. The local Scots took affectionately to *an Niseag,* as they called the creature, and, at first, were annoyed at the teams of newspaper reporters, scientists, students and curiosity seekers who poured into the district. But all of this observation did result in four photographs taken by a London surgeon, Dr. Robert Kenneth Wilson, which have since proved one of the main buttresses against those who scoff at the whole legend. They disproved one popular theory that the creature was a large gray seal, and added some weight to the suggestion of the Reverend David Blair, the Abbot of Dunfermline, that the monster was a survival of the postglacial period when the loch was still connected with the ocean. In the years since these first reports, much research has been carried out at Loch Ness by both scientists and amateur enthusiasts—the most recent study being made in 1973 by a fifteen-member Japanese party who spent $50,000 on equipment and time, but in the end could only report of hearing "some mysterious noises that suggest there is something there." A Loch Ness Phenomena Investigation Bureau has also been established in Inverness to look into reports of alleged sightings. They claim to have averaged one sighting for every 350 hours of observation and favor the conclusion reached by a study team from London University in 1970 that there may well be more than one monster in the loch. They are also fascinated by the report of a land sighting of the creature by a party of schoolchildren who recently crossed the loch. Passing Bracorina Point, the account says, the children shouted, "Oh, look! What is that big thing on the bank over there?" Their boatman, Mr. Macdonald Robertson, later told an investigator that what he saw was "about the size of a full-grown Indian elephant." It plunged off the rocks into the water with a mighty splash which rocked the boat over one hundred yards away. The mystery of the Loch Ness Monster shows every indication of puzzling laymen and scientists alike for a great many years to come, just as it has that master of detective fiction *Leslie Charteris* (1907–   ). And what more natural thing could Mr. Charteris do than to bring the wits and resources of his famous character The Saint to bear on the mystery? "The Convenient Monster," written in 1965, is like no other Simon Templar investigation, and it may just possibly contain the answers to some of those baffling questions about *an Niseag* . . .

THE CONVENIENT MONSTER
Leslie Charteris

"Of course," said Inspector Robert Mackenzie, of the Invernessshire Constabulary, with a burr as broad as his boots seeming to add an extra R to the word, "I know ye're only in Scotland as an ordinary visitor, and no' expectin' to be mixed up in any criminal business."

"That's right," said the Saint cheerfully.

He was so used to this sort of thing that the monotony sometimes became irritating, but Inspector Mackenzie made the conventional gambit with such courteous geniality that it almost sounded like an official welcome. He was a large and homely man with large red hands and small twinkling grey eyes and sandy hair carefully plastered over the bare patch above his forehead, and so very obviously and traditionally a policeman that Simon Templar actually felt a kind of nostalgic affection for him. Short of a call from Chief Inspector Claud Eustace Teal in person, nothing could have brought back more sharply what the Saint often thought of as the good days; and he took it as a compliment that even after so many years, and even as far away as Scotland itself, he was not lost to the telescopic eye of Scotland Yard.

"And I suppose," Mackenzie continued, "ye couldna even be bothered with a wee bit of a local mystery."

"What's your problem?" Simon asked. "Has somebody stolen the haggis you were fattening for the annual Police Banquet?"

The Inspector ignored this with the same stony dignity with which he would have greeted the hoary question about what a Scotsman wore under his kilt.

"It might be involvin' the Loch Ness Monster," he said with the utmost gravity.

"All right," said the Saint good-humouredly. "I started this. I suppose I had it coming. But you're the first policeman who ever tried to pull my leg. Didn't they tell you that I'm the guy who's supposed to do the pulling?"

"I'm no' makin' a joke," Mackenzie persisted aggrievedly, and the Saint stared at him.

It was in the spring of 1933 that a remarkable succession of sober and reputable witnesses began to testify that they had seen in Loch Ness a monstrous creature whose existence had been a legend of the region since ancient times, but which few persons in this century had claimed to have seen for themselves. The descriptions varied in detail, as human observations are prone to do, but they seemed generally to agree that the beast was roughly 30 feet long and could swim at about the same number of miles per hour; it was a dark grey in colour, with a small horse-like head on a long tapering neck, which it turned from side to side with the quick movements of an alert hen. There were divergencies as to whether it had one or more humps in its back, and whether it churned the water with flippers or a powerful tail; but all agreed that it could not be classified with anything known to modern natural history.

The reports culminated in December with a photograph showing a strange reptilian shape thrashing in the water, taken by a senior employee of the British Aluminium Company, which has a plant nearby. A number of experts certified the negative to be unretouched and unfaked, and the headline writers took it from there.

Within a fortnight a London newspaper had a correspondent on the scene with a highly publicized big-game authority in tow; some footprints were found and casts made of them—which before the New Year was three days old had been pronounced by the chief zoologists of the British Museum to have all been made by the right hind foot of a hippopotamus, and a stuffed hippopotamus at that. In the nationwide guffaw which followed the exposure of this hoax, the whole matter exploded into a theme for cartoonists and comedians, and that aura of hilarious incredulity still coloured the Saint's vague recollections of the subject.

It took a little while for him to convince himself that the Inspector's straight face was not part of an elaborate exercise in Highland humour.

"What has the Monster done that's illegal?" Simon inquired at length, with a gravity to match Mackenzie's own.

"A few weeks ago, it's thocht to ha' eaten a sheep. And last night it may ha' killed a dog."

"Where was this?"

"The sheep belonged to Fergus Clanraith, who has a farm by the loch beyond Foyers, and the dog belongs to his neighbours, a couple named Bastion from doon in England who settled here last summer.

'Tis only aboot twenty miles away, if ye could spairr the time with me."

The Saint sighed. In certain interludes, he thought that everything had already happened to him that could befall a man even with his exceptional gift for stumbling into fantastic situations and being offered bizarre assignments, but apparently there was always some still more preposterous imbroglio waiting to entangle him.

"Okay," he said resignedly. "I've been slugged with practically every other improbability you could raise an eyebrow at, so why should I draw the line at dog-slaying monsters. Lay on, Macduff."

"The name is Mackenzie," said the Inspector seriously.

Simon paid his hotel bill and took his own car, for he had been intending to continue his pleasantly aimless wandering that day anyhow, and it would not make much difference to him where he stopped along the way. He followed Mackenzie's somewhat venerable chariot out of Inverness on the road that takes the east bank of the Ness River, and in a few minutes the slaty grimness of the town had been gratefully forgotten in the green and gold loveliness of the countryside.

The road ran at a fairly straight tangent to the curves of the river and the Caledonoan Canal, giving only infrequent glimpses of the seven locks built to lift shipping to the level of the lake, until at Dores he had his first view of Loch Ness at its full breadth.

The Great Glen of Scotland transects the country diagonally from north-east to south-west, as if a giant had tried to break off the upper end of the land between the deep natural notches formed by Loch Linnhe and the Beauly Firth. On the map which Simon had seen, the chain of lochs stretched in an almost crow-flight line that had made him look twice to be sure that there was not in fact a clear channel across from the Eastern to the Western Sea. Loch Ness itself, a tremendous trough 24 miles long but only averaging about a mile in width, suggested nothing more than an enlargement of the Canal system which gave access to it at both ends.

But not many vessels seemed to avail themselves of the passage, for there was no boat in sight on the lake that afternoon. With the water as calm as a mill-pond and the fields and trees rising from its shores to a blue sky dappled with soft woolly clouds, it was as pretty as a picture postcard and utterly unconvincing to think of as a place which might be haunted by some outlandish horror from the mists of antiquity.

For a drive of twenty minutes, at the sedate pace set by Mackenzie the highway paralleled the edge of the loch a little way up its steep stony banks. The opposite shore widened slightly into the tranquil beauty of Urquhart Bay with its ancient castle standing out grey and stately on the far point, and then returned to the original almost uniform breadth. Then, within fortunately brief sight of the unpicturesque aluminium works, it bore away to the south through the small stark village of Foyers and went winding up the glen of one of the tumbling streams that feed the lake.

Several minutes further on, Mackenzie turned off into a narrow side road that twisted around and over a hill and swung down again, until suddenly the loch was spread out squarely before them once more and the lane curled past the first of two houses that could be seen standing solitarily apart from each other but each within a bowshot of the loch. Both of them stood out with equal harshness against the gentle curves and colours of the landscape with the same dark graceless austerity as the last village or the last town or any other buildings Simon had seen in Scotland, a country whose unbounded natural beauty seemed to have inspired no corresponding artistry in its architects, but rather to have goaded them into competition to offset it with the most contrasting ugliness into which bricks and stone and tile could be assembled. This was a paradox to which he had failed to fit a plausible theory for so long that he had finally given up trying.

Beside the first house a man in a stained shirt and corduroy trousers tucked into muddy canvas leggings was digging in a vegetable garden. He looked up as Mackenzie brought his rattletrap to a stop, and walked slowly over to the hedge. He was short but powerfully built, and his hair flamed like a stormy sunset.

Mackenzie climbed out and beckoned to the Saint. As Simon reached them, the red-haired man was saying: "Aye, I've been over and seen what's left o' the dog. It's more than they found of my sheep, I can tell ye."

"But could it ha' been the same thing that did it?" asked the Inspector.

"That' no' for me to say, Mackenzie. I'm no' a detective. But remember, it wasna me who said the Monster took my sheep. It was the Bastions who thocht o' that, it might be to head me off from askin' if *they* hadn't been the last to see it—pairhaps on their Sunday dinner table. There's nae such trick I wouldna put beyond the Sassenach."

Mackenzie introduced them: "This is Mr. Clanraith, whom I was tellin' ye aboot. Fergus, I'd like ye to meet Mr. Templar, who may be helpin' me to investigate."

Clanraith gave Simon a muscular and horny grip across the untrimmed hedge, appraising him shrewdly from under shaggy ginger brows.

"Ye dinna look like a policeman, Mr. Templar."

"I try not to," said Saint expressionlessly. "Did you mean by what you were just saying that you don't believe in the Monster at all?"

"I didna say that."

"Then apart from anything else, you think there might actually be such a thing."

"There might."

"Living where you do, I should think you'd have as good a chance as anyone of seeing it yourself—if it does exist."

The farmer peered at Simon suspiciously.

"Wad ye be a reporter, Mr. Templar, pairhaps?"

"No, I'm not," Simon assured him; but the other remained wary.

"When a man tells o' seein' monsters, his best friends are apt to wonder if he may ha' taken a wee drop too much. If I had seen anything, ever, I wadna be talkin' aboot it to every stranger, to be made a laughin'-stock of."

"But ye'll admit," Mackenzie put in, "it's no' exactly normal for a dog to be chewed up an' killed the way this one was."

"I wull say this," Clanraith conceded guardedly. "It's strange that nobody haird the dog bark, or e'en whimper."

Through the Saint's mind flickered an eerie vision of something amorphous and loathsome oozing soundlessly out of night-blackened water, flowing with obscene stealth towards a hound that slept unwarned by any of its senses.

"Do you mean it mightn't've had a chance to let out even a yip?"

"I'm no' sayin'," Clanraith maintained cautiously. "But it was a guid watchdog, if naught else."

A girl had stepped out of the house and come closer while they talked. She had Fergus Clanraith's fiery hair and greenish eyes, but her skin was pink and white where his was weatherbeaten and her lips were full where his were tight. She was a half a head taller than he, and her figure was slim where it should be.

Now she said: "That's right. He even barked whenever he heard me coming, although he saw me every day."

Her voice was low and well modulated, with only an attractive trace of her father's accent.

"Then if it was a pairson wha' killed him, Annie, 'twad only mean it was a body he was still more used to."

"But you can't really believe that any human being would do a thing like that to a dog that knew them—least of all to their own dog!"

"That's the trouble wi' lettin' a lass be brocht up an' schooled on the wrong side o' the Tweed," Clanraith said darkly. "She forgets what the English ha' done to honest Scotsmen no' so lang syne."

The girl's eyes had kept returning to the Saint with candid interest, and it was to him that she explained, smiling: "Father still wishes he could fight for Bonnie Prince Charlie. He's glad to let me do part-time secretarial work for Mr. Bastion because I can live at home and keep house as well, but he still feels I'm guilty of fraternizing with the Enemy."

"We'd best be gettin' on and talk to them ourselves," Mackenzie said. "And then we'll see if Mr. Templar has any more questions to ask."

There was something in Annie Clanraith's glance which seemed to say that she hoped that he would, and the Saint was inclined to be of the same sentiment. He had certainly not expected to find anyone so decorative in the cast of characters, and he began to feel a tentative quickening of optimism about this interruption in his travels. He could see her in his rear-view mirror, still standing by the hedge and following with her gaze after her father had turned back to his digging.

About three hundred yards and a few bends farther on, Mackenzie veered between a pair of stone gatepost and chugged to a standstill on the circular driveway in front of the second house. Simon stopped behind him and then strolled after him to the front door, which was opened almost at once by a tall thin man in a pullover and baggy grey flannel slacks.

"Good afternoon, sir," said the detective courteously. "I'm Inspector Mackenzie from Inverness. Are ye Mr. Bastion?"

"Yes."

Bastion had a bony face with a long aquiline nose, lank black hair flecked with grey, and a broad toothbrush moustache that gave him an indeterminately military appearance. His black eyes flickered to the Saint inquiringly.

"This is Mr. Templar, who may be assistin' me," Mackenzie said. "The constable who was here this morning told me all aboot what ye showed him, on the telephone, but could we ha' a wee look for ourselves?"

"Oh, yes, certainly. Will you come this way?"

The way was around the house, across an uninspired formal garden at the back which looked overdue for the attention of a gardener, and through a small orchard beyond which a stretch of rough grass sloped quickly down to the water. As the meadow fell away, a pebbly beach came into view, and Simon saw that this was one of the rare breaches in the steep average angle of the loch's sides. On either side of the little beach the ground swelled up again to form a shallow bowl that gave an easy natural access to the lake. The path that they traced led to a short rustic pier with a shabby skiff tied to it, and on the ground to one side of the pier was something covered with potato sacking.

"I haven't touched anything, as the constable asked me," Bastion said. "Except to cover him up."

He bent down and carefully lifted off the burlap.

They looked down in silence at what was uncovered.

"The puir beastie," Mackenzie said at last.

It had been a large dog of confused parentage in which the Alsatian may have predominated. What had happened to it was no nicer to look at than it is to catalogue. Its head and hindquarters were partly mashed to a red pulp; and plainly traceable across its chest was a row of slot-like gashes, each about an inch long and close together, from which blood had run and clotted in the short fur. Mackenzie squatted and stretched the skin with gentle fingers to see the slits more clearly. The Saint also felt the chest: it had an unnatural contour where the line of punctures crossed it, and his probing touch found only sponginess where there should have been a hard cage of ribs.

His eyes met Mackenzie's across the pitifully mangled form.

"That would be quite a row of teeth," he remarked.

"Aye," said the Inspector grimly. "But what lives here that has a mouth like that?"

They straightened up and surveyed the immediate surroundings. The ground here, only a stride or two from the beach, which in turn was less than a yard wide, was so moist that it was soggy, and pockets of muddy liquid stood in the deeper indentations with which it was plentifully rumpled. The carpet of coarse grass made individual impressions difficult to identify, but three or four shoe-heel prints could be positively distinguished.

"I'm afraid I made a lot of those tracks," Bastion said. "I know you're not supposed to go near anything, but all I could think of at the time was seeing if *he* was still alive and if I could do anything for him.

The constable tramped around a bit too, when he was here." He pointed past the body. "But neither of us had anything to do with those marks there."

Close to the beach was a place where the turf looked as if it had been raked by something with three gigantic claws. One talon had caught in the roots of a tuft of grass and torn it up bodily: the clump lay on the pebbles at the water's edge. Aside from that, the claws had left three parallel grooves, about four inches apart and each about half an inch wide. They dug into the ground at their upper ends to a depth of more than two inches, and dragged back toward the lake for a length of about ten inches as they tapered up.

Simon and Mackenzie stood on the pebbles to study the marks. Simon spanned them experimentally with his fingers while the detective took exact measurements with a tape and entered them in his notebook.

"Anything wi' a foot big enough to carry claws like that," Mackenzie said, "I'd no' wish to ha' comin' after me."

"Well, they call it a Monster, don't they?" said the Saint dryly. "It wouldn't impress anyone if it made tracks like a mouse."

Mackenzie unbent his knees stiffly, shooting the Saint a distrustful glance, and turned to Bastion.

"When did ye find all this, sir?" he asked.

"I suppose it was about six o'clock," Bastion said. "I woke up before dawn and couldn't get to sleep again, so I decided to try a little early fishing. I got up as soon as it was light—"

"Ye didna hear any noise before that?"

"No."

"It couldna ha' been the dog barkin' that woke ye?"

"Not that I'm aware of. And my wife is a very light sleeper, and she didn't hear anything. But I was rather surprised when I didn't see the dog outside. He doesn't sleep in the house, but he's always waiting on the doorstep in the morning. However, I came on down here—and that's how I found him."

"And you didn't see anything else?" Simon asked. "In the lake, I mean."

"No. I didn't see the Monster. And when I looked for it, there wasn't a ripple on the water. Of course, the dog may have been killed some time before, though his body was still warm."

"Mr. Bastion," Mackenzie said, "do *ye* believe it was the Monster that killed him?"

Bastion looked at him and at the Saint.

"I'm not a superstitious man," he replied. "But if it wasn't a monster of some kind, what else could it have been?"

The Inspector closed his notebook with a snap that seemed to be echoed by his clamping lips. It was evident that he felt that the situation was wandering far outside his professional province. He scowled at the Saint as though he expected Simon to do something about it.

"It might be interesting," Simon said thoughtfully, "if we got a vet to do a post-mortem."

"What for?" Bastion demanded brusquely.

"Let's face it," said the Saint. "Those claw marks *could* be fakes. And the dog *could* have been mashed up with some sort of club—even a club with spikes set in it to leave wounds that'd look as if they were made by teeth. But by all accounts, no one could have got near enough to the dog to do that without him barking. *Unless the dog was doped first.* So before we go overboard on this Monster theory, I'd like to rule everything else out. An autopsy would do that."

Bastion rubbed his scrubby moustache.

"I see your point. Yes, that might be a good idea."

He helped them to shift the dog on to the sack which had previously covered it, and Simon and Mackenzie carried it between them back to the driveway and laid it in the boot of the detective's car.

"D'ye think we could ha' a wurrd wi' Mrs. Bastion, sir?" Mackenzie asked, wiping his hands on a clean rag and passing it to the Saint.

"I suppose so," Bastion assented dubiously. "Although she's pretty upset about this, as you can imagine. It was really her dog more than mine. But come in, and I'll see if she'll talk to you for a minute."

But Mrs. Bastion herself settled that by meeting them in the hall, and she made it obvious that she had been watching them from a window.

"What are they doing with Golly, Noel?" she greeted her husband wildly. "Why are they taking him away?"

"They want to have him examined by a doctor, dear."

Bastion went on to explain why, until she interrupted him again:

"Then don't let them bring him back. It's bad enough to have seen him the way he is, without having to look at him dissected." She turned to Simon and Mackenzie. "You must understand how I feel. Golly was like a son to me. His name was really Goliath—I called him that because he was so big and fierce, but actually he was a pushover when you got on the right side of him."

Words came from her in a driving torrent that suggested the corollary of a power-house. She was a big-boned strong-featured woman who made no attempt to minimize any of her probable forty-five years. Her blonde hair was unwaved and pulled back into a tight bun, and her blue eyes were set in a nest of wrinkles that would have been called characterful on an outdoor man. Her lipstick, which needed renewing, had a slapdash air of being her one impatient concession to feminine artifice. But Bastion put a soothing arm around her as solicitously as if she had been a dimpled bride.

"I'm sure these officers will have him buried for us, Eleanor," he said. "But while they're here I think they wanted to ask you something."

"Only to confairrm what Mr. Bastion told us, ma'am," said Mackenzie. "That ye didna hear an disturrbance last night."

"Absolutely not. And if Golly had made a sound, I should have heard him. I always do. Why are you trying so hard to get around the facts? It's as plain as a pikestaff that the Monster did it."

"Some monsters have two legs," Simon remarked.

"And I suppose you're taught not to believe in any other kind. Even with the evidence under your very eyes."

"I mind a time when some other footprints were found, ma'am," Mackenzie put in deferentially, "which turned oot to be a fraud."

"I know exactly what you're referring to. And that stupid hoax made a lot of idiots disbelieve the authentic photograph which was taken just before it, and refuse to accept an even better picture that was taken by a thoroughly reputable London surgeon about four months later. I know what I'm talking about. As a matter of fact, the reason we took this house was mainly because I'm hoping to discover the Monster."

Two pairs of eyebrows shot up and lowered almost in unison, but it was the Saint who spoke for Mackenzie as well as himself.

"How would you do that, Mrs. Bastion?" he inquired with some circumspection. "If the Monster has been well known around here for a few centuries, at least to everyone who believes in him—"

"It still hasn't been scientifically and officially established. I'd like to have the credit for doing that, beyond any shadow of doubt, and naming it *monstrum eleanoris*."

"Probably you gentlemen don't know it," Bastion elucidated, with a kind of quaintly protective pride, "but Mrs. Bastion is a rather distinguished naturalist. She's hunted every kind of big game there is, and even holds a couple of world's records."

"But I never had a trophy as important as this would be," his better half took over again. "I expect you think I'm a little cracked—that there couldn't really be any animal of any size in the world that hasn't been discovered by this time. Tell them the facts of life, Noel."

Bastion cleared his throat like a schoolboy preparing to recite, and said with much the same awkward air: "The gorilla was only discovered in 1847, the giant panda in 1869, and the okapi wasn't discovered till 1901. Of course explorers brought back rumours of them, but people thought they were just native fairy tales. And you yourselves probably remember reading about the first coelacanth being caught. That was only in 1938."

"So why shouldn't there still be something else left that I could be the first to prove?" Eleanor Bastion concluded for him. "The obvious thing to go after, I suppose, was the Abominable Snowman; but Mr. Bastion can't stand high altitudes. So I'm making do with the Loch Ness Monster."

Inspector Mackenzie, who had for some time been looking progressively more confused and impatient in spite of his politely valiant efforts to conceal the fact, finally managed to interrupt the antiphonal barrage of what he could only be expected to regard as delirious irrelevancies.

"All that I'm consairned wi', ma'am," he said heavily, "is tryin' to detairrmine whether there's a human felon to be apprehended. If it should turrn oot to be a monster, as ye're thinkin', it wadna be in my jurisdeection. However, in that case, pairhaps Mr. Templar, who is no' a police officer, could be o' more help to ye."

"Templar," Bastion repeated slowly. "I feel as if I ought to recognize that name, now, but I was rather preoccupied with something else when I first heard it."

"Do you have a halo on you somewhere?" quizzed Mrs. Bastion, the huntress, in a tone which somehow suggested the aiming of a gun.

"Sometimes."

"Well, by Jove!" Bastion said. "I should've guessed it, of course, if I'd been thinking about it. You didn't sound like a policeman."

Mackenzie winced faintly, but both the Bastions were too openly absorbed in re-appraising the Saint to notice it.

Simon Templar should have been hardened to that kind of scrutiny, but as the years went on it was beginning to cause him a mixture of embarrassment and petty irritation. He wished that new acquaintances could dispense with the reactions and stay with their original problems.

He said, rather roughly: "It's just my bad luck that Mackenzie caught me as I was leaving Inverness. I was on my way to Loch Lomond, like any innocent tourist, to find out how bonnie the banks actually are. He talked me into taking the low road instead of the high road, and stopping here to stick my nose into your problem."

"But that's perfectly wonderful!" Mrs. Bastion announced like a bugle. "Noel, ask him to stay the night. I mean, for the week-end. Or for the rest of the week, if he can spare the time."

"Why—er—yes," Bastion concurred obediently. "Yes, of course. We'd be delighted. The Saint ought to have some good ideas about catching a monster."

Simon regarded him coolly, aware of the invisible glow of slightly malicious expectation emanating from Mackenzie, and made a reckless instant decision.

"Thank you," he said. "I'd love it. I'll bring in my things, and Mac can be on his way."

He sauntered out without further palaver, happily conscious that only Mrs. Bastion had not been moderately rocked by his casual acceptance.

They all ask for it, he thought. Cops and civilians alike, as soon as they hear the name. Well, let's oblige them. And see how they like whatever comes of it.

Mackenzie followed him outside, with a certain ponderous dubiety which indicated that some of the joke had already evaporated.

"Ye'll ha' no authorrity in this, ye underrstand," he emphasized, "except the rights o' any private investigator—which are no' the same in Scotland as in America, to judge by some o' the books I've read."

"I shall try very hard not to gang agley," Simon assured him. "Just phone me the result of the P.M. as soon as you possibly can. And while you're waiting for it, you might look up the law about shooting monsters. See if one has to take out a special licence, or anything like that."

He watched the detective drive away, and went back in with his two-suiter. He felt better already, with no official eyes and ears absorbing his most trivial responses. And it would be highly misleading to say that he found the bare facts of the case, as they had been presented to him, utterly banal and boring.

Noel Bastion showed him to a small but comfortable room upstairs, with a window that faced towards the home of Fergus Clanraith but which also afforded a sidelong glimpse of the loch. Mrs. Bastion was already busy there, making up the bed.

"You can't get any servants in a place like this," she explained. "I'm lucky to have a woman who bicycles up from Fort Augustus once a week to do the heavy cleaning. They all want to stay in the towns where they can have what they think of as a bit of life."

Simon looked at Bastion innocuously and remarked: "You're lucky to find a secretary right on the spot like the one I met up the road."

"Oh, you mean Annie Clanraith." Bastion scrubbed a knuckle on his upper lip. "Yes. She was working in Liverpool, but she came home at Christmas to spend the holidays with her father. I had to get some typing done in a hurry, and she helped me out. It was Clanraith who talked her into staying. I couldn't pay her as much as she'd been earning in Liverpool, but he pointed out that she'd end up with just as much in her pocket if she didn't have to pay for board and lodging, which he'd give her if she kept house. He's a widower, so it's not a bad deal for him."

"Noel's a writer," Mrs. Bastion said. "His big book isn't finished yet, but he works on it all the time."

"It's a life of Wellington," said the writer. "It's never been done, as I think it should be, by a professional soldier."

"Mackenzie didn't tell me anything about your background," said the Saint. "What should he have called you—Colonel?"

"Only Major. But that was in the Regular Army."

Simon did not miss the faintly defensive tone of the addendum. But the silent calculation he made was that the pension of a retired British Army Major, unless augmented by some more commercial form of authorship than an unfinished biography of distinctly limited appeal, would not finance enough big-game safaris to earn an ambitious huntress a great reputation.

"There," said Mrs. Bastion finally. "Now, if you'd like to settle in and make yourself at home, I'll have some tea ready in five minutes."

The Saint had embarked on his Scottish trip with an open mind and an attitude of benevolent optimism, but if anyone had prophesied that it would lead to him sipping tea in the drawing-room of two practically total strangers, with his valise unpacked in their guest bedroom, and solemnly chatting about a monster as if it were as real as a monkey, he would probably have been mildly derisive. His hostess, however, was obsessed with the topic.

"Listen to this," she said, fetching a well-worn volume from a bookcase. "It's a quotation from the biography of St. Columba, written about the middle of the seventh century. It tells about his visit to Inverness some hundred years before, and it says *he was obliged to cross the water of Nesa; and when he had come to the bank he sees some of the inhabitants bringing an unfortunate fellow whom, as those who were bringing him related, a little while before some aquatic monster seized and savagely bit while he was swimming. . . . The blessed man orders one of his companions to swim out and bring him from over the water a coble . . . Lugne Mocumin without delay takes off his clothes except his tunic and casts himself into the water. But the monster comes up and moves towards the man as he swam. . . . The blessed man, seeing it, commanded the ferocious monster saying, 'Go thou no further nor touch the man; go back at once.' Then on hearing this word of the Saint the monster was terrified and fled away again more quickly than if it had been dragged off by ropes.*"

"I must try to remember that formula," Simon murmured, "and hope the Monster can't tell one Saint from another."

"'Monster' is really a rather stupid name for it," Mrs. Bastion said. "It encourages people to be illogical about it. Actually, in the old days the local people called it *an Niseag,* which is simply the name 'Ness' in Gaelic with a feminine diminutive ending. You could literally translate it as 'Nessie'."

"That does sound a lot cuter," Simon agreed. "If you forget how it plays with dogs."

Eleanor Bastion's weathered face went pale, but the muscles under the skin did not flinch.

"I haven't forgotten Golly. But I was trying to keep my mind off him."

"Assuming this beastie does exist," said the Saint, "how did it get here?"

"Why did it have to 'get' here at all? I find it easier to believe that it always was here. The loch is 750 feet deep, which is twice the mean depth of the North Sea. *An Niseag* is a creature that obviously prefers the depths and only comes to the surface occasionally. I think its original home was always at the bottom of the loch, and it was trapped there when some prehistoric geological upheaval cut off the loch from the sea."

"And it's lived there ever since—for how many million years?"

"Not the original ones—I suppose we must assume at least a couple. But their descendants. Like many primitive creatures, it probably lives to a tremendous age."

"What do you think it is?"

"Most likely something of the plesiosaurus family. The descriptions sound more like that than anything—large body, long neck, paddle-like legs. Some people claim to have seen stumpy projections on its head, rather like the horns of a snail, which aren't part of the usual reconstruction of a plesiosaurus. But after all, we've never seen much of a plesiosaurus except its skeleton. You wouldn't know exactly what a snail looked like if you'd only seen its shell."

"But if Nessie has been here all this time, why wasn't she reported much longer ago?"

"She was. You heard that story about St. Columba. And if you think only modern observations are worth paying attention to, several reliable sightings were recorded from 1871 onwards."

"But there was no motor road along the loch until 1933," Bastion managed to contribute at last, "and a trip like you made today would have been quite an expedition. So there weren't many witnesses about until fairly recently, of the type that scientists would take seriously."

Simon lighted a cigarette. The picture was clear enough. Like the flying saucers, it depended on what you wanted to believe—and whom.

Except that here there was not only fantasy to be thought of. There could be felony.

"What would you have to do to make it an official discovery?"

"We have movie and still cameras with the most powerful telephoto lenses you can buy," said the woman. "I spend eight hours a day simply watching the lake, just like anyone might put in at a regular job, but I vary the times of day systematically. Noel sometimes puts in a few hours as well. We have a view for several miles in both directions, and by the law of averages *an Niseag* must come up eventually in the area we're covering. Whenever that happens, our lenses will get close-up pictures that'll show every detail beyond any possibility of argument. It's simply a matter of patience, and when I came here I made up my mind that I'd spend ten years on it if necessary."

"And now," said the Saint, "I guess you're more convinced than ever that you're on the right track and the scent is hot."

Mrs. Bastion looked him in the eyes with terrifying equanimity.

"Now," she said, "I'm going to watch with a Weatherby Magnum as well as the cameras. *An Niseag* can't be much bigger than an elephant, and it isn't any more bulletproof. I used to think it'd be a crime to kill the last survivor of a species, but since I saw what it did to poor Golly I'd like to have it as a trophy as well as a picture."

There was much more of this conversation, but nothing that would not seem repetitious in verbatim quotation. Mrs. Bastion had accumulated numerous other books on the subject, from any of which she was prepared to read excerpts in support of her convictions.

It was hardly eight-thirty, however, after a supper of cold meat and salad, when she announced that she was going to bed.

"I want to get up at two o'clock and be out at the loch well before daylight—the same time when that thing must have been there this morning."

"Okay," said the Saint. "Knock on my door, and I'll go with you."

He remained to accept a nightcap of Peter Dawson, which seemed to taste especially rich and smooth in the land where they made it. Probably this was his imagination, but it gave him a pleasant feeling of drinking the wine of the country on its own home ground.

"If you're going to be kind enough to look after her, I may sleep a bit later," Bastion said. "I must get some work done on my book tonight, while there's a little peace and quiet. Not that Eleanor can't take care of herself better than most women, but I wouldn't like her being out there alone after what's happened."

"You're thoroughly sold on this monster yourself, are you?"

The other stared into his glass.

"It's the sort of thing that all my instincts and experience would take with a grain of salt. But you've seen for yourself that it isn't easy to argue with Eleanor. And I must admit that she makes a terrific case for it. But until this morning I was keeping an open mind."

"And now it isn't so open?"

"Quite frankly, I'm pretty shaken. I feel it's got to be settled now, one way or the other. Perhaps you'll have some luck tomorrow."

It did in fact turn out to be a vigil that gave Simon goose-pimples, but they were caused almost entirely by the pre-dawn chill of the air. Daylight came slowly, through a grey and leaky-looking overcast. The lake remained unruffled, guarding its secrets under a pale pearly glaze.

"I wonder what we did wrong," Mrs. Bastion said at last, when the daylight was as broad as the clouds evidently intended to let it become. "The thing should have come back to where it made its last kill. Perhaps if we hadn't been so sentimental we should have left Golly right where he was and built a *machan* over him where we could have stood watch in turns."

Simon was not so disappointed. Indeed, if a monster had actually appeared almost on schedule under their expectant eyes, he would have been inclined to sense the hand of a Hollywood B-picture producer rather than the finger of Fate.

"As you said yesterday, it's a matter of patience," he observed philosophically. "But the odds are that the rest of your eight hours, now, will be just routine. So if you're not nervous I'll ramble around a while."

His rambling had brought him no nearer to the house than the orchard when the sight of a coppery-rosy head on top of a shapely free-swinging figure made his pulse fluctuate enjoyably with a reminder of the remotely possible promise of romantic compensation that had started to warm his interest the day before.

Annie Clanraith's smile was so eager and happy to see him that he might have been an old and close friend who had been away for a long time.

"Inspector Mackenzie told my father he'd left you here. I'm so glad you stayed!"

"I'm glad you're glad," said the Saint, and against her ingenuous sincerity it was impossible to make the reply sound even vestigially sceptical. "But what made it so important?"

"Just having someone new and alive to talk to. You haven't stayed long enough to find out how bored you can be here."

"But you've got a job that must be a little more attractive than going back to an office in Liverpool."

"Oh, it's not bad. And it helps to make father comfortable. And it's nice to live in such beautiful scenery, I expect you'll say. But I read books and I look at the TV, and I can't stop having my silly dreams."

"A gal like you," he said teasingly, "should have her hands full, fighting off other dreamers."

"All I get my hands full of is pages and pages of military strategy, about a man who only managed to beat Napoleon. But at least Napoleon had Josephine. The only thing Wellington gave his name to was an old boot."

Simon clucked sympathetically.

"He may have had moments with his boots off, you know. Or has your father taught you to believe nothing good of anyone who was ever born south of the Tweed?"

"You must have thought it was terrible, the way he talked about Mr. Bastion. And he's so nice, isn't he? It's too bad he's married!"

"Maybe his wife doesn't think so."

"I mean, I'm a normal girl and I'm not old-fashioned, and the one thing I do miss here is a man to fight off. In fact, I'm beginning to feel that if one did come along I wouldn't even struggle."

"You sound as if that Scottish song was written about you," said the Saint, and he sang softly:

> *"Ilka lassie has her laddie,*
> *   Ne'er a ane ha' I;*
> *But all the lads they smile at me,*
> *   Comin' through the rye."*

She laughed.

"Well, at least you smiled at me, and that makes today look a little better."

"Where were you going?"

"To work. I just walked over across the fields—it's much shorter than by the lane."

Now that she mentioned it, he could see a glimpse of the Clanraith house between the trees. He turned and walked with her through the untidy little garden toward the Bastions' entrance.

"I'm sorry that stops me offering to take you on a picnic."

"I don't have any luck, do I? There's a dance in Fort Augustus tomorrow night, and I haven't been dancing for months, but I don't know a soul who'd take me."

"I'd like to do something about that," he said. "But it rather depends on what develops around here. Don't give up hope yet, though."

As they entered the hall, Bastion came out of a back room and said: "Ah, good morning, Annie. There are some pages I was revising last night on my desk. I'll be with you in a moment."

She went on into the room he had just come from, and he turned to the Saint.

"I suppose you didn't see anything."

"If we had, you'd've heard plenty of gunfire and hollering."

"Did you leave Eleanor down there?"

"Yes. But I don't think she's in any danger in broad daylight. Did Mackenzie call?"

"Not yet. I expect you're anxious to hear from him. The telephone's in the drawing-room—why don't you settle down there? You might like to browse through some of Eleanor's collection of books about the Monster."

Simon accepted the suggestion, and soon found himself so absorbed that only his empty stomach was conscious of the time when Bastion came in and told him that lunch was ready. Mrs. Bastion had already returned and was dishing up an agreeably aromatic lamb stew which she apologized for having only warmed up.

"You were right, it was just routine," she said. "A lot of waiting for nothing. But one of these days it won't be for nothing."

"I was thinking about it myself, dear," Bastion said, "and it seems to me that there's one bad weakness in your eight-hour-a-day system. There are enough odds against you already in only being able to see about a quarter of the loch, which leaves the Monster another three-quarters where it could just as easily pop up. But on top of that, watching only eight hours out of the twenty-four only gives us a one-third chance of being there even if it does pop up within range of our observation post. That doesn't add to the odds against us, it multiplies them."

"I know; but what can we do about it?"

"Since Mr. Templar pointed out that anyone should really be safe enough with a high-powered rifle in their hands and everyone else within call, I thought that three of us could divide up the watches and cover the whole day from before dawn till after dusk, as long as one could possibly see anything. That is, if Mr. Templar would help out. I know he can't stay here indefinitely, but—"

"If it'll make anybody feel better, I'd be glad to take a turn that way," Simon said indifferently.

It might have been more polite to sound more enthusiastic, but he could not make himself believe that the Monster would actually be caught by any such system. He was impatient for Mackenzie's report, which he thought was the essential detail.

The call came about two o'clock, and it was climactically negative.

"The doctor canna find a trace o' drugs or poison in the puir animal."

Simon took a deep breath.

"What did he think of its injuries?"

"He said he'd ne'er seen the like o' them. He dinna ken anything in the wuruld wi' such crushin' power in its jaws as yon Monster must have. If 'twas no' for the teeth marrks, he wad ha' thocht it was done wi' a club. But the autopsy mak's that impossible."

"So I take it you figure that rules you officially out," said the Saint bluntly. "But give me a number where I can call you if the picture changes again."

He wrote it down on a pad beside the telephone before he turned and relayed the report.

"That settles it," said Mrs. Bastion. "It can't be anything else but *an Niseag*. And we've got all the more reason to try Noel's idea of keeping watch all day."

"I had a good sleep this morning, so I'll start right away," Bastion volunteered. "You're entitled to a siesta."

"I'll take over after that," she said. "I want to be out there again at twilight. I know I'm monopolizing the most promising times, but this matters more to me than to anyone else."

Simon helped her with the dishes after they had had coffee, and then she excused herself.

"I'll be fresher later if I do take a little nap. Why don't you do the same? It was awfully good of you to get up in the middle of the night with me."

"It sounds as if I won't be needed again until later tomorrow morning," said the Saint. "But I'll be reading and brooding. I'm almost as interested in *an Niseag* now as you are."

He went back to the book he had left in the drawing-room as the house settled into stillness. Annie Clanraith had already departed, before lunch, taking a sheaf of papers with her to type at home.

Presently he put the volume down on his thighs and lay passively thinking, stretched out on the couch. It was his uniquely personal method of tackling profound problems, to let himself relax into a state of blank receptiveness in which half-subconscious impressions could grow and flow together in delicately fluid adjustments that could presently mould a conclusion almost as concrete as knowledge. For some time he gazed sightlessly at the ceiling, and then he continued to meditate with his eyes closed.

He was awakened by Noel Bastion entering the room, humming tunelessly. The biographer of Wellington was instantly apologetic.

"I'm sorry, Templar—I thought you'd be in your room."

"That's all right." Simon glanced at his watch, and was mildly surprised to discover how sleepy he must have been. "I was doing some thinking, and the strain must have been too much for me."

"Eleanor relieved me an hour ago. I hadn't seen anything, I'm afraid."

"I didn't hear you come in."

"I'm pretty quiet on my feet. Must be a habit I got from commando training. Eleanor often says that if she could stalk like me she'd have a lot more trophies." Bastion went to the bookcase, took down a book, and thumbed through it for some reference. "I've been trying to do some work, but it isn't easy to concentrate."

Simon stood up and stretched himself.

"I guess you'll have to get used to working under difficulties if you're going to be a part-time monster hunter for ten years—isn't that how long Eleanor said she was ready to spend at it?"

"I'm hoping it'll be a good deal less than that."

"I was reading in this book *More Than A Legend* that in 1934, when the excitement about the Monster was at its height, a chap named Sir Edward Mountain hired a bunch of men and organized a systematic watch like you were suggesting, but spacing them all around the lake. It went on for a month or two, and they got a few pictures of distant splashings, but nothing that was scientifically accepted."

Bastion put his volume back on the shelf. "You're still sceptical, aren't you?"

"What I've been wondering," said the Saint, "is why this savage behemoth with the big sharp teeth and the nutcracker jaws chomped up a dog but didn't swallow even a little nibble of it."

"Perhaps it isn't carnivorous. An angry elephant will mash a man to a pulp, but it won't eat him. And that dog could be very irritating, barking at everything—"

"According to what I heard, there wasn't any barking. And I'm sure the sheep it's supposed to have taken didn't bark. But the sheep disappeared entirely, didn't it?"

"That's what Clanraith says. But for all we know, the sheep may have been stolen."

"But that could have given somebody the idea of building up the Monster legend from there."

Bastion shook his head.

"But the dog *did* bark at everyone," he insisted stubbornly.

"Except the people he knew," said the Saint, no less persistently. "Every dog is vulnerable to a few people. You yourself, for instance, if you'd wanted to, could have come along, and if he felt lazy he'd've opened one eye and then shut it again and gone back to sleep. Now, are you absolutely sure that nobody else was on those terms with him? Could a postman or a milkman have made friends with him? Or anyone else at all?"

The other man massaged his moustache.

"I don't know. . . . Well, perhaps Fergus Clanraith might."

Simon blinked.

"But it sounded to me as if he didn't exactly love the dog."

"Perhaps he didn't. But it must have known him pretty well. Eleanor likes to go hiking across country, and the dog always used to go with her. She's always crossing Clanraith's property and stopping to talk to him, she tells me. She gets on very well with him."

"What, that old curmudgeon?"

"I know, he's full of that Scottish Nationalist nonsense. But Eleanor is half Scots herself, and that makes her almost human in his estimation. I believe they talk for hours about salmon fishing and grouse shooting."

"I wondered if he had an appealing side hidden away somewhere," said the Saint thoughtfully, "or if Annie got it all from her mother."

Bastion's deep-set sooty eyes flickered over him appraisingly.

"She's rather an attractive filly, isn't she?"

"I have a feeling that to a certain type of man, in certain circumstances, and perhaps at a certain age, her appeal might be quite dangerous."

Noel Bastion had an odd expression of balancing some answer on the tip of his tongue, weighing it for advisability, changing his mind a couple of times about it, and finally swallowing it. He then tried to recover from the pause by making a business of consulting the clock on the mantelpiece.

"Will you excuse me? Eleanor asked me to bring her a thermos of tea about now. She hates to miss that, even for *an Niseag.*"

"Sure."

Simon followed him into the kitchen, where a kettle was already simmering on the black coal stove. He watched while his host carefully scalded a teapot and measured leaves into it from a canister.

"You know, Major," he said, "I'm not a detective by nature, even of the private variety."

"I know. In fact, I think you used to be just the opposite."

"That's true, too, I do get into situations, though, where I have to do a bit of deducing, and sometimes I startle everyone by coming up with a brilliant hunch. But as a general rule, I'd rather prevent a crime than solve one. As it says in your kind of text-books, a little preventive action can save a lot of counter-attacks."

The Major had poured boiling water into the pot with a steady hand, and was opening a vacuum flask while he waited for the brew.

"You're a bit late to prevent this one, aren't you?—if it *was* a crime."

"Not necessarily. Not if the death of Golly was only a stepping-stone—something to build on the story of a missing sheep, and pave the way for the Monster's next victim to be a person. If a person were killed in a similar way now, the Monster explanation would get a lot more believers than if it had just happened out of the blue."

Bastion put sugar and milk into the flask, without measuring, with the unhesitating positiveness of practice, and took the lid off the teapot to sniff and stir it.

"But, good heavens, Templar, who could treat a dog like that, except a sadistic maniac?"

Simon lighted a cigarette. He was very certain now, and the certainty made him very calm.

"A professional killer," he said. "There are quite a lot of them around who don't have police records. People whose temperament and habits have developed a great callousness about death. But they're not sadists. They're normally kind to animals and even to human beings, when it's normally useful to be. But fundamentally they see them as expendable, and when the time comes they can sacrifice them quite impersonally."

"I know Clanraith's a farmer, and he raises animals only to have them butchered," Bastion said slowly. "But it's hard to imagine him doing what you're talking about, much as I dislike him."

"Then you think we should discard him as a red herring?"

Bastion filled the thermos from the teapot, and capped it.

"I'm hanged if I know. I'd want to think some more about it. But first I've got to take this to Eleanor."

"I'll go with you," said the Saint.

He followed the other out of the back door. Outside, the dusk was deepening with a mistiness that was beginning to do more than the failing light to reduce visibility. From the garden, one could see into the orchard but not beyond it.

"It's equally hard for the ordinary man," Simon continued relentlessly, "to imagine anyone who's lived with another person as man and wife, making love and sharing the closest moments, suddenly turning around and killing the other one. But the prison cemeteries are full of 'em. And there are plenty more on the outside who didn't get caught—or who are still planning it. At least half the time, the marriage has been getting a bit dull, and someone more attractive has come along. And then, for some idiotic reason, often connected with money, murder begins to seem cleverer than divorce."

Bastion slackened his steps, half turning to peer at Simon from under heavily contracted brows, then spoke slowly.

"I'm not utterly dense, Templar, and I don't like what you seem to be hinting at."

"I don't expect you to, chum. But I'm trying to stop a murder. Let me make a confession. When you and Eleanor have been out or in bed at various times, I've done quite a lot of prying. Which may be a breach of hospitality, but it's less trouble than search warrants. You remember those scratches in the ground near the dead dog which I said could've been made with something that wasn't claws? Well, I found a gaff among somebody's fishing tackle that could've made them, and the point had fresh shiny scratches and even some mud smeared on it which can be analyzed. I haven't been in the attic and found an embalmed shark's head with several teeth missing, but I'll bet Mackenzie could find one. And I haven't yet found the club with the teeth set in it, because I haven't yet been allowed down by the lake alone; but I think it's there somewhere, probably stuffed under a bush, and just waiting to be hauled out when the right head is turned the wrong way."

Major Bastion had come to a complete halt by that time.

"You unmitigated bounder," he said shakily. "Are you going to have the impertinence to suggest that I'm trying to murder my wife, to come into her money and run off with a farmer's daughter? Let me tell you that I'm the one who has the private income, and—"

"You poor feeble egotist," Simon retorted harshly. "I didn't suspect that for one second after she made herself rather cutely available to me, a guest in your house. She obviously wasn't stupid, and no girl who wasn't would have gambled a solid understanding with you against a transient flirtation. But didn't you ever read *Lady Chatterley's Lover*? Or the Kinsey Report? And hasn't it dawned on you that a forceful woman like Eleanor, just because she isn't a glamour girl, couldn't be bored to frenzy with a husband who only cares about the campaigns of Wellington?"

Noel Bastion opened his mouth, and his fists clenched, but whatever was intended to come from either never materialized. For at that moment came the scream.

Shrill with unearthly terror and agony, it split the darkening haze with an eldritch intensity that seemed to turn every hair on the Saint's nape into an individual icicle. And it did not stop, but ululated again and again in weird cadences of hysteria.

For an immeasurable span they were both petrified; and then Bastion turned and began to run wildly across the meadow, towards the sound.

"Eleanor!" he yelled, insanely, in a voice almost as piercing as the screams.

He ran so frantically that the Saint had to call on all his reserves to make up for Bastion's split-second start. But he did close the gap as Bastion stumbled and almost fell over something that lay squarely across their path. Simon had seen it an instant sooner, and swerved, mechanically identifying the steely glint that had caught his eye as a reflection from a long gun-barrel.

And then, looking ahead and upwards, he saw through the blue fogginess something for which he would never completely believe his eyes, yet which would haunt him for the rest of his life. Something greyblack and scaly-slimy, an immense amorphous mass from which a reptilian neck and head with strange protuberances reared and swayed far up over him. And in the hideous dripping jaws something of human shape, from which the screams came, that writhed and flailed ineffectually with a peculiar-looking club. . . .

With a sort of incoherent sob, Bastion scooped up the rifle at his feet and fired it. The horrendous mass convulsed; and into Simon's eardrums, still buzzing from the heavy blast, came a sickening crunch that cut off the last shriek in the middle of a note.

The towering neck corkscrewed with frightful power, and the thing that had been human was flung dreadfully towards them. It fell with a kind of soggy limpness almost at their feet, as whatever had spat it out lurched backwards and was blotted out by the vaporous dimness with the sound of a gigantic splash while Bastion was still firing again at the place where it had been. . . .

As Bastion finally dropped the gun and sank slowly to his knees beside the body of his wife, Simon also looked down and saw that her hand was still spasmodically locked around the thinner end of the crude bludgeon in which had been set a row of shark's teeth. Now that he saw it better, he saw that it was no home-made affair, but probably a souvenir of some expedition to the South Pacific. But you couldn't be right all the time, about every last detail. Just as a few seconds ago, and until he saw Bastion with his head bowed like that over the woman who had plotted to murder him, he had never expected to be restrained in his comment by the irrational compassion that finally moved him.

"By God," he thought, "now I know I'm ageing."

But aloud he said: "She worked awful hard to sell everyone on the Monster. If you like, we can leave it that way. Luckily I'm a witness to what happened just now. But I don't have to say anything about—this."

He released the club gently from the grip of the dead fingers, and carried it away with him as he went to telephone Mackenzie.

IX

GODS FROM THE SKIES?

***

The Cave of History
By Theodore Sturgeon

Men Without Bones
By Gerald Kersh

17

In the introduction to the first story in this collection, which dealt with that most ancient of traditions, The Hollow Earth, I mentioned a theory, which has been advanced, that the phenomena known as Flying Saucers might originate there. Now, in this the last section of the book, we in a sense bring our survey back full circle and consider in detail stories about these mysterious objects. For, although the history of Flying Saucers is claimed to stretch back to the very earliest times, current sightings of these objects undoubtedly represent the most widely discussed mystery of our time. The beginning of the modern absorption in these aerial craft is easily traced to the afternoon of June 24, 1947, when Kenneth Arnold, a fire-appliance salesman, skilled pilot and U.S. marshal, saw some mysterious lights in the sky while flying over the Cascade Mountains of America. "I observed, far to my left and to the North," he said, "a formation of very bright objects coming from the vicinity of Mount Baker, flying very close to the mountaintops and traveling with tremendous speed. I could see no tails on them and they flew like no aircraft I had ever seen before. As I put it to newsmen in Pendleton, Oregon, they flew like a saucer would if you skipped it across the water." Thus was the crucial sighting made, and into the language went Arnold's description of these strange objects as "Flying Saucers." (It was officialdom that later named them, rather prosaically, "Unidentified Flying Objects" or "UFOs.") Public reaction to the story was, in the main, highly sceptical, and it needed many more sightings from airline pilots and reliable citizens to convince people that these were not crank tales and that there was something worth investigating behind the reports of mysterious objects in the skies. Kenneth Arnold himself made several more sightings, and even managed to obtain some snapshots of the UFOs. Other, even stranger, photographs were reported, too, and for a time the U.S. Government actually suppressed publication of some of these photographs without explanation. By this time a number of scientists and young enthusiasts were busy collecting eyewitness reports of Flying Saucers, and newspaper articles and books were soon pouring from the presses. The theories contained in these works on the origins of the craft varied from the initial fear that they were spy vessels belonging to a hostile nation

(Russia, of course), to spaceships from another world, and scoutships from the hollow earth. Writers like the Englishman Harold T. Wilkins also noted that the craft carried crews of experienced space travelers, while a number of Americans, including the renowned George Adamski, claimed to have actually encountered the craft and their occupants at close quarters. In the ensuing years, Flying Saucers quickly proved to be anything but an American phenomenon. Reports were collected in Europe and Scandinavia, over the whole of the Americas, in Africa and Asia, and even down under in Australia and New Zealand. (Russia, too, began to contribute examples to the ever-growing dossier, and actually provided the first report of the crash landing of a Flying Saucer and the recovery of its dead occupants—though no more specific details than these were released.) Researchers also began compiling lists of historical sightings which stretched back into the early days of mankind—thereby enabling them to compare modern sightings against ancient Sanskrit records and Egyptian papyrus rolls. From all this data, the indication seemed to emerge that those who controlled the saucers were at the very least observing the ways of humanity, and perhaps even trying to

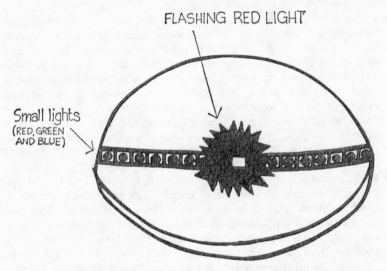

A flying saucer as sketched by Mrs. Ruby McNair, when it flew over her home in Montana in 1967.

make contact with us. The whole subject was, of course, one of enormous appeal to science-fiction writers, who had for years been dispatching men into the far realms of the universe in magazines and books. However, since Flying Saucers arrived on the contemporary scene before the advent of actual space flight, there was an added element of speculation. Not surprisingly, stories about UFOs which were wildly improbable and sensationally scarifying deluged the market. Of late, however, a few writers have debated both conscientiously and excitingly on the purpose of the saucers. One such is *Theodore Sturgeon* (1918–   ), regarded today as a master of the genre. He has written several stories on the theme, but none seems to me to possess such authenticity of plot or such gripping speculation as the tale hereunder, published in 1947 in *Thrilling Wonder Stories* shortly after Kenneth Arnold's first sighting.

THE CAVE OF HISTORY
Theodore Sturgeon

Sykes died, and after two years they tracked Gordon Kemp down and brought him back, because he was the only man who knew anything about the death. Kemp had to face a coroner's jury in Switchpath, Arizona, a crossroads just at the edge of the desert, and he wasn't too happy about it, being city-bred and not quite understanding the difference between "hicks" and "folks."

The atmosphere in the courtroom was tense. Had there been great wainscoted walls and a statue of blind Justice, it would have been more impersonal and, for Kemp, easier to take. But this courtroom was a crossroads grangers' hall in Switchpath, Arizona.

The presiding coroner was Bert Whelson, who held a corncob pipe instead of a gavel. At their ease around the room were other men, dirt-farmers and prospectors like Whelson. It was like a movie short. It needed only a comedy dance number and somebody playing a jig.

But there was nothing comic about it. These hicks were in a position to pile trouble on Kemp, trouble that might very easily wind up in the gas chamber.

The coroner leaned forward. "You got nothin' to be afeard of, son, if your conscience is clear."

"I still ain't talking. I brought the guy in, didn't I? Would I of done that if I'd killed him?"

The coroner stroked his stubble, with a soft rasping sound like a rope being pulled over a wooden beam.

"We don't know about that, Kemp. *Hmm.* Why can't you get it through your head that nobody's accusing you of anything? You're jest a feller knows something about the death of this here Alessandro Sykes. This court'd like to know exactly what happened."

He hesitated, shuffled.

"Sit down, son," said the coroner.

That did it. He slumped into the straight chair that one of the men pushed up for him, and told this story.

*   *   *

I guess I better go right back to the beginning, the first time I ever saw this here Sykes.

I was working in my shop one afternoon when he walked in. He watched what I was doing and spoke up.

"You Gordon Kemp?"

I said yes and looked him over. He was a scrawny feller, prob'ly sixty years old and wound up real tight. He talked fast, smoked fast, moved fast, as if there wasn't time for nothin', but he had to get on to somethin' else. I asked him what he wanted.

"You the man had that article in the magazine about the concentrated atomic torch?" he said.

"Yeah," I told him. "Only that guy from the magazine, he used an awful lot of loose talk. Says my torch was three hundred years ahead of its time." Actually it was something I stumbled on by accident, more or less. The ordinary atomic hydrogen torch—plenty hot.

I figured out a ring-shaped electromagnet set just in front of the jet, to concentrate it. It repelled the hydrogen particles and concentrated them. It'll cut anything—anything. And since it got patented, you'd be surprised at the calls I got. You got no idea how many people want to cut into bank vaults an' the side doors of hock shops. Well, about Sykes. . . .

I told him this magazine article went a little too far, but I did have quite a gadget. I gave him a demonstration or two, and he seemed satisfied. Finally I told him I was wasting my time unless he had a proposition.

He's lookin' real happy about this torch of mine, an' he nods.

"Sure. Only you'll have to take a couple of weeks off. Go out West. Arizona. Cut a way into a cave there."

"Cave, huh?" I said. "Is it legal?" I didn't want no trouble.

"Sure it's legal," he tells me.

"How much?"

He says he hates to argue.

"If you'll get me into that place—and you can satisfy yourself as to whether it's legal—I'll give you five thousand dollars," he says.

Now, five thousand berries cuts a lot of ice for me. Especially for only two weeks' work. And besides, I liked the old guy's looks. He was queer as a nine-dollar bill, mind you, and had a funny way of carryin' on, but I could see he was worth the kind of money he talked.

He looked like he really needed help, too. Aw, maybe I'm just a Boy Scout at heart. As I say, I liked him, money or no money, and chances are I'd have helped him out for free.

He came to see me a couple more times and we sweated out the details. It wound up with him and me on the train, and my torch and the other gear in the baggage car up front. Maybe some of you remember the day we arrived here. He seemed to know a lot of people here. Mm? I thought so. He told me how many years he had been coming out to Switchpath.

He told me lots of things. He was one of the talkin'est old geezers I ever did see. I understood about one ninth of what he said. He was lonely, I guess. I was the first man he ever called in to help him with his work, and he spilled the overflow of years of workin' by himself.

About this Switchpath proposition, he told me that when he was just a punk out of college, he was a archaeologist roamin' around the desert lookin' for old Indian stuff, vases and arrowheads and such stuff. And he run across this here room in the rock, at the bottom of a deep cleft.

He got all excited when he told me about this part of it. Went on a mile a minute about plasticine ages and messy zorics and pally o' lithographs or something. I called him down to earth, and he explained to me that this room was down in rock that was very old—a couple of hundred thousand years, or maybe a half million.

He said that rock had been there either before mankind had a start here on earth, or maybe about the same time as the missing link. Me, I don't care about dead people or dead people's great-grandfathers, but Sykes was all enthusiastic.

Anyhow, it seems that this cave had been opened by some sort of an earthquake or something, and the stuff in it must have been there all that time. What got him excited was that the stuff was machinery of some kind and must have been put there *way before there was any human beings on earth at all!*

That seemed silly to me. I wanted to know what kind of machinery.

"Well," he says, "I thought at first that it was some sort of a radio transmitter. Get this," he says. "Here is a machine with an antenna on top of it, just like a microwave job. And beside it is another machine.

"This second machine is shaped like a dumbbell standing on one end. The top of it is a sort of covered hopper, and at the waist of the machine is an arrangement of solenoids made out of some alloy that was never seen before on this earth.

"There's gearing between this machine and the other, the transmitter. I have figured out what this dumbbell thing is. It's a recorder."

I want to know what is it recording. He lays one finger on the side of his nose and winks at me.

"Thought," he says. "Raw thought. But that isn't all. Earthquakes, continental shifts, weather cycles, lots more stuff. It integrates all these things with thought."

I want to know how he knows all this. That was when he told me that he had been with this thing for the better part of the last thirty years. He'd figured it out all by himself. He was real touchy about that part of it.

Then I began to realize what was the matter with the poor old guy. He really figured he had something big here, and he wanted to find out about it. But it seems he was an ugly kid and a shy man, and he wanted to make the big splash all by himself. It wouldn't do for him just to be known as the man who discovered this thing.

"Any dolt could have stumbled across it," he'd say. He wanted to find out everything there was about this thing before he let a soul know about it. "Greater than the Rosetta Stone," he used to say. "Greater than the nuclear hypothesis." Oh, he was a great one for slinging the five-dollar words.

"And it will be Sykes who gave this to the world," he would say. "Sykes will give it to humanity, complete and provable, and history will be reckoned from the day I speak."

Oh, he was wacky, all right. I didn't mind, though. He was harmless, and a nicer little character you'd never want to meet.

Funny guy, that Sykes. What kind of a life he led I can only imagine. He had dough—inherited an income or something, so he didn't have the problems that bother most of the rest of us. He would spend days in that cavern, staring at the machines. He didn't want to touch them. He only wanted to find out what they were doing there. One of them was running.

The big machine, the dumbbell-shaped one, was running. It didn't make any noise. Both machines had a little disk set into the side; it was half red, half black. On the big machine, the one he called the recorder, this disk was turning. Not fast, but you could see it was moving. Sykes was all excited about that.

On the way out here, on the train, he spouted a lot of stuff. I don't know why. Maybe he thought I was too dumb to ever tell anybody about it. If that's what he thought, he had the right idea. I'm just a grease-monkey who happened to have a bright idea. Anyway, he showed me something he had taken from the cave.

It was a piece of wire about six feet long. But wire like I have never seen before or since. It was about 35 gauge—like a hair. And crooked. Crimped, I mean. Sykes said it was magnetized, too. It bent easy enough, but it wouldn't kink at all, and you couldn't put a tight bend in it. I imagine it'd dent a pair of pliers.

He asked me if I thought I could break it. I tried and got a gash in my lunch-hook for my trouble. So help me, it wouldn't break, and it wouldn't cut, and you couldn't get any of those crimps out of it. I don't mean you'd pull the wire and it would snap back. No. You couldn't pull it straight at all.

Sykes told me on the train that it had taken him eight months to cut that piece loose. It was more than just tough. It fused with itself. The first four times he managed to cut it through, he couldn't get the ends apart fast enough to keep them from fusing together again.

He finally had to clamp a pair of steel blocks around the wire, wait for enough wire to feed through to give him some slack and then put about twelve tons on some shears to cut through the wire. Forged iridium steel, those cutters were, and that wire left a heck of a hole in them.

But the wire parted. He had a big helical spring hauling the wire tight, so that the instant it parted it was snapped out of the way. It had to be cut twice to get the one piece out, and when he put the ends together they fused. I mean, both on the piece he took out and the two free ends in the machine—not a mark, not a bulge.

Well, you all remember when we arrived here with all that equipment, and how we hired a car and went off into the desert. All the while the old man was happy as a kid.

"Kemp, my boy," he says, "I got it decoded. I can read that tape.

Do you realize what that means? Every bit of human history—I can get it in detail. Every single thing that ever happened to this earth or the people in it.

"You have no idea in what detail that tape records," he said. "Want to know who put the bee on Alexander the Great? Want to know what the name of Pericles' girl friend really was? I have it all here. What about these Indian and old Greek legends about a lost continent? What about old Fort's fireballs? Who was the man in the iron mask? I have it, son, I have it."

That was what went on all the way out there, to that place in the dry gulch where the cave was.

You wouldn't believe what a place that was to get to. How that old guy ever had the energy to keep going back to it I'll never know. We had to stop the car about twenty miles from here and hoof it.

The country out there is all tore up. If I hadn't already seen the color of his money I'd have said the heck with it. Sand and heat and big rocks and more places to fall into and break your silly neck— *Lord!*

Me with a pack on my back too, the torch, the gas, and a power supply and all. We got to this cleft, see, and he outs with a length of rope and makes it fast to a stone column that's eroded nearby. He has a slip-snaffle on it. He lowers himself into the gulch and I drop the gear down after him, and then down I go.

Brother, it's dark in there. We go uphill about a hundred and fifty yards, and then Sykes pulls up in front of a facing. By the light of his flash I can see the remains of a flock of campfires he's made there over the years.

"There it is," he says. "It's all yours, Kemp. If that three-hundred-years-in-the-future torch of yours is any good—prove it."

I unlimbered my stuff and got to work, and believe me it was hard, slow goin'. But I got through. It took nine hours before I had a hole fit for us to crawl through, and another hour for it to cool enough so's we could use it.

All that time the old man talked. It was mostly bragging about the job he'd done decoding the wire he had. It was mostly Greek to me.

"I have a record here," he says, swishin' his hunk of wire around, "of a phase of the industrial revolution in Central Europe that will have the historians gnashing their teeth. But have I said anything? Not me. Not Sykes!

"I'll have the history of mankind written in such detail, with such authority, that the name of Sykes will go into the language as a synonym for the miraculously accurate." I remember that, because he said it so much. He said it like it tasted good.

I remember once I asked him why it was we had to bother cutting in. Where was the hole he had used?

"That, my boy," he says, "is an unforeseen quality of the machines. For some reason they closed themselves up. In a way I'm glad they did. I was unable to get back in and I was forced to concentrate on my sample. If it hadn't been for that, I doubt that I would ever have cracked the code."

So I asked him what about all this—what were the machines and who left them there and what for? All this while I was cutting away at that rock facing. And, man! I never seen rock like that. If it *was* rock—which, now, I doubt.

It come off in flakes, in front of my torch. *My* torch, that'll cut anything. Do you know that in those nine hours I only got through about seven and a half inches of that stuff? And my torch'll walk into laminated bank vaults like the door was open.

When I asked him, he shut up for a long time, but I guess he wanted to talk. He sure was enthusiastic. And besides, he figured I was too dumb to savvy what he was talking about. As I said before, he was right there. So he run off about it, and this is about how it went:

"Who left these machines here or how they operate, we may never know. It would be interesting to find out, but the important thing is to get the records and decode them all."

It had taken him a while to recognize that machine as a recorder. The tip-off was that it was running and the other one, the transmitter, was not.

He thought at first that maybe the transmitter was busted, but after a year or two of examining the machines without touching them he began to realize that there was a gear train waiting by the tape where it fed through the gismo that crimped it.

This gear train was fixed to start the transmitter, see? But it was keyed to a certain crimp in the tape. In other words, when something happened somewhere on earth that was just the right thing, the crimper would record it and the transmitter would get keyed off.

Sykes studied that setup for years before he figured the particular squiggle in that wire that would start that transmitter to sending.

Where was it sending to? Why? Sure, he thought about that. But that didn't matter to him.

What was supposed to happen, when the tape ran out? Who or what would come and look at it when it was all done? You know, he didn't care. He just wanted to read that tape, is all. Seems there's a lot of guys write history books and stuff. And he wanted to call them liars. He wanted to tell them the way it really was. Can you imagine?

So there I am, cutting away with my super-torch on what seems to be a solid wall made out of some stuff that has no right to be so tough. I can still see it.

So dark, and me with black goggles on, and the doc with his back to me so's he won't wreck his eyes, spoutin' along about history and the first unbiased account of it. And how he was going to thrust it on the world and just kill all those guys with all those theories.

I remember quitting once for a breather and letting the mercury cells juice up a bit while I had a smoke. Just to make talk, I ask Sykes when does he think that transmitter is going to go to work.

"Oh," he says. "It already did. It's finished. That's how I knew that my figuring was right. That tape has a certain rate through the machine. It's in millimeters per month. I have the figure. It wouldn't matter to you. But something happened a while ago that made it possible to check. July sixteenth, nineteen hundred and forty-five, to be exact."

"You don't tell me," I says.

"Oh," he says, real pleased, "but I do! That day something happened which put a wiggle in the wire there—the thing I was looking for all along. It was the crimp that triggered the transmitter. I happened to be in the cave at the time.

"The transmitter started up and the little disk spun around like mad. Then it stopped. I looked in the papers the next week to see what it was. Nothing I could find. It wasn't until the following August that I found out."

I suddenly caught wise.

"Oh—the atom bomb! You mean that rig was set up to send something as soon as an atomic explosion kicked off somewhere on earth!"

He nodded his head. By the glare of the red-hot rock he looked like a skinny old owl.

"That's right. That's why we've got to get in there in a hurry. It was after the second Bikini blast that the cave got sealed up. I don't know if that transmission is ever going to get picked up.

"I don't know if anything is going to happen if it is picked up. I do know that I have the wire decoded and I mean to get those records before anybody else does."

If that wall had been any thicker I never would've gotten through. When I got my circle cut and the cut-out piece dropped inside, my rig was about at its last gasp. So was Sykes. For the last two hours he'd been hoppin' up an' down with impatience.

"Thirty years' work," he kept saying. "I've waited for this for thirty years and I won't be stopped now. Hurry up! Hurry up!"

And when we had to wait for the opening to cool, I thought he'd go wild. I guess that's what built him up to his big breakdown. He sure was keyed up.

Well, at last we crawled into the place. He'd talked so much about it that I almost felt I was comin' back to something instead of seeing it for the first time.

There were the machines, the big one about seven feet tall, dumbbell-shaped, and the little one sort of a rounded cube with a bunch of macaroni on top that was this antenna he was talking about.

We lit a pressure lantern that flooded the place with light—it was small, with a floor about nine by nine—and he jumped over to the machines.

He scrabbles around and hauls out some wire. Then he stops and stands there looking stupid at me.

"What's the matter, Doc?" I say. I called him Doc.

He gulps and swallows.

"The reel's empty. It's empty! There's only eight inches of wire here. Only——" And that was when he fainted.

I jumped up right away and shook him and shoved him around a little until his eyes started to blink. He sits up and shakes himself.

"*Refilled*," he says. He is real hoarse. "Kemp! They've been here!"

I began to get the idea. The lower chamber is empty. The upper one is full. The whole setup is arranged to run off a new recording. And where is Sykes' thirty years' work?

He starts to laugh. I look at him. I can't take that. The place is too small for all that noise. I never heard anybody laugh like that. Like short screams, one after the other, fast. He laughs and laughs.

I carry him out. I put him down outside and go back in for my gear. I can hear him laughing out there and that busted-up voice of his echoing in the gulch. I get everything onto the backpack and go to put out the pressure lantern when I hear a little click.

It's that transmitter. The little red and black disk is turning around on it. I just stand there watching it. It only runs for three or four minutes. And then it begins to get hot in there.

I got scared. I ducked out of the hole and picked up Sykes. He didn't weigh much. I looked back in the hole. The cave was lit up. Red. The machines were cherry red, straw-color, white, just that quick. They melted. I saw it. I ran.

I don't hardly remember getting to the rope and tying Sykes on and climbing up and hauling him up after me. He was quiet then, but conscious. I carried him away until the light from the gulch stopped me. I turned around to watch.

I could see a ways down into the gulch. It was fillin' up with lava. It was lightin' up the whole desert. And I never felt such heat. I ran again.

I got to the car and dumped Sykes in. He shifted around on the seat some. I asked him how he felt. He didn't answer that but mumbled a lot of stuff.

Something like this.

"They knew we'd reached the atomic age. They wanted to be told when. The transmitter did just that. They came and took the recordings and refilled the machine.

"They sealed off the room with something they thought only controlled atomic power could break into. This time the transmitter was triggered to human beings in that room. Your torch did it, Kemp—that three-hundred-years-in-the-future torch! They think we have atomic power! They'll come back!"

"Who, Doc? Who?" I says.

"I don't know," he mumbles. "There'd be only one reason why someone—some creature—would want to know a thing like that. And that's so they could stop us."

So I laughed at him. I got in and started the car and laughed at him.

"Doc," I said, "we ain't goin' to be stopped now. Like the papers say, we're in the atomic age if it kills us. But we're in for keeps. Why, humanity would have to be killed off before it'd get out of this atomic age."

"I know that, Kemp—I know—that's what I mean! What have we done? What have we done?"

After that he's quiet a while and when I look at him again I see he's dead. So I brought him in. In the excitement I faded. It just didn't look good to me. I knew nobody would listen to a yarn like that.

*   *   *

There was silence in the courtroom until somebody coughed, and then everyone felt he had to make a sound with his throat or his feet. The coroner held up his hand.

"I kin see what Brother Kemp was worried about. If that story is true I, for one, would think twice about tellin' it."

"He's a liar!" roared a prospector from the benches. "He's a murderin' liar! I have a kid reads that kind of stuff, an' I never did like to see him at it. Believe me, he's a-goin' to cut it out as of right now. I think this Kemp feller needs a hangin'!"

"Now, Jed!" bellowed the coroner. "If we kill off this man we do it legal, hear?" The sudden hubbub quieted, and the coroner turned to the prisoner.

"Listen here, Kemp—somethin' jest occurred to me. How long was it from the time of the first atom blast until the time that room got sealed up?"

"I dunno. About two years. Little over. Why?"

"An' how long since that night you been talking about, when Sykes died?"

"Or was murdered," growled the prospector.

"Shut up, Jed. Well, Kemp?"

"About eighteen mon— No. Nearer two years."

"Well, then," said the coroner, spreading his hands. "If there was anything in your story, or in that goofy idea of the dead man's about someone comin' to kill us off—well, ain't it about time they did?"

There were guffaws, and the end of the grange hall disappeared in a burst of flame. Yelling, cursing, some of them screaming, they pushed and fought their way out into the moonlit road.

The sky was full of ships.

18

The most exciting speculations that have been made about Flying Saucers are those which have come from a school of writers led, figuratively speaking, by the Swiss archaeologist Erich von Daniken. Simply stated, they believe the craft to be the means of transport of extraterrestrial beings who have visited this planet since time immemorial. It was Daniken's book *Chariots of the Gods*, published in 1969, which focused worldwide attention on this theory, although, to be perfectly fair, earlier writers had advanced the same theory but without his dazzling array of facts or stylistic boldness. Drawing on modern astrological research and ancient records and monuments, Daniken propounded that there are "approximately 100,000,000 planets on which we can speculate that life exists—and among these perhaps 100,000 containing civilizations more advanced than our own." (He has received strong scientific support for this contention from no less a figure than Dr. Willy Ley, who says there may be 18,000 inhabited planets in the Milky Way *alone*.) Daniken believes that these extraterrestrials have possessed the ability for space travel for many centuries, and has produced a wealth of data which, he says, is evidence of their visits here. For example, he cites the famous Piri Reis maps, which date back to the time of Christ and yet show the shape of the Earth and the Antarctic almost exactly as if it had been photographed from outer space by an Apollo rocket. In a sentence, they contain information man could not have known until this century. Turning to ancient traditions, he points to the numerous legends that refer to gods who came from the skies "in chariots of fire." These, he maintains, were spacemen, and he emphasizes his claim with an impressive array of photographs and drawings of ancient religious stone carvings found in various countries, all bearing striking resemblances to modern astronauts in the style of dress and headgear. He has similarly devoted much study to strange monuments—locating ancient rock edifices constructed in a manner only the most sophisticated modern equipment might hope to duplicate: monuments made of unknown metals which have stood for centuries without decaying; and god figures with features unlike any to be found on Earth. From all this wealth of evidence, Daniken has concluded that the ancient astronauts certainly influenced the Christian religion—and perhaps most of the others—and that God himself may have been one of these space visitors, too. Of course, Daniken and his supporters have not been without their critics in both scientific and lay circles—and some of their claims have been seriously undermined by arguments that they have misread the signs or seen only what they wanted to see in carvings and monuments without allowing for contemporary influences. Only by reading both sides of this highly controversial argument can the reader hope to begin forming his own conclusions, and perhaps accepting Daniken's fundamental statement: "Let us get used to the idea that the world of ideas which has grown up over the millennia is going to collapse . . . for we now have the means to find out all about our past, without leaving any gaps, if we really want to." Perhaps no one is better suited to take up Daniken's standpoint in a fictional way than *Gerald Kersh* (1909–), whose writings have ranged from the bizarre to the ingenious and the amazingly prophetic. He is devoted to old legends and traditions and delights in turning theories inside out with skill and reason. No wonder he should have found the riddle of the Flying Saucers and their occupants so fascinating—and their intervention on Earth so intriguing. "Men Without Bones" (written in 1955) is the result, and I positively guarantee that no collection of fantasy stories has ever ended on such a provocative note . . .

MEN WITHOUT BONES
Gerald Kersh

We were loading bananas into the *Claire Dodge* at Puerto Pobre, when a feverish little fellow came aboard. Everyone stepped aside to let him pass—even the soldiers who guard the port with nickel-plated Remington rifles, and who go barefoot but wear polished leather leggings. They stood back from him because they believed that he was afflicted-of-God, mad; harmless but dangerous; best left alone.

All the time the naphtha flares were hissing, and from the hold came the reverberation of the roaring voice of the foreman of the gang down below crying: "Fruta! Fruta! FRUTA!" The leader of the dock gang bellowed the same cry, throwing down stem after stem of brilliant green bananas. The occasion would be memorable for this, if for nothing else—the magnificence of the night, the bronze of the Negro foreman shining under the flares, the jade green of that fruit, and the mixed odors of the waterfront. Out of one stem of bananas ran a hairy gray spider, which frightened the crew and broke the banana-chain, until a Nicaraguan boy, with a laugh, killed it with his foot. It was harmless, he said.

It was about then that the madman came aboard, unhindered, and asked me: "Bound for where?"

He spoke quietly and in a carefully modulated voice; but there was a certain blank, lost look in his eyes that suggested to me that I keep within ducking distance of his restless hands which, now that I think of them, put me in mind of that gray, hairy, bird-eating spider.

"Mobile, Alabama," I said.

"Take me along?" he asked.

"None of my affair. Sorry. Passenger myself," I said. "The skipper's ashore. Better wait for him on the wharf. He's the boss."

"Would you happen, by any chance, to have a drink about you?"

Giving him some rum, I asked: "How come they let you aboard?"

"I'm not crazy," he said. "Not actually . . . a little fever, nothing more. Malaria, dengue fever, jungle fever, rat-bite fever. Feverish country, this, and others of the same nature. Allow me to introduce myself. My name is Goodbody, Doctor of Science of Osbaldeston University. Does it convey nothing to you? No? Well then; I was assistant to Professor Yeoward. Does *that* convey anything to you?"

I said: "Yeoward, Professor Yeoward? Oh yes. He was lost, wasn't he, somewhere in the upland jungle beyond the source of the Amer River?"

"Correct!" cried the little man who called himself Goodbody. "I saw him get lost."

Fruta!—Fruta!—Fruta!—Fruta! came the voices of the men in the hold. There was rivalry between their leader and the big black stevedore ashore. The flares spluttered. The green bananas came down. And a kind of sickly sigh came out of the jungle, off the rotting river—not a wind, not a breeze—something like the foul breath of high fever.

Trembling with eagerness and, at the same time, shaking with fever chills, so that he had to use two hands to raise his glass to his lips—even so, he spilled most of the rum—Doctor Goodbody said: "For God's sake, get me out of this country—take me to Mobile—hide me in your cabin!"

"I have no authority," I said, "but you are an American citizen; you can identify yourself; the Consul will send you home."

"No doubt. But that would take time. The Consul thinks I am crazy too. And if I don't get away, I fear that I really will go out of my mind. Can't you help me? I'm afraid."

"Come on, now," I said. "No one shall hurt you while I'm around. What are you afraid of?"

"Men without bones," he said, and there was something in his voice that stirred the hairs on the back of my neck. "Little fat men without bones!"

I wrapped him in a blanket, gave him some quinine, and let him sweat and shiver for a while, before I asked, humoring him: "What men without bones?"

He talked in fits and starts in his fever, his reason staggering just this side of delirium:

". . . What men without bones? . . . They are nothing to be afraid of, actually. It is they who are afraid of you. You can kill them with your boot, or with a stick. . . . They are something like jelly. No, it is not really fear—it is the nausea, the disgust they inspire. It overwhelms. It paralyzes! I have seen a jaguar, I tell you—a full-grown jaguar—stand frozen, while they clung to him, in hundreds, and ate him up alive! Believe me, I saw it. Perhaps it is some oil they secrete, some odor they give out . . . I don't know . . ."

Then, weeping, Doctor Goodbody said: "Oh, nightmare—nightmare—nightmare! To think of the depths to which a noble creature can be degraded by hunger! Horrible, horrible!"

"Some debased form of life that you found in the jungle above the source of the Amer?" I suggested. "Some degenerate kind of anthropoid?"

"No, no, no. *Men!* Now surely you remember Professor Yeoward's ethnological expedition?"

"It was lost," I said.

"All but me," he said. ". . . We had bad luck. At the Anaña Rapids we lost two canoes, half our supplies and most of our instruments. And also Doctor Terry, and Jack Lambert, and eight of our carriers. . . .

"Then we were in Ahu territory where the Indians use poison darts, but we made friends with them and bribed them to carry our stuff westward through the jungle . . . because, you see, all science starts with a guess, a rumor, an old wives' tale; and the object of Professor Yeoward's expedition was to investigate a series of Indian folk tales that tallied. Legends of a race of gods that came down from the sky in a great flame when the world was very young. . . .

"Line by criss-cross line, and circle by concentric circle, Yeoward localized the place in which these tales had their root—an unexplored place that has no name because the Indians refuse to give it a name, it being what they call a 'bad place'."

His chills subsiding and his fever abating, Doctor Goodbody spoke calmly and rationally now. He said, with a short laugh: "I don't know why, whenever I get a touch of fever, the memory of those boneless men comes back in a nightmare to give me the horrors. . . .

"So, we went to look for the place where the gods came down in flame out of the night. The little tattooed Indians took us to the edge of the Ahu territory and then put down their packs and asked for their pay, and no consideration would induce them to go further. We were going, they said, to a very bad place. Their chief, who had been a great man in his day, sign-writing with a twig, told us that he had strayed there once, and drew a picture of something with an oval body and four limbs, at which he spat before rubbing it out with his foot in the dirt. Spiders? we asked. Crabs? What?

"So we were forced to leave what we could not carry with the old chief against our return, and go on unaccompanied, Yeoward and I, through thirty miles of the rottenest jungle in the world. We made about a quarter of a mile in a day . . . a pestilential place! When that stinking wind blows out of the jungle, I smell nothing but death, and panic. . . .

"But, at last, we cut our way to the plateau and climbed the slope, and there we saw something marvelous. It was something that had been a gigantic machine. Originally it must have been a pear-shaped thing, at least a thousand feet long and, in its widest part, six hundred feet in diameter. I don't know of what metal it had been made, because there was only a dusty outline of a hull and certain ghostly remains of unbelievably intricate mechanisms to prove that it had ever been. We could not guess from where it had come; but the impact of its landing had made a great valley in the middle of the plateau.

"It was the discovery of the age! It proved that countless ages ago, this planet had been visited by people from the stars! Wild with excitement, Yeoward and I plunged into this fabulous ruin. But whatever we touched fell away to fine powder.

"At last, on the third day, Yeoward found a semi-circular plate of some extraordinarily hard metal, which was covered with the most maddeningly familiar diagrams. We cleaned it, and for twenty-four hours, scarcely pausing to eat and drink, Yeoward studied it. And, then, before the dawn of the fifth day he awoke me, with a great cry, and said: 'It's a map, a map of the heavens, and a chart of a course from Mars to Earth!'

"And he showed me how those ancient explorers of space had proceeded from Mars to Earth, via the Moon. . . . To crash on this naked plateau in this green hell of a jungle? I wondered. 'Ah, but was it a jungle then?' said Yeoward. 'This may have happened five million years ago!'

"I said: 'Oh, but surely! it took only a few hundred years to bury Rome. How could this thing have stayed above ground for five thousand years, let alone five million?' Yeoward said: 'It didn't. The earth swallows things and regurgitates them. This is a volcanic region. One little upheaval can swallow a city, and one tiny peristalsis in the bowels of the earth can bring its remains to light again a million years later. So it must have been with the machine from Mars . . .'

" 'I wonder who was inside it,' I said. Yeoward replied: 'Very likely some utterly alien creatures that couldn't tolerate the Earth, and died, or else were killed in the crash. No skeleton could survive such a space of time.'

"So, we built up the fire, and Yeoward went to sleep. Having slept, I watched. Watched for what? I didn't know. Jaguars, peccaries, snakes? None of these beasts climbed up to the plateau; there was nothing for them up there. Still, unaccountably, I was afraid.

"There was the weight of ages on the place. *Respect old age,* one is told. . . . The greater the age, the deeper the respect, you might say. But it is not respect; it is dread, it is fear of time and death, sir! . . . I must have dozed, because the fire was burning low—I had been most careful to keep it alive and bright—when I caught my first glimpse of the boneless men.

"Starting up, I saw, at the rim of the plateau, a pair of eyes that picked up luminosity from the fading light of the fire. *A jaguar,* I thought, and took up my rifle. But it could not have been a jaguar because, when I looked left and right I saw that the plateau was ringed with pairs of shining eyes . . . as it might be, a collar of opals; and there came to my nostrils an odor of God knows what.

"Fear has its smell as any animal-trainer will tell you. Sickness has its smell—ask any nurse. These smells compel healthy animals to fight or to run away. This was a combination of the two, plus a stink of vegetation gone bad. I fired at the pair of eyes I had first seen. Then, all the eyes disappeared while, from the jungle, there came a chattering and a twittering of monkeys and birds, as the echoes of the shot went flapping away.

"And then, thank God, the dawn came. I should not have liked to see by artificial light the thing I had shot between the eyes.

"It was gray and, in texture, tough and gelatinous. Yet, in form, externally, it was not unlike a human being. It had eyes, and there were either vestiges—or rudiments—of head, and neck, and a kind of limbs.

"Yeoward told me that I must pull myself together; overcome my 'childish revulsion', as he called it; and look into the nature of the beast. I may say that he kept a long way away from it when I opened it. It was my job as zoologist of the expedition, and I had to do it. Microscopes and other delicate instruments had been lost with the canoes. I worked with a knife and forceps. And found? Nothing: a kind of digestive system enclosed in very tough jelly, a rudimentary nervous system, and a brain about the size of a walnut. The entire creature, stretched out, measured four feet.

"In a laboratory I could tell you, perhaps, something about it . . . with an assistant or two, to keep me company. As it was, I did what I could with a hunting-knife and forceps, without dyes or microscope, swallowing my nausea—it was a nauseating thing!—memorizing what I found. But, as the sun rose higher, the thing liquefied, melted, until by nine o'clock there was nothing but a glutinous gray puddle, with two green eyes swimming in it. . . . And these eyes—I can see them now—burst with a thick *pop,* making a detestable sticky ripple in that puddle of corruption. . . .

"After that, I went away for a while. When I came back, the sun had burned it all away, and there was nothing but something like what you see after a dead jellyfish has evaporated on a hot beach. Slime. Yeoward had a white face when he asked me: 'What the devil is it?' I told him that I didn't know, that it was something outside my experience, and that although I pretended to be a man of science with a detached mind, nothing would induce me ever to touch one of the things again.

"Yeoward said: 'You're getting hysterical, Goodbody. Adopt the proper attitude. God knows, we are not here for the good of our health. Science, man, science! Not a day passes but some doctor pokes his fingers into fouler things than that!' I said: 'Don't you believe it. Professor Yeoward, I have handled and dissected some pretty queer things in my time, but this is something repulsive. I have nerves? I dare say. Maybe we should have brought a psychiatrist . . . I notice, by the way, that you aren't too anxious to come close to me after I've tampered with that thing. I'll shoot one with pleasure, but if you want to investigate it, try it yourself and see!'

"Yeoward said that he was deeply occupied with his metal plate. There was no doubt, he told me, that this machine that had been had come from Mars. But, evidently, he preferred to keep the fire between himself and me, after I had touched that abomination of hard jelly.

"Yeoward kept himself to himself, rummaging in the ruin. I went about my business, which was to investigate forms of animal life. I do not know what I might have found, if I had had—I don't say the courage, because I didn't lack that—if I had had some company. Alone, my nerve broke.

"It happened one morning. I went into the jungle that surrounded us, trying to swallow the fear that choked me, and drive away the sense of revulsion that not only made me want to turn and run, but made me afraid to turn my back even to get away. You may or may not know that, of all the beasts that live in that jungle, the most impregnable is the sloth. He finds a stout limb, climbs out on it, and hangs from it by his twelve steely claws; a tardigrade that lives on leaves. Your tardigrade is so tenacious that even in death, shot through the heart, it will hang on to its branch. It has an immensely tough hide covered by an impenetrable coat of coarse, matted hair. A panther or a jaguar is helpless against the passive resistance of such a creature. It finds itself a tree, which it does not leave until it has eaten every leaf, and chooses for a sleeping place a branch exactly strong enough to bear its weight.

"In this detestable jungle, on one of my brief expeditions—brief, because I was alone and afraid—I stopped to watch a giant sloth hanging motionless from the largest bough of a half-denuded tree, asleep, impervious, indifferent. Then, out of that stinking green twilight came a horde of those jellyfish things. They *poured up* the tree, and writhed along the branch.

"Even the sloth, which generally knows no fear, was afraid. It tried to run away, hooked itself on to a thinner part of the branch, which broke. It fell, and at once was covered with a shuddering mass of jelly. Those boneless men do not bite: they suck. And, as they suck, their color changes from gray to pink and then to brown.

"But they are afraid of us. There is race-memory involved here. We repel them, and they repel us. When they became aware of my presence, they—I was going to say, ran away—they slid away, dissolved into the shadows that kept dancing and dancing and dancing under the trees. And the horror came upon me, so that I ran away, and arrived back at our camp, bloody about the face with thorns, and utterly exhausted.

"Yeoward was lancing a place in his ankle. A tourniquet was tied under his knee. Near-by lay a dead snake. He had broken its back with that same metal plate, but it had bitten him first. He said: 'What kind of a snake do you call this? I'm afraid it is venomous. I feel a numbness in my cheeks and around my heart, and I cannot feel my hands.'

"I said: 'Oh, my God! You've been bitten by a jarajaca!'

"'And we have lost our medical supplies,' he said, with regret. 'And there is so much work left to do. Oh, dear me, dear me! . . . Whatever happens, my dear fellow, take *this* and get back.'

"And he gave me that semi-circle of unknown metal as a sacred trust. Two hours later, he died. That night the circle of glowing eyes grew narrower. I emptied my rifle at it, time and again. At dawn, the boneless men disappeared.

"I heaped rocks on the body of Yeoward. I made a pylon, so that the men without bones could not get at him. Then—oh, so dreadfully lonely and afraid!—I shouldered my pack, and took my rifle and my machete, and ran away, down the trail we had covered. But I lost my way.

"Can by can of food, I shed weight. Then my rifle went, and my ammunition. After that, I threw away even my machete. A long time later, that semi-circular plate became too heavy for me, so I tied it to a tree with liana-vine, and went on.

"So I reached the Ahu territory, where the tattooed men nursed me and were kind to me. The women chewed my food for me, before they fed me, until I was strong again. Of the stores we had left there, I took only as much as I might need, leaving the rest as payment for guides and men to man the canoe down the river. And so I got back out of the jungle. . . .

"Please give me a little more rum." His hand was steady, now, as he drank, and his eyes were clear.

I said to him: "Assuming that what you say is true: these 'boneless men'—they were, I presume, the Martians? Yet it sounds unlikely, surely? Do invertebrates smelt hard metals and——"

"Who said anything about Martians?" cried Doctor Goodbody. "No, no, no! The Martians came here, adapted themselves to new conditions of life. Poor fellows, they changed, sank low; went through a whole new process—a painful process of evolution. What I'm trying to tell you, you fool, is that Yeoward and I did *not* discover Martians. Idiot, don't you see? *Those boneless things are men. We are Martians!"*